D1300756

Ed McBain is one of the most illustrious names in crime fiction. In 1998, he was the first non-British author to be awarded the Crime Writers' Association/Cartier Diamond Dagger Award and he is also holder of the Mystery Writers of America's coveted Grand Master Award. His latest novel in Orion paperback is *Fat Ollie's Book*, and his latest hardback novel, *The Frumious Bandersnatch*, is also available from Orion. Visit his website at www.edmcbain.com.

By Ed McBain

THE 87TH PRECINCT NOVELS

THE MATTHEW HOPE NOVELS

OTHER NOVELS

THE CON MAN

'TIL DEATH

Ed McBAIN

The Con Man
First published in Great Britain in 1963
by Penguin Books

'Til Death
First published in Great Britain in 1964
by Penguin Books

This omnibus edition published in 2008
by Orion Books Ltd
Orion House, 5 Upper St Martin's Lane
London WC2H 9EA

Copyright © Ed McBain 1957, 1959

A CIP catalogue record for this book is available from the British Library.

ISBN 978-1-4072-1710-9

Printed in Great Britain by Clays Ltd, St Ives plc

The Orion Publishing Group's policy is to use papers that are natural, renewable
and recyclable products and made from wood grown in sustainable forests.
The logging and manufacturing processes are expected to conform to the
environmental regulations of the country of origin.

www.orionbooks.co.uk

THE CON MAN
An 87th Precinct Novel

Ed McBAIN

This is for my dear wife, Dragica

The city in these pages is imaginary.
The people, the places are all fictitious.
Only the police routine is based on
established investigatory technique.

1.

EVERYBODY has a right to earn a living.

That's the American way. You get out there and sweat, and you make a buck. And you invest that buck in lemons and sugar. The water and ice, you get free. You've got yourself a little lemonade stand by the side of the road, and pretty soon you're pulling in five bucks a week. You take that five, and you buy more lemons and more sugar, and you spot your stands at intervals along the road, and pretty soon you can't handle all the business. You hire people to work for you. You start putting the lemonade up in bottles, and then cans, and before you know it you're freezing the stuff and it's being distributed in chain stores all over the country. You buy yourself a big house in the country with a swimming pool and a garbage disposal unit, and you go to cocktail parties where people serve your lemonade with a little bit of gin tossed in for kicks. You have arrived in spades.

That's the American way, and everybody has a right to earn a living.

The law doesn't quarrel with man's inalienable right to pursue the buck. The law only questions the method and means of acquiring the elusive green.

If, for example, your particular penchant is cracking safes, the law may cock a slightly disciplinary eyebrow in your direction.

Or if, for example, you like to hit people on the head

and take their wallets, you can't very well blame the law for looking at you somewhat disdainfully.

Or if, to stretch a point, you make your living by hiring out a gun, *your* gun, by squeezing the trigger of that gun, by using that gun to actually shoot people – well, really!

You can, after all, be a gentleman about all this. You can, if you figure crime is the quickest, safest, most exciting way of making the most money in the shortest time, go about it like a gent.

You can fool people.

You need not resort to violence.

You need not go out and buy a costly set of burglars' tools.

You need not acquire a pistol.

You need not draw up complicated plans for getting in and out of a bank.

You need not set up an expensive counterfeit printing press in your basement.

You can remain a gentleman, pursue a life of romantic criminal adventure, see the world, meet a lot of nice people and drink a lot of cool drinks, and still make a lot of money – all by fooling people.

You can, in short, become a con man.

The little Negro girl was very nervous. She was nervous because she was in a police station talking to two detectives. One of the detectives was Negro, too, but that didn't make her any less nervous. Both detectives were listening to her sympathetically, but that didn't make her feel any less a fool – and she supposed this feeling of foolishness was what made her feel so nervous.

She had been in the city for two years now. She had come up from North Carolina a long while ago, and she knew she'd looked green at the time, and she knew her speech was not Northern, but that was a long time ago and she'd thought she was quite cosmopolitan by now, quite the city slicker. Pride goeth before a fall, she supposed, and she sat with her foolishness inside her, and her nervousness breaking out on her hands which picked lint from the small black purse she carried.

She sat in the detective squad room of the 87th Precinct on a mild day in April. There had been rain just a little while before, and the greenery in Grover Park across the street had shoved its clean sweet scent on to the air, and the cleanness and sweetness had somehow managed to cross the street and filter in through the grilled windows of the squad room. The squad room did not very often smell sweet. The squad room housed sixteen detectives who, while they were not always all there at the same time, worked hard none the less in somewhat cramped quarters. Detectives sweat. That sounds almost sacrilegious because everyone knows only *living* human beings sweat. But even admitting that some detectives aren't quite human, let's be kind and allow that some of them are almost quite living. Which is why the sweet smell from the park was a welcome one on that April day which had miraculously turned to one of sunshine after a bad start.

'I feel awful silly about this,' the girl said.

'What was your name again, miss?' Kling asked. Kling was a Detective/3rd Grade. He was tall and blond, and somewhat young-looking, mainly because he *was* young. He was the newest detective on the squad, and sometimes his questions weren't exactly to the point because he was still learning the art of questioning. Sometimes, too, his questions made him feel a little foolish. So Bert Kling knew just how the young Negro girl in the straight-back chair felt.

'My name is Betty,' she said. 'Betty Prescott.'

'Where do you live, Betty?' Kling asked.

'Well, I work for some people in the next state. I'm a domestic, you know? I been working for them for six months now. Mr and Mrs Haines?' She made the last a question, and she raised her eyebrows as if expecting Kling to know who Mr and Mrs Haines were. Kling did not know. 'I'm supposed to be back there now,' Betty said. 'Thursday's my day off, you see. Thursdays and every other Sunday. I generally come into the city every Thursday. Mr Haines drives me to the station, and then Mrs Haines picks me up when I come back. I'm supposed to be back now, but I felt I should report this. I called Mrs Haines, and she said by all means I should report it. You see?'

'I see,' Kling said. 'Do you keep an apartment in the city?'

'I live with my cousin here. Isabel Johnson?' Again she made the name a question. Kling didn't know Isabel Johnson, either.

'All right, what happened, Betty?' Brown asked. He had been silent up to this point, giving Kling his head. But Arthur Brown was a Detective/2nd Grade with a known tendency toward impatience. He was impatient perhaps because his name was Brown and the accidentals of birth had tinted his complexion the same colour. He had taken a lot of ribbing from fellow Americans over the years, and had once considered changing his name to Lipschitz, so that the hate mongers could really have a ball. His impatience, as it related to his chosen profession, was sometimes a hindrance but it crossed a very subtle line into a second character trait and that

4

trait was doggedness. Once Brown got his teeth into a case, he wouldn't unclamp his jaws until the nut was cracked. His impatience was a peculiar thing. There was, for example, a detective named Meyer Meyer at the precinct. Meyer's surname was, of course, Meyer and Meyer's father had stuck him with the given name of Meyer, so that his offspring emerged as Meyer Meyer. Now if ever a man took guff because of a handle some unthinking parent had given him, Meyer Meyer was that man. But in Meyer, the years of guff had led to an almost supernatural attitude of patience. The only crack in Meyer's veneer of extreme patience emerged in a physical way. For Meyer Meyer was as bald as a cue ball, even though he was a young man. But that's the way it goes. Two men, two names, two extremes.

Impatiently, Brown asked, 'What happened?'

'I got off the train yesterday morning,' Betty said. 'I take the 8.17 in with Mr Haines. I don't sit with him because he's always talking business with his friends. He's in public relations?' Again the question mark. Kling nodded.

'Go on,' Brown said impatiently.

'Well, when we got here to the city, I got off the train and I was walking along when this man came up to me.'

'Where was this?' Brown asked.

'Right in the station,' Betty said.

'Go ahead.'

'He said hello, and he asked me was I new in the city? I said no I'd been up North for two years, but I was working out the state. He seemed like a very nice fellow, dressed nice, you know? Respectable?'

'Yes,' Kling said.

'Anyway, he said he was a preacher. He looked like a preacher, too. He started blessing me then. He said God

5

bless you, and all like that, and he said I should be very careful in the big city because there was all kinds of pitfalls for a young innocent girl. People who'd want to do me harm?'

Again the question mark, and again Kling said, 'Yes,' and immediately afterwards cursed himself for falling into the pitfall of the girl's speech pattern.

'He said I should be especially careful with money, because there was all sorts of people who'd do most anything to get their hands on it. He asked me if I had any money with me.'

'Was he white or Negro?' Brown asked.

Betty looked at Kling somewhat apologetically. 'He was white,' she said.

'Go ahead,' Brown told her.

'Well, I said I had a little money with me, and he asked me if I'd like him to bless it for me? He said do you have a ten dollar bill, and I said no. So he said do you have a five dollar bill, and I said yes. Then he took out his own five dollar bill, and he put it into this little white envelope. With a cross on the front. A crucifix?'

This time Kling did not say 'Yes.' He did not even nod.

'Then he said something like God bless this money and keep it safe from those who would, oh like that. We kept talking, and he put the envelope back in his pocket, and then he said Here, my child, you take this blessed five dollars and let me have your bill. I gave him my five dollars, and he reached into his pocket and gave me the envelope with the cross on it, the envelope with the blessed money.'

'And this morning?' Brown asked impatiently.

'Well, this morning I was ready to go to the train

station, and I saw the envelope in my purse, so I opened it up?'

'Yes,' Kling said.

'Surprise,' Brown said. 'No five dollars.'

'Why, no!' Betty said. 'There was just a folded paper napkin in the envelope. He must have switched that envelope while he was talking to me, after he'd blessed the money. I don't know what I'm going to do now. I needed that five dollars. Can't you catch him?'

'We'll try,' Kling said. 'Can you give us a description of the man?'

'Well, I didn't really look at him too hard. He was nice-looking, and very nicely dressed?'

'What was he wearing?'

'A dark blue suit. Or maybe black. It was dark, anyway.'

'Tie?'

'A bow-tie, I think.'

'Carrying a briefcase or anything?'

'No.'

'Where'd he get the envelope from?'

'His inside pocket.'

'Did he tell you his name?'

'If he did, I don't remember.'

'All right, Miss Prescott,' Brown said. 'If anything develops, we'll call you. In the meantime, I think you'd better forget all about that five dollars.'

'*Forget* it?' she asked with a great big question mark, and nobody answered her.

They led her to the slatted wooden railing which divided the squad room from the corridor outside, and they watched her walk down the corridor and then turn into the stairwell which led to the ground floor of the building.

'What do you think?' Kling asked Brown.

'The old switch game,' Brown said. 'There are a hundred variations. We'd better plant a few men at the station to watch for this preacher.'

'Think we'll get him?'

'I don't know. Chances are he won't be working the same place tomorrow. I tell you, Bert, I think there's an upswing in confidence men these days, you know it?'

'I thought they were dying out.'

'For a while, yeah. But all of a sudden, all the old confidence games are reappearing. Games that have beards on them, they're so old – all of a sudden, they start cropping up.' Brown shook his head. 'I don't know.'

'Well, they're not too serious,' Kling said.

'Crime is serious,' Brown said flatly.

'Oh sure,' Kling said. 'I just meant, well – aside from a few bucks lost – there's never any *real* harm done.'

The girl in the River Harb had had some real harm done to her.

She floated up on to the rocks near the Hamilton Bridge, and three young kids didn't know what she was at first, and then they realized, and they ran like hell for the nearest cop.

The girl was still on the rocks when the cop arrived. The cop did not like to look at dead bodies, especially dead bodies which had been in the water for any amount of time. Bloated and immense, the girl hardly looked like a girl at all. Her head hair had been completely washed away. Her body was decomposed and fibrous strands of flesh clung to her brassière which, snapped by the expanding gases in the body, miraculously clung to her though the rest of her clothing was gone. Her lower front teeth were gone, too.

The patrolman managed to keep down the bilious feeling which suddenly attacked his stomach. He went to the nearest call box and he phoned in to the 87th Precinct, which house he happened to work for.

Sullivan, the sergeant who was manning the desk, said, '87th Precinct, good morning.'

'This is Di Angelo,' the patrolman said.

'Yeah?'

'I've got a floater near the bridge.'

He gave Sullivan all the details, and then he went back to stand alongside the dead girl on the rocks which were washed with April sunshine.

2.

DETECTIVE STEVE CARELLA was glad the sun was shining.

It was not that Carella didn't like rain. After all, the farmers sure needed it. And, though it may sound a bit poetic, walking hatless in the spring rain had been one of Carella's favourite pastimes before the day of his idiocy.

The day of his idiocy had been Friday, 22 December.

He would never think of it without referring to it as the day of his idiocy because that was the day he'd allowed a young punk pusher to take his service revolver away from him and fire three shots into his chest. That had been a fine Christmas, all right. That had been a Christmas when Carella could almost hear the angels, so imbued was he with the season's spirit. That had been a Christmas when he thought he wouldn't quite make it, when he thought sure he was a goner. And then somehow, the clouds had blown away. And where there was a painful mist before, there was a slow clearing and Teddy's face in that clearing, streaked with tears. He had recognized his wife Teddy first, and then slowly the rest of the hospital room had come into focus. She had leaned over the bed and rested her cheek against his, and he could feel her tears hot on his face, and he whispered hoarsely, 'Cancel the wreath,' in an attempt at wit that was unfunny. She had clung to him fiercely, wordlessly — wordlessly because Teddy could neither speak nor hear. She had clung to him, and then she had kissed his unfunny humour off his mouth, and then she had covered his face with kisses, holding his hand all the while, careful not to lean on his bandaged, wounded chest.

He had healed. Time heals all wounds, the wise men say.

Of course, the wise men didn't know about rain and bullet holes. When it rained, Carella's healed wounds ached. He always thought that was a bunch of bull, wounds aching when it rained. Well, it was not a bunch of bull. His wounds ached when it rained, and so he was glad the rain had stopped and the sun was shining.

The sun was shining on what had once been a girl, and Carella looked down at the travesty death had wrought and there was momentary pain in his eyes, and momentary anger, and both passed.

To Di Angelo, he said, 'You find the body, Fred?'

'Some kids,' Di Angelo said. 'They come running to me. Jesus, it's a mess, ain't it?'

'It almost always is,' Carella said. He looked at the body again and then, because certain police formalities had to be followed whenever an unknown body turned up, he took a small black pad from his back pocket. He opened the pad, slid the pencil out from under its leather loop and wrote:

1. *Place where body found*: washed ashore on rock pile in River Harb.
2. *Time when found*:

He looked up at Di Angelo. 'When did you get here, Fred?'

Di Angelo looked at his watch. 'I'd say around 1.15, Steve. I was just a little bit off Silvermine, and I'm generally there around . . .'

'1.15 it is,' Carella said, and he wrote down the information. He then wrote '3. *Cause of death:*' and '4. *Time when death occurred:*' and left both those items to be filled in by the m.e. or the coroner.

He next wrote:

5. *Supposed age:* 25–35.
6. *Supposed profession:* ?
7. *Description of body:*

   (a) *Sex:* female.
   (b) *Colour:* white.
   (c) *Nationality:* ?
   (d) *Height:* ?
   (e) *Weight:* ?

There were a lot of question marks.

There were also a good many other items Carella could have listed under a description of the body. Items like build and complexion and hair and eyes and eyebrows and nose and chin and face and neck and lips and mouth and many more. And to these he could have given answers ranging from short and stocky to stout and square-shouldered; or small and pug; or square and dimpled; or thick and puffy; or any one of a hundred combinations for each category.

The trouble was that the body was a floater and pretty badly decomposed. Where an unknown body would automatically have called for a description of the eyes, the colour, the shape, etc. Carella could give no such description here because the eyes had already decomposed. Where he would have liked to list the colour of the girl's hair, that hair had been washed away, and he settled for a brief note: *Head hair gone. Pubic hair blonde.* He terminated his description of the body with the boldly printed word: FLOATER. That, for anyone in the know, summed up the story. Then he went on to the next item.

> 8. *Description of clothing*: single article of clothing is brassière. Have lab check for laundry and dry-cleaning marks.
> 9. *Jewellery and other objects on person*: none.

Carella closed the notebook.

'What do you make of it?' Di Angelo asked.

'You want statistics or guesses?' Carella said.

'Gee, I don't know. I was just asking.'

'Well, by statistics, this girl shouldn't be dead,' Carella said. 'It's all a mistake.'

'How so?'

'From the looks of her, I'd say she's been in the water maybe three, four months. Somebody probably reported her missing during that time – assuming she's got family or friends – so that makes her technically a missing person.'

'Yeah?' Di Angelo asked, impressed as always by Carella. Di Angelo respected Carella a great deal. Part of this respect was due to the fact that they were both of Italian descent, and there was something immensely gratifying – to Di Angelo's way of thinking – about an Italian boy making good. Di Angelo felt about Carella much the same way he felt about Frank Sinatra. But the major part of Di Angelo's respect came from a thorough appreciation of the fact that Carella was a smart cop, a well-informed cop and, on occasion, a tough cop. This, in Di Angelo's book, was a tough combination to beat.

'So let's look at the missing persons statistics,' Carella said. 'We've got a girl here. Well, there are usually twenty-five per cent more males than females among missing persons.'

'Yeah?' Di Angelo said.

'Two: she's probably somewhere between twenty-five and thirty years old. The peak age for missing persons is fifteen.'

'Yeah?' Di Angelo said.

'Three: this is April. The peak month for missing persons is May, and the second peak month is September.'

'How you like that?' Di Angelo said.

'So, statistically, this is all wrong.' Carella sighed, and again there was a passing film of pain in his eyes. 'That doesn't make her any less dead, though,' he said.

'No,' Di Angelo said, shaking his head.

'One guess of a semi-technical nature,' Carella said. 'Five'll get you ten she's an out-of-towner.'

Di Angelo nodded and then glanced up to the highway where two police sedans had pulled up. 'Here's the lab boys and the photographers,' he said and then, as if he were certain such would not be the case now that they were on the scene, he looked down at the dead girl and said, 'Rest in peace.'

If Carella's interest in the floater, at this stage of the game, was a more or less fleeting one, there were those involved in police work who gave the decomposed body and its single article of clothing a much closer and more thorough inspection.

The girl's brassière was sent to the Police Laboratory. The girl's body was sent to the morgue.

Sam Grossman was a police lieutenant, and also a skilled laboratory technician. He was a big man with a rough-hewn face and big hands. He wore glasses because his eyes were not too good. There was a gentility about him which belied the fact that he dealt with cold scientific facts and often with the facts of death. He ran a clean laboratory, and his men got results. His laboratory was divided into seven sections, and it covered a good deal of the first floor of the Headquarters building on High Street downtown. The seven sections were:

1. CHEMICAL AND PHYSICAL
2. BIOLOGICAL
3. GENERAL
4. FIREARMS
5. QUESTIONED DOCUMENTS
6. PHOTOGRAPHIC
7. MECHANICAL

The brassière was turned over to the physical section first. The gentlemen who examined it there paid little or no attention to the fact that this single item of clothing is responsible for one of the most widespread and nationally advertised fetishes in America. They didn't care whether or not the secret was in the circle or whether or not anyone had dreamt she was a ballerina in this particular brassière or whether or not there was any hidden treasure to be found. They were interested in the undergarment as it applied to one thing and one thing alone: the identity of the dead girl.

Most articles of clothing, you see, will carry either laundry or dry-cleaning marks. Sam Grossman was proud of the fact that his lab had the most comprehensive file of laundry marks in the nation. In a matter of minutes, provided there was a mark in the article of clothing, Sam's men could pinpoint the exact laundry which had stamped the mark.

The brassière carried no visible laundry marks. It

would have been simpler if it had. It's always simpler when you can see something with the naked eye. In truth, though, it wasn't very much more difficult to put the brassière on the long white counter over which hung the ultra-violet lights. A flip of the switch, and the counter turned a lovely shade of purple, and the brassière turned a lovely shade of purple, and Sam's men turned it over and over, searching for the luminous Phantom Fast laundry mark which many laundries use. The Phantom Fast mark is a good idea since it leaves no unsightly numbers on the back of your shirt collar or the seat of your underpants. It means compiling a separate set of marks for police files, but think of how pretty your shirts look. The only thing that'll bring out a Phantom Fast mark is ultra-violet light and hell, police labs are crawling with that kind of light.

The only trouble with the dead girl's brassière was that it didn't carry a Phantom Fast mark either.

Faced with the fact that the girl probably did her own laundry, but otherwise unfazed, Sam's men began putting the bra through a series of chemical tests to determine whether or not it held any peculiar stains.

Meanwhile, back at the morgue . . .

The assistant medical examiner was a man named Paul Blaney. He had been examining dead bodies for a good many years, but he still could not get used to floaters. He had been examining this particular dead body for nigh on two hours, and he still could not get used to floaters. He had estimated that the dead girl was approximately thirty-five years of age, that her weight while she was alive (according to her five-foot-three-and-a-half inches height and her large bone structure) was probably somewhere around 125 pounds, and that her head hair (judging from the colour of her pubic hair) was probably blonde.

Her lower front teeth had been lost in the water, and

her upper front teeth were in good condition although her upper back teeth and her lower back teeth had a good many fillings and a good many cavities. The upper right second molar had been extracted a long time ago and never replaced. Blaney had prepared a dental chart to be compared with the dental chart of any suspected missing person.

He had also made a methodical scrutiny of the girl's body for identifying marks or scars and had concluded that she'd once had an appendectomy (there was a long scar across her belly), that she'd been vaccinated on her left thigh rather than on either of her arms, that there was a cluster of birth marks at the base of her spinal column and, unusual in a woman, there was a small tattoo on the fold of skin between her right thumb and forefinger. The tattoo was a simple heart, the point of which ran toward the arm. There was a single word within the heart. The tattoo looked like this:

Blaney estimated that the body had been submerged for at least three to four months. The epidermis of both hands was lost, and he sighed a forlorn sigh for his brothers of toil in the police laboratory because he knew this would mean extra work for them. And then, with a great show of distaste and a maximum of somehow remarkably detached efficiency, he cut off the fingers and thumb of each hand and wrapped them up for delivery to Sam Grossman.

Then he began working on the dead girl's heart.

It requires a certain amount of dispassionate, emotionless

patience to lift finger-print impressions from fingers and thumbs which have been cut from a cadaver.

If the dead girl had been in the water for a comparatively short period of time, Sam Grossman's men could have dried off each finger with a soft towel and then – in order to smooth out the so-called washerwoman's skin effect – have injected glycerine beneath the fingertip skin. They could then have taken their prints with ease.

Unfortunately, the girl had not been in the water for a short period of time.

Nor had she been in the water only long enough to wear away the friction ridges of her fingers. Had this been the case, the lab boys would have cut away the skin of each fingertip, placing these snips in separate test tubes with formaldehyde solution. Assuming the papillary ridges were intact on the outer surface of the skin, one of Sam's men would have put on a rubber glove, placed the piece of skin on his index finger, and then rolled finger, glove, and skin on an inking plate – as if the piece of skin were actually his own finger – and then recorded it on the finger-print form.

Even if the papillary ridges had been destroyed, the papillary pattern would be found on the inner surface of the skin and a good photograph could be had if the skin were attached to a piece of cardboard, inner surface out, and the picture taken in oblique light.

Unfortunately, the unidentified dead girl had been in the water for close to four months and the laboratory technicians had to turn to more tedious and inventive methods of getting their finger-prints.

In the hands of less skilled operators than Sam Grossman's men, an attempt at the papillary method may have proved less expedient and less fruitful. But Sam's men were whizzes, and so they took each finger and each thumb, and they stood over Bunsen burners and slowly, methodically, doggedly dried the fingers, passing them over the flame, their hands moving in short arcs, back and forth, back and forth, until each finger had shrunk and dried.

Then, at last, they were able to touch each finger lightly with printer's ink and take their impressions.

Their impressions did not tell them who the dead girl was.

One copy of her prints was sent to the Bureau of Criminal Identification.

One copy was sent to the F.B.I.

A third copy was sent to the Bureau of Missing Persons.

A fourth was sent to Homicide North – since all suicides or suspected suicides are treated exactly like homicides.

And finally, a copy was sent to the Detective Division of the 87th Precinct, in which territory the body had been found.

Sam Grossman's men washed their hands.

There was something about Paul Blaney that made Carella's flesh crawl. Perhaps it was the idea of Blaney dealing with death as an occupation, but Carella suspected it was the man's personality and not his job. He had, after all, dealt with many men whose occupation was death. With Blaney, however, it seemed to be more a preoccupation than an occupation, and so Carella stood before him, towering over him, and he could feel a nest of spiders in his stomach, and he wanted to scratch himself or take a bath.

The two men stood in the clean antiseptic examination-room of the morgue, alongside the stainless-steel table with its troughs to gather in the flow of blood, with its stainless-steel basin to capture the blood and hold it in a ruby pool. Blaney was a short man with a balding head and a scraggly black moustache. He was the only man Carella had ever met who owned violet eyes.

Carella stood opposite him, a big man but not a heavy one. He gave an impression of athletic tightness, every muscle and sinew in his body pulled into a wiry bundle of power. His eyes were brown, slanting downward to meet high cheek bones, so that his face had an almost Oriental look. He wore his brown hair short. He wore a grey sports jacket and charcoal slacks, and the jacket stretched wide across the breadth of his shoulders, angled in sharply to cover narrow hips and a flat hard stomach.

'What do you make of it?' he asked Blaney.

'I hate floaters,' Blaney said. 'I hate to look at them. The goddamned things make me sick.'

'Nobody likes floaters,' Carella said.

'Me especially,' Blaney said, nodding vigorously. 'They always give me the floaters. If you've got seniority around here, you can pull anything you want. So I'm low man on the totem pole. So whenever a goddamned floater comes in, everybody else suddenly has corpses in Siberia. Is that fair? That I should get the floaters?'

'Somebody's got to get them.'

'Sure, but why me? Listen, I don't complain about anything they give me. We've had stiffs in here so burned up, you wouldn't even know they were human. You ever handle charred flesh? Okay, but do I complain? We get automobile accident victims where a guy's head is hanging from his neck by one strand of skin. I take it in stride. I'm an m.e., and you've got to take the good ones with the bad ones. But why should I get all the floaters? How come nobody else gets the floaters?'

'Look ...' Carella started, but Blaney was just gathering steam, just picking up speed.

'There isn't anybody in the goddamn department who does a better job than me. Trouble is, I haven't got seniority. It's all politics. Who do you think gets the nice posh jobs? The old fuddies who've been cutting up stiffs for forty years. But I do a neat, thorough job. Thorough. I'm thorough. I don't overlook anything. Not a thing. So I get the floaters!'

'Maybe they figure you're so expert, they wouldn't trust them to anyone else,' Carella said drily.

'Huh?' Blaney said. 'Expert?'

'Certainly. You're a good man, Blaney. Floaters are tough. You can't trust them with just any damn butcher.'

Blaney's violet eyes softened a shade. 'I never thought of it that way,' he said. He smiled slightly, and then the smile vanished before a suspicious lowering of his brows as he thought the problem over again.

'What about this one?' Carella asked, not wanting Blaney to start thinking too hard.

'Oh,' Blaney said. 'Yeah. Well, I got a report there – all the junk. Been in the water about four months, I would say. I just got done with the heart.'

'And?'

'You know anything about the heart?'

'Not very much, no.'

'Right and left chambers, you see. Blood passes through, gets pumped around the body, oh hell, I can't give a layman an anatomy lesson.'

'I didn't ask for one,' Carella said.

'Anyway, I did the Gettler test. Idea is that if someone

drowns, water passes from the lungs into the blood. We can tell pretty well this way whether a person drowned in fresh water or salt water.'

'How so?'

'If it was fresh water, the blood in the left side of the heart will have a lower-than-normal chloride content. Salt water, the blood in the left side of the heart will have a higher-than-normal amount of chloride.'

'This girl was found in the River Harb,' Carella said. 'That's fresh water, isn't it?'

'Sure. But according to Smith – you know, Smith, Glaister and Von Neureiter . . .'

'Go ahead,' Carella said.

'According to Smith, if a person is already dead when he's thrown into the water, it's impossible for any water to get into that person's left heart.' Blaney paused. 'In other words, if we find no water in the left heart during autopsy, we can safely assume that person didn't drown. That person was dead before he hit the water.'

'Yes?' Carella said, interested now.

'This little girl didn't have a drop of water there, Carella. This little girl didn't drown.'

Carella stared deep into Blaney's violet eyes. 'How'd she die?' he asked.

'Acute arsenic poisoning,' Blaney said. 'Greatest amount of it was found in the stomach and intestines. Indicates oral ingestion. The whole system was not impregnated, so we can chalk off chronic poisoning. This was acute. She may, in fact, have died just a few hours after she swallowed the stuff.'

Blaney scratched the top of his balding head.

'In fact,' he added, 'you may even have yourself a homicide here.'

3.

LIFE, if you take a somewhat dim and cynical view of it, is something like a big con game.

Look around you, friends, and see the confidence men.

'I have in my hand right here, ladies and gentlemen, a bar of So-Soap. This is the only soap on the market which contains neocenephrotaneticin which we call Neo # 7. Neo # 7 puts an invisible film of visible filmy acentodoids on the epidermal glottifram . . .'

'If I am elected, friends, I can promise you good clean government. And why can I promise you good abusive government? Because I am sincere and untrustworthy. I am honest and selfishly domineering. I am the biggest, the most attentive, the most fastidious violator of the Mann Act, and I can promise . . .'

'Look, George, where else can you get a deal like this one? We are willing to construct the whole damned thing, take full responsibility for the job, and all it'll cost you is a round two million dollars. And with that you get my own personal guarantee. My own personal guarantee.'

'Baby, what I'm trying to tell you is I never felt like this before. I mean, when you walk into a room, Jesus, the room lights up, do you know what I mean? My heart begins to go up and down like a yo-yo. There's a light that comes from you, baby, a light that fills up the sky. If that ain't love, I don't know what love is. Believe me, baby, I never felt like this. Like walking on air with my head in the clouds, like wanting to sing all the time. I love you, sweetheart, I love you like crazy. So why don't you be a good girl and take off that dress, huh?'

'I'll be honest with you. That car had 75,000 miles on it before we turned back the speedometer. Also, that's a new paint job. We don't trust new paint jobs. Who knows what's under that paint, friend. I wouldn't sell you that dog if you begged me. But step over here a minute and take a look at this lavender and red convertible which was owned by the maiden aunt of a Protestant minister who used it only once a week to do her marketing around the corner. Now this car . . .'

NOW

FOR THE FIRST TIME IN PUBLISHING HISTORY
We are proud to announce the most compelling novel since *Gone with the Wind*.

'THE TATTERED PICCOLO'

A Book of the Month Club selection . . .
A Literary Guild selection . . .
A Reader's Digest Book Club selection . . .
Purchased by a major movie company as a vehicle for Tab Hunter . . .
6,000,000 copies now in print!
Rush to your bookseller. He may still have a few in stock!

'The trouble with this guy's parties is he doesn't know how to mix martinis. It takes a certain amount of finesse, you know. Now here's my formula. You take a water glass full of gin . . .'

'Hello, friends, I'm George Grosnick. This is my brother Louie Grosnick. We make Grosnick Beer . . . all right, Louie, you tell them . . .'

*

It's the hard sell and the soft sell, anywhere you go, everywhere you go. It comes at you a hundred times a day, and maybe it's stretching a point to say that every human being has his own confidence game, that every human being has a tiny touch of larceny in his soul, but be careful, friend; the television is on, and that man is pointing at *you*!

The man in the dark blue suit was a con man.

He sat in the hotel lobby waiting for a man named Jamison. He had first seen Jamison at the railroad station when the train from Boston pulled in. He had followed Jamison to the hotel, and now he sat in the lobby and waited for him to appear because the man in the dark blue suit had plans for Jamison.

He was a good-looking man, tall, with even features and a friendly mouth and eyes. He dressed immaculately. His white shirt was spotless, and his suit was freshly pressed. His black shoes were highly polished and, amazing in this elastic-top-socked age, his socks were held firmly in place with garters.

He was holding a guide book to the city in his hand.

He looked at his watch. It was close to six-thirty, and Jamison should be down soon if he planned on having dinner at all. The lobby bustled with activity. A beer company was holding eliminations for its yearly glamour-girl contest, and models swarmed over the thick rugs, accompanied by Press agents and photographers. All of the models looked the same. The hair-colouring varied, but otherwise they all looked the same. They were, in essence, symbols created by con men. They were too, in essence, con men themselves.

He saw Jamison come out of one of the elevators. Quickly he rose and stood with the guide book open at the top of the steps leading to the street. He could see Jamison from the corner of his eye, moving toward the steps. He buried himself in the guide book and when Jamison was abreast of him, he moved sharply to the left, colliding with him.

Jamison looked startled. He was a stout man with a red face, dressed in a brown pin stripe. The con man fumbled for the fallen guide book, and then – from his knees – said, 'Gosh, I'm sorry. Excuse me, please.'

'That's all right,' Jamison said.

The con man stood up. 'I got so involved in this book, I guess I wasn't watching where I . . . say, you're all right, aren't you?'

'Yes, I'm fine,' Jamison said.

'Well, I'm certainly glad to hear that. This darn book is Greek to me, I can tell you that. I'm from Boston, you see. I've been trying to make out the street . . .'

'Boston?' Jamison said, interested. 'Really?'

'Well, not exactly. A suburb. West Newton. Do you know it?'

'Why, sure I do,' Jamison said. 'I've lived in Boston all my life.'

The con man's face opened with delighted surprise. 'Is that right? Well, I'll be . . . say, how do you like that?'

'Small world, ain't it?' Jamison said, grinning.

'Listen, this calls for something,' the con man said. 'I'm superstitious that way. Something like this happens, it calls for something. Let me buy you a drink.'

'Well, I was just on my way to dinner,' Jamison said.

'Fine, we'll have a drink together and then you can go on your way. Tell you the truth, I'm tickled I ran into you. I don't know a soul in this town.'

'I suppose we could have a drink,' Jamison said. 'You here on business?'

26

'Yes,' the con man said. 'Marlboro Tractor Corporation, know them?'

'No. I'm in textiles myself,' Jamison said.

'Well, no matter. Shall we try the hotel bar, or do you want to scout up something else? Hotel bars are a little stiff, don't you think?' He had already taken Jamison's arm and was leading him down the steps.

'Well, I never really . . .'

'Sure. Seemed to me there were a lot of bars on the next street. Why don't we try one of them?' He passed Jamison through the revolving doors, and when they reached the sidewalk, he looked up at the buildings, seemingly bewildered. 'Now, let me see,' he said. 'Which is East and which is West?'

'That's East,' Jamison said, pointing.

'Fine.'

The con man introduced himself as Charlie Parsons, Jamison said his first name was Elliot. Together, they walked up the street, looking at the various bars, deciding against one or another for various reasons — most of which Parsons offered.

When they came to a place called the Red Cockatoo, Parsons took Jamison's arm and said, 'Now this looks like a nice place. How about it?'

'Suits me fine,' Jamison said. 'One bar's just about as good as another, the way I look at it.'

They were heading for the entrance door when the door opened and a man in a grey suit stepped out on to the sidewalk. He was a pleasant looking man in his late thirties, a shock of red hair topping his head. He seemed very much in a hurry.

'Say,' Parsons said, 'excuse me a minute.'

The redheaded man stopped. 'Yes?' he said. He still seemed in a hurry.

'What kind of a place is this?' Parsons asked.

'Huh?'

'The bar. You just came out of it. Is it a nice place?'

'Oh,' the redheaded man said. 'The bar. Tell you the truth, I don't know. I just stopped in there to make a phone call.'

'Oh, I see,' Parsons said. 'Well, thank you,' and he turned away from the redheaded man, seemingly to enter the bar with Jamison.

'It's the damnedest thing, ain't it?' the redhead said. 'I haven't been in this city for close to five years. So I come in on a trip, and I've been calling old friends since the minute I arrived, and all of them are busy tonight.'

Parsons turned, smiling. 'Oh?' he said. 'Where you from?'

'Wilmington,' the redhead said.

'We're out-of-towners, too,' Parsons explained. 'Listen, if you haven't anything else to do, why don't you join us for a drink?'

'Well, gee, that's awfully kind of you,' the redhead said. 'But I wouldn't want to impose.'

'No imposition at all,' Parsons said. He turned to Jamison. 'You don't mind, do you, Elliot?'

'Not at all,' Jamison said. 'More the merrier.'

'Well, in that case, I'd enjoy it a lot,' the redhead said.

'I'm Charlie Parsons,' Parsons said, 'and this is Elliot Jamison.'

'Pleased to know you,' the redhead said. 'I'm Frank O'Neill.'

The men shook hands all round.

'Well, let's get those drinks,' Parsons said, and they went into the bar. They took a table in the corner, and after they'd made themselves comfortable, Parsons said, 'Are you here on business, Frank?'

'No, no,' O'Neill said. 'Pleasure. Strictly pleasure. Some stock I've been holding took a big jump, and I decided to take those extra dividends and have myself a hell of a time.' He leaned over the table, and his voice lowered. 'I've got more than three thousand dollars with me. I think I'll be able to have a whopper with that, eh?' He burst out laughing, and Parsons and Jamison laughed with him, and then they ordered a round of drinks.

'Drink whatever you like and as much as you like,' O'Neill said, 'because this is all on me.'

'Oh, no,' Parsons said. 'We invited you to join us.'

'I don't care,' O'Neill insisted. 'If it wasn't for you fellows, I'd be on the town alone. Hell, that's no fun.'

'Well,' Jamison said, 'I really don't think it's fair for you . . .'

'It certainly wouldn't be fair, Elliot. We'll each pay for a round, how's that?'

'No, sir!' O'Neill objected. He seemed to be a pretty hot-tempered fellow, and somehow this business of who should pay for the drinks was upsetting him. He raised his voice and said, 'I'm paying for everything. I've got three thousand dollars, and if that's not enough to pay for a few lousy drinks, I'd like to know what is.'

'That's not the point, Frank,' Parsons said. 'Really. You'd embarrass me.'

'Me, too,' Jamison said. 'I think Charlie's right. We'll each pay for a round.'

'I'll tell you what I'll do,' O'Neill said. 'I'll match you for the drinks. How's that?'

'Match us?' Parsons said. 'What do you mean?'

'We'll match coins. Here.' He reached into his pocket and pulled out a quarter. The drinks had come by this time, and the men sipped a little from their glasses.

Parsons took a quarter from his pocket, and then Jamison took a quarter from his.

'Here's the way we'll work it,' O'Neill said. 'We'll all flip together. Odd man, the fellow who has a head when the other two have tails – or tails when the other two have heads – doesn't pay. Then the other two flip to see who does pay. Okay?'

'Fair enough,' Parsons said.

'Okay, here we go,' O'Neill said. The three men flipped their coins and covered them. When they uncovered, Parsons and O'Neill were showing heads. Jamison was showing tails.

'Well, you're out of it,' O'Neill said. 'It's between you and me now, Charlie.'

They flipped.

'How do we work this?' Parsons asked.

'You have to say whether we match or don't match,' O'Neill said.

'I say we match.'

They uncovered the coins. Both men were showing tails.

'You lose,' Parsons said.

'I always do,' O'Neill said, and somehow – in spite of his earlier eagerness to pay for the drinks – he seemed miffed now that he actually *had* to pay for them. 'I'm just plain unlucky,' he said. 'Some fellows go to carnivals, throw a few baseballs at a stuffed monkey, come home winning a power lawn mower. They buy one ticket in a raffle, and they win the new Dodge convertible. Me, I buy six books of tickets. I get nothing. I ain't never won anything in my whole life. I'm an unlucky son of a gun, all right.'

'Well,' Parsons said in a seeming attempt to cajole O'Neill, 'I'll pay for the next round.'

'Oh, no,' O'Neill said. 'We'll match for the next round.'

'We haven't even finished this round,' Jamison said politely.

'Makes no never mind,' O'Neill said. 'I'm gonna lose anyway. Come on, let's match.'

'You shouldn't take that attitude,' Parsons said. 'I believe that in matching, or in cards, or in things like that, you can control your own luck. No, really, you can. It's all in the mind. If you go into this thinking you're going to lose, why you *will* lose.'

'I'll lose no matter what,' O'Neill said. 'Come on, let's match.'

The men flipped their coins.

Parsons showed heads.

O'Neill showed heads.

Jamison showed tails.

'You're a real lucky fink,' O'Neill said, his irritation mounting. 'You could jump into a tub of horseshit and come out smelling of lavender.'

'Well, I'm not usually lucky,' Jamison said apologetically. He exchanged a quick glance with Parsons, whose uplifted eyebrows clearly expressed the opinion that O'Neill was a strange duck indeed.

'Come on, come on,' O'Neill said, 'let's get this over with. This time I'll call.' He and Parsons flipped their coins and covered them. 'We match,' O'Neill said.

Parsons uncovered heads.

O'Neill uncovered tails and said, 'Son of a bitch! You see? I never win, never! Goddamnit, let's match for the next round.'

'We're already a round ahead of ourselves,' Parsons said gently.

'You want me to pay for all the damn drinks, is that it?' O'Neill shouted.

'Well, no, no, that's not it.'

'Why won't you give me a chance to win back what I've lost?'

Parsons smiled gently and looked to Jamison for assistance.

Jamison cleared his throat. 'You misunderstand, Frank,' he said genially. 'We hadn't planned on making this a big drinking night. As a matter of fact, I haven't even had dinner yet.'

'Is three rounds of drinks a big drinking night?' O'Neill asked irritably. 'I say we match for the third round. I *insist* we match for the third round.'

Parsons smiled weakly. 'Frank, it's really academic. We may not even get to the third round. Look, let me pay for the last two rounds, huh? This party was my idea, and I'm a little embarrassed . . .'

'I lost, and I'll pay!' O'Neill said firmly. 'Now, come on, let's match for the third round.'

Parsons sighed. Jamison shrugged and caught Parsons' eye. The men flipped their coins.

'Heads,' Jamison said.

'Tails,' Parsons said.

'Tails,' O'Neill said sourly. 'This Jamison never loses, does he? By God, he never loses. Come on, it's between you and me, Charlie.'

'It's my turn to call, isn't it?' Parsons asked.

'Yes, yes,' O'Neill said impatiently. 'It's your god-damn turn to call.' He flipped and covered his coin. Parsons flipped, covered the coin and said, 'We won't match this time.' He lifted his hand: tails.

O'Neill uncovered his coin. 'Heads! I could have told you! I could have told you even before I looked at the damn thing. I never win! Never!' He rose angrily. 'Where's the men's room? I'm going to the men's room!'

He stalked away from the table, and Parsons watched him.

'I'd like to apologize,' Parsons said. 'When I invited him, I had no idea he was such a sore loser.'

'Hell, the matching was all his idea, anyway,' Jamison said.

'God, he really got riled up, didn't he?'

'He's a peculiar fellow,' Jamison said, shaking his head.

Parsons seemed to have a sudden idea. 'Listen,' he said, 'let's have some fun with him.'

'What kind of fun?'

'Well, he's a sore loser – worst I've ever seen.'

'Me, too,' Jamison said.

'He said he's got three thousand dollars with him. Let's take it away from him.'

'What?' Jamison said, suddenly righteously indignant.

'Not for keeps. We'll take it away from him and then give it all back later.'

'Take it away? But I don't understand.'

'We'll change the matching rules when he comes back. We'll make it odd man *loses*. All right, we'll make sure that your coin and my coin always match. Nine times out of ten, *he'll* be odd man. And loser.'

'How we going to do that?' Jamison asked, beginning to get interested in the idea of a little sport.

'Simple. Keep your coin on end, so you can shove it down to either heads or tails. If I touch my nose with my finger, make your coin show heads. If I don't touch it, show tails.'

'I see,' Jamison said, grinning.

'We'll keep raising the stakes. We'll clean him out, and then we'll give him back his money. Okay?'

Jamison couldn't keep the grin off his face. 'Boy,' he said, 'he's really going to blow his stack.'

'Until he knows it's all a gag,' Parsons said. He patted Jamison on the back. 'Here he comes. Now let me handle this.'

'All right,' Jamison said, secretly beginning to enjoy himself.

O'Neill came back to the table and sat. He seemed angry as hell. 'The second round come yet?' he asked.

'No,' Parsons said. 'You know, Frank, it's your attitude that makes you lose. I was just telling that to Elliot here.'

'Attitude, my ass,' O'Neill said. 'I'm just unlucky.'

'I can prove it to you,' Parsons said. 'Come on, let's match a little more.'

'I thought you said this wasn't going to be a drinking night,' O'Neill said suspiciously.

'We'll match for a few bucks, all right?'

'I'll lose,' O'Neill said.

'Why not give Charlie's theory a chance?' Jamison put in.

'Sure,' Parsons said. 'I've got a little money with me. Let's see how fast you can take it away from me, using my theory.' He paused, then turned to Jamison. 'You've got some money with you, haven't you, Elliot?'

'About two hundred and fifty dollars,' Jamison said. 'I don't like to carry too much with me. You never know.'

'That's wise,' Parsons said, nodding. 'What do you say, Frank?'

'All right, all right, what's your theory?'

'Just concentrate on winning, that's all. Think with

all your might. Just think *I'm going to win, I'm going to win*, that's all.'

'It won't work, but I'm game. How much do we bet?'

'Let's start with five,' Parsons said. 'To make it quicker, we'll do it this way. Odd man loses. He pays each of the other players five bucks. How does that sound?'

'Well, that sounds a little stee . . .' Jamison started.

'That sounds fine to me,' O'Neill said. Parsons winked at Jamison. Jamison gave a slight nod of acknowledgement, and then hastily said, 'Yes, that sounds fine to me, too.'

They began matching.

With remarkable regularity, O'Neill kept losing. Then, perhaps because Parsons wanted to make it look good, Jamison began to lose a little too. The men matched silently. Their table was in a corner of the place, protected from sight by a translucent glass wall. It is doubtful, anyway, that anyone would have stopped the men from their innocent coin-matching. They flipped, uncovered, exchanged bills. In a short while, O'Neill had lost something like four hundred dollars. Jamison had lost close to two hundred dollars. Parsons winked at Jamison every now and then, just to let him know that everything was proceeding according to plan. O'Neill kept complaining to Jamison – who was losing along with him – about Parsons' theory. 'The only one that goddamn theory works for is him himself,' O'Neill said.

They kept matching.

Jamison did not lose as much now. O'Neill kept losing, and he got angrier with each flip of the coin. Finally, he looked at both men and said, 'Say, what is this?'

'What's what?' Parsons asked.

'I've dropped nearly six hundred dollars so far.' He turned to Jamison. 'How much have you lost?'

Jamison did a little mental calculation. 'Oh, about two hundred thirty-five, something like that.'

'And you?' O'Neill said to Parsons.

'I'm winning,' Parsons said.

O'Neill looked at his two companions with a long, steady gaze. 'You wouldn't be trying to fleece me by any chance would you?' he asked.

'Fleece?' Parsons asked.

'You wouldn't be a pair of swindlers by any chance, would you?' O'Neill asked.

Jamison could hardly keep the grin off his face. Parsons winked at him.

'What makes you say that?' Parsons asked.

O'Neill rose suddenly. 'I'm calling a cop,' he said.

The grin dropped from Jamison's face. 'Hey now,' he said, 'wait a minute. We were just . . .'

Parsons, sitting secure with Jamison's $235 and O'Neill's $600 in his pocket, said, 'No need to get sore, Frank. A game's a game.'

'Besides,' Jamison said, 'we were only . . .'

Parsons put an arm on his sleeve and winked at him. 'The breaks are the breaks, Frank,' he said to O'Neill.

'And crooks are crooks,' O'Neill said. 'I'm getting a cop.' He started away from the table.

Jamison's face went white. 'Charlie,' he said, 'we've got to stop him. A joke is a joke, but Jesus . . .'

'I'll get him,' Parsons said, rising. He chuckled. 'God, he's a weird duck, isn't he? I'll bring him right back. You wait here.'

O'Neill had already reached the door. As he stepped outside, Parsons called, 'Hey, Frank! Wait a minute!' and ran out after him.

Jamison sat at the table alone, still frightened, telling himself he would never again be a party to a practical joke.

It wasn't until a half-hour later that he realized the joke was on him.

He told himself it couldn't be.

Then he sat for another half-hour.

Then he went to the nearest police station and told a detective named Arthur Brown the story.

Brown listened patiently, and then took a description of the two professional coin matchers who had conned Jamison out of two hundred and thirty-five dollars.

P. T. Barnum rolled over in his grave, chuckling.

4.

THE Missing Persons Bureau is a part of the Detective Division, and so the two men Bert Kling talked to were detectives.

One was called Ambrose.

The other was called Bartholdi.

'Naturally,' Bartholdi said, 'we got nothing to do here but concern ourselves with floaters.'

'Naturally,' Ambrose said.

'We only got reports on sixteen missing kids under the age of ten today, but we got nothing to do but worry about a stiff been in the water for six months.'

'Four months,' Kling corrected.

'Pardon me,' Bartholdi said.

'With dicks from the 87th,' Ambrose said, 'you got to be careful. You slip up by a couple of months, they jump down your throat. They got very technical flatfoots at the 87th.'

'We try our hardest,' Kling said drily.

'Humanitarians all,' Bartholdi said. 'They worry about floaters. They got concern for the human race.'

'Us,' Ambrose said, 'all we got to worry about is the three-year-old kids who vanish from their front stoops. That's all we got to worry about.'

'You'd think I was asking to spend the night with your sister,' Kling said. 'All I want is a look at your files.'

'I'd rather you spent the night with my sister,'

Bartholdi said. 'You might be disappointed since she's only eight years old, but I'd still rather.'

'It ain't that we don't believe in inter-departmental cooperation,' Ambrose said. 'There ain't nothing we like better than helping out fellow flatfoots. Ain't that a fact, Romeo?'

Romeo Bartholdi nodded. 'Tell him about our war record, Mike.'

Ambrose said, 'It was us who went to the Pacific after World War II to help clear up all that unidentified dead problem.'

'If you cleaned up the whole Pacific Theatre,' Kling said, 'you should be able to help me with one floater.'

'The trouble with flatfoots,' Bartholdi said, 'is they got no heads for clerical work. We've got a dandy filing system here, you see? If we let dicks from all over the city come in and foul it up, we'd never be able to identify *anybody* anymore.'

'Well, I'm glad you've got such a real nice filing system,' Kling said. 'Do you plan on keeping it a secret from the rest of the department, or will you throw open the files during Open School Week?'

'Another thing I like about the bulls from the 87th,' Ambrose said, 'is that they are all so comical. When one of them is around, you can hardly keep from wetting your pants.'

'With glee,' Bartholdi said.

'That's what makes a good cop,' Ambrose expanded. 'Humour, humaneness, and devotion to detail.'

'Plus the patience of Job,' Kling said. 'Do I get a peek at the goddamn files, or don't I?'

'Temper, temper,' Bartholdi said.

'How far back do you want to go?' Ambrose asked.

'About six months.'

'I thought she was in the water for only four?'

'She may have been reported missing before then.'

'Clever, clever,' Bartholdi said. 'God, this city would fall to smouldering ashes were it not for the 87th Precinct.'

'All right, screw you,' Kling said, turning. 'I'll tell the lieutenant your files aren't open for our inspection. So long, fellers.'

'He's running home to mama,' Bartholdi said, unfazed.

'Mama's liable to be upset,' Kling said. 'Mama doesn't mind a good joke but not on the city's time.'

'All work and no play . . .' Bartholdi started, and then cut himself short when he saw that Kling actually was leaving. 'All right, sorehead,' he said, 'come look at the files. Come drown in the files. We've got enough missing persons here to keep you going for a year.'

'Thanks a lot,' Kling said, and he followed the detectives down the corridor.

'We try to keep them cross-indexed,' Ambrose said. 'This ain't the I.B., but we do our level best. We got 'em alphabetically, and we got 'em chronologically – according to when they were reported missing – and we got 'em broken down male and female.'

'The boys with the boys, and the girls with the girls,' Bartholdi said.

'There's everything you need in each of the separate folders. Medical reports where we could get 'em, dental charts, even letters and documents in some of the folders.'

'Don't mix the folders up,' Bartholdi said. 'That would mean getting a beautiful blonde police stenographer in to straighten them out again.'

'And we don't cotton to beautiful blondes around here,' Ambrose said.

'We kick 'em out in the street whenever they come knocking.'

'That's because we're both respectable married men.'

'Who resist all temptations,' Bartholdi concluded. 'Here are the files.' He made a grandiloquent sweeping gesture with one arm, indicating the banks and banks of green filing cabinets which lined the walls of the room. 'This is April, and you want to go back six months. That'd put you in November.' He made a vague gesture with one hand. 'That's over there someplace.' He winked at Ambrose. 'Now, are we cooperating, or *are* we?'

'You're the most cooperative,' Kling said.

'Hope you find what you need,' Ambrose said, opening the door. 'Come on, Romeo.'

Bartholdi followed him out. Kling sighed, looked at the filing cabinets, and then lighted a cigarette. There was a sign on one of the walls and the sign read: SHUFFLE THEM, JIGGLE THEM, MAUL THEM, CARESS THEM — BUT LEAVE THEM THE WAY YOU FOUND THEM!

He walked around the room until he came to the cabinet containing the file of persons who were reported missing in November of the preceding year. He opened the top drawer of the cabinet, pulled up a straight-back wooden chair upon which to prop his foot and doggedly began leafing through the folders.

The work was not exactly unpleasant, but it was far from exciting. The average misconception of the city detective, of course, is one of a tough, big man wearing a shoulder holster, facing a desperate criminal and shooting it out in the streets. Kling was big, not so tough, and he carried his service revolver in a leather holster clipped into his right back pocket. He was not shooting it out with anyone at the moment, desperate or not. The only desperation he knew was of a quiet sort which drives many city detectives into the nearest loony bin where they silently pick at the coverlets. Kling, at the moment, was involved in routine – and routine is the most routine thing in the world.

Routine is what makes you wash your face and shave and brush your teeth in the morning.

Routine is the business of inserting a key into the ignition switch, twisting the key, starting the car, and putting it into Drive before you can go anyplace.

Routine is answering a letter with a polite 'Thank you,' and then answering the resultant 'Thank you' letter with another letter stating 'You're welcome.'

Routine is the list of questions you ask the surviving wife of an automobile accident victim.

Routine is the tag you fill out and attach to a piece of evidence.

Routine is the report you type back at the squad room.

Routine is a deadly dull bore, and it isn't even crashing, and detectives know routine in triplicate and the detective who isn't patient with a typewriter – no matter what his method of typing may be – doesn't last very long in the detective division.

When you've looked at missing-person report after missing-person report, you begin to wish you were missing yourself. After a while, they all begin to blend together into a big mass of humanity which has formed a conspiracy to bore you to death. After a while, you don't know who has the birthmark on her left breast or who has the tattoo on his big toe. After a while, you don't even care. There are amusing breaks in the routine, of course, but these are few and far between. Like the husband and wife, for example, who both vanished on the same day and who later filed missing-person reports for each other. Very comical, and Kling grinned, picturing the husband as an Alec Guinness type of character lolling with a brunette in Brazil. He formed no mental picture of the wife. He lighted another cigarette and continued his search for someone who might possibly resemble the 87th's floater.

He consumed two packages of cigarettes while perusing the files. He had finished the first pack before lunch. He went out for a ham sandwich and a cup of coffee which he took back to the bureau with him, together with a fresh package of cigarettes and a warning to himself to go slow on the coffin nails. By the end of the day, he had finished the second pack, and he'd also collected a sizeable pile of folders which could possibly tie in with the floater. One report looked particularly promising. Kling opened the folder again and went over the material inside it.

There were, Kling noticed, certain inconsistencies in the report. Early in the report, for example, the girl was 'last seen at' her 'home address' on 31 October at 11.45 p.m. Later in the report, under REMARKS, the girl was last seen at the Scranton railroad station the next morning. Kling surmised, as he was forced to surmise, that police procedure was responsible for the foul-up. Henry Proschek was the man who'd reported his daughter missing. And he had probably last seen her in his own home on the night of 31 October. Someone else, apparently, had seen her at the railroad station the next morning, had observed her carefully enough to describe what she was wearing. But this someone else was not the person filing the complaint, hence the inconsistency. There was, Kling further noticed, a question mark under

POLICE DEPARTMENT
REPORT OF MISSING PERSON

Bel./Dist. —— Squad ——
Case No. ——
M.P. Bur. No. 72165018
Date of This Report 11/7

Surname PROSCHEK	First Name MARY LOUISE	Initials	Nativity U.S.A.	Sex	Age 34	Color

| Address 1112 Main Scranton, Pa. | Home address At? | | | | | |
| Probable Destination This city | Cause of Absence ? | | Date and Time Seen 10/31 | | | |

| | | Date and Time Reported 11/7 11:45 8:15 a.m. p.m. | | | | |

PHYSICAL note peculiarities	Headgear	CLOTHING—give color, fabric, style, label, where possible	strike out irrelevant words	MISCELLANEOUS INFORMATION
Height Ft. 5 in. 3¼	Headgear Hatless			Occupation or School File clerk
Weight 128	Jacket or Sweater None			Ever Fingerprinted? Where & When? Never
Build Stout	Overcoat Top Coat Blue reversible—red inside			Dry Cleaner Marks Dress and coat—X3175 Do-Brite Cleaners, Scranton
	Suit or Dress Navy blue shantung, white buttons up front			
Complexion Fair	Shirt or Blouse None	Vest		Laundry Marks
Hair Blond	Scarf Red silk			Photo Rcv'd Yes Prev. Missing No
Eyes Blue	Tie or Fur Piece None			Publicity Desired? Yes
Glasses, Type ——	Trousers or Skirt None	Gloves Red cotton		Soc. Sec. # 119-16-4683
Mustache—Beard ——	Hose Natural nylon, seamless			Preliminary Investigation
Teeth See dental	Shoes Navy blue calf pump, with rhinestone crescent			Desk Officer Sgt. Davis, 11th Pct. Telegraph Bureau Dept./3rd Gr. P. Levine

chart in folder		Handbag	Navy blue calf, sling strap
			Bureau of Information Det./Lst
			Gr. R. Nicholson
		Others	
		Luggage ?	
Scars		Jewelry Worn	Marley High
Appendectory scar			School ring—class of June, 1939—worn on right ring finger
			Notification to M.P. Bureau
Deformities	None		
Tattoo Marks	None	Money Carried	$4,375.00 be-lleved to be withdrawn from Scranton bank
			By: Det.-Lt. B. Raphael, 14th Detective Squad
			Received at M.P. Bureau
			by: Sgt. L. Norris
		Characteristics, Habits, Mannerisms	
Physical	None		Assigned Det./
			By: Sgt. L. Norris
			Squad
Condition			Assigned Date./
Physical Good	Mental Good		M.P. Bur.
			2nd Gr., John Phillips
Reported by		Address	Telephone No.
Henry Proschek		Scranton, Pa.	SC 2-7185
			Relationship
		1112 Main	Father

Remarks

Girl gave no indication she was leaving home. Was seen at train station next morning. Subsequent letter from this city (no return address) advised parents she had come here to start "a new life." Also said "longer" letter will follow." (See letter in folder.) This was last contact parents had with girl. Father, in city week later, phoned 14th nearest precinct.

Det. John Phillips
Signature of Assigned Detective

Lt. Samuel Barker
Commis.   Civilian

the word 'LUGGAGE'. He wondered if she had indeed gone baggageless, or if the observer at the station had simply failed to notice any luggage.

The report was somewhat vague when it said 'See letter in folder.' Did this mean the first letter the girl had written, or the longer letter she'd promised? And which of these letters was the last contact the parents had had? The answer, obviously, was in the folder.

Kling opened it again.

There was only one letter in the folder. Apparently, the second longer letter had never been written. And apparently it was this lack of further clarifying communication which had brought Henry Proschek to the city in search of his daughter, culminating in his phone call to the closest police station.

Feeling somewhat like a Peeping Tom, Kling began reading Mary Louise Proschek's letter to her parents:

1 November

Dear Mom and Daddy:

I know your not worried I was kidnapped or anything because Betty Anders happened to spy me at the station this morning and by now it is probly all over town. So I know your not worried but I suppose you are wondering why I have left and when I am coming back.

I suppose I shouldn't have left without an explanation, but I don't think you would understand or improve what Im about to do. I have been planing on it for a long time, and it is something I have to do which is also why I have been staying on at Johnson's because I was saving my money all these years. I now have more than $4,000 dollars, you have to hand it to me for being persistint, ha ha.

I will write you a longer letter when everything here is

*settled. I am starting a new life here, Daddy, so please
don't be too angry with me. Try to understand. Love and
kisses.*

Your loving dghtr,
Mary Louise

Whoever Detective Phillips of the Missing Persons
Bureau was, he had done a good job on the missing
Proschek girl. He had put a call through to the Scranton
police, who had then checked with the girl's bank and
discovered that $4,375.00 had been withdrawn from her
account on 31 October, the day before she'd left. The
withdrawal slip had been signed by her and presented by
her together with her pass book. Detective Phillips had
then put a check on every bank in the city in an attempt
to locate a new account started by Mary Louise Proschek.
Each bank reported negatively. Phillips had checked on
the stationery the girl used, and found it to be five and
dime stuff. The letter had been mailed Special Delivery
and postmarked from a station in the heart of the city. A
check had been made of hock shops in the hope the
high-school graduation ring would turn up. It had not.
Phillips had acquired a dental chart from the girl's
parents, and that was in her folder. Kling removed it and
gave it a summary glance.

He remembered that the floater's lower front teeth had
been lost in the water, but he couldn't remember which
of her other teeth had fillings, or which had been
extracted. He sighed and turned to some of the other
information in the folder.

The preliminary investigatory work had been handled
by people other than the Missing Persons Bureau, of

48

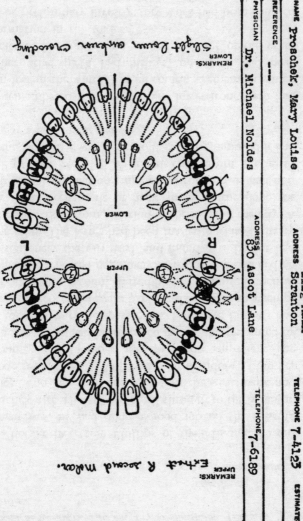

REMARKS: Slight lower anterior crowding

LOWER

UPPER

REMARKS: Extract R second molar.

L

R

UPPER

LOWER

course. When Henry Proschek had reported his daughter's absence to the 14th Precinct, the detective he'd spoken to had immediately checked with the desk officer to ascertain whether or not Mary Louise had been either arrested or hospitalized in his precinct. He then checked with Communications and the Bureau of Information to find out if anyone answering her description was in a hospital or a morgue at the moment. When his efforts to locate her had proved fruitless, he had then phoned the information in to the M.P. Bureau where the routine business of preparing forms in triplicate had then followed. And, to confirm his phone call, he mailed on the next day one of the triplicate copies of his own report to the M.P. Bureau.

The M.P. Bureau had sent out a teletype alarm throughout the city and to nearby police areas. And the name of Mary Louise Proschek had been added to the daily mimeographed list of missing persons which is distributed to transportation terminals, hospitals and any place where a refugee might seek help or shelter.

The girl was still missing. Perhaps she was the 87th's floater.

But if Kling could remember very little about the floater's teeth, he could remember one important point about her right hand. There had been a tattoo on the flap of skin between the girl's right thumb and forefinger — the word MAC in a heart.

On Mary Louise Proschek's missing person report, under the heading TATTOOS, there was one word — and that word was 'None'.

5.

HENRY PROSCHEK was a small thin man with deep brown eyes and a bald head. He was a coal miner and the grime of three decades had permanently lodged beneath his fingernails and in the seams of his face. He was dressed in his Sunday best, and he had scrubbed himself vigorously before coming up from Scranton, but he still looked grubby and if you didn't know his trade was the honest occupation of extracting coal from the earth, you would have considered him a dirty little man.

He sat in the squad room of the 87th Precinct, and Carella watched him. There was indignation in Proschek's eyes, a flaring indignation which Carella had not thought the miner capable of. Proschek had just listened to Kling's little speech, and now there was indignation in his eyes, and Carella wondered whether or not Kling had delivered his talk wrong. He decided that Kling had done it in the only way possible. The kid was new, but he was learning, and there are only so many ways to tell a man his daughter is dead.

Proschek sat with his indignation in his eyes, and then his anger spread to his mouth and bubbled from his lips. 'She's not dead,' he said.

'She *is*, Mr Proschek,' Kling said. 'Sir, I'm sorry, but . . .'

'She's not dead,' Proschek said firmly.

'Sir . . .'

And again he said, '*She's not dead!*'

Kling turned to Carella. Carella shoved himself off the

50

desk effortlessly. 'Mr Proschek,' he said, 'we've compared the dead girl's teeth with the dental chart you gave to the Missing Persons Bureau. They're identical, sir. Believe me, we wouldn't have had this happen . . .'

'There's been a mistake,' Proschek said.

'There's been no mistake, sir.'

'How could she be dead?' Proschek asked. 'She came here to start a new life. She said so. She wrote that to me. So how could she be dead?'

'Her body . . .'

'And you wouldn't find my daughter drowned. My daughter was an excellent swimmer. My daughter won a medal in high school for her swimming. I don't know who that girl is, but she's not Mary Louise.'

'Sir . . .'

'I'd have broke her neck if she wore a tattoo. You said this dead girl has a tattoo on her hand. My Mary Louise would never even have considered a thing like that.'

'That's what we wanted to find out from you, sir,' Carella said. 'You told us she didn't have a tattoo. In that case, she must have acquired the tattoo in this city. We know she wasn't drowned, you see. She was dead before she entered the water. So if we can tie in the tattoo with . . .'

'That dead girl isn't my daughter,' Proschek said. 'You brought me all the way from Pennsylvania, and she isn't even my daughter. Why are you wasting my time? I had to lose a whole day, just to come here.'

'Sir,' Carella said firmly, 'that girl *is* your daughter. Please try to understand that.' Proschek stared at him hostilely. 'Did she have any friends named Mac?' Carella asked.

'None,' Proschek said.

'MacDonald, MacDougall, McMorrow, McManus, McThing, Mc-Anything?'

'No.'

'Are you certain?'

'My daughter didn't have many boy friends,' Proschek said. 'She . . . she wasn't a very pretty girl. She had good colouring, fair, like her mother – blue eyes and blonde hair, that's a good combination – but she didn't . . . she wasn't very pretty. I . . . I used to feel sorry for her. A man . . . it doesn't matter if a man isn't good-looking. But to a girl, looks are everything. I used to feel sorry for her.' He paused and looked up at Carella and then repeated, as if to clarify his earlier statements, 'She wasn't very pretty, my daughter.'

Carella looked down at Proschek, knowing the coal miner had used the past tense, knowing that the girl was already dead in Proschek's mind, and wondering why the man fought the knowledge now, fought the indisputable knowledge that his daughter was dead and had been dead for at least three months.

'Please think, Mr Proschek,' he said. 'Did she ever mention anyone named Mac?'

'No,' Proschek said. 'Why should Mary Louise mention a Mac? That girl isn't Mary Louise.' He paused, got a sudden idea, and said, 'I want to see that girl.'

'We'd rather you didn't,' Carella said.

'I want to see her. You say she's my daughter, and you show me dental charts, and that's all a lot of crap. I want to see that girl. I can tell you whether or not she's Mary Louise.'

'Is that what you called her?' Carella asked. 'Mary Louise?'

'That's what I baptized her. Mary Louise. Everybody else called her just plain Mary, but that wasn't the way I intended it. I intended it Mary Louise. That's a pretty name, isn't it? Mary Louise. Mary is too . . . plain.' He blinked. 'Too plain.' He blinked again. 'I want to see that girl. Where is that girl?'

'At the mortuary,' Kling said.

'Then take me there. A relative's supposed to identify a . . . a body, isn't he? Isn't that the case?'

Kling looked at Carella.

'We'll check out a car and take Mr Proschek to the hospital,' Carella said wearily.

They did not talk much on the ride to the hospital. The three men sat on the front seat of the Mercury sedan, and the city burst with April greenery around them, but the inside of the car was curiously cheerless. They drove into the hospital parking lot, and Carella parked the police sedan in a space reserved for the hospital staff. Mr Proschek blinked against the sunshine when he got out of the car. Then he followed Carella and Kling to the morgue.

The detectives did not have to identify themselves to the attendant. They had both been there many times before. They told the attendant the number they wanted, and then they followed him past the rows of doors set into the corridor wall, the small refrigerator doors behind each one of which was a corpse.

'We don't advise this, Mr Proschek,' Carella said. 'Your daughter was in the water for a long time. I don't think . . .'

Proschek was not listening to him. They had stopped before a door marked 28, and Proschek was watching the attendant.

'Yes or no, Steve?' the attendant asked, reaching for the handle of the door.

Carella sighed. 'Show it to him, Buddy,' he said, and the attendant opened the door and rolled out the slab.

Proschek looked at the decomposed, hairless body of

the girl on the slab. Carella watched him, and for a brief second he saw recognition leap into the coal miner's eyes, shocking, sudden recognition and he felt some of the pain the old man was feeling.

And then Proschek turned to face Carella, and his eyes were like agate, and his mouth was set into a hard, tight line.

'No,' he said. 'She's not my daughter.'

His words echoed down the long corridor. The attendant rolled the slab back into the refrigerator compartment, and the rollers squeaked.

'He claiming the body?' the attendant asked.

'Mr Proschek?' Carella asked.

'What?' Proschek said.

'Are you claiming the body?'

'What?'

'Are you . . .?'

'No,' Proschek said. 'She's not my daughter.' He turned and started down the corridor, his heels clacking on the concrete floor. 'She's not my daughter,' he said, his voice rising, 'she's not my daughter, she's not my daughter, she's not my daughter.'

And then he reached the door at the end of the corridor, and he fell to his knees, his hand clutching the knob, and he began sobbing bitterly. Carella ran to him, and he stooped and put his arm around the old man, and Proschek buried his face in Carella's chest, weeping, and he said, 'Oh, my God, she's dead, my Mary Louise is dead, my daughter is dead, my daughter . . .' and then he couldn't say anything else because his body was trembling and his tears were choking him.

The beauty of being a shoemaker, Teddy Carella thought, is that you don't take your work home with you. You cobble so many shoes, and then you go home to your wife, and you don't think about soles and heels until the next day.

A cop thinks about heels all the time.

A cop like Steve Carella thinks about souls, too.

She would not, of course, have been married to anyone else but it pained her none the less to see him sitting by the window brooding. His brooding position was almost classical, almost like the Rodin statue. He sat slumped in the easy chair, his chin cupped in one large hand, his legs crossed. He sat barefoot, and she loved his feet, that was ridiculous, you don't love a man's feet, well the hell with you, I love his feet. They've got good clean arches and nice toes, sue me.

She walked to where he was sitting.

She was not a tall girl, but she somehow gave an impression of height. She held her head high, and her shoulders erect, and she walked lightly with a regal grace that added inches to her stature. Her hair was black, and her eyes were brown, and she wore no lipstick now on full lips which needed none anyway. The lips of Teddy Carella were decorative – decorative in that they were beautiful, and decorative in that they could never form words. She had been born deaf, and she could neither hear nor speak and so her entire face, her entire body served as her means of communication.

Her face spoke in exaggerated syllables. Her eyes gave tongue to words she could not utter. Her hands moved fluidly, expressively, to convey meaning. When Teddy Carella listened, her eyes never left your face. When Teddy Carella 'spoke', you were compelled to give her your complete attention because her pantomime some-how enhanced the delicacy of her loveliness.

Now, standing spread-legged before her brooding

husband, she put her hands on her hips and stared down at him. She wore a red wrap-around skirt, a huge gold safety-pin fastening it just above her left knee. She wore red Capezio flats, and a white blouse swooped low at the throat to the first swelling rise of her breasts. She had caught her hair back with a bright red ribbon, and she stood before him now and defied him to continue with his sullen brooding.

Neither spoke. Teddy because she could not, and Carella because he would not. The silent skirmish filled the small apartment.

At last, Carella said, 'All right, all right.'

Teddy nodded and cocked one eyebrow.

'Yes,' he said, 'I'm emerging from my shell.'

She hinged her hands together at the wrist and opened them slowly, and then snapped them shut.

'You're right,' Carella said. 'I'm a clam.'

She pointed a pistol-finger at him and squeezed the trigger.

'Yes, my work,' he said.

Abruptly, without warning, she moved on to his lap. His arms circled her, and she cuddled up into a warm ball, pulling her knees up, snuggling her head against his chest. She looked up at him, and her eyes said *Tell me*.

'This girl,' he said. 'Mary Louise Proschek.'

Teddy nodded.

'Thirty-three years old, comes to the city to start a new life. Turns up floating in the Harb. Letter to her folks was full of good spirits. Even if we suspected suicide, which we don't, the letter would fairly well eliminate that. The m.e. says she was dead before she hit the water. Cause of death was acute arsenic poisoning. You following me?'

Teddy nodded, her eyes wide.

'She's got a tattoo mark right here . . .' He showed the

spot on his right hand. '. . . the word Mac in a heart. Didn't have it when she left Scranton, her home town. How many Macs do you suppose there are in this city?'

Teddy rolled her eyes.

'You said it. Did she come here to meet this Mac? Did she just run into him by accident? Is he the one who threw her in the river after poisoning her? How do you go about locating a guy named Mac?'

Teddy pointed to the flap of skin between her thumb and forefinger.

'The tattoo parlours? I've already started checking them. We may get a break because not many women wear tattoos.'

Quickly, Teddy unbuttoned the top button of her blouse and then pulled it open, using both hands, spreading it in a wide dramatic 'V'.

'The Rose Tattoo?' Carella asked. 'That's fiction.'

Teddy shrugged.

Carella grinned. 'Besides, I think you just wanted an excuse to bare your bosom.'

Teddy shrugged again, impishly.

'Not that it isn't a lovely bosom.'

Teddy's eyebrows wagged seductively. She curved her hands through the air and moistened her lips.

'Of course,' Carella said, 'I've seen better.'

Oh? Teddy's face asked, suddenly coldly aloof.

'There was this girl in burlesque,' Carella expanded. 'She could set them going in opposite directions, one swinging to the right, the other to the left. Had a little light on each one. They'd turn out all the house lights and you'd just see these two circles of light in the darkness. Fantastic!' He grinned at his wife. 'Now that's what I call talent.'

Teddy shrugged, telling her husband that that was what she didn't call any talent whatever.

'You, on the other hand . . .' His hand came up suddenly to cup her breast. Gingerly, delicately, Teddy picked up his hand with her thumb and forefinger and deposited it on the arm of the chair.

'Angry?' Carella asked.

Teddy shook her head.

'Love me?' Carella asked.

Teddy shook her head most vigorously.

'Hate me?'

No.

'Who then?'

Teddy swung her forefingers in opposite directions, and Carella burst out laughing. 'You hate the burlesque dancer?'

Teddy gave one emphatic nod.

'I don't blame you,' he said. 'She was an old bag.'

Teddy beamed and threw her arms around his neck.

'Now do you love me?'

Yes, yes, yes.

'What'd you do all day?' he asked, holding her close, beginning to relax, succumbing to the warmth of her.

Teddy opened her hands like a book.

'Read?' Carella watched while she nodded. 'What'd you read?'

Teddy scrambled off his lap and then clutched her middle, indicating that she had read something that was very funny. She walked across the room and he watched her when she stooped alongside the magazine rack.

'If you're not careful,' he said, 'I'm going to undo that damn safety-pin.'

She put the magazines on the floor, stood up, and undid the safety-pin. The skirt hung loose, one flap over the other. When she stooped to pick up the magazine again, it opened in a wide slit from her knee to almost her waist. Wiggling like the burlesque queen Carella had described, she walked back to him and dumped the magazines in his lap.

'Pen-pal magazines?' Carella asked, astonished.

Teddy hunched up her shoulders, grinned, and then covered her mouth with one hand.

'My God!' he said. 'Why?'

With her hands on her hips, Teddy kicked at the ceiling with one foot, the skirt opening over the clean line of her leg.

'For kicks?' Carella asked, shrugging. 'What kind of stuff is in here? "*Dear Pen Pal; I am a cocker spaniel who always wanted to be in the movies . . .*"'

Teddy grinned and opened one of the magazines for him. Carella thumbed through it. She sat on the arm of his chair, and the skirt opened again. He looked at the magazine, and then he looked at his woman, and then he said, 'The hell with this noise,' and he threw the magazine to the floor and pulled Teddy on to his lap.

The magazine fell open to the Personals column.

It lay on the floor while Steve Carella kissed his wife. It lay on the floor when he picked her up and carried her into the next room.

There was a small ad in the Personals column.

It read:

Widower. Mature. Attractive. 35 years old. Seeks alliance with understanding woman of good background. Write P.O. Box 137.

6.

THE girl had read the advertisement six times, and she was now on her fifth revision of the letter she was writing in answer to it.

She was not a stupid girl, nor did she particularly believe anything romantic or exciting would happen after she mailed her letter. She was, after all, thirty-seven years old and she had come to believe – once she'd turned thirty-five – that romance and excitement would never be a part of her life.

There was, in the girl's mind, a certain cynicism. There were some who would call her cynicism a simple case of sour grapes, but she honestly believed it was a good deal more than that. She had been weaned on the Big Romance legend, had had it bleated at her in radio serials, flashed before her eyes at the local movie house, seen it and heard it since she was old enough to understand the English language. She had been more susceptible to the legend because she was a girl, and a rather imaginative girl at that. For her, the knight in shining armour *did* exist – and she would wait until he came along.

When you're not so pretty, the waiting can take a long time.

'Marty' is a nice enough fiction, but the girls outnumber the men in this world of ours and not many people care whether or not you can do Differential Calculus so long as you've got a beautiful phizz. Besides, she couldn't do Differential Calculus. Nor had she ever considered herself a particularly intelligent girl. She had gone to business school and scraped through, and she was a fair enough secretary at a small hardware concern, and she was convinced at the age of thirty-seven that the Big Romance legend which had been foisted upon her by the fiction con men was just a great big crock.

She didn't mind it being a great big crock.

She told herself she didn't mind.

She had said good-bye to her virginity when she turned twenty-nine. She had been disappointed. No trumpets blasting, no banners unfurling, no clamorous medley of gonging bells. Just pain. Since that time, she had dabbled. She considered sex the periodic gratification of a purely natural urge. She approached sex with the paradoxical relentlessness of an uncaged jungle beast and the precise aloofness of a Quaker bride. Sex was like sleep. You needed both, but you didn't spend your life in bed.

And now, at thirty-seven, long since her parents had given up all hope for her, long since she herself had abandoned the Big Romance, the Wedding in June, the Honeymoon at Lovely Lake Lewis legend, she felt lonely.

She kept her own apartment, primarily because her jousting with sex would never have been understood by her parents, partly because she wanted complete independence – and alone in the apartment she could hear the creaking of the floorboards and the unrelenting drip of the water tap, and she knew complete aloneness.

It is a big world.

From somewhere out in that big world, a mature attractive man of thirty-five sought an alliance with an understanding woman of good background.

Cut and dried, cold and impersonal, stripped of all the

fictional hoop-dee-dah. The man could have been advertising for a Pontiac convertible or a slightly used power mower. She supposed it was this directness of approach which appealed to her. Understanding. Could she understand his appeal? Could she understand his loneliness, the single cipher in a teeming world of matched and mismatched couples? She thought she could. She thought she could detect honesty in his simple appeal.

And because she detected honesty there, her own dishonesty left her feeling somewhat guilty. This was the fifth draft of her letter, and her age had changed with each draft. In the first letter, she'd claimed to be thirty. The second letter advanced her age by two years. The third letter went back to thirty again. Number four admitted to thirty-one. She had done a bit of soul-searching before starting on the fifth rewrite.

He was, when you considered it, thirty-five. But he'd said he was mature. A mature man of thirty-five isn't a college kid with a briar pipe. A mature man of thirty-five wanted and needed a woman of understanding. Could this not mean a woman who was slightly older than he, a woman who could . . . mother him? Sort of? Besides, wasn't complete honesty essential at this stage of the game? Especially with this man whose plea was devoid of all frills and fripperies?

But thirty-seven sounded so close to forty.

Who wants a forty-year-old spinster? (*Should she mention that she was wise in the ways of the world?*)

Thirty-three, on the other hand, sounded too suburban housewife – skirt and blouse and nylons and loafers, going to meet the 6.10. Was that what he wanted? A scatter-brained little blonde who hopped into the station wagon in compliance with the Commuter Romance

Legend – the automaton who set the roast according to her husband's train schedule? The robot who had the shakerful of martinis waiting for dear tired old hubby, *hard day at the mine today, sweetheart?*

Or was he looking for the sleeker model? The silver-toned beauty in the red Thunderbird rushing over country lanes. Grey flannel pedal pushers, white blouse, bright red scarf at the throat, push button control, push-pull-click-click. *Dahling, we're terribly late for the Samalsons. Do tie your tie.*

He wanted honesty.

'I am thirty-six years old,' she wrote.

Well, almost honesty.

She crossed out the words. This man deserved *complete* honesty. She tore up the fifth letter, picked up the pen, and in a neat precise hand – except for the t's which were crossed with somewhat animalistic ferocity – she began writing her letter again.

> *Dear Sir:*
>
> *I am thirty-seven years old.*
>
> *I start my letter with this fact because I do not wish to waste your time. Your appeal seemed, to me, an honest one – and so I am being completely honest in return. I am thirty-seven. That is the fact of the matter. If you are now tearing up this letter and throwing it into the waste basket, so be it.*
>
> *You asked for an understanding woman. I ask for an understanding man. It is not easy to write this letter. I can imagine how difficult it was for you to place your ad, and I can understand what led you to do so. I can only ask for the same understanding on your part.*
>
> *I feel almost as if I were applying for a position somewhere. I don't want to feel that way, but I can see no*

other way of letting you know what I am like and I wish (if you decide to answer my letter) that you will follow the same pattern. I am going to tell you what I am, and who I am.

Physically, I am five-feet-four inches tall. I am one hundred and ten pounds without dieting. I mention that because I'm not one of these women who have to watch everything they eat. I always stay slim. I've been the same weight, give or take a few pounds, for the longest time. I can still wear skirts I bought when I was twenty-one.

My hair is brown, and my eyes are brown. I wear glasses. I had to start wearing them when I was twelve because I ruined my eyes reading so much. I don't read very much anymore. I've become disillusioned with fiction, and the non-fiction is either inspirational stuff or stuff about mountain climbing, and I neither want to be inspired nor do I desire to climb Everest. I thought for a while that foreign novels might offer me something American novels didn't — but everyone is selling the same thing these days, and the product usually suffers in translation. Perhaps you've run across some reading which I haven't discovered yet, and which could offer me the deep pleasure I got from books when I was a little girl. If so, I'd appreciate knowing about it.

I dress quietly. The brightest dress I own is a yellow taffeta, and I haven't worn that for ages. I usually prefer suits. I work in an office you see, and it's a somewhat staid place. I have a lot of clothes, incidentally, which I've accumulated over the years. I wouldn't call myself exactly penniless, either. I'm a secretary, and I've been earning close to ninety dollars a week for a long time. Twenty of that I send to my parents, but the remaining seventy or so is more than enough to keep me going. This may sound ridiculously businesslike, but I do have almost five thousand dollars in

*the bank, and I'd honestly like to know what your
financial setup is, too.*

*My tastes are simple. I like good music. I don't mean
Rock and Roll. I've sort of outgrown the candy stick and
dungaree set. I like Brahms and I like Wagner — Wagner
especially. There is something wild in his music, and I find
it exciting. I like pop music on the sentimental side. I don't
mean the current hit parade rages. I mean old standards
done up in albums. Stuff like* Smoke Gets In Your Eyes
and Stardust *and* This Love Of Mine, *you get the idea.
I think my favourite record album is Sinatra's* In The
Wee Small Hours. *I've always liked him, and whatever
his trouble with Ava Gardner, it's none of my business. I
listen to records a lot. Living alone can be too quiet. I play
my albums at night, and they help to pass the time.*

*I generally sew while I'm listening. I'm a good
seamstress and I've made many of my own clothes. I hate
darning socks, I feel I should tell you that right now. I
feel I should also tell you that my indoor activities are not
confined to playing records alone.*

She stopped here, wondering if she had said too much,
wondering if she sounded too bold. Would he understand what she meant? A widower couldn't possibly
want a girl with absolutely no experience! Still . . .

*I do a lot of other things indoors. Like cooking. And
other things. I'm a good cook. I can make potatoes forty-two
different ways, I'm not exaggerating, and my speciality is
Southern fried chicken, though I have never been down
South. My ambition is to travel around the United States
someday. I half think that's why I've been saving my
money so religiously.*

Oh . . . religion.

I'm Protestant.

I hope you're Protestant, too, but it really doesn't matter that much. I hope you're white, too, because I am *and* that would matter to me — not that I'm prejudiced or anything. Honestly, I'm not. But I'm too mature to be defiant, and I don't feel like battling the good fight for democracy, not at this late stage of the game. I hope you understand this isn't bigotry. It's caution, it's fear, it's wanting to belong, it's whatever you choose to call it. But it's not bigotry.

I ride a little, usually in the Spring and in the Fall. I like the outdoors, though I'm not a very good athlete. I swim pretty well. I have a fast crawl. I was once a swimming counsellor at a children's camp, and I learned to dislike children that Summer. Of course, I've never had any of my own so I wouldn't know. I imagine it's different with your own. You said you are a widower. Do you have any children?

So far, you are just a post-office box-number, and here I've told you almost everything I could think of about myself. I like movies. John Wayne is my favourite. He's not very good-looking, but there is a manliness about him, and I think that's very important.

Well, I suppose that's it.

I hope you'll answer this letter. I'll send you a picture if you like after I hear from you again. I say 'again', because I feel by reading your ad I've already heard from you once. And I honestly feel I did 'hear' you, if you know what I mean.

Sincerely,

Priscilla Ames
41 La Mesa Street
Phoenix, Arizona

Priscilla Ames read her letter over. It seemed honest

and sincere to her. She had no desire to make herself sound more attractive than she really was. Why start out with a bunch of lies and then get tangled up in them later? No, this was the best way.

Priscilla Ames folded the letter – which ran to some six pages – and then put it into the envelope. She copied the address from the magazine on to the face of the envelope, sealed the envelope, and then went out to mail it.

Priscilla Ames didn't know what she was asking for.

7.

IT'S the little things in life that get you down.

The big problems are the easy ones to solve. There's a lot at stake with the big problems. It's the little ones that are the tough bastards. Should I shave tonight for the big date with Buxom Blonde, or should I wait until tomorrow morning for the big conference with Amalgamated Aluminium? God, a man can go nuts!

The 87th's big problem was the floater. It's not often you get a floater.

The 87th's little problem was the con man.

It was the con man who was driving Detective Arthur Brown nuts. Brown didn't like to be conned, and he didn't like other people to be conned, either. The man – or men, more accurately – who were fleecing honest citizens of Brown's fair city rankled him. They invaded his sleep. They dulled his appetite. They were even ruining his sex life. He was surly and out of sorts, more impatient than ever, scowling, snapping, a very difficult man to work with. The men who worked with him, being kindly, considerate, thoughtful bulls, did everything in their power to make his working day even more difficult. A moment did not go by but what one or another of the 87th's bulls would make some passing crack to Brown about the difficulties he was experiencing with the con man.

'Catch him yet, Artie?' they would ask.

'Hey, some guy conned my grandmother out of her

false teeth yesterday,' they would say. 'Think it's your buzzard, Brown?'

Brown took all the patter and all the jive with enviable discourteousness, admirable lack of self-control and remarkable short temper. His usual answer was short and to the point and consisted of a combination of two words, one of which was unprintable. Brown had no time for jokes. He only had time for the files.

Somewhere in those files was the man he wanted.

Bert Kling was occupied with another kind of reading matter.

Bert Kling stood before the bulletin board in the Detective Squad Room. It was raining again, and the rain oozed against the window panes and the harsh light behind the panes cast a sliding, running, dripping silhouette on the floor at his feet, so that the room itself seemed to be slowly dissolving.

The vacations schedule had been posted on the bulletin board.

Kling studied it now. Two detectives studied it with him. One of the detectives was Meyer Meyer. The other was Roger Havilland.

'What'd you draw, kid?' Havilland asked.

'10 June,' Kling replied.

'10 June? Well, well, well, ain't that a dandy time to start a holiday?' Havilland said, winking at Meyer.

'Yeah, dandy,' Kling said disgustedly. He had honestly not expected a more choice spot. He was the newest man on the squad, promoted from a rookie at that, and so he could hardly have hoped to compete with the cops who had seniority. But he was none the less disappointed. 10 June! Hell, that wasn't even summer yet!

'I like my vacations at the early part of June,'

Havilland went on. 'Excellent time for vacations. I always ask for the end of April. I like it chilly. I wouldn't think of leaving this lovely squad room during the suffocating months of July and August. I like heat, don't you, Meyer?'

Meyer's blue eyes twinkled. He was always willing to go along with a gag, even when the gag originated with a man like Havilland whom Meyer did not particularly like. 'Heat is wonderful,' Meyer said. 'Last year was marvellous. I'll never forget last year. A cop hater loose, and the temperature in the nineties. That makes for a memorable summer.'

'Just think, kid,' Havilland said. 'Maybe this summer'll be a hot one, too. You can sit over there by the windows, where you get a nice breeze from the park. And you can think back over your nice cool vacation in the beginning of June.'

'You slay me, Havilland,' Kling said. He turned to start away from the bulletin board, and Havilland laid a beefy hand on his arm. There was strength in Havilland's fingers. He was a big cop with a cherubic face, and a leerlike smile was on that face now. Kling disliked Havilland. He had disliked him even when he'd been a patrolman and had only heard of Havilland's questioning tactics with suspects. Since he'd made 3rd Grade, he had had the opportunity to see Havilland in action, and his dislike had mounted in proportion to the number of times Havilland used his hamlike fists on helpless prisoners. Havilland, you see, was a bull. He roared like a bull, and he gored like a bull, and he probably even snored like a bull. In truth, he had once been a gentle cop. But he'd once tried to break up a street fight, and the fighters had ganged up on him, taken away his service revolver, and broken his arm with a lead pipe.

The compound fracture had to be broken and reset at the hospital. It healed painfully and slowly. It left Havilland with a philosophy: Hit first, ask later.

The broken arm, to Kling's way of thinking, bought neither benediction nor salvation for Havilland. Neither did it buy understanding. It bought, perhaps, a little bit of insight into a man who was basically a son of a bitch. Kling wasn't a psychiatrist. He only knew that he didn't like the leer on Havilland's face, and he didn't like Havilland's hand on his arm.

'Where you going on your vacation, kid?' Havilland asked. 'You don't want to waste that nice cool month of June, do you? Remember, it gets to be summer along about the 21st. Where you going, huh?'

'We haven't decided yet,' Kling said.

'We? *We?* You going with somebody?'

'I'm going with my fiancée,' Kling said tightly.

'Your girl, huh?' Havilland said. He winked at Meyer, including him in a secret fraternity which Meyer did not feel like joining.

'Yes,' Kling said. 'My girl.'

'Whatever you do,' Havilland said, winking at Kling this time, 'don't take her out of the state.'

'Why not?' Kling asked, the implication escaping him for a moment, immediately sorry as soon as Havilland opened his mouth in reply.

'Why, the Mann Act, kid!' Havilland said. 'Watch out for those state lines.'

Kling stared at Havilland and then said, 'How would you like a punch in the mouth, Havilland?'

'Oh, Jesus!' Havilland roared, 'the kid breaks me up! There's nothing dishonest about screwing, kid, unless you cross a state line!'

'Lay off, Rog,' Meyer said.

'What's the matter?' Havilland asked. 'I envy the kid. Vacation in June, and a sweet little shackup waiting for . . .'

'Lay off!' Meyer said, more loudly this time. He had seen the spark of sudden anger in Kling's eyes, and he had seen the involuntary clenching of Kling's right fist. Havilland outweighed and outreached Kling, and Havilland was not famous for the purity of his fighting tactics. Meyer did not want blood on the squad-room floor. Not Kling's blood, anyway.

'Nobody's got any sense of humour in this dump,' Havilland said surlily. 'You got to have a sense of humour here or you don't survive.'

'Go help Brown with his con man troubles,' Meyer said.

'Brown ain't got no humour either,' Havilland said, and he stalked off.

'That big turd,' Kling said. 'Some day . . .'

'Well,' Meyer said, his eyes twinkling, 'in a sense he's right. The Mann Act is a serious thing. Very serious.'

Kling looked at him. Meyer had used almost the same words as Havilland, but somehow there was a difference. 'A very serious thing,' he answered. 'I'll be careful, Meyer.'

'Caution is the watchword,' Meyer said, grinning.

'The truth is,' Kling said, 'this damn June 10th spot might screw things up. Claire goes to college, you know. She may be in the middle of finals or something right then.'

'You been planning on this for some time?' Meyer asked.

'Yeah,' Kling said, thinking of the 10 June spot, and hoping it would jibe with Claire's schedule, and wondering what he could do about it if it didn't.

Meyer nodded sympathetically. 'Is it a special occasion?' he asked. 'Your going away together, I mean?'

Kling, immersed in his thoughts, answered automatically, forgetting he was talking to a fellow cop. 'Yes,' he said. 'We're in love.'

'The trouble with you,' Havilland said to Brown, 'is you're in love with your work.'

'I spend almost all my waking hours in this room,' Brown said. 'It'd be a sad goddamn thing if I didn't like what I was doing.'

'It wouldn't be sad at all,' Havilland said. 'I hate being a cop.'

'Then why don't you quit the force?' Brown asked flatly.

'They need me too much,' Havilland said.

'Sure.'

'They do. This squad would go to pieces in a week if I wasn't around to hold its hand.'

'Hold this a while,' Brown said.

'Crime would flourish,' Havilland continued, unfazed. 'The city would be overrun by cheap thieves.'

'Roger Havilland, Protector of the People,' Brown said.

'That's me,' Havilland confessed.

'Here, Protector,' Brown said, 'take a look at this.'

'What?'

'This R.K.C. card. How does it look to you?'

'What am I supposed to be looking for?' Havilland asked.

'A con man,' Brown said. He handed the card to Havilland. With the casual scrutiny born of years of detective work, Havilland studied the face of the card:

'Tells me nothing,' Havilland said.

RESIDENT KNOWN CRIMINAL

Name **Frederick Deutsch** Command **2**

Alias **Fritzie, Dutch, The Dutchman**

Address **67 South 4th Street** Precinct **87th**

Floor **1st** Apartment No. **1C** House ———

CHANGE OF ADDRESS

Moved to Hotel Carter, Culver and South 11th

Criminal Specialty **Confidence man**

Names of Associates ——— Prison (In or Out) **Out**

D.D. 64b Note—If criminal moves, forward card to Resident Precinct.
(Over)

Gallery No. **73471-3R**   **DESCRIPTION**

Where born **U.S.A.**

Sex **Male** Age **31** Color **White**

Eyes **Blue** Hair **Brown** Ht. **5'11¼"**

Weight **145** Occup. **Waiter**

Right- or Left-Handed **Right**

Distinctive Marks or Scars **Small scar under chin**

Operator or Chauffeur License **Operator**

Automobile License No. **7295-BN** Model **1954**

Make **Nash** Color **Red and black**

REMARKS **Young but highly skilled in all confidence games. M.O. varies with each game. Operates alone or in pair, but partner never apprehended. Served 18 mos., released 1951.**

74

'Flip it over,' Brown told him.

Havilland turned over the card and began reading again.

'Could be,' Havilland said.

'Thing that interests me about him is that he's a jack of all trades,' Brown said. 'You get a con man, he usually sticks to one game if it's working for him. This guy varies his game. Like the louse we got roaming the 87th. He must be pretty smooth, too, because he's barely a kid and he only took one fall.' Brown looked at the card. 'Who the hell made out this thing? It's supposed to tell you where he was sentenced and what for.'

'What difference does it make?' Havilland asked airily.

'I like to know what I'm dealing with,' Brown said. 'Why?'

'Because I'm heading for the Hotel Carter right now to pick him up.'

8.

THE Hotel Carter was, in many respects, a very sleazy dump.

On the other hand, to those of its inhabitants who had recently arrived from Skid Row it had all the glamour and impressiveness of the Waldorf Astoria. It all depended how you looked at it.

If you stood on the sidewalk at the corner of Culver Avenue and South 11th Street, and it happened to be raining, and you happened to be a cop out to make a pinch, the Hotel Carter looked like a very sleazy dump.

Brown sighed, pulled up the collar of his trenchcoat, remarked to himself silently that he looked something like a private eye and then walked into the hotel lobby. An old man sat in a soiled easy chair looking out at the rain, remembering kisses from Marjorie Morningstar under the lilacs. The lobby smelled. Brown suspected the old man contributed to the smell. He adjusted his nostrils the way he would adjust his shoulder holster, glanced around quickly, and then walked to the desk.

The clerk watched him as he crossed the lobby. The clerk watched him carefully. An April fly, not yet feeling its summer oats, buzzed lazily around the desk. A brass spittoon at the base of the desk dripped with misaimed spittle. The smell in the lobby was a smell of slovenliness and dissolution. Brown reached the desk. He started to open his mouth.

'I'll give it to you straight,' the desk clerk said. 'We don't take niggers.'

Brown didn't even blink. 'You don't, huh?' he asked.

'We don't.' The clerk was a young man, his hair line receding even though he was not yet twenty-six. He had a hawkish nose and pale green eyes. An acne pimple festered near his right nose flap. 'Nothing personal,' he said. 'I only work here, and those are the orders.'

'Glad to know how you feel,' Brown said, smiling. 'Trouble is, I didn't ask.'

'Huh?' the clerk said.

'Now you have to understand there's nothing I'd like better than a room in this hotel. I just come up from a cotton patch down south where we fertilize our cotton with human excrement. I lived in a leaky tarpaper shack, and so you can imagine what a palace your fine, splendid hotel looks like to me. I think it would be too much for me to bear, just being allowed to stay in one of your rooms. Why, just being here in the lobby is like coming close to paradise.'

'Go ahead,' the clerk said, 'make wise-cracks. You still don't get a room. I'm being honest with you. You should thank me.'

'Oh, I do, I do,' Brown said. 'I thank you from the bottom of my cotton-pickin' heart. Is there a man named Frederick Deutsch registered here?'

'Who wants to know?' the clerk asked.

Brown smiled and sweetly said, '*I* want to know. Jus' li'l ol' cotton-pickin' me.' He reached into his back pocket and flipped his wallet open to his shield. The clerk blinked. Brown continued smiling.

'I was only joking about the room,' the clerk said. 'We got lots of Negro people staying here.'

'I'll bet the place is just packed with them,' Brown said. 'Is Deutsch registered here, or isn't he?'

'The name don't ring a bell,' the clerk said. 'He a transient?'

'A regular,' Brown said.

'I got no Deutsches in my regulars.'

'Let's see the list.'

'Sure, but there ain't a Deutsch on it. I know my steadies by heart.'

'Let's see it anyway, huh?' Brown said.

The clerk sighed, dug under the counter, and came up with a register. He turned it on the desk top so that Brown could see it. Rapidly, Brown ran his finger down the page.

'Who's Frank Darren?' he asked.

'Huh?'

'Frank Darren.' Brown pointed at the name. 'This one.'

'Oh.' The clerk shrugged. 'A guy. One of the guests.'

'How long's he been here?'

'Couple years now, I guess. Even more than that.'

'He register as Darren when he checked in?'

'Sure.'

'What's he look like?'

'Tall guy, kind of skinny. Blue eyes, long hair. Why?'

'He in now?'

'I think so, yeah. Why?'

'What room's he in?'

'312,' the clerk said. 'I thought you was looking for somebody named Deutsch?'

'I am,' Brown said. 'Give me the key to 312.'

'What for? You need a warrant before you go busting in on . . .'

'If I have to go all the way home for a warrant,' Brown

said levelly, 'I'll also pick up one for violation of P.L. 514, excluding a citizen by reason of colour from the equal enjoyment of any accommodation furnished by innkeepers or . . .'

Hastily, the clerk handed him the key. Brown nodded and crossed to the elevator. He stabbed at the button and waited patiently while the elevator crept down to the lobby. When it opened, a blonde chambermaid stepped out of it, winking at the elevator operator.

'Three,' Brown said.

The elevator operator stared at him. 'Did you see the clerk?'

'I saw the clerk and the clerk saw me. Now let's cut the bull and get this car in motion.'

The elevator operator stepped back, and Brown entered the car. He leaned back against the back wall as the car climbed. Darren, of course, might very well be Darren and not Deutsch, he reasoned. But an elementary piece of police knowledge was that a man registering under a phoney name – especially if his luggage, shirts, or handkerchiefs were monogrammed – would generally pick a name with the same initials as his real name. Frederick Deutsch, Frank Darren – it was worth a try. Besides, the R.K.C. card had given this as Deutsch's last address. Maybe the card was wrong. Or, if it was right, why hadn't the master mind who'd figured out where Deutsch was staying also mentioned the fact that he was registered under an alias? Brown did not like sloppy police work. Sloppiness made him impatient. Slow elevators also made him impatient.

When they reached the third floor, he said, 'Doesn't it hurt your ear-drums?'

'Doesn't what hurt my ear-drums?' the elevator operator asked.

'Breaking the sound barrier like this?' Brown said, and then he stepped into the corridor. He waited until the doors slid shut behind him. He looked at the two doors closest to him in the corridor, to ascertain which way the numbers were running, and then he turned right.

302, 304, 306, 308, 310 . . .

He stopped outside room 312 and reached under his coat. He pulled the .38 from its shoulder rig, thumbed off the safety catch, and then took the key the clerk had given him and inserted it into the latch with his left hand.

Inside the room, there was sudden movement. Brown turned the key quickly and kicked open the door. There was a man on the bed, and the man was in the process of reaching for a gun which lay on the night table.

'Better leave it where it is,' Brown said.

'What is this?' the man asked. He was somewhat better-looking than his photo, but not much. He looked a little older, possibly because the photo had been taken many years back when he'd been mugged and printed before his arraignment. He wore a white-on-white shirt open at the throat, the sleeves rolled up just past his wrists, bulging with the cuff links which had been rolled up with the material. A small monogram was on the man's left breast pocket, the red letters F.D. in a black diamond.

'Put on your coat,' Brown said. 'I want to talk to you back at the squad.'

'What about?'

'Swindling,' Brown said.

'You can just blow it out,' the man said.

'Can I?'

'Damn right you can. I'm as legitimate as the Virgin Mary.'

'Is that why you carry a gun?' Brown asked.

'I've got a permit,' the man said.

'We'll check that back at the precinct, too.'

'Go get a warrant for my arrest,' the man said.

'I don't need any goddamn warrant!' Brown snapped. 'Now get the hell off that bed and into your coat, or I'll have to help you. And you won't like my help, believe me.'

'Listen, what the hell . . .'

'Come on, Fritzie,' Brown said.

The man looked up sharply.

'It is Fritzie, isn't it?' Brown asked. 'Or is it Dutch?'

'My name's Frank Darren,' the man said.

'And mine's Peter Pan. Put on your coat.'

'You're making a mistake, pal,' the man said. 'I've got friends.'

'A judge?' Brown asked. 'A senator? What?'

'Friends,' the man said.

'I got friends, too,' Brown said. 'I got a good friend who runs a butcher shop in Diamondback. He'll be as much help to you as your judge. Now come on, we're wasting time.'

The man slid off the bed. 'I got nothing to hide,' he said. 'You got nothing on me.'

'I hope not,' Brown said. 'I hope you're clean, and I hope you've got a permit for that gun, and I hope you went to confession last week. In the meantime, let's go back to the precinct.'

'Jesus, can't we talk here?' the man asked.

'No,' Brown said. He grinned. 'They don't allow niggers in this hotel.'

The man's licence and registration were made out to Frederick Deutsch.

81

Brown looked them over and said, 'All right, why were you registered under an alias?'

'You wouldn't understand,' Deutsch said.

'Try me.'

'What the hell for. I'm innocent until I'm proved guilty. Is there any law against using a phoney name to register in a hotel?'

'As a matter of fact,' Brown said, 'it's a misdemeanour, violation of P.L. 964. Use of name or address with intent to deceive.'

'I wasn't trying to deceive anybody,' Deutsch said.

'I can get a court injunction without any proof that you've deceived and misled anybody.'

'So get one,' Deutsch said.

'What for? I don't care if you use the name forever. I'd just like to know why you felt it was necessary to hide behind an alias.'

'You hit it, cop,' Deutsch said.

'If I hit it, I don't know it,' Brown answered. 'What's the story?'

'I'm going straight,' Deutsch said.

'Hold it a minute,' Brown said. 'Let me get the string quartet in here. We're going to need violins for this one.'

'I told you you wouldn't understand,' Deutsch said, wagging his head.

Brown studied him seriously for a moment. 'Go ahead,' he said. 'I'm listening.'

'I took a fall in 1950,' Deutsch said. 'I was twenty-four years old. I'd been working the confidence game since I was seventeen. First time I fell. I got off with eighteen months. On Walker Island.' Deutsch shrugged.

'So?'

'So I didn't like it. Is that so hard to understand? I didn't like being cooped up. Eighteen months with

82

every kind of crazy bastard you could imagine. Queers and winos and junkies and guys who'd axe their own mothers. Eighteen months of it. When I got out, I'd had it. I'd had it, and I didn't want any more of it.'

'So?'

'So I decided to play it straight. I figured I take another fall, it ain't going to be eighteen months this time. This time it'll be a little longer. The third time, who knows? Maybe they throw away the key. Maybe they begin to figure Fritzie Deutsch is just another guy like these queers and winos and junkies.'

'But you weren't,' Brown said, a faint smile on his mouth.

'No, I wasn't. I conned a lot of people, but I was a gent and you can go to hell if you don't believe me. Working the game was the same as having a job with me. That's why I got so good at it.'

'I imagine it paid pretty well, too,' Brown said.

'I'm still wearing the clothes I bought when things were going good,' Deutsch said. 'But what's the percentage? A few years of good living, and the rest of my life cooped up with slobs? Is that what I wanted? That's what I asked myself. So I decided to straighten out.'

'I'm listening.'

'It ain't so easy,' Deutsch said, sighing. 'Guys don't want ex-cons working for them. I know that sounds corny as hell. I see it in a lot of movies even. Where Robert Taylor or somebody can't get a job because he once was a con. Only, of course, with him it's like he was a con by mistake. You know, he took the fall when he was really clean. Anyway, it's true. It's tough to get a job when you got a record. They make a few phone calls, and they find out Fritzie Deutsch done time, well, so long Fritzie, it's been nice knowing you.'

'So you assumed the Frank Darren alias, is that right?'

'Yeah,' Deutsch said.

'And you've got a job now?'

'I work in a bank.'

'Doing what?'

'I'm a guard.' Deutsch looked up quickly, to see if Brown was smiling. Brown was not. 'That's how come I've got a permit for the gun,' Deutsch added. 'I ain't snowing you. That's one thing you can check.'

'We can check a lot of things,' Brown said. 'What bank do you work for?'

'You going to tell them my real name?' Deutsch asked. A sudden fear had come into his eyes, and he put his hand on Brown's arm, and the fingers there were tense and tight.

'No,' Brown said.

'First National. The Mason Avenue branch.'

'I'll check that, and I'll check the permit,' Brown said. 'But there's one other thing.'

'What?'

'I want some mooches to meet you.'

'What for? I ain't conned anybody since . . .'

'They may think differently. If you're clean, you won't mind them looking you over.'

'At the Line-up? Jesus, do I have to go to the Line-up?'

'No. I'll ask the victims to come down here.'

'I'm clean,' Deutsch said. 'I got nothing to worry about. It's just I hate the Line-up.'

'Why?'

Deutsch looked up at Brown, and his eyes were wide and serious. 'It's full of bums, you know that?' He paused and sucked in a deep breath. 'And I ain't a bum anymore.'

Murder will out, and it was a fine day for the outing of murder. The fiction con men could not have chosen a better day. They would have written it just this way, with the rain a fine drilling drizzle that swept in over the River Harb, and the sky an ominous roiling grey behind it. The tugboats on the river moaned occasionally, and the playgrounds on the other side of the River Highway were empty, the black asphalt glistening slickly under the steady wash of the rain. The movie con men would have panned their cameras down over the empty silent playgrounds, across the concrete of the River Highway, down the slopes of the embankments leading to the river. The sound track would pick up the wail of the tugs and the sullen swish of the rain and the murmur of the river lapping at rotted wooden beams.

There would be a close-up, and the close-up would show a hand suddenly breaking the surface of the water, the fingers stiff and widespread.

And then a body would appear, and the water would nudge the body until it washed ashore and lay lifeless with the other debris while the rain drilled down unrelentingly. The con men would have written it with flourish and filmed it with style and they had a fine day for the plying of their trades.

The men of the 87th Precinct weren't con men.

They only knew they had another floater.

9.

THE tattoo was obviously a mistake.

Mary Louise Proschek had had an almost identical tattoo. It had nestled snugly on the fold of skin between her right thumb and forefinger. The tattoo had been a heart, and the word 'MAC' had decorated that heart. Mac – and a heart. A man – and love. For the con men throughout the ages have built a legend about the heart, have made the hard-working sump pump of the body the centre of emotion, have disassociated love from the mind, have given a veneer of glamour to a bundle of muscle. It could have been worse. Their efforts could have descended upon the liver. In fact the bile or the intestinal tract could have become the citadel of romance. The con men knew their trade. The shape of the heart makes a good symbol, easily recognized, easily worshipped. The eyes, the ears, the nose, the mind – the organs which see and hear and smell and know another human being, the organs which make another human being a living breathing part of yourself, a part as vital as your brain – these are discounted. St Valentine had a good Press agent.

The second floater was a girl.

There was a tattoo on the flap of skin between her right thumb and forefinger.

The tattoo was a heart.

There was a word in the heart.

And the word was 'NAC'.

And obviously, the tattoo was a mistake. Obviously the man or woman who had been paid to decorate the skin had made a mistake. Obviously, he had been told to needle the word 'MAC' into that heart, to fasten indelibly that man's name on to that girl's flesh. He had goofed. Perhaps he'd been drunk, or perhaps he'd been tired, or perhaps he simply didn't give a damn, some people *are* that way, you know – no pride in their work. Whatever the case, the name had come out all wrong. Not a 'MAC' this time, but a 'NAC'. The man who'd thrown those girls into the water must have been absolutely furious.

Nobody likes his byline misspelled.

The idea was to combine business with pleasure.

It was an idea Steve Carella didn't particularly relish, but he'd promised Teddy he'd meet her downtown at eight on the button, and the call from the tattoo parlour had been clocked in at 7.45, and he knew it was too late to reach her at the house. He couldn't have called her in any case because the telephone was one instrument Carella's wife could never use. But he had, on other occasions, illegally dispatched a radio motor patrol car to his own apartment with the express purpose of delivering a message to Teddy. The police commissioner, even while allowing that Carella was a good cop, might have frowned upon such extra-curricular squad car activity. So Carella, sneak that he was, never told him.

He stood now on the corner under the big bank clock partially covered by the canopy which spread out over the entrance, shielding the big metal doors. He hoped there would not be an attempted bank robbery. If there was anything he disliked, it was foiling attempted bank robberies when he was off duty and waiting for the most beautiful woman in the world. Naturally, he was never off duty. A cop, as he well knew, is on duty twenty-four hours a day, three hundred and sixty-five days a year, three hundred and sixty-six days in leap year. Then, too, there was the tattoo parlour to visit, and he couldn't consider himself officially clocked out until he'd made that call, and then reported the findings back to whoever was catching at the squad.

He hoped there would not be an attempted bank robbery, and he also hoped it would stop drizzling because the rain was seeping into his bones and making his wounds ache. Oh, my aching wounds!

He put his aches out of his mind and fell to wool-gathering. Carella's favourite form of wool-gathering was thinking about his wife. He knew there was something hopelessly adolescent about the way he loved her, but those were the facts, ma'm, and there wasn't much he could do to change his feelings. There were probably more beautiful women in the world, but he didn't know who they were. There were probably sweeter, purer, warmer, more passionate women too. He doubted it. He very strongly doubted it. The simple truth was that she pleased him. Hell, she delighted him. She had a face he would never tire of watching, a face which was a thousand faces, each linked subtly by a slender chain of beauty. Fully made up, her brown eyes glowing, the lashes darkened with mascara, her lips cleanly stamped with lipstick, she was one person – and he loved the meticulously calculated beauty, the freshly combed, freshly powdered veneer of that person.

In the morning, she was another person. Warm with sleep, her eyes would open, and her face would be undecorated, her full lips swollen, the black hair tangled like wild weeds, her body supple and pliable. He loved her this way, too, loved the small smile on her mouth and the sudden eager alertness of her eyes.

Her face was a thousand faces, quiet and introspective when they walked along a lonely shore barefoot and the only sound was the distant sound of breakers on the beach, a sound she could not hear in her silent world. Alive with fury, her face could change in an instant, the black brows swooping down over suddenly incandescent eyes, her lips skinning back over even white teeth, her body taut with invective she could not hurl because she could not speak, her fists clenched. Tears transformed her face again. She did not cry often, and when she did cry it was with completely unselfconscious anguish. It was almost as if, secure in the knowledge of her beauty, she could allow her face to be torn by agony.

Many men longed for the day when their ship would come in.

Carella's ship *had* come in – and it had launched a thousand faces.

There were times, of course, like *now* when he wished the ship could do a little more than fifteen knots. It was eight-twenty, and she'd promised to be there at eight on the dot, and whereas he never grew weary of her mental image he much preferred her in person.

Now! For the first time! Live! On our stage! In person! Imported from the Cirque d'Hiver in Paris . . .

There must be something wrong with me, Carella thought. *I'm never really here. I'm always . . .*

He spotted her instantly. By this time, he was not surprised by what the sight of her could do to him. He had come to accept the instant quickening of his heart and the automatic smile on his face. She had not yet seen him, and he watched her from his secret vantage point, feeling somewhat sneaky, but what the hell!

She wore a black skirt and a red sweater, and over that a black cardigan with red piping. The cardigan hung open, ending just below her hips. She had a feminine walk which was completely unconscious, completely uncalculated. She walked rapidly because she was late, and he heard the steady clatter of the black pumps on the pavement and he watched with delighted amusement the men who turned for a second look at his wife.

When she saw him, she broke into a run. He did not know what it was between them that made the shortest separation seem like a ten-year stretch at Alcatraz. Whatever it was, they had it. She came into his arms, and he kissed her soundly, and he wouldn't have given a damn if Twentieth Century Fox had been filming the entire sequence for a film titled *The Mating Season Jungle*.

'You're late,' he said. 'Don't apologize. You look lovely. We have to make a stop, do you mind?'

Her eyes questioned his face.

'A tattoo parlour downtown. Guy thinks he may remember Mary Louise Proschek. We're lucky. This is business, so I was able to check out a sedan. Means we don't have to take the train home tonight. Some provider, your husband, huh?'

Teddy grinned and squeezed his arm.

'The car's around the corner. You look beautiful. You smell nice, too. What've you got on?'

Teddy dry washed her hands.

'Just soap and water? You're amazing! Look how nice you can make soap smell. Honey, this won't take more than a few minutes. I've got some pictures of the Proschek girl in the car, and maybe we can get a make on them from this guy. After that, we'll eat and whatever you like. I can use a drink, can't you?'

Teddy nodded.

'Why do people always say they can "use" a drink? What, when you get right down to it, can they use it for?' He studied her and added, 'I'm too talkative tonight. I guess I'm excited. We haven't had a night out in a long while. And you look beautiful. Don't you get tired of my saying that?'

Teddy shook her head, and there was a curious tenderness in the movement. He had grown used to her eyes, and perhaps he missed what they were saying to him, over and over again, repeatedly. Teddy Carella didn't need a tongue.

They walked to the car, and he opened the door for her, went around to the other side, and then started the motor. The police radio erupted into the closed sedan.

'Car 21, Car 21, Signal 1. Silvermine at North 40th . . .'

'I'll be conscientious and leave it on,' Carella said to Teddy. 'Some pretty redhead may be trying to reach me.'

Teddy's brows lowered menacingly.

'In connexion with a case, of course,' he explained.

Of course, she nodded mockingly.

'God, I love you,' he said, his hand moving to her thigh. He squeezed her quickly, an almost unconscious gesture, and then he put his hand back on the wheel.

They drove steadily through the maze of city traffic. At one stop light, a traffic cop yelled at Carella because he anticipated the changing of the light from red to green. The cop's raingear was slick with water. Carella felt suddenly like a heel.

The windshield wipers snicked at the steady drizzle. The tyres whispered against the asphalt of the city. The city was locked in against the rain. People stood in doorways, leaned out of windows. There was a grey quietness to the city, as if the rain had suspended all activity, had caused the game of life to be called off.

There was a rain smell to the city, too, all the smells of the day captured in the steady canopy of water and washed clean by it. There was, too, and strange for the city, a curious sense of peace.

'I love Paris when it drizzles,' Carella said suddenly, and he did not have to explain the meaning of his words because she knew at once what he meant, she knew that he was not talking about Paris or Wichita, that he was talking about this city, his city, and that he had been born in it and into it and that it, in turn, had been born into him.

The expensive apartment houses fell away behind them, as did the line of high fashion stores, and the advertising agency towers, and the publishing shrines, and the gaudy brilliance of the amusement area, and the stilled emptiness of the garment district at night, and the tangled intricacy of the narrow side-streets far downtown, the pushcarts lining the streets, filled with fruits and vegetables, the store windows behind them, the Italian *salami*, and the *provoloni*, and the *pepperoni* hanging in bright red strings.

The tattoo parlour nestled in a side-street on the fringe of Chinatown, straddled by a bar and a laundromat. The combination of the three was somewhat absurd, ranging from the exotica of tattooing into the nether world of intoxication and from there to the plebeian task of laundering clothes. The neighbourhood had seen its days of glory perhaps, but they were all behind it. Far behind it. Like an old man with cancer, the neighbourhood patiently and painfully awaited the end – and the end was the inevitable city housing project. And in the meantime, nobody bothered to change the soiled bedclothes. Why bother when something was going to die anyway?

The man who ran the tattoo parlour was Chinese. The name on the plate glass window was Charlie Chen.

'Everybody call me Charlie Chan,' he explained. 'Big detective, Charlie Chan. But me *Chen*, Chen. You know Charlie Chan, detective?'

'Yes,' Carella said, smiling.

'Big detective,' Chen said. 'Got stupid sons.' Chen laughed. 'Me got stupid sons, too, but me no detective.' He was a round fat man, and everything he owned shook when he laughed. He had a small moustache on his upper lip, and he had thick fingers, and there was an oval jade ring on the forefinger of his left hand. 'You detective, huh?' he asked.

'Yes,' Carella said.

'This lady police lady?' Chen asked.

'No. This lady's my wife.'

'Oh. Very good. Very good,' Chen said. 'Very pretty. She wants tattoo, maybe? Do nice butterfly for her on shoulder. Very good for strapless gowns. Very pretty. Very decorative.'

Teddy shook her head, smiling.

'Very pretty lady. You very lucky detective,' Chen said. He turned to Teddy. 'Nice yellow butterfly maybe? Very pretty?' He opened his eyes seductively. 'Everybody say very pretty.'

Teddy shook her head again.

'Maybe you like red better? Red your colour, maybe? Nice red butterfly?'

Teddy could not keep herself from smiling. She kept shaking her head and smiling, feeling very much a part of her husband's work, happy that he'd had to make the call, and happy that he'd taken her with him. It was curious, she supposed, but she did not know him as a cop. His function as a cop was something almost completely alien to her, even though he talked about his work. She knew that he dealt with crime, and the perpetrators of crime, and she often wondered what kind of man he was when he was on the job. Heartless? She could not imagine that in her man. Cruel? No. Hard, tough? Perhaps.

'About this girl,' Carella said to Chen. 'When did she come in for the tattoo?'

'Oh, long time ago,' Chen said. 'Maybe five months, maybe six. Nice lady. Not so pretty like your lady, but very nice.'

'Was she alone?'

'No. She with tall man.' Chen scrutinized Carella's face. 'Prettier than you, detective.'

Carella grinned. 'What did he look like?'

'Tall. Movie star. Very handsome. Muscles.'

'What colour was his hair?'

'Yellow,' Chen said.

'His eyes?'

Chen shrugged.

'Anything you remember about him?'

'He smile all the time,' Chen said. 'Big white teeth. Very pretty teeth. Very handsome man. Movie star.'

'Tell me what happened?'

'They come in together. She hold his arm. She look at him, stars in her eyes.' Chen paused. 'Like your lady. But not so pretty.'

'Were they married?'

Chen shrugged.

'Did you see an engagement ring or a wedding band on her finger?'

'I don't see,' Chen said. He grinned at Teddy. Teddy grinned back. 'You like black butterfly? Pretty black wings? Come, I show you.' He led them into the shop. A

94

beaded curtain led to the back room. The walls of the shop were covered with tattoo designs. A calendar with a nude girl on it hung on the wall near the beaded curtain. Someone had jokingly inked tattoos on to her entire body. The tattooer had drawn a pair of clutching hands on the girl's full breasts. Chen pointed to a butterfly design on one of the walls.

'This butterfly. You like? You pick colour. Any colour. I do. I put on your shoulder. Very pretty.'

'Tell me what happened with the girl,' Carella said, gently insistent. Teddy looked at him curiously. Her husband was enjoying the byplay between herself and Chen, but he was not losing sight of his objective. He was here in this shop for a possible lead on the man who had killed Mary Louise Proschek. She suddenly felt that if the byplay got too involved, her husband would call a screaming halt to it.

'They come in shop. He say the girl want tattoo. I show them designs on wall. I try to sell her butterfly. Nobody like butterfly. Butterfly my own design. Very pretty. Good for shoulder. I do butterfly on one lady's back, near base of spine. Very pretty, only nobody see. Good for shoulder. I try to sell her butterfly, but man say he wants heart. She say she wants heart, too. Stars in eyes, you know? Big love, big thing, shining all over. I show them big hearts. Very pretty hearts, very complicated, many colours.'

'They didn't want a big heart?'

'Man wants small heart. He show me where.' Chen spread his thumb and forefinger. 'Here. Very difficult. Skinny flesh, needle could go through. Very painful. Very difficult. He say he wants it there. She say if he wants it there, she wants it there. Crazy.'

'Who suggested what lettering to put into the heart?'

'Man. He say you put M-A-C in heart.'

'He said to put the name Mac into that heart?'

'He no say name Mac. He say put M-A-C.'

'And what did she say?'

'She say yes, M-A-C.'

'Go on.'

'I do. Very painful. Girl scream. He hold her shoulders. Very painful. Tender spot.' Chen shrugged. 'Butterfly on shoulder better.'

'Did she mention his name while she was here?'

'No.'

'Did she call him Mac?'

'She call him nothing.' Chen thought a moment. 'Yes, she call him darling, dear, sweetheart. Love words. No name.'

Carella sighed. He lifted the flap of the manila envelope in his hands and drew out the glossy prints that were inside it. 'Is this the girl?' he asked Chen.

Chen looked at the pictures. 'That she,' he said. 'She dead, huh?'

'Yes, she's dead.'

'He kill her?'

'We don't know.'

'She love him,' Chen said, wagging his head. 'Love very special. Nobody should kill love.'

Teddy looked at the little round Chinese, and she suddenly felt very much like allowing him to tattoo his prize butterfly design on her shoulder. Carella took the pictures back and put them into the envelope.

'Has this man ever come into your shop again?' Carella asked. 'With another woman perhaps?'

'No, never,' Chen said.

'Well,' Carella said, 'thanks a lot, Mr Chen. If you remember anything more about him, give me a call, won't you?' He opened his wallet. 'Here's my card. Just ask for Detective Carella.'

'You come back,' Chen said, 'you ask for Charlie Chan, big detective with stupid sons. You bring wife. I make pretty butterfly on shoulder.' He extended his hand and Carella took it. For a moment, Chen's eyes went serious. 'You lucky,' he said. 'You not so pretty, have very pretty lady. Love very special.' He turned to Teddy. 'Someday, if you want butterfly, you come back. I make very pretty.' He winked. 'Detective husband like. I promise. Any colour. Ask for Charlie Chan. That's me.'

He grinned and wagged his head, and Carella and Teddy left the shop, heading for the police sedan up the street.

10.

'NICE guy, wasn't he?' Carella said.

Teddy nodded.

'I wish they were all like him. A lot of them aren't. With many people, the presence of a cop automatically produces a feeling of guilt. That's the truth, Teddy. They instantly feel that they're under suspicion, and everything they say becomes defensive. I guess that's because there are skeletons in the cleanest closets. Are you very hungry?'

Teddy made a face which indicated she was famished.

'Shall we find a place in the neighbourhood, or do you want to wait until we get uptown?'

Teddy pointed to the ground.

'Here?'

Yes, she nodded.

'Chinese?'

No.

'Italian?'

Yes.

'You shouldn't have married a guy of Italian descent,' Carella said. 'Whenever such a guy eats in an Italian restaurant, he can't help comparing his spaghetti with what his mother used to cook. He then becomes dissatisfied with what he's eating, and the dissatisfaction spreads to include his wife. The next thing you know, he's suing for divorce.'

Teddy put her forefingers to her eyes, stretching the skin so that her eyes became slitted.

'Right,' Carella said. 'You should have married a Chinese. But then, of course, you wouldn't be able to eat in Chinese restaurants.' He paused and grinned. 'All this eating talk is making me hungry. How about that place up the street?'

They walked to it rapidly, and Carella looked through the plate glass window.

'Not too crowded,' he said, 'and it looks clean. You game?'

Teddy took his arm, and he led her into the place.

It was, perhaps, not the cleanest place in the world. As sharp as Carella's eyes were, a cursory glance through a plate glass window is not always a good evaluation of cleanliness. And, perhaps, the reason it wasn't too crowded was that the food wasn't too good. Not that it mattered very much, since both Carella and Teddy were really very hungry and probably would have eaten sautéed grasshoppers if they were served.

The place did have nice chequered tablecloths and candles stuck into the necks of old wine bottles, the wax frozen to the glass. The place did have a long bar which ran the length of the wall opposite the dining-room, bottles stacked behind it, amber lights illuminating the bottles. The place did have a phone booth, and Carella still had to make his call back to the squad.

The waiter who came over to their table seemed happy to see them.

'Something to drink before you order?' he asked.

'Two martinis,' Carella said. 'Olives.'

'Would you care to see a menu now or later, sir?'

'Might as well look at it now,' Carella said. The waiter brought them two menus. Carella glanced at his briefly and then put it down. 'I'm bucking for a divorce,' he said. 'I'll have spaghetti.'

While Teddy scanned the menu, Carella looked around the room. An elderly couple were quietly eating at a table near the phone booth. There was no one else in the dining-room. At the bar, a man in a leather jacket sat with a shot glass and a glass of water before him. The man was looking into the bar mirror. His eyes were on Teddy. Behind the bar, the bartender was mixing the martinis Carella had ordered.

'I'm so damn hungry I could eat the bartender,' Carella said.

When the waiter came with their drinks, he ordered spaghetti for himself and then asked Teddy what she wanted. Teddy pointed to the lasagna dish on the menu, and Carella gave it to the waiter. When the waiter was gone, they picked up their glasses.

'Here's to ships that come in,' Carella said.

Teddy stared at him, puzzled.

'All loaded with treasures from the East,' he went on, 'smelling of rich spices, with golden sails.'

She was still staring at him, still puzzled.

'I'm drinking to you, darling,' he explained. He watched the smile form on her mouth. 'Poetic cops this city can do without,' he said, and he sipped at the martini and then put the glass down. 'I want to call the squad, honey. I'll be back in a minute.' He touched her hand briefly, and then went toward the phone booth, digging in his pocket for change as he walked away from the table.

She watched him walk from her, pleased with the long athletic strides he took, pleased with the impatience of his hand as it dug for change, pleased with the way he held his head. She realized abruptly that one of the first things that had attracted her to Carella was the way he moved. There was an economy and simplicity of motion about him, a sense of directness. You got the feeling that before he moved he knew exactly where he was going and what he was going to do, and so there was a tremendous sense of security attached to being with him.

Teddy sipped at the martini and then took a long swallow. She had not eaten since noon, and so she was not surprised by the rapidity with which the martini worked its alcoholic wonders. She watched her husband enter the phone booth, watched as he dialled quickly. She wondered how he would speak to the desk sergeant and then to the detective who was watching in the squad room. Would they know he'd been talking of treasure ships just a few moments before? What kind of a cop was he? What did the other cops think of him? She felt a sudden exclusion. Faced with the impenetrable privacy which was any man's work, she felt alone and unwanted. Quickly, she drained the martini glass.

A shadow fell over the table.

At first she thought it was only a trick of her eyes, and then she looked up. The man who'd been sitting at the bar, the man in the leather jacket, was standing at the table, grinning.

'Hi,' he said.

She glanced hastily at the phone booth. Carella had his back to the dining-room.

'What're you doing with a creep like that?' the man said.

Teddy turned away from him and fastened her eyes to the napkin in her lap.

'You're just about the cutest doll that ever walked into this dump,' the man in the leather jacket said. 'Why don't you ditch that creep and meet me later. How about it?'

She could smell whisky on the man's breath. There was something frightening about his eyes, something insulting about the way they roamed her body with open candour. She wished she were not wearing a sweater. Unconsciously, she pulled the cardigan closed over the jutting cones of her breasts.

'Come on,' the man said, 'don't cover them up.'

She looked up at him and shook her head. Her eyes pleaded with him to go away. She glanced again to the phone booth. Carella was talking animatedly.

'My name's Dave,' the man said. 'That's a nice name, ain't it? Dave. What's your name?'

She could not answer him. She would not have answered him even if she could.

'Come on, loosen up,' Dave said. He stared at her, and his eyes changed, and he said, 'Jesus, you're beautiful, you know that? Ditch him, will you? Ditch him and meet me.'

Teddy shook her head.

'Let me hear you talk,' Dave said.

She shook her head again, pleadingly this time.

'I want to hear your voice. I'll bet it's the sexiest goddamn voice in the world. Let me hear it.'

Teddy squeezed her eyes shut tightly. Her hands were trembling in her lap. She wanted this man to go away, wanted him to leave her alone, wanted him to be gone before Steve came out of that booth, before Steve came back to the table. She was slightly dizzy from the martini, and her mind could only think that Steve would be displeased, Steve might think she had invited this.

'Look, what do you have to be such a cold tomato for,

huh? I'll bet you're not so cold. I'll bet you're pretty warm. Let me hear your voice.'

She shook her head again, and then she saw Carella hang up the phone and open the door of the booth. He was grinning, and then he looked toward the table and the grin dropped from his mouth, and she felt a sudden sick panic at the pit of her stomach. Carella moved out of the booth quickly. His eyes had tightened into focus on the man with the leather jacket.

'Come on,' Dave said, 'what you got to be that way for, huh? All I'm asking . . .'

'What's the trouble, mister?' Carella said suddenly. She looked up at her husband, wanting him to know she had not asked for this, hoping it was in her eyes. Carella did not turn to look at her. His eyes were riveted to Dave's face.

'No trouble at all,' Dave said, turning, facing Carella with an arrogant smile.

'You're annoying my wife,' Carella said. 'Take off.'

'Oh, was I annoying her? Is the little lady your wife?' He spread his legs wide and let his arms dangle at his sides, and Carella knew instantly that he was looking for trouble and wouldn't be happy until he found it.

'You were, and she is,' Carella said. 'Go crawl back to the bar. It's been nice knowing you.'

Dave continued smiling. 'I ain't crawling back nowhere,' he said. 'This is a free country. I'm staying right here.'

Carella shrugged and pulled out his chair. Dave continued standing by the table. Carella took Teddy's hand.

'Are you all right?' he asked.

Teddy nodded.

'Ain't that sweet?' Dave said 'Big handsome hubby comes back from . . .'

Carella dropped his wife's hand and stood suddenly. At the other end of the dining-room, the elderly couple looked up from their meal.

'Mister,' Carella said slowly, 'you're bothering the hell out of me. You'd better . . .'

'Am I bothering you?' Dave said. 'Hell, all I'm doing is admiring a nice piece of . . .' and Carella hit him.

He hit him suddenly with the full force of his arm and shoulder behind the blow. He hit him suddenly and full in the mouth, and Dave staggered back from the table and slammed into the next table, knocking the wine bottle candle to the floor. He leaned on the table for a moment, and when he looked up his mouth was bleeding, but he was still smiling.

'I was hoping you'd do that, pal,' he said. He studied Carella for a moment, and then he lunged at him.

Teddy sat with her hands clenched in her lap, her face white. She saw her husband's face, and it was not the face of the man she knew and loved. The face was completely expressionless, the mouth a hard tight line that slashed it horizontally, the eyes narrowed so that the pupils were barely visible, the nostrils wide and flaring. He stood spread-legged with his fists balled, and she looked at his hands and they seemed bigger than they'd ever seemed before, big and powerful, lethal weapons which hung at his sides, waiting. His entire body seemed to be waiting. She could feel the coiled-spring tautness of him as he waited for Dave's rush, and he seemed like a smoothly functioning, well-oiled machine in that moment, a machine which would react automatically as soon as the right button were pushed, as soon as the right lever were pressed. There was nothing human about the machine.

All humanity had left Steve Carella the moment his fist had lashed out at Dave. What Teddy saw now was a highly trained and a highly skilled technician about to do his work, waiting for the response buttons to be pushed.

Dave did not know he was fighting a machine. Ignorantly, he pushed out at the buttons.

Carella's left fist hit him in the gut, and he doubled over in pain and then Carella threw a flashing uppercut which caught Dave under the chin and sent him sprawling backwards against the table again. Carella moved quickly and effortlessly, like a cue ball under the hands of an expert pool player, sinking one ball and then rolling to position for a good shot at the next ball. Before Dave clambered off the table, Carella was in position again, waiting.

When Teddy saw Dave pick up the wine bottle, her mouth opened in shocked anguish. But she knew somehow this did not come as a surprise to her husband. His eyes, his face did not change. He watched dispassionately while Dave hit the bottle against the table. The jagged shards of the bottle neck clutched in Dave's fist frightened her until she wanted to scream, until she wished she had a voice so that she could scream until her throat ached. She knew her husband would be cut, she knew that Dave was drunk enough to cut him, and she watched Dave advancing with the broken bottle, but Carella did not budge an inch, he stood there motionless, his body balanced on the balls of his feet, his right hand open, the fingers widespread, his left hand flat and stiff at his side.

Dave lunged with the broken bottle. He passed low, aiming for Carella's groin. A look of surprise crossed his face when he felt Carella's right hand clamp on to his wrist. He felt himself falling forward suddenly, pulled by Carella who had stepped back lightly on his right foot, and who was raising his left hand high over his head, the hand still stiff and rigid.

And then Carella's left hand descended. Hard and straight, like the sharp biting edge of an axe, it moved downward with remarkable swiftness. Dave felt the impact of the blow. The hard calloused edge of Carella's hand struck him on the side of his neck, and then Dave bellowed and Carella swung his left hand across his own body and again the hand fell, this time on the opposite side of Dave's neck, and he fell to the floor, both arms paralysed for the moment, unable to move.

Carella stood over him, waiting.

'Lay . . . lay off,' Dave said.

The waiter stood at the entrance to the dining-room, his eyes wide.

'Get the police,' Carella said, his voice curiously toneless.

'But . . .' the waiter started.

'I'm a detective,' Carella said. 'Get the patrolman on the beat. Hurry up!'

'Yes,' the waiter said. 'Yes, sir.'

Carella did not move from where he stood over Dave. He did not once look at Teddy. When the patrolman arrived, he showed his shield and told him to book Dave for disorderly conduct, generously neglecting to mention assault. He gave the patrolman all the information he needed, walked out with him to the squad car, was gone for some five minutes. When he came back to the table, the elderly couple had gone. Teddy sat staring at her napkin.

'Hi,' he said, and he grinned.

She looked across the table at him.

'I'm sorry,' he said. 'I didn't want trouble.'

She shook her head.

'He'll be better off locked up for the night. He'd only have picked on someone else, hon. He was spoiling for a fight.' He paused. 'The next guy he might have succeeded in cutting.'

Teddy Carella nodded and sighed heavily. She had just had a visit to her husband's office and seen him at work. And she could still remember the terrible swiftness of his hands, hands which she had only known tenderly before.

And so she sighed heavily because she had just discovered the world was not populated with gentle little boys playing games.

And then she reached across the table, and she took his right hand and brought it to her mouth, and she kissed the knuckles, and she kissed the palm, and Carella was surprised to feel the wetness of her tears against his flesh.

11.

IT was unfortunate, perhaps, that Arthur Brown was so zealous in his pursuit of the con man. Had he not been such an eager beaver, he would not have asked to replace Carella when Carella drew Line-up that week. Line-up means a trip downtown to headquarters on High Street, and Line-up means sitting in a room with a pile of other detectives from all over the city, watching the parade of felony offenders. Line-up is sometimes exciting; usually, it's a bore.

Brown, as it happened, had just held his personal Line-up in the squad room of the 87th Precinct, whereat he paraded Frederick 'Fritzie' Deutsch before a little Negro girl named Betty Prescott and a big businessman named Elliot Jamison. Both victims had cleared Deutsch at once. He was not the man (or in Jamison's case, *either* of the men) who had conned them. Brown was secretly pleased. He had thanked both Miss Prescott and Mr Jamison, and then clapped Deutsch on the back and gruffly said, 'Keep your nose clean.'

And then he had asked Carella if he could take his place at the Line-up the next day. Carella, who considered the Line-up a necessary evil – something like a mother-in-law who comes to live with you – readily relinquished the duty. Had Carella been the sort of cop who loved Line-up, had Carella been more conscientious, more devoted to detail, had Carella felt any real purpose would be served by his appearance at headquarters that Wednesday, things might have worked out differently.

Actually, Carella *was* conscientious, and he *was* devoted to detail – but he was up to his ears in floaters and the Line-up very rarely turned up any good murder suspects. His time, he assumed, could be better spent in a thorough rundown of the city's tattoo parlours in an effort to track down the 'NAC' which had appeared on the second floater's hand.

So he allowed Brown to take his place, and that was most unfortunate.

It was unfortunate in that there were two handsome blond men who were shown at the Line-up that Wednesday.

One of them had killed Mary Louise Proschek and the second unidentified floater.

Brown was interested, at the moment, in con men – not murderers.

Carella was interested in tattoo parlours.

Kling was a new cop.

He accompanied Brown to headquarters on that Wednesday. The city was again blanketed with a dreary drizzle, and the men spoke very little on the long ride downtown. Kling, for the most part, was thinking of breaking his vacation date to Claire, and wondering how she would react to it. Brown was thinking about his con man, who had acted singly once and in concert a second time, and wondering if the Line-up would turn up anything. Brown drove slowly because of the slick pavement. They did not reach headquarters until 9.05. By the time the elevator had taken them to the ninth floor, the Line-up had been under-way for some ten minutes. They pinned their shields to their jackets and passed through the patrolman outside at the desk in the corridor. The patrolman said nothing. He simply looked at his watch condemningly.

The large, gymnasium-like room was dark when they entered it. The only area of light was at the far end of the room, where the stage was brilliantly illuminated.

'. . . third stick-up in 1949,' the Chief of Detectives said from his raised dais behind the rows and rows of folding chairs upon which detectives from every precinct in the city sat. 'Thought we'd cured you that time, Alphonse, but apparently you never learn. Now how about that gas station last night?'

The man on the stage was silent. The microphone hung before his face on a solid steel pipe, and the graduated height markers on the wall behind him told the assembled bulls that he was five-feet-eight inches tall.

Kling and Brown made their way unobtrusively past the dais and speaking stand, and then shuffled into one of the rows, sitting as quickly and quietly as they could.

'I'm talking to you, Alphonse,' the Chief of Detectives said. 'Never mind the late-comers,' he added sarcastically, and Kling felt a hot flush over his face.

'I hear you fine,' Alphonse said.

'Then how about it?'

'I don't have to say nothing at a Line-up, and you know it.'

'You've been to a lot of Line-ups, huh?'

'A couple.'

'On these other stick-ups?'

'Yeah.'

'Never thought you'd be here again on a stick-up, did you?'

'I got nothing to say,' Alphonse said. 'You got to prove there was a stick-up and that I done it.'

'That shouldn't be too hard,' the Chief of Detectives said. 'It might go a little easier on you if you told us what we wanted to know, though.'

'Snow jobs I can do without so early in the morning,' Alphonse said. 'I know the set-up. Don't ask questions, 'cause I know I don't have to answer them.'

'All right,' the Chief of Detectives conceded. 'Next case.'

Alphonse walked off the stage, his movements followed by every eye in the room. For the purpose of these Monday-to-Thursday early-morning parades was simply to acquaint every detective in the city with the men who were committing crime in their city. Sometimes, a victim was invited to the Line-up in an attempt to identify a suspect, but such occasions were rare and usually fruitless. They were rare because a victim generally had a thousand good reasons for not wanting to be at the Line-up. They were usually fruitless because a victim generally had a thousand good reasons for not wanting to identify a suspect. The least valid of these reasons, if the most popularly accepted, was fear of reprisal. In any case, not many suspects were identified by victims. Were this the sole purpose of the Line-up, the whole affair would have been a dreadful flop. On the other hand, the bulls who congregated at headquarters every Monday-to-Thursday morning – as much as they disliked the task – studied the felony offenders of the day before with close scrutiny. You never knew when you'd get a lead to the case you were working on. And you never knew when it might be important to recognize a cheap thief on the street. Such recognition might, in rare cases, even save your life.

And so the Chief of Detectives went through the prescribed ritual, and the bulls listened and watched.

'Riverhead, one,' the Chief of Detectives said, calling off the area of the city in which the arrest had been made, and the number of the case from that area that day. 'Riverhead, one. Hunter, Curt, thirty-five. Drinking heavily in a bar on Shelter Place. Got into an argument with the bartender and hurled a chair at the bar mirror. No statement. What happened, Curt?'

Hunter had been led to the steps at the side of the stage by his arresting officer, a burly patrolman. The patrolman would have had to be burly to arrest Hunter, who cleared the six-foot-two marker and who must have weighed about two hundred pounds. He had broad shoulders and a narrow waist, and he took aggressive strides to where the microphone hung. He had blond hair, combed slickly back from a wide forehead. He had a straight nose, and steel grey eyes. His cheek bones were high, and his mouth was a strong mouth, and his chin was cleft. He looked as if he were walking on stage to take instructions from a director, rather than to face the fire of the Chief of Detectives.

'How about what?' he asked.

'What'd you argue about?' the Chief of Detectives said.

Hunter crowded the microphone. 'That jail I was in last night was a pig-sty. Somebody puked all over the floor.'

'We're not here to discuss . . .'

'I'm no goddamn criminal,' Hunter shouted. 'I got into a little fray, all right. That's no reason to put me in a cell smelling of somebody's goddamn vomit!'

'You should have thought of that before you committed a felony,' the Chief of Detectives said.

'Felony?' Hunter shouted. 'Is getting drunk a felony?'

'No, but assault is. You hit that bartender, didn't you?'

'All right, I hit him,' Hunter said.

'That's assault.'

'I didn't hit him with anything but my fist!'

'That's second-degree assault.'

'There are guys hitting guys every day of the week,' Hunter said. 'I don't see them getting pulled in on first-degree or second-degree or even third-degree assault.'

'This is your first offence, isn't it?' the Chief of Detectives asked.

'Yeah, yeah,' Hunter said.

'Relax, you may get off with just a fine. Now let's hear the story.'

'The bartender called me Pretty Boy,' Hunter said.

'So you hit him?'

'No, not then. I hit him later.'

'Why?'

'He said something about us big handsome hunks of men never being any good with a woman. He said you could never judge a book by its cover. That's when I hit him.'

'Why'd you throw the chair at the bar mirror?'

'Well, I hit him, and he called me a name.'

'What name?'

'A name.'

'We've heard them all,' the Chief of Detectives said. 'Let's have it.'

'It's a name I associate with abnormal men,' Hunter said. 'That's when I threw the chair. I wasn't aiming at the mirror, I was aiming at him. That son of a bitch! I can get any woman I want!'

'You always lose your temper so easily?' the Chief of Detectives asked.

'Not usually,' Hunter said.

'What made you so touchy last night?'

'I was just touchy,' Hunter said.

'The arresting officer found a thousand dollars in small bills in your pocket. How about that?'

'Yeah, how about that?' Hunter shouted. 'When do I get it back? I hit a guy, and next thing you know I'm being robbed and thrown into a cell that smells of vomit.'

'Where'd you get that thousand?'

'From the bank,' Hunter said.

'Which bank?'

'My bank.. The bank where I save.'

'When did you withdraw it?'

'Yesterday afternoon.'

'Why?'

Hunter hesitated.

'Well?'

'I thought I might take a little trip,' Hunter said. His voice had become suddenly subdued. He squinted into the lights, as if trying to read the face of his questioner.

'What kind of a trip?'

'Pleasure.'

'Where?'

'Upstate.'

'Alone?'

Hunter hesitated again.

'How about it, Curt? Alone or with somebody?'

'With somebody,' Hunter said.

'Who?'

'A girl.'

'*Who?*'

'That's my business.'

'That's your pleasure,' the Chief of Detectives corrected, and all the bulls – including Brown and Kling – laughed. 'What happened to change your plans?'

'Nothing,' Hunter said, annoyed by the laughter, on guard now, waiting for the next question.

'You drew a thousand dollars from your bank yesterday afternoon, is that right?'

'Yes.'

'Because you thought you just *might* take a little trip with a girl. Last night, you're drinking alone in a bar, the thousand dollars in your pocket, and a bartender says something about your inability to please a woman, so you haul off and sock him. Is that right?'

'Yes, that's right.'

'Okay. What happened? The girl call it off?'

'That's my business,' Hunter said again.

'Do you like girls?' the Chief of Detectives asked.

Hunter's eyes were narrow now, peering into the lights suspiciously. 'Don't *you?*' he asked.

'I love 'em,' the Chief of Detectives said. 'But I'm asking you.'

'I like 'em fine,' Hunter said.

'This girl you planned the trip with? A special friend?'

'A doll,' Hunter said, his face blank.

'But a friend?'

'A doll,' he repeated, and the Chief of Detectives knew that was all he'd get from Hunter. The tall handsome blond man waited. Kling watched him, never once connecting him with the blond man who had allegedly led Mary Louise Proschek into Charlie Chen's tattoo parlour. Kling had read Carella's report, but his mind simply did not make any connexion.

'Next case,' the Chief of Detectives said, and Hunter

115

walked across the stage. When he reached the steps on the other side, he turned and shouted, 'The city hasn't heard the end of that goddamn pukey prison!' and then he went down the steps.

'Riverhead, two,' the Chief of Detectives said, 'Donaldson, Chris, thirty-five. Tried to pick a man's pocket in the subway. Transit cop made the pinch. Donaldson stated it was a mistake. How about it, Chris?'

Chris Donaldson could have been a double for Curt Hunter. As he walked across the stage, in fact, the Chief of Detectives murmured, 'What is this? A twin act?' Donaldson was tall and blond and handsome. If there were any detectives in the audience with inferiority complexes, the combination of Hunter and Donaldson should have been enough to shove them over the thin line to psychosis. It was doubtful that the Line-up had ever had such a combined display of masculine splendour since its inception. Donaldson seemed as unruffled as Hunter had been. He walked to the microphone. His head crossed the six-foot-three inch marker on the white wall behind him.

'There's been a mistake,' Donaldson said.

'Really?'

'Yes,' he said calmly. 'I didn't pick anybody's pocket, nor did I attempt to. I'm a gainfully employed citizen. The man whose pocket was picked simply accused the wrong person.'

'Then how come we found his wallet in your jacket pocket?'

'I have no idea,' Donaldson said. 'Unless the real pickpocket dropped it there when he felt he was about to be discovered.'

'Tell us what happened,' the Chief of Detectives said,

and then in an aside to the assembled bulls, he added, 'This man has no record.'

'I was riding the subway home from work,' Donaldson said. 'I work in Isola, live in Riverhead. I was reading my newspaper. The man standing in front of me suddenly wheeled around and said, "Where's my wallet? Somebody took my wallet!"'

'Then what?'

'The car was packed. A man standing alongside us said he was a transit cop, and before you knew it, another man and I were grabbed and held. The cop searched us and found the wallet in my pocket.'

'Where'd the other man go?'

'I have no idea. When the transit cop found the wallet on me, he lost all interest in the other man.'

'And your story is that the other man was the pickpocket.'

'I don't know who the pickpocket was. I only know that he wasn't me. As I told you, I *work* for a living.'

'What do you do?'

'I'm an accountant.'

'For whom?'

'Binks and Lederle. It's one of the oldest accounting firms in the city. I've worked there for a good many years.'

'Well, Chris,' the Chief of Detectives said, 'it sounds good. It's up to the judge, though.'

'There are people, you know,' Donaldson said, 'who sue the city for false arrest.'

'We don't know if it's false arrest yet, do we?'

'*I'm* quite sure of it,' Donaldson said. 'I've led an honest life, and I have no desire to get involved with the police.'

'Nobody does,' the Chief of Detectives said. 'Next case.'

Donaldson walked off the stage. Kling watched him, wondering if his story were true, again making no connexion between Mary Louise Proschek's blond escort and the man who'd claimed he'd been falsely accused of pickpocketing.

'Diamondback, one,' the Chief of Detectives said. 'Pereira, Genevieve, forty-seven, slashed her husband with a bread knife. No statement. What happened, Jenny?'

Genevieve Pereira was a short woman with shrewd blue eyes. She stood with her lips pursed and her hands clasped. She was dressed neatly and quietly, the only garish thing about her being a smear of blood across the front of her dress.

'I detect an error in your notations, sir,' she said.

'Do you?'

'You've misrepresented me chronologically by two years. My age is only forty-five.'

'Forgive me, Jenny,' the Chief of Detectives said.

'I feel, too, that your familiarity is somewhat uncalled-for. Only my closest acquaintances call me Jenny. The appellation, for your exclusive benefit, is Genevieve.'

'Thank you,' the Chief of Detectives said, a smile in his voice. 'And may I call you that?'

'If the necessity is so overwhelming,' Genevieve said.

'Why'd you stab your husband, Genevieve?'

'I did not stab him,' Genevieve answered. 'He suffered, at best, a surface scratch. I'm sure he'll convalesce.'

'You speak English beautifully,' the Chief of Detectives said.

'Your praise, though unsolicited,' Genevieve said, 'is

none the less appreciated. I've always tried to avoid dull clichés and transparent repetition.'

'Well, it certainly comes out beautifully,' the Chief of Detectives said, and Kling detected a new note of sarcasm.

'Any perseverant person can master the English tongue,' Genevieve said. 'Application is all that is required. Plus an abundant amount of native intelligence. And a detestation of the obvious.'

'Like what?'

'I'm sure I could not readily produce any examples.' She paused. 'I would have to cogitate on it momentarily. I suggest instead, that you read some of the various works of literature which have aided me.'

'Books like what?' the Chief of Detectives asked, and this time the sarcasm was unmistakable. *English for Martians?* Or *The English Language As A Lethal Weapon?*'

'I find sarcastic males vulgar,' Genevieve said.

'Did you find stabbing your husband vulgar?'

'I did not stab him. I scratched him with a knife. I see no reason for promoting this case to federal proportions.'

'Why'd you stab him?'

'Nor do I see,' Genevieve persisted, 'any pertinent reasons for discussing my marital affairs before an assemblage of barbarians.' She paused and cleared her throat. 'If you would relinquish my wrapper, I assure you I would depart without . . .'

'Sure,' the Chief of Detectives said. 'Next case.'

And that's the way it went.

When it was all over, Kling and Brown went downstairs and lighted cigarettes.

'No con man,' Brown said.

'These Line-ups are a waste of time,' Kling offered. He

blew out a stream of smoke. 'How'd you like those two handsome bastards?'

Brown shrugged. 'Come on,' he said, 'we better get back to the squad.'

The two handsome bastards, considering the fact that one of them was a murderer, got off pretty lightly.

Curt Hunter was found guilty and paid a five-hundred-dollar fine, plus damages.

Chris Donaldson was found not guilty.

Both men were once again free to roam the city.

12.

BERT KLING expected trouble, and he was getting it.

Usually, he and Claire Townsend got along just jim-dandy. They'd had their quarrels, true, but who was there to claim that the path of true love ever ran smooth? In fact, considering the bad start their romance had had, their love was chugging along on a remarkably even keel. Kling had had a rough time in the beginning trying to dislodge the torch Claire was carrying from the firm grip with which she'd carried it. He'd succeeded. They had passed through the getting-acquainted stages, and had then progressed rapidly through the con man's legend of going steady, and then through the con man's formality of getting engaged, and – if they weren't careful – they would enter the con man's legality of getting married, and then the con man's nightmare of having children.

Provided they could leap this particular hurdle which confronted them on that Wednesday night.

The hurdle was a very high one.

Kling was learning, perhaps a little late to do anything about it, that hell hath no fury like a woman scorned.

The woman scorned was rather tall by American standards. Not too tall for Kling, but she'd have given the run-of-the-mill unheroic American male trouble unless she wore flats on her dates. The woman scorned had black hair cut close to her head, and brown eyes which were aglow now with an inner fury, and a good mouth which was twisted into a somewhat sardonic grin. The woman scorned was slender without being skinny, bosomy without being busty, leggy without being gangly. The woman scorned was, as a matter of fact, damned pretty even when she was venting her fury.

'You *know*,' she said, 'that this probably means no vacation, don't you?'

'I don't know that at all,' Kling said. 'I have no reason to believe that.'

'You are not, if you'll pardon my pointing it out, writing up a traffic ticket at the moment.'

'Nor did I intend to sound as if I were,' Kling said, amazed by the high level of their argument, thinking at the same time that Claire looked quite lovely when she was angry and wanting simultaneously to kiss the fury off her mouth.

'I realize that the 87th Precinct is just *loaded* with super master minds who have all sorts of priority over a dumb rookie who just got promoted. But for God's sake, Bert . . .'

'Claire . . .'

'You *did* crack a murder case, you know! And the commissioner *did* personally commend you, and *did* personally promote you! What do you have to do in order to get a vacation spot that jibes with your fiancée's schedule? Stop mass fratricide? Cure the common cold?'

'Claire, it's not a question of . . .'

'Whatever you have to do, you should have *done* it!' Claire snapped. 'Of all the idiotic times for a vacation, 10 June absolutely takes the brass bologna! Of all the incredibly ridiculous . . .'

'It's not my fault, Claire. Claire, the schedule is made out by Lieutenant . . .'

'. . . incredibly ridiculous times for a vacation, 10 June positively wins the fur-lined bathtub!'

'All right,' Kling said.

'All right?' she repeated. 'What's all right about it? It reeks! It's bureaucracy in action! Hell, it's totalitarianism!'

'It's a hell of a thing, all right,' Kling agreed. 'Would you like me to quit my job? Shall I get a nice democratic position like shoemaker or butcher or . . .'

'Oh, stop it.'

'If I were a midget,' Kling said, 'I could probably get a job stuffing Vienna sausages. Trouble is . . .'

'Stop it,' she said again, but she was smiling.

'You better?' he asked hopefully.

'I'm sick,' she answered.

'It's a tough break.'

'Let's have a drink.'

'Rye neat,' he said.

Claire looked at him. 'No need to go all to pieces, officer,' she said. 'It's not the end of the world. Worst comes to worst, you can go on vacation with some other girl.'

'That sounds like a good idea,' Kling said, snapping his fingers.

'And all I'll do is break both your arms,' Claire said. She poured two hookers of rye and handed one of them to Kling. 'Here's to a solution.'

'You just hit the solution,' Kling said, raising the glass to his lips. 'Another girl.'

'Don't you dare drink to that!' Claire said.

'You're sure finals don't begin until the 17th?'

'Positive.'

'Can you swing something?'

'Like what?'

'I don't know.' Kling looked into the eye of his glass. 'Aw, hell,' he said, 'here's to a solution,' and he threw it down.

Claire swallowed hers without batting an eyelid. 'Let's think,' she said.

'How many tests are there?' Kling asked.

'Five,' she answered.

'When is school over?'

'Classes end on 7 June. The next week is a reading week. And then finals start on the 17th.'

'When do they end?'

'Two weeks later. That's when the semester is officially over.'

'28 June?'

'Yes.'

'That's great. I need another drink.'

'No more. We need clear heads.'

'How about you taking your tests during that last week of classes?'

'Impossible.'

'Why?'

'I don't know. It just is.'

'Has it ever been done before?'

'I doubt it strongly.'

'Hell, this is an emergency.'

'Is it? Bert, Women's U. is an all-girls school. Can I go to the dean and say I'd like to have permission to take my finals the week of the 3rd because my boy-friend and I are leaving on vacation the following week?'

'Why not?'

'They'd probably expel me. Girls have been expelled for less.'

'Hell, I can't see anything wrong with that.' Kling thought it over for a moment and then nodded emphatically. 'There is nothing at all wrong with going on vacation with your fiancé – not boy-friend, if you please, but *fiancé* – especially if you plan on getting married soon.'

'You make it sound worse than I did.'

'Then your mind is as evil as your dean's.'

'And yours, of course, is simon pure.'

Kling grinned. 'Absolutely,' he said.

'It still wouldn't work.'

'Then give me another drink and we'll resort to all kinds of subterfuge.'

Claire poured two more hookers. 'Here's to all kinds of subterfuge,' she toasted. Together, they tossed off the shots and she refilled the glasses.

'We could, of course, say you were having a baby.'

'We could?'

'Yes. And that you were going to be confined to the hospital during finals, so could you please take them a little earlier? How does that sound?'

'Very good,' Claire said. 'The dean would appreciate that.' She tossed off her drink and poured another.

'Go easy there,' Kling advised. He drank his whisky and held out his glass for a refill. 'We need a clear head here. Heads, I mean.'

'Suppose . . .' Claire said thoughtfully.

'Um?'

'No, that wouldn't work.'

'Let me hear it.'

'No, no, it wouldn't work.'

'What?'

'Well, I was thinking we could get married and say I had to miss finals because I was going on my honeymoon. How's that?'

'If you're trying to scare me,' Kling said, 'you're not.'

'I thought you wanted to wait until I graduated.'

'I do. Don't tempt me.'

'Okay,' Claire said. 'Whoosh, I'm beginning to feel that booze.'

'Keep a tight grip,' Kling said. He thought silently for a moment. 'Get me a pen and some paper, will you?'

'What for?'

'Letter to the dean,' Kling said.

'All right,' Claire answered. She walked across the room to the secretary and Kling said, 'You wiggle very nice.'

'Keep your mind on your work,' Claire said.

'You *are* my work. You're my life's work.'

Claire giggled and came back to him. She put her hands on his shoulders, leaned over, and kissed him fiercely on the mouth.

'You'd better go get the pen and paper,' he said.

'I'd better,' she answered. She walked away again, and again he watched her. This time, she returned with a fountain pen and two sheets of stationery. Kling put the paper on the coffee table, uncapped the pen and asked, 'What's the dean's name?'

'Which one? We have several.'

'The one in charge of vacations.'

'None such.'

'Permissions?'

'Anna Kale.'

'Miss or Mrs?'

'Miss,' Claire said. 'There are no such things as married deans.'

'Dear Miss Kale,' Kling said out loud as he wrote. 'How's that for a beginning?'

'Brilliant,' Claire said.

'Dear Miss Kale: I am writing to you on behalf of my daughter, Claire Townsend . . .'

'What's the penalty for forgery?' Claire asked.

'Shhhh,' Kling said. 'On behalf of my daughter, Claire Townsend, who requests permission to take her final examinations during the week of 3 June, rather than during the scheduled examination period.'

'You should have been a writer,' Claire said. 'You have a natural style.'

'As you know,' Kling went on, writing, 'Claire is an honour student . . .' He paused. 'Are you?'

'Phi Bete in my junior year,' Claire said.

'A bloody genius,' Kling said, and then went back to the letter. 'Claire is an honour student and can be trusted to take her exams without revealing their content to any students who will be tested at a later date. I would not make such an urgent request were it not for the fact that my sister is leaving for a tour of the West on 10 June . . .'

'A tour of the West!' Claire said.

'. . . a tour of the West on 10 June,' Kling went on, 'and has offered to take her niece with her. This is an opportunity which should not be bypassed, adding – I feel – more to a young girl's education than a strict compliance to schedule could offer. I hope you will agree the experience should be a rewarding one, and I know you would not put red tape into the way of a trip which would undoubtedly enrich one of your students. Trusting your decision will be the right one, I remain respectfully yours, Ralph Townsend.' Kling held the letter at arm's length. 'How's that?' he asked.

'It'll make a fine Exhibit A for the state,' Claire said.

'Screw the state,' Kling said. 'How about the letter?'

'My father hasn't got any sisters,' Claire said.

'A slight oversight,' Kling said. 'What about the drama of the appeal?'

'Excellent,' Claire said.

'Think she'll buy it?'

'What have we got to lose?'

'Nothing. I need an envelope.' Claire rose and went to the secretary. 'Stop wiggling,' he called after her.

'It's natural,' she answered.

'It's *too* natural,' Kling said. 'That's the trouble.'

He began doodling while she searched for an envelope. She found the envelope and started back across the room, walking as rigidly as she could, inhibiting the instinctive sway of her hips.

'That's better,' Kling said.

'I feel like a robot.'

She handed him the envelope, and he quickly scrawled 'Miss Anna Kale' across its face. He folded the letter, put it into the envelope, sealed the envelope, and then handed it to Claire. 'You are to deliver this tomorrow,' he said. 'Without fail. The fate of a nation hinges on your mission.'

'I'm more interested in your doodling,' Claire said, looking down at the drawing Kling had inked on to one of the stationery sheets.

'Oh, that,' Kling said. He expanded his chest. 'I was an ace in Art Appreciation, you know.'

He had drawn a heart on the sheet of paper. He had put lettering into the heart. The completed masterpiece looked like this:

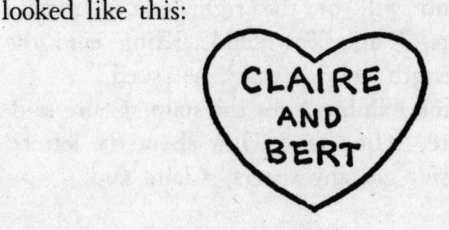

'For that,' Claire said, 'you deserve a kiss.'

She kissed him. She probably would have kissed him, anyway, heart or no. Kling was, none the less, surprised and delighted. He accepted Claire's kiss, and her lips completely wiped out of his mind any connexion he may have made between his own artistic endeavour and the tattoos found on the 87th's floaters.

He never knew how close he'd come to solving at least one mystery.

13.

THE second floater's name was Nancy Mortimer.

Her body had been identified by her parents who'd come from Ohio at the request of the police. She was thirty-three years old, a plain girl with simple tastes. She had left home two months ago, heading for the city. She had taken two thousand dollars in cash with her. She had told her parents she was going to meet a friend. If things went well, she'd told them, she would bring the friend home for them to meet.

Things, apparently, had not gone well.

The girl had been in the River Harb, according to the autopsy report, for at least a month.

And, according to the same report, the girl had died of arsenic poisoning.

There is an old Arab saying.

Actually, it is said by young Arabs, too. It fits many occasions, and so it is probably used with regularity. It is:

'Show them the death, and they will accept the fever.'

We don't have to look for hidden meanings in this gem of Arabian wisdom. The Freudian con men would probably impart thanatopsic values to what is undoubtedly an old folk saying. We don't have to do that. We can simply look at it for what it is, and understand it for what it says.

It says:

Feed a man gravel, and he will then appreciate hardtack.

It says:

Bed a man down with an aged old crone, and he will then appreciate a middle-aged mahjong player.

It says:

Show them the death, and they will accept the fever.

Priscilla Ames had seen the death and was ready to accept the fever. In her native town of Phoenix, Priscilla Ames had gone out with many men who had considerably lowered her estimation of the species. She had seen the death, and after a considerably lengthy correspondence with a man whose address she'd got from a pen-pal magazine, she was now ready to accept the fever.

To her delighted surprise, the fever turned out to be a delirium.

A blind date, after all, is something about which you exercise a little caution. When you travel away the hell from Phoenix to meet a man – even though you've already seen that man's picture, even though the picture looked good, but hadn't she sent a somewhat exotic pose, too, hadn't she cheated a little in the exchange of photos – you don't expect to meet a knight in shining armour. You approach cautiously.

Especially if you were Priscilla Ames who had long ago dismissed such knights as figments of the imagination.

But here, by God, was a knight in shining armour.

Here, by all that was holy, was a shining resplendent man among men, a towering blond giant with a wide white grin and laughing eyes, and a gentle voice, and a body like Apollo!

Here, by the saints, was the answer to every young maiden's prayer, the devoutly sought answer, the be-all and the end-all!

Here – was a man!

131

You could have knocked Priscilla over with a Mack truck. She had stepped off the plane, and there he was, coming toward her, grinning, and she had felt her heart quickening and then immediately thought, *No, he's made a mistake, it's the wrong man*, and then she knew it was the right man, the right man, the man she'd possibly been waiting for all her life.

That first day had sung, absolutely sung. Being in this magic, wonderful city, and drinking in the sights, and hearing the noise and the clamour and feeling wonderfully alive again, and feeling above all his presence beside her, the tentative touch of his fingers on her arm, gentle with the promise of force. He had taken her to lunch, and then to her hotel, and she had not been out of his sight since. It had been two weeks now, and she still could not adjust to the miracle of him. Ecstatically, she wondered if her life with this man would always be like this, would always be accompanied by a reckless headiness, good Lord, she was drunk on him!

She stood before the mirror in her hotel bedroom now, waiting for him. She looked prettier, she felt. Her hair looked browner and her eyes had more sparkle, and her breasts seemed fuller, and her hips seemed more feminine, and all because of him, all because of what he did to her, she wore his love like bright white armour.

When she heard his knock on the door, she ran to open it. He was wearing a deep blue trenchcoat, and the rain had loosened a wisp of his blond hair so that it hung boyishly on his forehead. She went into his arms instantly, her mouth reaching for his.

'Darling, darling,' she said, and he held her close to him, and she could smell tobacco on him, and aftershave, and she could smell too the close smell of rain-impregnated cloth.

'Pris,' he said, and the word was a caress. No one had ever said her name the way he said it. No one had ever made it an important name, a name that was hers alone. He held her at arm's length and looked down at her. 'You're beautiful,' he said. 'How come I'm so lucky?'

She never knew what to say in answer to his compliments. At first she suspected he was simply flattering her. But there was sincerity and honesty about this man, and she could read truth in his eyes. Whatever her shortcomings, she felt this man honestly believed she was beautiful, and witty, and vivacious.

'I'll get an umbrella,' she said.

'We don't need one,' he answered. 'It's a nice rain, Pris, warm. Do you mind? I like to walk in the rain. I'd like to walk in the rain with you.'

'Whatever you say,' she answered. She looked up at him. I must look like a complete idiot, she thought. He must surely see adoration in my eyes, he must think I'm a stupid child instead of a grown woman. 'Where . . . where are we going tonight?' she asked.

'A wonderful place for dinner,' he said. 'We have a lot of talking to do.'

'Talking?'

'Yes,' he said. He saw the frown on her face, and his eyes twinkled. His fingers touched her forehead, smoothing out the frown. 'Stop looking so serious,' he chided. 'Don't you know I love you?'

'Do you?' she asked, and there was fear in her eyes for a moment, and then he pulled her to him and said, 'Of course, I love you. Pris, Pris, I love you,' and the fear vanished and she buried her head in his shoulder and there was a small smile of contentment on her mouth.

They walked in the rain.

It was, as he had promised, a warm rain. It touched

133

the city gently. It roved the concrete canyons like a wistful maiden looking for her lost lover. It spoke in whispers, spoke to the buildings and the gutters and the park benches deserted and alone, and it spoke to the new green of the trees and to the growing things pushing to the sky, pushing through the warm moist earth. It spoke in syllables as old as time, and it spoke to Priscilla and her man, spoke to two lovers who threaded their way across the city arm in arm, cradled in the warmth of the song of the rain.

He shook out his trenchcoat when they entered the restaurant. There was a pretty redheaded hat-check girl, and he handed her his coat, and she smiled up at him, somewhat dazed by his good looks. But he turned from her without returning her smile, and he helped Priscilla out of her coat and then slung it over his arm and looked for the head waiter.

The waiter led the couple to a table in the corner of the restaurant. The floors were decorated with a huge chequerboard tile in black and white. The walls were done in rich Italian mosaic, and clerestory windows threw the mottled light of dusk into the room. A candle burned brightly in the centre of the round marble table. From somewhere near the bar, Pris heard the screech of a parrot. She craned her neck, looking past the tiers of huge apothecary jars filled with coloured liquids, purples and reds and oranges and yellows and bright vivid living greens.

'Would you like to order now, sir?' the head waiter asked. 'Some drinks first,' he replied. 'Rémy Martin for me,' he said. 'Pris?'

She was lost in the way he pronounced the drink, giving it the proper French twist. 'What?' she asked.

'Something to drink?' he said, smiling.

'A whisky sour,' she said.

'Yes, miss,' the head waiter said. 'A whisky sour for the lady, and *what* was it for the gentleman, please?'

He looked up at the head waiter, and for a moment there was unmasked impatience in his eyes. And then, with something akin to cruelty, he viciously said, 'Reeeeeemy Martin,' pronouncing the words like a guttersnipe.

'Yes, sir. Of course, sir,' the head waiter said, and he bowed away from the table.

Priscilla watched her man, fascinated by his boldness and his quickness, and his sureness.

'What was it you wanted to discuss?' she asked.

'First the drinks,' he said smiling. 'Do you like this place?'

'Yes, it's wonderful. It's so different. There aren't any places like this in Phoenix.'

'This is the most marvellous city in the world,' he told her. 'It's the only city that's really alive. And if you're in love, there's no place that can come near it. Even Paris. Paris is touted as the spot for lovers, but nothing can beat this city.'

'Have you been to Paris?'

'I was there during the war,' he said. 'I was a Commando.'

'Wasn't that terribly dangerous?' she asked, feeling a foolish dread and knowing that the dread was idiotic because the danger was long past.

He shrugged. 'Here are the drinks,' he said.

The head waiter brought their drinks and carefully placed them down. 'Would you care to see a menu now?' he asked.

'Please.'

He left the menus, and tiptoed away.

Priscilla lifted her glass. He lifted his.

'To us,' he said.

'Is that all?'

'That's everything, Pris,' he said, and again the sincerity shone in his eyes. 'Everything I want. Us.' He drank. 'Good.'

She drank with him, staring at him idiotically. 'What . . . what did you want to discuss?'

'The date,' he said simply.

'The . . . the date?'

'I want to marry you,' he said, reaching across the table suddenly and clasping her hand under his. 'Pris, you saw my plea, you answered my plea. Oh, Pris, there were dozens who answered it, believe me, you have no idea how many lonely wom . . . lonely people there are in this world. But out of those dozens, and out of all the hundreds and thousands and millions of people who crawl over the face of this earth, *we* happened to come together. Like a couple of stars colliding in space, Pris, going their separate ways and then *wham*!' He lifted his hand from the table suddenly and slammed his fist into the open palm. The sudden noise frightened her, but it also thrilled her. He was dynamic and unpredictable, and as one of the television brothers would have said, he certainly did have a flair for the dramatic.

'Like that,' he said, 'and there's a sudden shower of sparks, and all at once you've been part of my life always, all at once I can't bear to be apart from you, all at once I want you to be mine forever. I've got a job, you know that. A good job. I'm not the handsomest man in the world, but . . .'

'Oh, please,' she said, 'please . . .'

'. . . but I'm a hard worker, and I'll care for you always, Pris. This is why you came here to my city, to

136

find me. And we've found each other, Pris, and I don't want to wait any longer. Not another minute.'

'Wh . . . what do you mean?' she asked.

'I want to hear you say you'll marry me.'

'You know I will,' she answered, reaching across the table for his hand.

'Tomorrow,' he said.

'Wh . . .'

'Tomorrow.'

She looked at him steadily across the table. His eyes were glowing. His mouth looked sweet and tender.

'All right,' she said in a small voice.

'Good.' He grinned. 'Damnit,' he said, 'I feel like kissing you.' He rose suddenly, walked around the table and kissed her just as the waiter approached to take their order. The waiter didn't clear his throat. He simply stood there looking at them, watching them kiss. When they were finished, he said, 'Did you . . . ah . . . care for anything else?'

They laughed and then gave the waiter their orders.

'I feel wonderful,' she said.

'I feel great,' he told her. 'I feel as if I can lick this city with my bare hands. Pris, with you by my side, I can do anything, do you know that? Anything!'

'I . . . I'm glad you feel that way.'

'Do you know why? Because I've got your love, and your love makes me feel strong.'

'I . . . I feel strong, too,' she said.

'How much do you love me?' he asked.

'Don't you know how much I love you?'

'How much?' he persisted.

'You're . . . you're the only thing that matters,' she said.

'Pris,' he said, his eyes gleaming now, 'I've got

something like ten thousand dollars in the bank. I'm going to ask for a vacation, by God! I'll ask for a month, and we'll go to Bermuda or some place, how about that? Maybe Europe. What do you say, Pris?'

'I couldn't let you do that,' she answered.

'Why not?'

'I couldn't let you spend your money so foolishly.'

'My money?' he asked. A puzzled frown crossed his face. '*My* money? Pris darling, once we're married, everything I've got is yours. Everything.'

'Well, still . . .'

'Don't you look at it that way? Don't you feel we own everything together?'

'Certainly. But . . .'

'Then not another word about it. It's settled. We're going to Bermuda.'

'I'd rather . . . I'd much rather start looking for a place . . . and . . . and furnishing it. We could take a short honeymoon, darling, but shouldn't we . . .?'

'Of course, what an idiot I am! Of course, we've got to find a place of our own. My apartment is much too small, especially if we plan on a family later on.' He looked at her as if he'd made a *faux pas*. 'I . . . I remember your letter . . . the first one. You don't like children.'

'Oh, I'd love your children,' she said.

He smiled tremulously. 'Well, I . . . I just wasn't sure. I . . .' He cocked his head to one side, as if his emotions were too much for him to bear, as if the pressure of his emotions had forced the movement of his head, the way a tidal wave causes a buoy to bob. 'In any case, we've still got my ten thousand. That should furnish an apartment, all right.'

'And my money,' she added quietly.

'Your what?'

'The money I brought with me,' she said.

'Oh, yes. I'd forgotten completely about it.' He smiled indulgently. 'What is it, darling, something like five hundred dollars?'

Her eyes opened wide in surprise. 'You know very well it's closer to five *thousand* dollars,' she said.

'You're joking!'

'I'm not, I'm serious.' She grinned, enjoying his boyish surprise, feeling as if she had given him an unexpected present.

'You took . . . you carried so much *cash* with you?'

'Of course not. Don't you remember, darling? In one of my letters I told you I would be closing out my bank account, and you suggested I carry it in travellers' cheques.'

'Yes, but I had no idea . . . five thousand dollars.'

'It's really about forty-seven hundred,' she said.

'Still . . . honey, you've got to put that in the bank right away.'

'Why?'

'So that it can start collecting interest. For God's sake, why do you need forty-seven hundred dollars in travellers' cheques?'

'You're right,' she said.

'Tomorrow, early in the morning,' he said, 'before the wedding. We'll open an account for you at my bank.'

'A separate account, do you mean?' she asked.

'Naturally. It's your money, isn't it?'

'A little while ago, you said . . . you said when we were married everything you had was mine.'

'Of course it is. You know that, darling. I meant every word I said.'

'Then aren't you being a bit unfair?' she asked.

'Unfair? How?' He seemed very troubled. 'What have I done, Pris? Have I said something wrong?'

'You said separate account.'

'I don't understand.'

She leaned across the table, and her eyes held his in a steady gaze. 'Tomorrow,' she said, 'we'll be married. I'll go wherever you want to go and do whatever you want to do. I'll be yours – forever. And that means completely. No games, no kidding. Forever. I've waited a long time for you, darling, and I expect this to be for keeps. Tomorrow morning, we'll go to your bank. I'll endorse the travellers' cheques, and deposit the forty-seven hundred dollars in your account.'

He was already shaking his head.

'Yes,' she said. 'Yes.'

'I can't allow you to do that,' he told her. 'I'm sorry, Pris. I want you, *not* a dowry.'

'But it isn't a dowry,' she said. 'It's simply a stake in our future together. Don't you think I have a right to invest in our future?'

'Well . . .'

'You mustn't be stubborn about this, darling, really. It's the least I can bring to you. Besides, I'll feel as if all those lonely years of working and saving haven't gone for nothing. They'll have been worth while; they'll have been building for you . . . and for me.'

'We'll talk about it in the morning,' he said.

'It's settled, as far as I'm concerned. That's the first thing we'll do, before we do anything else.'

He seemed very worried about something. She squeezed his hand and said, 'What is it, darling?'

'I feel like a positive . . . I don't know . . . a . . . a moneylender or something!' he said vehemently.

'How silly you are,' she said gently.

'To go into a bank with you, and stand by while you endorse those cheques, and then to deposit them in my account.' He shook his head. 'I'd feel like a . . . like a gigolo! No, I won't do it, Pris.'

'Would it embarrass you?'

'Yes.'

'I'll cash them at the hotel then.'

'I don't want you to cash them at all,' he said. 'But I suppose I'd feel a lot easier if you cash them there.'

'All right, I'll have them cashed at the hotel. I'll have the money in good American currency when you come to call for me. To take me to my wedding.'

He grinned. 'I suppose I am being foolish. All right, cash them at the hotel. Then we'll go to the bank, deposit the money, and away we go. To our wedding.'

'There's a waiting period in this state, isn't there?' she asked.

'Yes. We'll drive out of the state. Look, let's do it right. I'll call for you at about ten. You'll have the cheques cashed by then?'

'Yes.'

'Good. We'll go to the bank and deposit them in my account, if that's what you want, and then we'll make a day of it. We'll have lunch downtown someplace, I know some very nice places, and then we'll drive out of the state. We'll just take our honeymoon as it comes, shall we? We'll stop wherever we feel like stopping.'

'It sounds wonderful,' she said.

'Good. Let's have another drink to it, shall we?'

He snapped his fingers for the waiter, and while they waited for him to come to their table, she leaned over and whispered the three most expensive words in the English language.

'I love you.'

And he looked at her with tender guile and answered with the three cheapest words in the English language.

'I love you.'

There was, in Teddy Carella, the constant fear that she didn't do enough for her husband.

Perhaps it was because she lacked the power of speech. She could not whisper the expensive words or the cheap words or any words. She could only show him how much she loved him, could only invent for him a thousand and one ways to show that she was his. She felt, you see, that she would eventually bore him. She felt that he would eventually seek a woman who could tell him the things his ears undoubtedly longed to hear – and she couldn't have been more wrong. Her face told him all he had to know.

Her devotion to invention, however, made her an excellent wife, a wife full of surprises, a wife who constantly delighted Carella and diverted Carella and made his life a day-by-day birthday party. In all truth, Teddy Carella would have been that kind of a wife even if she *could* speak. She was simply that kind of a person. Her ancestry was part Irish and part Scotch, but there was something of the Oriental philosophy in her attitude toward her husband. She wanted to please him. If he were pleased, she in turn would be pleased. She didn't have to read a book to know that love was a many-splendoured thing.

And since her attitude was definitely Oriental, it was not surprising that her mind often returned to the jovial Charlie Chen and to the cherished butterfly design which adorned the wall of his shop.

What would Steve's reactions be if he came to her one night, found her in a flimsy nightgown and, upon lowering one of the delicate straps to kiss her shoulder, discovered there a lacy black butterfly?

The prospect delighted her imagination.

The more she thought of it, the better the idea seemed. She was sure that Steve would be pleased. And, too, she was sure that Charlie Chen would be pleased. And, without a doubt, she herself would be pleased. There was something terribly risky and ridiculous about having a butterfly tattoo put on your shoulder. The idea was exciting. Even thinking about it, she could hardly contain her excitement.

But would it be very painful?

Yes, it probably would be very painful. Although Chen seemed like a man you could trust. Chen seemed like a man who would not hurt her. And Chen knew how much she loved her husband. That was important somehow. The butterfly would be a gift to Steve, and it should rightfully be tattooed by a man who knew and understood a woman's love for her man.

Pain be damned, she thought, *I shall do it!* NOW!

She glanced at the clock. No, not now. Steve would be home for dinner soon, so not now. She went to the desk calendar and flipped the pages. She had a dental appointment day after tomorrow, but she was free all day tomorrow.

Would it really look attractive in a strapless gown?

Yes, if Chen did it delicately, a small black butterfly poised for flight.

She made her mental assignation. Tomorrow, after lunch, she would visit Charlie Chen.

And then, a live dark butterfly poised for flight, she busied herself around the apartment, waiting for Steve, her secret humming inside her.

14.

THE young man had problems of his own.

He walked the streets of the city, and he concentrated on his problems, and he considered what happened to him the greatest kind of good fortune.

The young man was dressed neatly and conservatively. He looked as if he might have money in the bank. He didn't look overly bright. He walked the streets of the city, and now that the rain had stopped it wasn't so bad at all. People were beginning to appear in the streets, like victims of a siege after the shelling has stopped. The sky was still grey, but the clouds were tearing away in spots like gauzy cheesecloth, and the sun was trying desperately to push its way through. In the gutters, the accumulation of water sped for the sewers, carrying the miscellaneous refuse of the day. The kids rolled up their trouser legs and splashed in the water, stomping their feet. Store owners came out on to the sidewalk, stood looking up at the sky with hands on hips for a moment, and then went to roll up their awnings. A pair of lovers emerged from a dark hallway where they had stopped to wait out the rain. The girl's mouth had been kissed hard, and the boy's mouth carried lipstick which had been bruised into the skin. Together they walked briskly up the street, navigating the large puddles that dotted the sidewalk.

Everything stops, the young man thought. The rain stops, and the sun comes out, and then the sun stops, and the rain begins. When will my particular problem stop?

A boy on a bicycle rode past, his wheels creating hissing canopies of water as he raced alongside the sidewalk.

The young man watched the boy on the bicycle. He sighed heavily. There were two men standing on the sidewalk near the corner. One of the men was a redhead. The other man was tall, with dark hair, and he wore a dark blue suit.

The young man gave them a cursory glance. As he approached them, the man in the blue suit stepped into his path.

'Excuse me,' he said.

The young man looked up.

'My name is Charlie Parsons. I wonder if you'd do me a favour.'

'What's that?' the young man asked.

'This fellow here,' Parsons said, indicating the redhead, 'has a gold coin, and I might be interested in buying it from him. Trouble is, I left my glasses home and I can't read the date on it. I wonder if you'd be so kind.'

The young man shrugged. 'Well, I'm in sort of a hurry,' he said.

'It'll only take a minute, and I'd certainly appreciate it.'

'Well,' the young man said, 'where's the coin?'

The redhead produced a large gold coin. 'Picked it up in Japan,' he said. 'I just got back from there. I was in the Army until last week. Just got discharged.' The redhead grinned disarmingly. He seemed like a simple country boy. 'My name's Frank O'Neill.'

The young man simply nodded and took the coin. 'What am I supposed to look for?' he asked.

'The date,' Parsons told him. 'Should be on the bottom there someplace.'

'On the bott . . .? Oh yes, here it is. 1801.'

'1801?' Parsons said. 'Are you sure?'

'That's what it says. 1801.'

'Why, that's . . .' Parsons stopped himself. O'Neill was looking at him.

'That makes it pretty old, don't it?' O'Neill asked innocently.

Parsons cleared his throat. Obviously, he had stumbled upon something of real value and was now trying to hide his find. 'No, that's not very old at all. In fact, I'd say that's a pretty common coin. The only surprising thing about it is that you were able to find a Russian coin in Japan.'

The young man looked at Parsons and then at O'Neill. 'Russia once had a war with Japan, you know,' he said.

'Say, that's right,' O'Neill said. 'Bet that's how the coin happened to be there. Damn, if you can't pick up all kinds of junk in the interior of that country.'

'I might still be interested in buying the coin,' Parsons said guardedly. 'Just as a curiosity piece, you understand. You know, a Russian coin which found its way to Japan.'

'Well,' O'Neill said, 'I got it for a pack of cigarettes.' His candid naïveté was remarkable. 'That's all it cost me.'

'I couldn't let you have more than ten dollars for it,' Parsons said judiciously. In an aside, he winked at the young man. The young man stared at him, a puzzled expression on his face.

'I'd say you just bought yourself a gold coin,' O'Neill said, grinning.

Parsons reached into his wallet, trying to hide his haste. He pulled out a twenty-dollar bill and handed it to O'Neill. 'Do you have any change?' he asked.

'No, I don't,' O'Neill said. 'Let me have the bill, and I'll cash it in that cigar store.'

Parsons gave him the bill, and O'Neill went into the cigar store on the corner. As soon as he was gone, Parsons turned to the young man.

'Jesus,' he said, 'do you know what that coin is worth?'

'No,' the young man said.

'At least two hundred dollars! And he's letting me have it for ten!'

'You're pretty lucky,' the young man said.

'Lucky, hell. I spotted him for a hick from the minute I saw him. I'm just wondering what else he's got to sell.'

'I doubt if he's got anything else,' the young man said.

'I don't. He's just back from Japan. Who knows what else he may have picked up? I'm going to pump him when he gets back.'

'Well, I'll be running along,' the young man said.

'No, stick around, will you? I may need your eyesight. What a time to forget my glasses, huh?'

O'Neill was coming out of the cigar store. He had got two tens for the twenty, and he handed one of the tens and the gold coin to Parsons. The other ten he put into his pocket. 'Well,' he said, 'much obliged.' He started to go, and Parsons laid a hand on his arm.

'You said . . . uh . . . that you could get all kinds of junk in the interior. What . . . uh . . . did you have in mind?'

'Oh, all kinds of junk,' O'Neill said.

'Like what?'

'Well, I picked up some pearls,' O'Neill said. 'As a matter of fact, I'm sorry I did.'

'Why?'

'Damn things cost me a fortune, and I could use some money right now.'

'How much did they cost you?' Parsons asked.

'Five hundred dollars,' O'Neill said, as if that were all the money in the world.

'Real pearls?'

'Sure. Black ones.'

'Black pearls?' Parsons asked.

'Yeah. Here, you want to see them?' He reached into his pocket and pulled out a leather bag. He unloosened the drawstrings on the bag, and poured some of its contents into the palm of his hand. The pearls were not exactly black. They glowed with grey luminescence.

'There they are,' O'Neill said.

'That bag is full of them?' Parsons asked, taking one of the pearls and studying it.

'Yeah. Got about a hundred of them in there. Fellow I bought them from was an old Jap.'

'Are you sure they're genuine?'

'Oh, sure,' O'Neill said.

'They're not paste?'

'Would I pay five hundred dollars for paste?'

'Well, no. No, I guess not.' Parsons looked hastily to the young man. Then he turned to O'Neill. 'Are you . . . are you . . . did you want to sell these?'

'I tell you,' O'Neill said, 'the Army discharged me here, and I live down South. I lost all my money on the boat took us back, and I'll be damned if I know how I'm going to get home.'

'I'd be . . . ah . . . happy to give you five hundred

dollars for these,' Parsons said. Quickly, he licked his lips, as if his mouth had suddenly gone dry. 'Provided they're genuine.'

'Oh, they're real all right. But I couldn't let you have them for five hundred.'

'That's what they cost you,' Parsons pointed out.

'Sure, but I had the trouble of making the deal, and of carting them all the way back to the States. I wouldn't let them go for less than a thousand.'

'Well, that's kind of high,' Parsons said. 'We don't even know they're genuine. They may be paste.'

'Hell, I wouldn't try to stick you,' O'Neill said.

'I've been stuck before,' Parsons said. 'After all, I don't know you from a hole in the wall.'

'That's true,' O'Neill said, 'but I hope you don't think I'd let you buy these pearls without having a jeweller look at them first.'

Parsons looked at him suspiciously. 'How do I know the jeweller isn't a friend of yours?'

'You can pick any jeweller you like. I won't even come into the shop with you. I'll give you the pearls, and I'll wait outside. Listen, these are the real articles. Only reason I'm letting you have them so cheap is because I don't want to fool around. I want to go home.'

'What do you think?' Parsons asked, turning to the young man.

'I don't know,' the young man said.

'Will you come with us to a jeweller?'

'What for?'

'Come along,' Parsons said. 'Please.'

The young man shrugged. 'Well, all right,' he said.

They walked up the street until they came to a jewellery shop. The sign outside said 'REPAIRS, APPRAISALS.'

'This should do it,' Parsons said. 'Let me have the pearls.'

O'Neill handed him the sack.

'You coming?' Parsons asked the young man.

'All right,' the young man said.

'You'll see,' O'Neill said. 'He'll tell you they're worth a thousand dollars.'

Together, Parsons and the young man went into the shop. O'Neill waited outside on the sidewalk.

The jeweller was a wizened old man bent over a watch. He did not look up. He kept his brow squeezed tight against the black eyepiece, and he picked at the watch like a man pulling meat from a lobster claw. Parsons cleared his throat. The jeweller did not look up. Together they waited. A cuckoo clock on the wall chirped the time. It was 2 p.m.

Finally the jeweller looked up. He opened his eyes wide, and the eyepiece fell into his open palm.

'Yes?' he asked.

'I'd like some pearls appraised,' Parsons said.

'Where are they?'

'Right here,' Parsons said, extending the sack.

The jeweller loosened the drawstrings. He shook a few of the smokey grey globes into the palm of his hand.

'Nice size,' he said. 'Nice sheen. Nice smoothness. What do you want to know?'

'Are they real?'

'They're not paste, I can tell you that immediately.' He nodded. 'Impossible to say whether they're cultured or genuine Oriental without having them X-rayed, though. I'd have to send out of the shop for that.'

'How much are they worth?' Parsons asked.

The jeweller shrugged. 'If they're cultured, you can

get between ten and twenty-five dollars for each pearl. If they're genuine Oriental, the price is much higher.'

'How much higher?'

'Judging from the size of these, I'd say between a hundred and two hundred for each pearl. At least a hundred.' He paused. 'How much did you want for them?'

'A thousand,' Parsons said.

'You've got a sale,' the jeweller answered.

'I'm not selling,' Parsons said. 'I'm buying.'

'How many are in that sack?' the jeweller asked. 'About seventy-five pearls?'

'A hundred,' Parsons said.

'Then you can't go wrong. Even if they're cultured, you'd get at least ten dollars for each pearl – so there's your thousand right there. And if they're genuine Oriental, you stand to make a phenomenal profit. If they're genuine Oriental, you can get back ten times your investment. I'd have them X-rayed at once if I were you.'

Parsons grinned. 'Thank you,' he said. 'Thanks a lot.'

'Don't mention it,' the jeweller said. He put his eyepiece back in place and bent over his watch again.

Parsons took the young man to one side. 'What do you think?' he asked.

'Looks like a good deal,' the young man said.

'I know. Listen, I can't let this hick get away from me.'

'He's willing to sell. What makes you think he'll try to get away?'

'That's just it. If these pearls are genuine Oriental, he's sitting on a fortune. I've got to buy them before he has them X-rayed himself.'

'I see what you mean,' the young man said.

'The trouble is, I live in the next state. By the time I got to my bank, it'd be closed. This fellow isn't going to wait until tomorrow, that's for sure.'

'I guess not,' the young man said.

'Do you live in the city?'

'Yes.'

'Do you bank here?'

'Yes.'

'Have you got a thousand dollars in the bank?'

'Yes.'

'I hate to do this,' Parsons said.

'Hate to do what?'

Parsons smiled. 'I hate to cut you in on such a sweet deal.'

'Would you?' the young man asked, interest showing in his eyes.

'What choice do I have? If I asked our hick to wait until tomorrow, I'd lose him.'

'Fifty-fifty split?' the young man asked.

'Now wait a minute,' Parsons said.

'Why not? I'll be putting up the money.'

'Only until tomorrow. Besides, he's my hick. You wouldn't have known anything about this if I hadn't stopped you.'

'Sure, but you can't buy those pearls if I don't go to the bank.'

'That's true.' Parsons' eyes narrowed. 'How do I know you won't take the pearls and then refuse to sell me my half tomorrow?'

'I wouldn't do a thing like that,' the young man said.

'I want your address and telephone number,' Parsons said.

'All right,' the young man said. He gave them to Parsons, and Parsons wrote them down.

'How do I know these are legitimate?' Parsons asked. 'Let me see your driver's licence.'

'I don't drive. You can check it in the phone book.' He turned to the jeweller. 'Have you got an Isola directory?'

'Never mind,' Parsons said. 'I trust you. But I'll be at your apartment first thing tomorrow morning to give you my five hundred dollars and to get my share of the pearls.'

'All right,' the young man said. 'I'll be there.'

'God, this is a great deal, isn't it? If they're genuine, we'll be rich. And if they're cultured, we break even. We can't lose.'

'It's a good deal,' the young man agreed.

'Let's get to the bank before he changes his mind.'

O'Neill was waiting for them outside. 'Well?' he asked.

'He said they're not paste,' Parsons told him.

'See? What'd I tell you? Did he say they're worth a thousand?'

'He said they might be worth about that.'

'Well, do we have a deal or don't we?'

'I'll have to go home for my pass book,' the young man said.

'All right. We'll go with you.'

The three men hailed a cab, and the cab took them uptown. The young man got out, and the cab waited. When he came down again, he had his bank book with him. He gave the cabbie instructions, and the three men drove to the bank. They all got out then, and Parsons paid the cabbie. The young man went into the bank, and when he came out, he had a thousand dollars in cash with him.

'Here's the money,' he said.

Parsons grinned happily.

The young man handed the thousand dollars to O'Neill.

'And here're the pearls,' O'Neill said, reaching into his pocket and handing the young man a leather sack. 'I'm certainly much obliged to you fellows. This means I'll be able to go home.'

'Not for a long while,' the young man said.

O'Neill looked up. He was staring into the open end of a .38 Detective Special. 'What?' he said.

The young man grinned. 'The old diamond switch,' he said, 'only with pearls. You've got my thousand, and the pearls in this sack you gave me are undoubtedly paste. Where are the real ones the jeweller appraised?'

'Listen,' Parsons said, 'you're making a mistake, Mac. You're . . .'

'Am I?' The young man was already frisking O'Neill. In two seconds, he located the sack of real pearls. 'Tomorrow morning, I'd be sitting around in my apartment waiting for my *partner* to arrive with his five hundred dollars. Only my partner would never show up. My partner would be out spending his share of the thousand dollars he conned from me.'

'This is the first time we ever done anything like this,' O'Neill said, beginning to panic.

'Is it? I've got a few other people who may be willing to identify you,' the young man said. 'Come on, we're taking a little ride.'

'Where to?' Parsons asked.

'To the 87th Precinct,' the young man said. The young man's name was Arthur Brown.

15.

THE tattoo parlour was near the Navy yards, and so the specialities of the house were anchors, mermaids, and fish. There were also dagger designs, and ship designs, and Mothers in hearts.

The man who ran the place was called Popeye. He was called Popeye because a drunken sailor had once jabbed out his left eye with his own tattooing needle. Judging from Popeye's present condition, he may very well have been drunk himself when he'd lost his eye. He was certainly ossified now. Carella reflected upon the man's profession, and concluded that he wouldn't trust him to remove a small splinter with a heated needle, no less decorate his flesh with a tattooing tool.

'Come and go, come and go,' Popeye said. 'All th' time. In an' out, in an' out. From all ov' the worl'. I decorate 'em. Me. I colour their fleshes.'

Carella was not interested in those who came and went from all over the world. He was interested in what Popeye had told him just a few minutes before.

'This couple,' he said. 'Tell me more about them.'

'Han'some guy,' Popeye said. 'Ver' han'some. Big tall blond feller. Walk like a king. Rish. You can tell when they rish. He had money, this feller.'

'You tattooed the girl?'

'Nancy. Tha' was her name. Nancy.'

'How do you know?'

'He called her that. I heard him.'

'Tell me exactly what happened?'

'She in trouble? Nancy in trouble?'

'She's in the biggest kind of trouble,' Carella said. 'She's dead.'

'Oh.' Popeye squinched up his face and looked at Carella with his good eye. 'Tha's a shame,' he said. 'Li'l Nancy's dead. Automobile accident?'

'No,' Carella said. 'Arsenic.'

'Wha's that?' Popeye asked.

'A deadly poison.'

'Too bad. Li'l girls should'n take poison. She cried, you know? When I was doin' the job. Bawled like a baby. Big han'some bassard jus' stood there an' grinned. Like as if I was brandin' her for him. Like as if I was puttin' a trade mark or somethin' on her. Sick as a dog, poor li'l Nancy.'

'What do you mean sick?'

'Sick, sick.'

'How?'

'Pukin',' Popeye said.

'The girl vomited?' Carella asked.

'Right here in th' shop,' Popeye said. 'Got th' can all slobbed up.'

'When was this?'

'They'd jus' come from lunch,' Popeye said. 'She was talkin' about it when they come in th' shop. Said they didn't have no Chinese res'rants in her home town.'

'Is there a Chinese restaurant in the neighbourhood?'

'One aroun' th' corner. Looks like a dump, but has real good food. Cantonese. You dig Cantonese?'

'What else did she say?'

'Said th' food was ver' spicy. Tha' figgers, don't it?'

'Go on.'

'Han'some said he wanted a tattoo on the li'l girl's hand. A heart an' N-A-C.'

'He said that?'

'Yeah.'

'Why NAC?'

Popeye cocked his head so that his dead socket stared Carella directly in the face. 'Why, tha's their names,' he said.

'What do you mean, names?'

''Nitials, I mean. N is her initial. N for Nancy.'

Carella felt as if he'd been struck by lightning.

'The "A" is jus' "and", you know. Nancy *and* Chris. Tha' was his name. Chris. N-A-C.'

'Goddamnit!' Carella said. 'Then the Proschek girl's tattoo meant *Mary* and Chris. I'll be a son of a bitch!'

'Wha'?' Popeye said.

'How do you know his name was Chris?' Carella asked.

'She said so. When he said "NAC," she said, "Why don't we put th' whole names, Nancy and Chris?" Tha's what she said.'

'What did he say?'

'Said there wasn't enough space. Said it was just a tiny li'l heart. Hell, that li'l girl was goofy about him. He'da tole her to lay down an' take off her bloomers, she'da done it ri' here in the shop.'

'You said she cried while you were working on her?'

'Yeah. Bawled like a baby. Hurt like hell.'

'Were you drunk?'

'Me? Drunk? Hell, no. Wha' makes you think I was drunk?'

'Nothing. What happened next?'

'She was cryin', and I was working, and then all of a sudden, she feels sick. Han'some looked kind of worried.

He kep' tryin' to rush her out of the shop, but the poor girl had to puke, you know? So I took her in back. Slobbed up the whole damn can.'

'Then what?'

'He wanted to take her away. Kep' sayin', "Come on, Nancy, we'll go to my place. Come on." She wouldn' go withim. Said she wanted me to finish th' tattoo. Game kid, huh?'

'Did you finish it?'

'Yeah. She was sick as hell all the way through. You could see she was tryin' to keep from pukin' again.' Popeye paused. 'But I finished it. Nice job, too. Han'some paid me, an' away they went.'

'Into a car?'

'Yeah.'

'What make?'

'I dinn notice,' Popeye said.

'God damn,' Carella said.

'I'm sorry,' Popeye said. 'I dinn notice.'

'Did she mention the man's last name? This Chris fellow.'

Popeye thought for a moment. 'Yeah, yeah,' he said. 'She did. She said something about the future Mrs Somebody.'

'Mrs *who*?' Carella asked.

'I don't remember.'

'God damn,' Carella said again. He snorted heavily. He bit his lower lip. 'Can you give me a full description of the man?' he asked finally.

'Much's I can remember,' Popeye said.

'Blond hair,' Carella said. 'Right?'

'Yeah.'

'Long or short?'

'Average.'

'He wasn't wearing a crew-cut or anything like that?'

'No.'

'All right, what about his eyes? What colour?'

'Blue, I think. Or grey. One or th' other.'

'What kind of a nose?'

'Good nose. Not long, not short. Good nose. He was a han'some guy.'

'Mouth?'

'Good mouth.'

'Was he smoking?'

'No.'

'Any scars or birthmarks on his face?'

'No.'

'Anywhere on his body?'

'I dinn undress him,' Popeye said.

'I meant visible. On his hands perhaps? Tattoos? Any tattoos on his hands?'

'Nope.'

'What was he wearing?'

'Topcoat. This was back in February, you know. A black topcoat. Had a kind of a red lining. Red silk, I think, and those straps you slip your hands through.'

'What straps?'

'Inside the coat. You know, so you can slip it over your shoulders while you're at the track. That's what I mean.'

'What kind of a suit?'

'A tweed. Grey.'

'Shirt?'

'White.'

'Tie?'

'Black tie. I remember asking him if he was in mourning. He jus' grinned.'

'He would, the bastard. Are you sure you can't

remember the make of the car he was driving? That would be very helpful.'

'I ain't good on cars,' Popeye said.

'Did you happen to notice the licence plate?'

'Nope.'

'But I'll bet you can tell me what kind of a tie-clasp he was wearing,' Carella said, sighing.

'Yeah. Silver bar with a horse's head on it. Nice. I figured him for a horse player.'

'What else do you remember?'

'Tha's about it.'

'Did they mention where they were going?'

'Yeah. To his place. He said she could lay down there an' he'd get her something cool to put on her forehead.'

'Where? Did he say where?'

'No. He only said his place. That could be anyplace in the city.'

'You're telling me?' Carella asked.

'I'm sorry,' Popeye said. 'Guy wants to take care of a girl with a stomach ache, that's his business. Wants to get her something for her head, ain't none of my affair.'

'He got her something for her *feet*,' Carella said.

'Huh?'

'A hundred-pound weight to carry her to the bottom of the river.'

'He drowned her?' Popeye asked. 'You mean he drowned that nice li'l girl?'

'No, he . . .'

'Bravest li'l thing ever come in here. Even the sailors I get whimper. She bawled, an' she got sick, but she come right back for more. That takes guts. To come back for more when you're so scared you're sick.'

'You don't know just how much guts it took,' Carella said.

'An' he drowned her, huh? How do you like that?'

'I didn't say he . . .'

'What a way to die,' Popeye said, shaking his head. His nose was red and bulging with aggravated veins. His one good eye was watery and bloodshot. His breath stank of cheap wine. 'What a way to die,' he repeated. 'Drownin'.'

'You're well on the way,' Carella said.

Then he thanked him and left the shop.

16.

CHRIS DONALDSON had already fed her the arsenic.

He had fed it to her in a half-dozen dishes: the tea, the fried rice, the chow mein, every dish he could get to while she was in the ladies' room. When the food had come, he'd simply said, 'Let's wash up,' and then he'd taken Priscilla by the elbow and led her away from the table. He'd doubled back almost instantly and done his work, and she had consumed the odourless and almost tasteless arsenic with apparent relish.

They had gone to the Chinese restaurant directly after they'd left the bank. They had deposited Priscilla's money in his account, and now she had consumed the arsenic, and now it was all a matter of time.

He watched her with the flat look of a reptile, a slight smile on his face. He hoped she would not get sick too soon, like the last one. That had been an embarrassing episode. Even beautiful women lost all their charm when they became violently ill, and the women he had murdered and was now murdering were far from beautiful.

'That was good,' Priscilla said.

'More tea, darling?' he asked.

'Yes, please.' He poured from the small round pot. 'Don't you like tea?' she asked. 'You haven't had any.'

'Not particularly,' he said. 'I'm a coffee drinker.'

She took the cup from him. 'Did you put sugar in it?' she asked.

'Yes,' he said. 'Everything's in it,' and he smiled at his own grim humour.

'You'll make a good husband,' Priscilla said. She felt full and warm and drowsy. This afternoon she would be married. She felt lazy and content and at complete peace with the world. 'You'll make a wonderful husband.'

'I'm going to try my damnedest,' he said. 'I'm going to make you the happiest woman in the world.'

'I'm the happiest woman in the world right now.'

'I want everyone to know you're mine,' Donaldson said. 'Everyone. I want to shout it at them. I want big signs telling them.'

Priscilla grinned. He watched her grin, and he thought *Do you know you've been poisoned, my dear? Do you know what metallic poisoning is?* He watched her, and he felt neither pity nor compassion. It would not be long now. A few hours at the most. Tonight he would dispose of her, the way he had disposed of the others. There was just one thing remaining, one concession to his ego. Like a great painter, he must sign his work. He must lead her into helping him sign his work.

'I get crazy ideas sometimes,' he said.

'Ah-ha,' she answered. 'Now he tells me there's insanity in his family. A few hours before the wedding, and he trots out the skeletons.'

'I really *do* get crazy ideas,' he persisted, as if his speech were rehearsed, a speech that had worked for him before and which he was sure would work now, annoyed because she had interrupted the smooth rehearsed flow of his speech with her silly witticism. 'Like I . . . I want to brand you. I want to put my name on you, so that people will know you're mine.'

'They'll know anyway. They can see it in my eyes.'

'Yes, but . . . well, it's silly, I admit it. It's crazy. Didn't I tell you it was crazy? Didn't I warn you?'

'If I were a cow, darling,' she said, 'I wouldn't at all mind being branded.'

'There must be some way,' he said, as if mulling the problem over. He reached across the table for her hand, toyed with her fingers. 'Oh, I don't mean a red hot branding iron. Pris, that would kill me. Any pain to you would kill me. But . . .' He stopped, studying her hand. 'Say,' he said. 'Saaaay . . .'

'What?'

'A tattoo. How about that?'

Priscilla smiled. 'A *what*?'

'A tattoo.'

'Well . . .' Priscilla was puzzled. 'What about a tattoo?'

'How would you like one?'

'I wouldn't,' she said firmly.

'Oh.' His voice fell.

'Why on earth would I want a tattoo?'

'No,' he said. 'Never mind.'

She stared at him, confused. 'What's the matter, darling?'

'Nothing.'

'Are you angry?'

'No.'

'You are, I can see it. Do you . . . do you *want* me to have a . . . a tattoo?'

'Yes,' he said.

'I'm not sure I understand.'

'A small one. Someplace on your hand.' He took her hand again. 'Right here perhaps, between the thumb and forefinger.'

'I . . . I'm afraid of needles,' Priscilla said.

'Then forget it.' He stared at the tablecloth. 'Finish your tea, won't you, darling?' he said, and he smiled up at her, a defeated boyish smile.

'If I . . .' She stopped, thinking. 'It's just that I'm afraid of needles.'

'It doesn't hurt at all, you know,' he said. 'I thought perhaps a little heart. With our initials in it. Priscilla and Chris. PAC. So that everyone would know. Everyone would know you're my woman.'

'I'm afraid of needles,' she said.

'It doesn't hurt,' he assured her.

'Chris, I . . . I'll do anything else you want. Anything, really. It's just that I've always been afraid of needles. Even getting a shot from the doctor.'

'Then forget it,' he said pleasantly.

She looked into his eyes. 'You're angry, aren't you?'

'No, no, not at all.'

'You are.'

'Pris, really I'm not. I'm just a little . . . disappointed.'

'In me?'

'No, of course not in you. How could I be disappointed in you?'

'In what then?'

'Well, I thought you'd like the idea.'

'I *do* like it, Chris. I *want* people to know I belong to you. But . . .'

'Yes, I know.'

'I feel like such a baby.'

'No, you're perfectly right. If you have a fear of . . .'

'Chris, please, I feel so silly. It probably . . .' She bit her lip. 'It probably doesn't hurt at all.'

'Not at all,' he said.

'I am . . . I am being a baby.'

'Forget it,' he said, but there was an aloofness about

him which chilled her. Desperately, she wanted to reach him again, wanted to be safe and secure in the warmth of his respect.

'I'll . . . I'll do whatever you say,' she told him.

'No, don't be ridiculous,' he said. He snapped his fingers and called, 'Waiter,' and to her he said, 'Let's get out of here.'

'I'll do it, Chris. I'll . . . I'll do it. The tattoo. Whatever you want.'

His eyes softened. He took her hands and said, 'Would you, Pris? It would really make me very happy.'

'I want to make you happy,' she said.

'Good. There's a tattoo parlour right on the edge of Chinatown. It won't hurt, Pris. I can promise you that.'

She nodded. 'I'm petrified,' she said.

'Don't be. I'll be right there with you.'

She covered her mouth and swallowed hard. 'This food was awfully heavy,' she said. She smiled apologetically. 'Very good, but heavy. I feel a little queasy.'

He looked at her, and there was concern in his eyes. The waiter approached the table, quietly depositing the check face down. Donaldson picked up the check, glanced at it, left a tip on the table, and then took Priscilla's arm. He paid the check at the cashier's booth.

As they left the restaurant, he said, 'Do you know the story about the man who goes to a Chinese brothel?'

'Oh, Chris,' she said.

'He goes there, and then the madam is surprised to see him returning five minutes later. She says to him, "But you were here just five minutes ago with Ming Toy, our most beautiful girl." And the fellow looks at her and says, "Well, you know how it is with a Chinese meal."'

Priscilla laughed, and then sobered almost instantly. 'I still feel queasy,' she said.

He took her elbow and glanced at her quickly. Then he quickened his pace and said, 'We'd better hurry.'

To say that Charlie Chen was surprised to see Teddy Carella would be complete understatement.

The door to his shop had been closed, and he heard the small tinkle of the bell when the door opened, and he glanced up momentarily and then lifted his hulk from the chair in which he sat smoking and went to the front of the shop.

'Oh!' he said, and then his round face broke into a delighted grin. 'Pretty detective lady come back,' he said. 'Charlie Chen is much honoured. Charlie Chen is much flattered. Come, sit down, Mrs . . .' He paused. 'Charlie Chen forget name.'

Teddy touched her lips with the tips of her fingers and then shook her head. Chen stared at her, uncomprehending. She repeated the gesture.

'You can't talk maybe?' he asked. 'Laryngitis?'

Teddy smiled, shook her head, and then her hand travelled swiftly from her mouth to her ears, and Chen at last understood.

'Oh,' he said. 'Oh.' His eyes clouded. 'Very sorry, very sorry.'

Teddy gave a slight shake of her head and a slight lift of her shoulders and a slight twist of her hands, explaining to Chen that there was nothing to be sorry for.

'But you understand me?' he asked. 'You know what I say?'

Yes, she nodded.

'Good. You most beautiful lady ever come into Charlie Chen's poor shop. I speak this from my heart. Beauty is not plentiful in the world today. There is not much beauty. To see true beauty, this gladdens me. Makes me very happy, very happy. I talk too fast for you?'

Teddy shook her head.

'You read my lips?' He nodded appreciatively. 'That very clever. Very clever. Why you come visit Charlie Chen?'

Teddy looped her thumbs together and then moved her hands as if they were in flight.

'The butterfly?' Chen asked, astounded. 'You want the butterfly?'

Yes, she nodded, delighted by his response.

'Oh,' he said, 'ohhhhhh,' as if her acknowledgement were the fulfilment of his wildest dream. 'I make very pretty. I make pretty big butterfly.'

Teddy shook her head.

'No big butterfly? Small butterfly?'

Yes.

'Ah, very clever, very clever. Delicate butterfly for pretty lady. Big butterfly no good. Small, little, pretty butterfly better. You very smart. You very beautiful, and you very smart. I do. Come. Come in. Please. Come in.'

He parted the curtains leading to the back of the shop, and then gallantly bowed and stepped aside while Teddy passed through. She went directly to the butterfly design pinned to the wall. Chen smiled, and then seemed to notice for the first time the calendar with its naked woman on the other wall.

'Excuse other pretty lady, please,' he said. 'Stupid sons do.'

Teddy glanced at the calendar and smiled.

'You decide colour?' Chen asked.

She nodded.

'Which?'

Teddy touched her hair.

'Black? Ah, good. Black very good. Little black butterfly. Come, sit. I do. No pain. Charlie Chen be very careful.'

He sat her down, and she watched him, beginning to get a little frightened now. Deciding to get one's shoulder decorated was one thing. Going ahead with it was another thing again. She watched his movements as he walked around the shop preparing his tools. Her eyes were saucer wide.

'You frightened?' he asked.

She gave a very small nod.

'No be. Everything go hunky-dory. I promise. Very clean, very sanitary, very harmless.' He smiled. 'Very painless, too.'

Teddy kept watching him, her heart in her mouth.

'I use very deep black. Black no good unless really black. Otherwise is grey. Life is all full of greys, pretty lady. No sharp whites, no sharp blacks. All greys. Very sad, life is.' Chen brought a pencil and a sheet of paper to the table. He drew several circles on it, one the size of a dime, the next the size of a nickel, then the size of a quarter, and lastly the size of a half-dollar.

'Which size do you want butterfly?' he asked.

Teddy studied the circles.

'Biggest one too big, no?' Chen asked.

Teddy nodded.

'Okay. We disintegrate.' He made a large cross over the half-dollar circle.

'Littlest one too little, yes?' he asked.

Again, Teddy nodded.

'Poof!' Chen said, and he crossed out the dime-sized circle. 'Which of these two?' he asked, pointing to the nickel and the quarter.

Teddy shrugged.

'I think bigger one, no? Then Charlie can do nice lace on wings. Too small, is difficult. Can do, but is difficult. Bigger one, we get nice effect, all lacy. Very pretty.' He cocked his head to one side and extended his forefinger. 'But not too big. Too big, no good.' He nodded. 'Most things in life too big. Grey, and too big. People forget blacks and whites, people forget little things. I tell you something.'

Teddy watched him, wondering if he were talking to put her at ease, realizing at the same time that he was succeeding. The panic she had felt just a few moments earlier was rapidly dissolving.

'You want listen?' Chen asked.

Teddy nodded.

'I was married very pretty lady. Shanghai. You know Shanghai?'

Teddy nodded again.

'Very nice city, Shanghai. I was tattoo there, too. Very skill art in China, tattoo. I tattoo many people. Then I marry very pretty lady. Prettiest lady in all Shanghai. Prettiest lady in all China! She give me three sons. She make me very happy. Life blacks and whites with her. Sharp good contrast. Everything clear and bright. Everything clean. No greys. Big concern for little things. Very joyous, very happy.' Chen was nodding, lost in his reminiscence. His eyes had glazed somewhat, and Teddy watched him, feeling a sadness in the man even before he spoke his next words.

'She die,' he said. 'Life very funny. Good things die early, bad ones never die. She die, life is grey again. Have three sons, but no laughter. No more lights in Shanghai. No more people talking. No more happiness. Only empty Charlie Chen. Empty.'

He paused, and she wanted to reach out to touch his hand, to comfort him.

'I come here America. Very good country. I have trade, tattoo.' He wagged his head. 'I get by, make living. Send oldest son to college, he not so stupid as I say. Younger ones good in school, too. I learn to live. Only one thing missing. Beauty. Very hard to find beauty.' Chen smiled. 'You bring beauty to my shop. I am very grateful. I do beautiful butterfly. My fingers wither and dry if I do not do beautiful butterfly. This I promise. I promise, too, no pain. This, too, I promise. You relax, yes? You unbutton blouse just a little, move off shoulder.' He paused. 'Which shoulder? Left or right? Very important to decide.'

Teddy touched her left shoulder.

'Ah, no, butterfly on left shoulder bad omen. We do right, okay? You no mind? We put pretty small black lacy butterfly on right shoulder, okay?'

Teddy nodded. She unbuttoned the top button of her blouse, and then slipped the blouse off her shoulder.

Chen looked up from his needle suddenly.

The bell over his front door had just sounded.

Someone had entered the shop.

17.

CHEN may not have recognized the tall blond man were it not for the fact that Teddy Carella was in the back of his shop, waiting to be tattooed.

For whereas the handsome blond had been an impressive figure, Chen had only seen him once and that had been a long time ago. But now, with Teddy in the rear of the shop, with Chen keenly reminded of Teddy's relationship to a husband who was a cop, he recognized the blond man the instant he stepped through the beaded curtains to confront him.

'Yes?' he said, and he saw the man's face and, curiously, he automatically began thinking in Chinese. *This is the man the detective seeks,* he thought. *The husband of the beauty who now waits to be tattooed. This is the man.*

'Hello, there,' Donaldson said. 'We've got some work for you.'

Chen's eyes fled to the girl beside Donaldson. She was not pretty. Her hair was a mousy brown, and her eyes were a faded brown, and she wore glasses, and she peered through the glasses, she was not pretty at all. She also looked a little sick. There was a tight drawn expression to her face, and her skin was pallid, she did not look well at all.

'What kind of work, please?' Chen asked.

'A tattoo,' Donaldson said, smiling.

Chen nodded. 'A tattoo for the gentleman, yes, sir,' he said.

'No,' Donaldson corrected, 'a tattoo for the lady,' and there was no longer the slightest doubt in Chen's mind. This was the man. A girl was dead, perhaps because of this man. Chen eyed him narrowly. This man was dangerous.

'You will sit down, please?' he asked. 'I be with you in one minute.'

'Hurry, won't you?' Donaldson said. 'We haven't got much time.'

'I be with you two shakes,' Chen said, and he parted the curtains and moved quickly to the back of the shop. He walked directly to Teddy. She saw the anxiety on his face immediately. She gave him her complete attention at once. Something had happened, and Chen was very troubled.

In a whisper, he said, 'Man here. One your husband wants. Do you understand?'

For a moment, she didn't understand. *Man here? One my husband . . .?* And then the meaning became clear, and she felt a sudden chill at the base of her spine, felt her scalp begin to prickle.

'He here with girl,' Chen said. 'Want tattoo. You understand?'

She swallowed hard, and then she nodded.

'What I should do?' Chen asked.

'I . . . I don't feel too well,' Priscilla Ames said.

'This won't take but a moment,' Donaldson assured her.

'Chris, I really don't feel well. My stomach . . .' She shook her head. 'Do you suppose that food was all right?'

'I'm sure it was, darling. Look, we'll get the tattoo, and then we'll stop for a bromo or something, all right?

We have a long drive ahead, and I wouldn't want you to be sick.'

'Chris, do we . . . do we have to get the tattoo? I feel awful. I've never felt like this before in my life.'

'It'll pass, darling. Perhaps the food was a little too rich.'

'Yes, it must have been something. Chris, I feel awful.'

Carella opened the door to his apartment.

'Teddy?' he called, and then he realized that calling her name was useless if she could not see his lips. He closed the door behind him and walked into the living-room. He took off his jacket, threw it on to one of the easy chairs, and then walked through to the kitchen.

The kitchen was empty.

Carella shrugged, went back to the living-room, and then opened the door leading to their bedroom. Teddy wasn't in the bedroom, either.

He stood looking into the room for several moments, then he sighed, went into the living-room again and opened the window wide. He picked up the newspaper, kicked off his shoes, loosened his tie, and then sat down to read and wait for his wayward wife.

He was dog tired.

In ten minutes, he was sound asleep in the easy chair.

Bert Kling was making a call on the company's time.

'How'd it go?' he asked Claire.

'It's too early to tell,' she said.

'Did she read it?'

'Yes, I think so.'

'And?'

'No expression.'

'None?'

'None. She read it and said she would let my father know. Period.'

'What do you think?'

'I think I love you,' Claire said.

'Don't get mushy,' Kling told her. 'Do you think it'll work?'

'Time will tell,' Claire said. 'I adore you.'

'I adore you, Chris,' Priscilla said, 'and I want to do this for you, but I just . . . don't . . . feel well.'

'You'll feel better in a little while,' Donaldson said. He paused and smiled. 'Would you like some chewing gum?' he asked pleasantly.

'Call him, would you, Chris? Please call him. Let's get this over with.'

Call him, Teddy Carella wrote on the sheet of paper under the circles Chen had drawn. *My husband, Detective Carella. Call him. FRederick 7-8024. Tell him.*

'Now?' Chen whispered.

Teddy nodded urgently. On the paper, she wrote *You must keep that man here. You must not allow him to leave the shop.*

'The phone,' Chen said. 'The phone is out front. How I can call?'

'Hey there!' Donaldson said. 'Are you coming out?'

The beaded curtains parted. Chen stepped through them. 'Sorry, sir,' he said. 'Slight delay. Sit a moment, please. Must call friend.'

'Can't that wait?' Donaldson asked. 'We're in something of a hurry.'

'No can wait, sir, sorry. Be with you one moment. Promised dear friend to call. Must do.' He moved toward the phone quickly. Quickly, he dialled. FR 7-8024. He waited. He could hear the phone ringing on the other end. Then . . .

'87th Precinct, Sergeant Murchison.'

'I speak to Mr Carella, please?' Chen said. Donaldson stood not three feet from him, impatiently toeing the floor. The girl sat in the chair opposite the phone, her head cradled in her hands.

'Just a second,' the desk sergeant said. 'I'll connect you with the Detective Division.'

Chen listened to the clicking on the line.

A voice said, '87th Squad, Havilland speaking.'

'Mr Carella, please,' Chen said.

'Carella's not here right now,' Havilland said. 'Can I help you?'

Chen looked at Donaldson. Donaldson looked at his watch. 'The . . . ah . . . the tattoo design he wanted,' Chen said. 'Is in the shop now.'

'Just a minute,' Havilland said. 'Let me take that down. Tattoo design he wanted, in shop now. Okay. Who's this, please?'

'Charlie Chen.'

'Charlie Chan? What is this, a gag?'

'No, no. You tell Mr Carella. You tell him call me back soon as he get there. Tell him I try to hold design.'

'He may not even come back to the squad,' Havilland said. 'He's . . .'

'You tell him,' Chen said. 'Please.'

'Okay,' Havilland said, sighing. 'I'll tell him.'

'Thank you,' Chen said, and he hung up.

Bert Kling walked over to Havilland's desk.

'Who was that?' he asked.

'Charlie Chan,' Havilland said. 'A crackpot.'

'Oh,' Kling said. He had half hoped it was Claire, even though he'd talked to her not five minutes earlier.

'Guys got nothing to do but bug police stations,' Havilland said. 'There ought to be a law against some of the calls we get!'

'Was your friend out?' Donaldson asked.

'Yes. He call me back. What kind tattoo you want?'

'A small heart with initials in it,' Donaldson said.

'What initials?'

'P-A-C.'

'Where you want heart?'

'On the young lady's hand.' Donaldson smiled. 'Right here between the thumb and forefinger.'

'Very difficult to do,' Chen said. 'Hurt young lady.'

Priscilla Ames looked up. 'Chris,' she said, 'I . . . I don't feel well, honestly I don't. Couldn't we . . . couldn't we let this wait?'

Donaldson took one quick look at Priscilla. His face grew suddenly hard. 'Yes,' he said, 'it will have to wait. Until another time. Come, Pris.' He took her elbow, pulled her to her feet, held her arm in a firm grip. He turned to Chen. 'Thank you,' he said. 'We'll have to go now.'

'Can do now,' Chen said desperately. 'You sit lady down, I make tattoo. Do very pretty heart with initials. Very pretty.'

'No,' Donaldson said. 'Not now.'

Chen grabbed Donaldson's arm. 'Take very quick. I do good job.'

'Take your hand off me,' Donaldson said, and he opened the door. The tinkle of the bell was loud in the small shop. The door slammed. Chen rushed into the back room.

'They go!' he said. 'Can't keep them! They go!'

Teddy was buttoning her blouse. She scooped the pencil and paper from the tabletop and threw them into her bag.

'His name Chris,' Chen said. 'She call him Chris.'

Teddy nodded and started for the door.

'Where you go?' Chen shouted. 'Where you go?'

She turned and smiled at him fleetingly. Then the door slammed again, and she was gone.

Chen stood in the middle of his shop, listening to the reverberating tinkle of the bell.

'What I do now?' he said aloud.

She followed behind them closely. They were not easy to lose, he as tall as a giant, his blond hair catching the afternoon sunlight. She, unsteady on her feet, his arm circling her waist, holding her. She followed behind them closely, and she could feel her heart hammering inside her rib cage.

What do I do now? she wondered, but she kept following because this was the man her husband wanted.

When she saw them stop before an automobile, she suddenly lost heart. The chase seemed to be a futile one. He opened the door for the girl and helped her in, and Teddy watched as he walked to the other side of the car and then the taxicab appeared and she knew the chase was not over but that it was just beginning. She hailed the cab, and it pulled to the side of the kerb, and the cabbie flicked open the rear door, and Teddy climbed in. He turned to face her and quickly she gestured to her ears and her mouth, and miraculously he understood her at once. She pointed through the windshield where Donaldson was just entering his car. She took a long hard look at the rear of the car.

'What, lady?' the cabbie asked.

Again, she pointed.

'You want me to follow him?' The cabbie watched Teddy nod, watched the door of Donaldson's car slam shut, and then watched as the sedan pulled away from the kerb. The cabbie couldn't resist the crack.

'What happened, lady?' he asked. 'That guy steal your voice?'

He gunned away from the kerb, following Donaldson, and then he glanced over his shoulder to see if Teddy had appreciated his humour.

Teddy wasn't even looking at him.

She had taken Chen's pencil and paper from her purse and was scribbling furiously.

He hoped she would not die in the car.

It did not seem possible or likely that she would, but he planned ahead for the eventuality because if it happened he didn't want to be caught short. It would be difficult getting her out of the car. This had never happened to him before, and he felt a tenseness in his hands as he gripped the wheel and navigated the car through the afternoon traffic. He must not panic. Whatever happened, he must not panic. Things had gone too well up to now. Panic could throw everything out the window. Whatever happened, he had to keep a clear head. Whatever happened, there was too much at stake, too much to lose. He had to think clearly and coolly. He had to face each situation as it presented itself. He had to face it and handle it.

'I'm sick, Chris,' Priscilla said. 'I'm very sick.'

You don't know just how sick, he thought. He kept his eyes on the road and his hands on the wheel. He did not answer her.

'Chris, I'm . . . I'm going to throw up.'

'Can't you . . .?'

'Please stop the car, Chris. I'm going to throw up.'

'I can't stop the car,' he said. He looked at her briefly, a side-glance that took in the pale white face, the watery eyes. Roughly, he pulled a neatly folded white handkerchief from his breast pocket, thrusting it at her. 'Use this,' he said.

'Chris, can't you stop? Can't you please . . .'

'Use the handkerchief,' he said, and there was something strange and new in his voice, and she was suddenly frightened. She could not think of her fright very long. In the next moment, she was violently ill and violently ashamed of herself for being ill.

'That guy's going to Riverhead,' the cabbie said, turning to Teddy. 'See, he's crossing the bridge. You sure you want me to follow him?'

Teddy nodded. Riverhead. She lived in Riverhead. She and Steve lived in Riverhead, but Riverhead was a big part of the city, where in Riverhead was the man taking the girl? And where was Steve? Was he at the squad? Was he home? Was he still out canvassing tattoo parlours? Was it possible he'd visit Charlie Chen again? She tore off a slip of paper, put it with the growing pile of slips beside her on the seat. Then she began writing again.

And then, as if to check the accuracy of her first observation, she looked at the rear of Donaldson's car again.

'Are you a writer or something?' the cabbie asked.

It bothered Kling.

He got up and walked to where Havilland was

reading a true detective magazine, his feet propped up on the desk.

'What'd you say that guy's name was?'

'What?' Havilland asked, looking up from the magazine. 'Here's a case about a guy who cut up his victims. Put them in trunks.'

'This guy who called for Steve,' Kling said. 'What'd you say his name was?'

'A crackpot. Sam Spade or something.'

'Didn't you say Charlie Chan?'

'Yeah, Charlie Chan. A crackpot.'

'What'd he say to you?'

'Said Carella's tattoo design was in the shop. Said he'd try to keep it there.'

'Charlie Chen,' Kling said, thoughtfully. 'Carella questioned him. Chen. He was the man who tattooed Mary Proschek.' He thought again. Then he said, 'What's his number?'

'He didn't leave any,' Havilland said.

'It's probably in the book,' Kling said, starting back for his own desk.

'The hell of this thing is that the cops didn't tip to this guy for three years,' Havilland said, wagging his head. 'Cutting up dames for three years, and didn't tip.' He wagged his head again. 'Jesus, how could they be so stupid!'

'It looks like he's pulling over, lady,' the cabbie said. 'You want I should pull in right behind him?'

Teddy shook her head.

The cabbie sighed. 'So where then? Right here okay?' Teddy nodded. The cabbie pulled in and stopped his meter. Up ahead, Donaldson had parked and was helping Priscilla from the car. Teddy watched them as she fished in her purse for money to pay the cabbie. She paid him, and then she scooped up the pile of paper slips from the seat beside her. She handed one to the cabbie, stepped out, and began running because Donaldson and Priscilla had just turned the corner.

'What . . .?' the cabbie said, but his fare was gone.

He looked at the narrow slip of paper. In a hurried hand, Teddy had written:

Call Detective Steve Carella, FRederick 7-8024. Tell him licence number is DN 1556. Hurry please!

The cabbie stared at the note.

He sighed heavily.

'Women writers!' he said aloud, and he crumpled the slip, threw it out the window, and gunned away from the kerb.

18.

KLING found the number in the classified. He asked the desk sergeant for a line, and then he dialled.

He could hear the phone ringing on the other end. Methodically, he began counting the rings.

Three . . . four . . . five . . .

Kling waited.

Six . . . seven . . . eight . . .

Come on, Chen, he thought. *Answer the damn thing!*

And then he remembered the message Chen had given Havilland. *He would try to keep the tattoo design in the shop.* Jesus, had something happened to Chen?

He hung up on the tenth ring.

'I'm checking out a car,' he shouted to Havilland. 'I'll be back later.'

Havilland looked up from his magazine. 'What?' he asked.

But Kling was already through the gate in the slatted railing and heading for the steps leading to the first floor.

Besides, the phone on Havilland's desk was ringing.

Chen was walking away from the shop when he heard the telephone. He had left the shop a moment earlier, fired with the decision to go directly to the 87th Precinct, find Carella, and tell him what had happened. He had locked up, and was walking toward his car when the telephone began ringing.

Perhaps there is no difference in the way a telephone

rings. It does not ring differently for sweethearts making lovers' calls, it does not ring differently when it carries bad news, or when it carries news of a big deal being closed.

Chen was in a hurry. He had to see Carella, had to talk to him.

So perhaps the ring of the telephone in his closed and locked shop was not really so urgent. Perhaps it did not really sound so terribly important. It was, after all, only a telephone ring.

It was, none the less, urgent-sounding enough to pull him back from the kerb and over to the locked door. It sounded urgent enough to force him to reach for his keys rapidly, find the right key, shove it into the hanging padlock, snap open the lock, and then throw open the door and rush to the phone.

It sounded urgent as hell until it stopped ringing.

By the time Chen lifted the receiver, all he got was a dial tone.

And since he had a dial tone, he used it.

He called FRederick 7-8024.

'87th Precinct, Sergeant Murchison,' the voice said.

'Detective Carella, please,' Chen said.

'Second,' the desk sergeant answered. Chen waited. He was right then. Carella was back. He listened to the clicking on the line.

'87th Squad, Detective Havilland,' Havilland said.

'I speak to Detective Carella, please?'

'Not here,' Havilland said. 'Who's this?' From the corner of his eye, he saw Kling disappear into the stairwell leading to the first floor.

'Charlie Chen. When he be back?'

'Just a second,' Havilland said. He covered the

mouthpiece. 'Hey, Bert!' he shouted. 'Bert!' There was no answer from the stairwell. Into the phone, Havilland said, 'I'm a cop, too, mister. What's on your mind?'

'Man who tattoo girl,' Chen said. 'He was here shop. With Mrs Carella.'

'Slow down,' Havilland said. 'What man? What girl?'

'Carella knows,' Chen said. 'Tell him man's name is Chris. Big blond man. Tell him wife follows. When he be back? Don't you know when he be back?'

'Listen . . .' Havilland started, and Chen impatiently said, 'I come. I come tell him. You ask him wait.'

'He may not even . . .' Havilland said, but he was talking to a dead line.

The girl was bent over double, the handkerchief pressed to her mouth. The tall blond man kept his arm around her waist, holding her up, half walking her, half dragging her down the street.

Behind them, Teddy Carella followed.

Teddy Carella knew very little about con men.

She knew, though, that you could stand on a corner and offer to sell five-dollar gold pieces for ten cents, and you wouldn't get a buyer all day. She knew that the city was an inherently distrustful place, that strangers did not talk to strangers in restaurants, that people somehow did not trust people.

And so she had taken out insurance.

If she had a tongue, she'd have shouted her message.

She could not speak, and so she'd taken insurance that would shout her message, a dozen narrow slips of paper, with the identical message on each slip:

Call Detective Carella, FRederick 7-8024. Tell him licence number is DN 1556. Hurry please!

And now, as she followed along behind Donaldson

and the girl, she began to shout her message. She could not linger long with each passer-by because she could not afford to lose sight of the pair. She could only touch the sleeve of an old man and hand him the paper, and then walk off. She could only gently press the slip into the hand of a matron in a grey dress, and leave her puzzled and somewhat amused. She could only stop a teenager, avoid the open invitation in his eyes, and hand him the message. She left behind her a trail of people with a scrap of paper in their hands. She hoped that one of them would call the 87th. She hoped the licence number would reach her husband. In the meantime, she followed a sick girl and a killer, and she didn't know what she would do if her husband didn't reach her, if her husband didn't somehow reach her.

'Sick . . . I . . .' Priscilla Ames could barely speak. She clung to the reassurance of his arm around her waist, and she staggered along the street with him, wondering where he was taking her, wondering why she was so deathly ill.

'Listen to me,' he said. There was a hard edge to his voice. He was breathing heavily, and she did not recognize his voice. Her throat burned, and she could only think of the churning in her stomach, why should she be so sick, why, why, 'I'm talking to you do you hear me?' she'd never been sick in her life, never a day's serious illness, why then this sudden 'Goddamnit, listen to me! You start throwing up again, I swear to Christ I'll leave you here in the gutter!'

'Wh . . . wh . . .' She swallowed. She was ashamed of herself, the food, it must have been the food, that and the fear of the needle, he shouldn't have asked her to be tattooed, always afraid of needles . . .

'It's the next house,' he said, 'the big apartment house. I'm taking you in the back way. We'll use the service elevator. I don't want anyone to see you like this. Do you hear me? Can you understand me?'

She nodded, swallowing hard, wondering why he was telling her all this, squeezing her eyes shut tightly, knowing only excruciating pain, feeling weak all over, suddenly so very weak, my purse, my purse Chris, I've . . .

She stopped.

She gestured limply with one hand.

'What is it?' he snapped. 'What . . .?' His eyes followed her gesture. He saw her purse where she'd dropped it to the sidewalk. 'Oh, goddamnit,' he said, and he braced her with one arm and stooped, half-turning, for the purse.

He saw the pretty brunette then.

She was not more than fifty feet behind them, and when he stooped to pick up the purse, the girl stopped, stared at him for a moment; and then quickly turned away to look into one of the store windows.

Slowly, he picked up the purse, his eyes narrowed with thought.

He began walking again.

Behind him, he could hear the clatter of the girl's heels.

'87th Precinct, Sergeant Murchison.'

'Detective Carella, please,' the young voice said.

'He's not here right now,' Murchison answered. 'Talk to anyone else?'

'The note said Carella,' the young voice said.

'What note, son?'

'Aw, never mind,' the boy replied. 'It's probably a gag.'

'Well, what . . .?'

The line went dead.

A fly was buzzing around the nose of Steve Carella. Carella swatted at it in his sleep.

The fly zoomed up toward the ceiling, and then swooped down again. Sssssszzzzzzzzz. It landed on Carella's ear.

Still sleeping, Carella brushed at it.

'87th Precinct, Sergeant Murchison.'

'Is there a Detective Carella there?' the voice asked.

'Just a minute,' Murchison said. He plugged into the bull's wire. Havilland picked up the phone.

'87th Detective Squad, Havilland,' he said.

'Rog, this is Dave,' Murchison said. 'Has Carella come back yet?'

'Nope,' Havilland said.

'I've got another call for him. You want to take it?'

'I'm busy,' Havilland said.

'Doing what? Picking your nose?'

'All right, give me the call,' Havilland said, putting down the magazine and the story about the trunk murderer.

'Here's the Detective Division,' he heard Murchison say.

'This is Detective Havilland,' Havilland said. 'Can I help you?'

'Some dame handed me a note,' the voice said.

'Yeah?'

'Said to call Detective Carella and tell him the licence number is DN 1556. Is this on the level? Is there really a Carella?'

'Yeah,' Havilland said. 'What was that number again?'

'What?'

'The licence number.'

'Oh. DN 1556. What's it all about?'

'Mister,' Havilland said, 'your guess is as good as mine. Thanks for calling.'

Kling sat in the squad car alongside the patrolman.

'Can't you make this thing go any faster?' he asked.

'I'm sorry, *sir*,' the patrolman said with broad sarcasm, somewhat miffed with the knowledge that not too many months ago Kling had been a patrolman, too. 'I wouldn't want to get a speeding ticket.'

Kling studied the patrolman with an implacable eye. 'Put on your goddamn siren,' he said harshly, 'and get this thing to Chinatown or your ass is going to be in a great big sling!'

The patrolman blinked.

The squad car's siren suddenly erupted. The patrolman's foot came down on to the accelerator.

Kling leaned forward, staring through the windshield.

Charlie Chen leaned forward, staring through the windshield.

He did not like to drive in city traffic.

Doggedly, he headed uptown.

When he heard the siren, he thought it was a fire engine, and he started to pull over to his right.

Then he saw that it was a police car, and not even on his side of the avenue. The police car sped by him, heading downtown, its siren blaring.

It strengthened Chen's resolve. He gritted his teeth,

leaned over the wheel, and stepped on the accelerator more firmly.

Carella swatted at the fly, and then sat upright in his chair, suddenly wide awake. He blinked.

The apartment was very silent.

He stood and yawned. What the hell time was it, anyway? Where the hell was Teddy? He looked at his watch. She was usually home by this time, preparing supper. Had she left a note? He yawned again and began looking through the apartment for a note.

He could find none. He looked at his watch again, then he went to his jacket and fished for his cigarettes. He reached into the package. It was empty. His fingers explored the sides. It was still empty.

Wearily, he sat down and put on his shoes.

He took his pad from his back pocket, slid the pencil out from under the leather loop, and wrote, '*Dear Teddy: I've gone down for some cigarettes. Be right back. Steve.*' He propped the note on the kitchen table. Then he went into the bathroom to wash his face.

'87th Squad, Detective Havilland.'

'I wanted Carella,' the woman's voice said.

'He's out,' Havilland said.

'A young lady stopped me and gave me a note,' the woman said. 'I really don't know whether or not it's serious, but I felt I should call. May I read the note to you?'

'Please do,' Havilland said.

'It says, "*Call Detective Steve Carella, FRederick 7-8024. Tell him licence number is DN 1556. Hurry please!*" Does that mean anything?'

'You say a young lady gave this to you?' Havilland asked.

'Yes, a quite beautiful young lady. Dark hair and dark eyes. She seemed rather in a hurry herself.'

For the first time that afternoon, Havilland forgot his trunk murderer. He remembered instead that the Chinaman who'd called had said, 'Man who tattoo girl. He was here shop. With Mrs Carella.'

And now a girl who answered the description of Steve's wife was going around handing out messages. That made sense. Carella's wife was a deaf mute.

'I'll get on it right away,' Havilland said. 'Thanks for calling.'

He hung up, consulted his list of numbers, and then dialled the Bureau of Motor Vehicles. He gave them the licence number and asked them to check it. Then he hung up and looked up another number.

He was dialling Steve Carella's home when Charlie Chen walked down the corridor and came to a breathless stop outside the slatted rail divider.

Steve Carella put on his jacket.

He went into the kitchen again to check the note and then, because he was there, he checked the handles on the gas range, to make sure all the jets were out.

He walked out of the kitchen and into the living-room and then to the front door. He was in the corridor and closing the door behind him when the telephone rang. He cursed mildly, went to the phone, and lifted the receiver.

'Hello?' he said.

'Steve?'

'Yeah.'

'Rog Havilland.'

'What's up, Rog?'

'Got a man here named Charlie Chen who says your killer was in his shop this afternoon. Teddy was there at the time, and . . .'

'What!'

'Teddy. Your wife. She trailed the guy when he left. Chen says the girl with him was very sick. I've gotten half a dozen phone calls in the past half-hour. Girl who answers Teddy's description has been handing out notes asking people to call you with a licence number. I've got the M.V.B. checking it now. What do you think?'

'Teddy!' Carella said, and that was all he could think of. He heard a phone ringing someplace, and then Havilland said, 'There's the other line going now. Might be the licence information. Hold on, Steve.'

He heard the click as the 'Hold' button was pressed, and he waited, squeezing the plastic of the phone, thinking over and over again, *Teddy, Teddy, Teddy*.

Havilland came back on in a minute.

'It's a black 1955 Cadillac hardtop,' Havilland said. 'Registered to a guy named Chris Donaldson.'

'That's the bird,' Carella said, his mind beginning to function again. 'What address have you got for him?'

'41-18 Ranier. That's in Riverhead.'

'That's about ten minutes from here,' Carella said. 'I'm starting now. Get a call in to whichever precinct owns that street. Get an ambulance going, too. If that girl is sick, it's probably from arsenic.'

'Right,' Havilland said. 'Anything else, Steve?'

'Yeah. Start praying he hasn't spotted my wife!'

He hung up, slapped his hip pocket to make sure he still had his .38 and then left the apartment without closing the door.

19.

STANDING in the concrete and cinder block basement of the building, Teddy Carella watched the indicator needle of the service elevator. She could see the washing machines going in another part of the basement, and beyond that she could feel the steady thrum of the apartment building's oil burner, and she watched the needle as it moved from numeral to numeral and then stopped at 4.

She pressed the 'Down' button.

Donaldson and the girl had entered that service elevator and had got off at the fourth floor. And now, as the elevator dropped to the basement again, Teddy wondered what she would do when she discovered what apartment he was in, wondered too just how sick the girl was, just how much time she had. The elevator door slid open.

Teddy got in, pressed the number '4' in the panel. The door slid shut. The elevator began its climb. Oddly, she felt no fear, no apprehension. She wished only that Steve were with her, because Steve would know what to do. The elevator climbed and then shuddered to a stop. The door slid open. She started out of the car, and then she saw Donaldson.

He was standing just outside the elevator, waiting for the door to open, waiting for her. In blind panic, she stabbed at the panel with the floor buttons. Donaldson's arm lashed out. His fingers clamped on her wrist, and he pulled her out of the car.

'Why are you following me?' he asked.

She shook her head dumbly. Donaldson was pulling her down the hallway. He stopped before Apartment 4C, threw open the door, and then shoved her into the apartment. Priscilla Ames was lying on the couch face down. The apartment smelled of human waste.

'There she is,' Donaldson said. 'Is that who you're looking for?'

He snatched Teddy's purse from her hands and began going through it, scattering lipstick, change, mascara, address book on to the floor. When he came upon her wallet, he unsnapped it and went through it quickly.

'Mrs Stephen Carella,' he read from the identification card. 'Resident of Riverhead, eh? So we're neighbours. Meet Miss Ames, Mrs Carella. Or have you already met?' He looked at the card again. 'In case of emergency, call . . .' His voice stopped. Then, like a slow trickle of a faulty water spout, it came on again. 'Detective Steve Carella, 87th Precinct, Frederick 7-802 . . .' He looked up at Teddy. 'Your husband's a cop, huh?'

Teddy nodded.

'What's the matter? Too scared to speak?' He studied her again. 'I said . . .' He stopped, watching her. 'Is something wrong with your voice?'

Teddy nodded.

'What is it? Can you talk?'

She shook her head. Her eyes lingered on his mouth, and following her gaze he suddenly knew.

'Are you deaf?' he asked.

Teddy nodded.

'Good,' Donaldson said flatly. He was silent again,

watching her. 'Did your husband put you up to following me?'

Teddy made no motion, no gesture. She stood as silent as a stone.

'Does he know about me?'

Again no answer.

'Why were you following me?' Donaldson asked, moving closer to her. 'Who put you on to me? Where'd I slip up?' He took her wrist. 'Answer me, goddamnit!'

His fingers were tight on her wrist. On the couch, Priscilla Ames moaned weakly. He turned abruptly.

'She's been poisoned, you know that, don't you?' he said to Teddy. '*I* poisoned her. She'll be dead in a little while, and tonight she goes into the river.' He saw Teddy's involuntary shudder. 'What's the matter? Does that frighten you? Don't be frightened. She's in pain, but she hardly knows what the hell's happening anymore. All she can think about right now is her own sickness. Christ, it smells vile in here! How can you stand it?' He laughed a short harsh laugh. The laugh was over almost before it began. His voice grew hard again. There was no compromise in it now. 'What does your husband know?' he asked. '*What does your husband know?*'

Teddy made no motion. Her face remained expressionless.

Donaldson watched her. 'All right,' he said. 'I'll assume the worst. I'll assume he's headed here right now with a whole damn battalion of police. Okay?'

Again, there was nothing on Teddy's face, nothing in her eyes.

'He won't find a damn thing when he gets here. I'll be gone, and Miss Ames'll be gone, and you'll be gone. He'll find the four walls.' He went to the closet, opened it quickly and pulled out a suitcase. 'Come with me,' he said. He shoved Teddy ahead of him, into the bedroom. 'Sit down,' he said. 'On the bed. Hurry up.'

Teddy sat.

Donaldson went to the dresser, threw open the top drawer. He began shovelling clothes into the suitcase. 'You're a pretty one,' he said. 'If I came on to something like you . . .' He didn't complete the sentence. 'The trouble with my business is that you can't enjoy yourself,' he said vaguely. 'Plain girls are good. They buy whatever you sell. Get involved with a beauty, and your secret's in danger. Murder is a big secret, don't you think? It pays well, too. Don't let anyone tell you crime doesn't pay. It pays excellently. If you don't get caught.' He grinned. 'I have no intention of getting caught.' He looked at her again. 'You're a pretty one. And you can't talk. A secret could be told to you.' He shook his head. 'It's too bad we haven't got more time.' He shook his head again. 'You're a pretty one,' he repeated.

Teddy sat on the bed motionless.

'You must know how it is,' he said. 'Being good-looking. It's a pain sometimes, isn't it? Men get to hate you, distrust you. Me, I mean. They don't like a man who's too good-looking. Makes them feel uncomfortable. Too much virility for them. Points up their own petty quarrels with the world, makes them feel inadequate.' He paused. 'I can get any girl I want, do you know that? Any girl. I just flutter my lashes, they fall down dead.' He chuckled. 'Dead. That's a laugh, isn't it? You must know, I guess. Men fall all over you, don't they?' He looked at her questioningly. 'Okay, sit there in your shell. You're coming with me, you know that, don't you? You're my insurance.' He laughed again. 'We'll make a good couple. We'll really give the spectators something to ogle. We offset each other. Blond and brunette. That's very good. It won't be bad, being seen with a pretty girl for a change. I get tired of these goddamn witches. But they pay well. I've got a nice bank balance.'

On the couch, Priscilla Ames moaned. Donaldson went to the doorway and looked into the living-room. 'Relax, lover,' he called. 'In a little while, you'll go for a nice refreshing swim.' He burst out laughing and turned to Teddy. 'Nice girl,' he said. 'Ugly as sin. Nice.' He went back to packing the bag, silent now, working rapidly. Teddy watched him. He had not packed a gun, so perhaps he didn't own one.

'You'll help me downstairs with her,' he said suddenly. 'The service elevator again. In and out, and whoosh, we're on our way. You'll stay with me for a while. You can't talk, that's good. No phone calls, no idle gossip to waiters, good, good. Just have to keep you away from pen and paper, I guess, huh?' He studied her again, his eyes changing. 'Be good to have a ball for a change,' he said. 'I get so goddamn tired of these witches, and you can't trust the beauties. If you want to know something, you can't trust *any*body. The world is full of con men. But we'll have a ball.' He looked at her face. 'Don't like the idea, huh? That's rough. It'll make it more interesting. You should consider yourself lucky. You *could* be scheduled for a swim with Miss Ames, you know. You should consider yourself lucky. Most women fall down when I come into a room. Consider yourself lucky. I'm pleasant company, and I know the nicest places in town. That's my business, you know. My avocation. I'm really an accountant. Actually, *accounting* is my avocation, I suppose. Women are my business. The lonely ones. The plain Janes. You're a surprise. I'm glad you followed me.' He grinned boyishly. 'Nice having somebody to talk to who doesn't talk back. That's the secret of the Catholic confession, and also the secret of psycho-analysis. You can tell the truth and the worst that'll happen to you is twelve Hail Marys or the discovery that you hate your mother. With you, there's no punishment. I can talk, and you can listen, and I don't have to spout the love phrases or the undying bliss bit. You look sexy, too. Still water. Deep, deep.'

He heard the sudden sharp snap of the front-door lock. He whirled quickly and ran into the living-room.

Carella saw a blond giant appear in the doorframe, eyes alert, fists clenched. The giant took in the .38 in Carella's fist, took in the unwavering glint in Carella's eye, and then lunged across the room.

Carella was no fool. This man was a powerhouse. This man could rip him in two.

Steadily, calmly, Carella levelled the .38.

And then he fired.

20.

APRIL was dying.

The rains had come and gone, and the cruellest month was being put to rest. May would burst with flowers. In June, there would be sunshine.

Priscilla Ames sat in the squad room of the 87th Precinct. Steve Carella sat opposite her.

'Will he live?' she asked.

'Yes,' Carella said.

'That's unfortunate,' she replied.

'It depends how you look at it,' Carella said. 'He'll go to trial, and he'll be convicted. He'll die, anyway.'

'I was a fool, I suppose. I should have known better. I should have known there's no such thing as love.'

'You're a fool if you believe that,' Carella said.

'I should have known,' Priscilla said, nodding. 'It took a stomach pump to teach me.'

'Love is for the birds, huh?' Carella said.

'Yes,' she answered. She lifted her head, and her eyes behind the glasses glared defiance. But they asked for something else, too, and Carella gave it to her.

'I love my wife,' he said simply. 'It may be for the birds, but it's for the humans, too. Don't let Donaldson sour you. Love is the biggest American industry. I know.' He grinned. 'I'm a stockholder.'

'I suppose . . .' Priscilla sighed. 'Anyway, thank you. That's why I came by. To thank you.'

'Where to now?' Carella asked.

'Back home,' Priscilla said. 'Phoenix.' She paused, and then smiled for the first time that afternoon. 'There are a lot of birds in Phoenix.'

Arthur Brown was conducting a post-mortem.

'I couldn't figure why two big con men who are knocking over marks in the two hundred to a thousand-dollar category should bother with a little coloured girl. Five bucks he got! He worked it as a single, without his partner, and all he got was five bucks!'

'So?' Havilland said.

'So it annoyed me. What the hell, a cop's got to bank on something, doesn't he? I asked Parsons. I asked him why the hell he bothered conning a little girl out of five bucks. You know what he said?'

'No, what?' Havilland asked.

'He said he wanted to teach the girl a lesson. Now how the hell do you like that? He wanted to teach her a lesson!'

'We're losing a great teacher,' Havilland said. 'The world is losing a great teacher.'

'You mustn't look at it that way,' Brown said. 'I prefer to think that the state penitentiary is *gaining* one.'

On the telephone, Bert Kling said, 'So?'

'It worked!'

'What!'

'It worked. She bought it. She's letting me go with my aunt,' Claire said.

'You're kidding!'

'I'm dead serious.'

'We leave on 10 June?'

'We do,' Claire said.

'Yippppeeeee!' Kling shouted, and Havilland turned

to him and said, 'For Christ's sake, pipe down! I'm trying to read!'

The working day was over.

There was May mixed in the April air. It touched the cheeks mildly, it lingered on the mouth. Carella walked and drank of it, and the draught was heady.

When he opened the door to his apartment, he was greeted with silence. He turned out the light in the living-room and went into the bedroom.

Teddy was asleep.

He undressed quietly and then got into bed beside her. She wore a fluffy white gown, and he lowered the strap of the gown from her right shoulder and kissed the warm flesh there. A cloud passed from the moon, filling the room with pale yellow. Carella moved back from his wife's shoulder and blinked. He blinked again.

'I'll be goddamned!' he said.

The warm April moonlight illuminated a small, lacy black butterfly on Teddy's shoulder.

'I'll be goddamned!' Carella said again, and he kissed her so hard that she woke up.

And, big detective that he was, he never once suspected she'd been awake all the while.

'Til Death
An 87th Precinct Novel

Ed McBAIN

CAST OF CHARACTERS

Detective Steve Carella
The brother of the bride, and the pride of the 87th Precinct, hated violence in any form — most of all when it threatened to crash his sister's garden wedding

Teddy Carella
Steve's beautiful, dark-haired wife could neither hear nor speak, but she knew that danger stalked her sister-in-law's wedding

Angela Carella
The lovely bride might have danced less gaily had she known that someone wanted to make her a widow on her wedding day

Tommy Giordano
The shy young bridegroom had butterflies in his stomach, until a black widow spider spun them into a web of suspicion

Marty Sokolin
The bitter, crazed ex-G.I. was determined to fulfil his promise — even if his only reward was a cell in the death house

Detective Meyer Meyer
The policeman had not become too tough to help a friend, despite the life-long hazing his gag-type name had subjected him to

Detective Bob O'Brien
The jinxed cop — so called because he'd had to kill seven men since he'd joined the force — prayed he wouldn't have to add an eighth name to his guilt-heavy conscience

Detective Cotton Hawes
The ladies' man of the 87th Precinct came to the wedding as an incognito bodyguard, but found himself struggling with the most tempting body he'd ever encountered

Christine Maxwell
The flirtatious merry widow figured a walk in the woods could lead only to a kiss – but she figured wrong

Joseph Birnbaum
The Carellas' warm-hearted friend and neighbour grew even more warm-hearted on champagne – until he ran into a chilling surprise

Ben Darcy
The bride's childhood beau, with all the charm of the boy next door, tried desperately to rekindle an old flame – but he used the wrong kind of fuel

Sam Jones
The groom's best man – and the beneficiary of his will – pulled a convenient, and suspicious, disappearing act when trouble started

Oona Blake
The tall, luscious blonde had a figure that could dazzle any man – and if that didn't work, she had a powerful left

This is for my dear wife, Dragica

The city in these pages is imaginary.
The people, the places are all fictitious.
Only the police routine is based on
established investigatory technique.

1.

DETECTIVE STEVE CARELLA blinked at the early Sunday morning sunshine, cursed himself for not having closed the blinds the night before, and then rolled over on to his left side. Relentlessly, the sunlight followed him, throwing alternating bars of black and gold across the white sheet. Like the detention cells at the 87th, he thought. God, my bed has become a prison.

No, that isn't fair, he thought. And besides, it'll be over soon – but Teddy, I wish to hell you'd hurry.

He propped himself on one elbow and looked at his sleeping wife. Teddy, he thought. Theodora. Whom I used to call my *little* Theodora. How you have changed, my love. He studied her face, framed with short black hair recklessly cushioned against the stark white pillow. Her eyes were closed, thick-fringed with long black lashes. There was a faint smile on the full pout of her lips. Her throat swept in an immaculate arc to breasts covered by the sheet – and then the mountain began.

Really, darling, he thought, you do look like a mountain.

It is amazing how much you resemble a mountain. A very beautiful mountain, to be sure, but a mountain none the less. I wish I were a mountain climber. I wish, honey, oh how I wish I could get *near* you! How long has it been now? Cut it out, Stev-o, he told himself.

1

Just cut it out because this sort of erotic rambling doesn't do anyone a damn bit of good, least of all me.

Steve Carella, the celebrated celibate.

Well, he thought, the baby is due at the end of the month, by God, that's next week! is it the end of June already? sure it is, my how the time flies when you've got nothing to do in bed but sleep. I wonder if it'll be a boy. Well, a girl would be nice, too, but oh would Papa raise a stink, he'd probably consider it a blot on Italy's honour if his only son Steve had a girl child first time out.

What were those names we discussed?

Mark if it's a boy and April if it's a girl. And Papa will raise a stink about the names, too, because he's probably got something like Rudolpho or Serafina in mind. Stefano Luigi Carella, that's me, and thank you, Pop.

Today is the wedding, he thought suddenly, and that makes me the most inconsiderate big brother in the world because all I can think of is my own libido when my kid sister is about to take the plunge. Well, if I know Angela, the prime concern on her mind today is probably *her* libido, so we're even.

The telephone rang.

It startled him for a moment, and he turned sharply toward Teddy, forgetting, thinking the sudden ringing would awaken her, and then remembering that his wife was a deaf mute, immune to little civilized annoyances like the telephone.

'I'm coming,' he said to the persistent clamour. He swung his long legs over the side of the bed. He was a tall man with wide shoulders and narrow hips, his pyjama trousers taut over a flat hard abdomen. Bare-chested and barefoot, he walked to the phone in nonchalant athletic ease, lifted the receiver, and hoped the call was not from the precinct. His mother would have a fit if he missed the wedding.

'Hello?' he said.

'Steve?'

'Yes. Who's this?'

'Tommy. Did I wake you?'

'No, no, I was awake.' He paused. 'How's the imminent bridegroom this morning?'

'I . . . Steve, I'm worried about something.'

'Uh-oh,' Carella said. 'You're not planning on leaving my sister waiting at the altar, are you?'

'No, nothing like that. Steve, could you come over here?'

'Before we go to the church, you mean?'

'No. No, I mean now.'

'Now?' Carella paused. A frown crossed his face. In his years with the police department, he had heard many anxious voices on the telephone. He had attributed the tone of Tommy's voice to the normal pre-conjugal jitters at first, but he sensed now that this was something more. 'What is it?' he asked. 'What's the matter?'

'I . . . I don't want to talk about it on the phone. Can you come over?'

'I'll be right there,' he said. 'As soon as I dress.'

'Thank you, Steve,' Tommy said, and he hung up.

Carella cradled the phone. He stared at it thoughtfully for a moment and then went into the bathroom to wash. When he came back into the bedroom, he tilted the blinds shut so that the sunshine would not disturb

3

his sleeping wife. He dressed and wrote a note for her and then – just before he left – he caressed her breast with longing tenderness, sighed, and propped the note up against his pillow. She was still sleeping when he went out of the apartment.

Tommy Giordano lived alone in a private house in the suburb of Riverhead, not three miles from Carella's home. He was a Korean war veteran who'd had a macabre switch pulled on him while he was overseas. At a time when every American parent with a soldier son was worrying about mud and bullets, and every soldier son was worrying about Mongolian cavalry charges accompanied by the pounding of drums and the bleating of bugles – at a time like that, it was unthinkable to suppose that everyday living in the United States held its own nightmarish dangers. Tommy came to the realization with shocking suddenness.

His captain called him into the muddy command tent on a bleak rainy day. As gently as he knew how, he informed Tommy that both his parents had been killed in an automobile accident the day before, and that he was being flown home for the funeral. Tommy was an only child. He went home to watch them lower two people he had loved into the receptive earth, and then the Army flew him back to Korea again. He was despondent and uncommunicative throughout the remainder of the war. When he was finally discharged, he went back to the house he'd inherited from his parents. His only friend was a boy he'd known for years – until he met Angela Carella.

And one night, in Angela's arms, he cried bitterly,

releasing the tears to which he could not succumb while wearing the uniform of a soldier. And then he was all right. And now he was Tommy Giordano, a pleasant-faced kid of twenty-seven with a disarming grin and an easygoing manner.

He opened the door the moment Carella rang as if he'd been waiting behind it, listening for the bell.

'Gee, Steve,' he said, 'I'm glad you came. Come on in. You want a drink or something?'

'At nine o'clock in the morning?' Carella asked.

'Is it that early? Gee, I must have got you out of bed. I'm sorry, Steve. I didn't mean to trouble you. A hell of a brother-in-law I'm going to make.'

'Why'd you call, Tommy?'

'Sit down, Steve. You want some coffee? Have you had breakfast?'

'I can use a cup of coffee.'

'Good. I'll make some toast, too. Look, I'm sorry as hell I woke you. I've been tossing and turning all night long myself, so I guess I didn't realize how early it was. Man, this getting married is murder. I swear to God, I'd rather face a mortar attack.'

'But this isn't why you called me.'

'No. No. It's something else. I'm a little worried, to tell the truth, Steve. Not for myself, but for Angela. I mean, I just can't make it out.'

'Make *what* out?'

'Well, like I said . . . listen, can you come in the kitchen? So I can make the coffee and toast? Would that be okay with you?'

'Sure.'

They went into the kitchen. Carella sat at the table

5

and lighted a cigarette. Tommy began measuring coffee into the percolator.

'I couldn't sleep all night,' Tommy said. 'I kept thinking of the honeymoon. When we're alone. What the hell do I do, Steve? I mean, I know she's your sister and all, but what do I do? How do I start? I love that girl. I don't want to hurt her or anything!'

'You won't. Just relax, Tommy. Just remember that you love her, and that you married her, and that you're going to be together for the rest of your lives.'

'Gee, I'll tell you the truth, Steve, even *that* scares me.'

'Don't let it.' He paused. 'Adam and Eve didn't have an instruction booklet, Tommy. And they made out all right.'

'Yeah, well I hope so. I sure hope so. I just wish I knew what the hell to *say* to her.' A pained look crossed his face, and Carella was momentarily amused.

'Maybe you won't have to say anything,' Carella said. 'Maybe she'll get the idea.'

'Boy, I hope so.' Tommy put the coffee-pot on the stove and then slid two slices of bread into the toaster. 'But I didn't call you so you could hold my hand. There's something else.'

'What is it?'

'Well, I told you I couldn't sleep all night. So I guess I got up kind of early, and I went to take in the milk. They leave it right outside the door. When I first got out of the Army, I used to go down to the grocery store each morning. But now I have it delivered. It's a little more expensive, but . . .'

'Go ahead, Tommy.'

'Yeah, well I was taking in the milk when I saw this little box resting on the floor, just outside the door.'

'What kind of a box?'

'A little tiny box. Like the boxes rings come in, you know? So I picked it up and looked at it and there was a note on it.'

'What did the note say?' Carella asked.

'Well, I'll show it to you in a few minutes. I took in the milk, and I carried the box into the bedroom. It was very nicely wrapped, Steve, fancy paper and a big bow and the note sticking up out of the bow. I couldn't figure out who'd left it. I thought it was probably a gag. One of the fellows. You know.'

'Did you open it?'

'Yes.'

'What was in it?'

'I'll let you see for yourself, Steve.'

He walked out of the kitchen and through the apartment. Carella heard a drawer opening and then closing in the bedroom. Tommy came back into the kitchen. 'Here's the note,' he said.

Carella studied the handwritten message on the small rectangle:

For the Groom!

'And the box?' he said.

'Here,' Tommy said. He extended the small box to

7

Carella. Carella put it on the kitchen table and lifted the lid. Then, quickly, he snapped the lid into place again.

Crouched in one corner of the box was a black widow spider.

2.

CARELLA SHOVED THE box away from him instantly. A look of utter horror had crossed his face, and it lingered still in his eyes and around the corners of his mouth.

'Yeah,' Tommy said. 'That's just the way I felt.'

'You could have told me what was in the box,' Carella said, beginning to think his future brother-in-law was something of a sadist. He had never liked spiders. During the war, stationed on a Pacific island, he had fought as bitterly against crawling jungle arachnids as he had against the Japanese. 'You think this is a gag somebody played?' he asked incredulously.

'I did before I opened the box. Now I don't know. You'd have to have a pretty queer sense of humour to give somebody a black widow spider. Or *any* kind of a spider, for Christ's sake!'

'Is that coffee ready?'

'Just about.'

'I'm really going to need a cup. Spiders have two effects on me. My mouth dries up, and I get itchy all over.'

'I just get itchy,' Tommy said. 'When I was in basic training in Texas, we had to shake our shoes out every morning before we put them on. To make sure no tarantulas had crawled into them during the—'

'Please!' Carella said.

'Yeah, it gives you the creeps, don't it?'

'Do any of your friends have ... odd senses of humour?' He swallowed hard. There seemed to be no saliva in his mouth.

'Well, I know some crazy people,' Tommy said, 'but this is a little far out, don't you think? I mean, this is slightly off-beat.'

'Slightly,' Carella said. 'How's the coffee?'

'In a minute.'

'Of course it *may* be a gag, who knows?' Carella said. 'A sort of a wedding joke. After all, the spider is a classic symbol.'

'Of what?'

'Of the vagina,' Carella said.

Tommy blushed. A bright crimson smear started at his throat and quickly worked its way on to his face. If Carella had not seen it with his own eyes, he wouldn't have believed it. He quickly changed the topic.

'Or maybe it's just a feeble pun on marriage in general. You know. The female black widow is supposed to devour her mate.'

Again Tommy blushed, and Carella realized there was no safe ground with a prospective bridegroom. Besides, he felt itchy. And his throat was dry. And no future brother-in-law had the goddamn right to spring a spider on a man so early in the morning – especially on Sunday morning.

'And of course,' Carella went on, 'there are more ominous overtones – if we're looking for them.'

'Yeah,' Tommy said. He glanced at the stove. 'Coffee's ready.' He carried the pot to the table and began pouring. 'A gag is a gag, but suppose I'd reached into that box and got bit? The black widow is poisonous.'

'Suppose *I'd* reached into it?' Carella asked.

'I wouldn't have let you, don't worry. But there was no one here when I opened it. I could've got bit.'

'I doubt if it would have killed you.'

'No, but it could have made me pretty sick.'

'Maybe somebody wants you to miss your own wedding,' Carella said.

'I thought of that. I also thought of something else.'

'What?'

'Why send a black widow? A *widow*, do you follow me? It's almost as if . . . well . . . maybe it's a hint that Angela's gonna be a bride and a widow on the same day.'

'You're talking like a man with a lot of enemies, Tommy.'

'No. But I thought it might be a hint.'

'A warning, you mean.'

'Yes. And I've been racking my brain ever since I opened that box, trying to think of anybody who'd . . . who'd want me dead.'

'And who'd you come up with?'

'Only one guy. And he's three thousand miles away from here.'

'Who?'

'A guy I knew in the Army. He said I was responsible for his buddy getting shot. I wasn't, Steve. We were on patrol together when a sniper opened up. I ducked the minute I heard the shot, and this other guy got hit. So his buddy claimed I was responsible. Said I should have yelled there was a sniper. How the hell was I supposed to yell it? I didn't even know it until I heard the shot – and then it was too late.'

'Was the man killed?'

11

Tommy hesitated. 'Yeah,' he said at last.

'And his buddy threatened you?'

'He said he was gonna kill me one day.'

'What happened after that?'

'He got shipped back home. Frostbite or something, I don't know. He lives in California.'

'Have you ever heard from him since?'

'No.'

'Was he the kind of a person who'd do a thing like this? Send a spider?'

'I didn't know him very well. From what I did know, he seemed like the kind of guy who *ate* spiders for breakfast.'

Carella almost choked on his coffee. He put down his cup and said, 'Tommy, I'm going to give you some advice. Angela is a very sensitive girl. I guess it runs in the Carella family. Unless you want to wind up getting a divorce real soon, I wouldn't discuss hairy or crawly or . . .'

'I'm sorry, Steve,' Tommy said.

'Okay. What was this guy's name? The one who threatened you?'

'Sokolin. Marty Sokolin.'

'Have any pictures of him?'

'No. What would I be doing with his picture?'

'Were you in the same company?'

'Yes.'

'Do you have one of these company group pictures where everybody's grinning and wishing he was out of the Army?'

'No.'

'Can you describe him?'

'He was a very big, beefy guy with a broken nose. He

12

looked like a wrestler. Black hair, very dark eyes. A small scar near his right eye. He was always smoking cigars.'

'Think he had a police record?'

'I don't know.'

'Well, we'll check on it.' Carella was pensive for a moment. 'It doesn't seem likely, though, that he's the guy. I mean, what the hell, how would he know you were getting married today?' He shrugged. 'Hell, this may just be a gag, anyway. Somebody with a warped sense of humour.'

'Maybe,' Tommy said, but he didn't seem convinced.

'Where's your phone?' Carella asked.

'In the bedroom.'

Carella started out of the kitchen. He paused. 'Tommy, would you mind a few extra guests at your wedding?' he asked.

'No. Why?'

'Well, if this *isn't* a gag – and it probably is – but if it isn't, we don't want anything happening to the groom, do we?' He grinned. 'And the nice thing about having a cop for a brother-in-law is that he can get bodyguards whenever he needs them. Even on a Sunday.'

There is no such day as Sunday in the police department. Sunday is exactly the same as Monday and Tuesday and all those other days. If you happen to have the duty on Sunday, that's it. You don't go to the commissioner or the chaplain or the mayor. You go to the squadroom. If Christmas happens to fall on one of your duty days, that's extremely unfortunate, too, unless you can arrange a switch with a cop who isn't celebrating Christmas. Life is just one merry round in the police department.

On Sunday morning, June 22, Detective 2nd/Grade Meyer Meyer was catching in the squadroom of the 87th Precinct. It was not a bad day to be in charge of the six-man detective team which had begun its shift at 8.00 A.M. and which would work through until 6.00 P.M. that evening. There was a mild breeze on the air, and the sky was a cloudless blue, and sunlight was pouring through the meshed grille screening over the squadroom's windows. The squadroom, shoddy with time and use, was quite comfortable on a day such as this. There were days when the city's temperature soared into the nineties, and on those days the squadroom of the 87th Precinct resembled nothing so much as a big iron coffin. But not today. Today, a man could sit without his trousers crawling up his behind. Today, a man could type up reports or answer phones or dig in the files without danger of melting into a small unidentifiable puddle on the squadroom floor.

Meyer Meyer was quite content. Puffing on his pipe, he studied the *Wanted* circulars on his desk and thought about how nice it was to be alive in June.

Bob O'Brien, six feet and one inch tall in his bare feet, weighing in at two hundred and ten pounds, stomped across the room and collapsed into the chair beside Meyer's desk. Meyer felt an immediate sense of doom, because if ever there was a jinxed cop it was O'Brien. Since the time he'd been forced to kill a neighbourhood butcher years ago – a man he'd known since he was a boy – O'Brien seemed to find himself constantly in the kind of scrapes wherein gunplay was absolutely necessary. He had not wanted to kill Eddie

14

the butcher. But Eddie'd been a little out of his head and had come raving out of his shop swinging a meat cleaver at an innocent woman. O'Brien tried to stop him, but it was no use. Eddie knocked him to the pavement and then raised the meat cleaver and O'Brien, acting reflexively, drew his service revolver and fired. He killed Eddie with a single shot. And that night he went home and wept like a baby. He had killed six men since that time. In each of the shootings, he had not wanted to draw his gun – but circumstances so combined to force him into the act of legal murder. And whenever he was forced to kill, he still wept. Not openly. He wept inside where it hurts most.

The cops of the 87th Squad were not a superstitious bunch, but they none the less shied away from answering a complaint with Bob O'Brien along. With O'Brien along, there was bound to be shooting. They did not know why. It certainly wasn't Bob's fault. He was always the last person on the scene to draw a gun, and he never did so until it became absolutely necessary. But with O'Brien along, there would undoubtedly be shooting and the cops of the 87th were normal-type human beings who did not long to become involved in gun duels. They knew that if O'Brien went out to break up a marble game being played by six-year-old tots, one of those tots would miraculously draw a sub-machine-gun and begin blasting away. That was Bob O'Brien. A hard-luck cop.

And that, of course, was pure police exaggeration because O'Brien had been a cop for ten years, four of them with the 87th, and he'd only shot seven men in all that time. Still, that was a pretty good average.

'How's it going, Meyer?' he asked.

'Oh, very nicely,' Meyer said. 'Very nicely, thank you.'

'I've been wondering.'

'What about?'

'Miscolo.'

Miscolo was the patrolman in charge of the Clerical Office just down the corridor. Meyer very rarely wondered about him. In fact, he very rarely even thought about him.

'What's the matter with Miscolo?' he asked now.

'His coffee,' O'Brien said.

'Something wrong with his coffee?'

'He used to make a good cup of coffee,' O'Brien said wistfully. 'I can remember times, especially during the winter, when I'd come in here off a plant or something and there was a cup of Miscolo's coffee waiting for me and I'm telling you, Meyer, it made a man feel like a prince, a regular prince. It had rich body, and aroma, and flavour.'

'You're wasting your time with police work,' Meyer said. 'I'm serious, Bob. You should become a television announcer. You can sell coffee the way—'

'Come on, I'm trying to be serious.'

'Excuse me. So what's wrong with his coffee now?'

'I don't know. It just isn't the same any more. You know when it changed?'

'When?'

'When he got shot. Remember when that nutty dame was up here with a bottle of T.N.T. and she shot Miscolo? Remember that time?'

'I remember,' Meyer said. He remembered very well. He still had scars as mementos of the pistol whipping

16

he'd received from Virginia Dodge on that day last October. 'Yes, I remember.'

'Well, right after Miscolo got out of the hospital, the first day he was on the job again, the coffee began to stink. Now what do you suppose causes something like that, Meyer?'

'Gee, I don't know, Bob.'

'Because, to me, it's a phenomenon, I mean it. A man gets shot, and suddenly he can't make good coffee any more. Now, to me, that's one of the eight wonders of the world.'

'Why don't you ask Miscolo?'

'Now how can I do that, Meyer? He takes pride in the cup of coffee he makes. Can I ask him how come his coffee is suddenly no good? How can I do that, Meyer?'

'I guess you can't.'

'And I can't go out to *buy* coffee or he'll be offended. What should I do, Meyer?'

'Gee, Bob, I don't know. It seems to me you've got a problem. Why don't you try some occupational therapy?'

'Huh?'

'Why don't you call up some of the witnesses to that hold-up we had the other day and see if you can't get something more out of them?'

'You think I'm goofing, you mean?'

'Did I say that, Bob?'

'I'm not goofing, Meyer,' O'Brien said. 'I've just got a thirst for some coffee, and the thought of drinking Miscolo's is making me sick.'

'Have a glass of water instead.'

'At nine-thirty in the morning?' O'Brien looked

shocked. 'Do you think we can call the desk and ask Murchison to sneak in some coffee from outside?'

The telephone on Meyer's desk rang. He snatched it from the cradle and said, '87th Squad, Detective Meyer.'

'Meyer, this is Steve.'

'Hi, boy. Lonely for the place, huh? Can't resist calling in even on your day off.'

'It's your twinkling blue eyes I miss,' Carella said.

'Yeah, everybody's charmed by my eyes. I thought your sister was getting married today.'

'She is.'

'So what can I do for you? Need a few bucks for a wedding present?'

'No. Meyer, would you take a look at the new schedule and see who's on my team this week? I want to know who else is off today.'

'You need a fourth for bridge? Hold on a second.' He opened his top desk drawer and pulled out a clip-board to which a mimeographed sheet was attached. He studied the grid, his index finger running down the page:

	Sunday 6/21	Monday 6/22	Tuesday 6/23	Wednesday 6/24	Thursday 6/25
8.00 A.M. to 6.00 P.M.	Meyer * O'Brien Willis	Fields * Di Maeo Levine	Carella * Hawes Kling	Brown Meredith * Kapek	Meyer O'Brien * Willis
6.00 P.M. to 8.00 A.M.	Brown * Meredith Kapek	Meyer * O'Brien Willis	Fields * Di Maeo Levine	Carella * Hawes Kling	Brown Meredith * Kapek'
Off duty	Carella Hawes Kling	Brown Meredith Kapek	Meyer O'Brien Willis	Fields Di Maeo Levine	Carella Hawes Kling
Patrol Day	Fields Di Maeo Levine	Carella Hawes Kling	Brown Meredith Kapek	Meyer O'Brien Willis	Fields Di Maeo Levine

SPECIAL ASSIGNMENT: Alexander, Parker, Kasoukian, Masterson
* Catcher

'Oh, I pity these poor bastards,' Meyer said into the phone. 'Having to work with a *shnook* like—'

'Come on, come on, who are they?' Carella asked.

'Kling and Hawes.'

'Have you got their home numbers handy?'

'Is there anything else you'd like, sir? Shoes shined? Pants pressed? Loan of my wife for the weekend?'

'Now that isn't a bad idea,' Carella said, grinning.

'Hold on. You got a pencil to take this down?'

'Sarah's number?'

'Leave Sarah out of this.'

'You were the one who brought her up.'

'Listen, horny, you want these numbers or not? We're trying to run a tight little squad here.'

'Shoot,' Carella said, and Meyer gave him the numbers. 'Thank you. Now there are a few more things I'd like you to do for me. First, will you see what you can get on a guy named Marty Sokolin. You may draw a blank because he's a resident of California and we haven't got time to check with the F.B.I. But give our own I.B. a buzz and see if he's turned up here in the past few years. Most important, try to find out if he's here now.'

'I thought this was your day off,' Meyer said wearily.

'A conscientious cop never has a day off,' Carella said conscientiously. 'The last thing is this. Can you send a patrolman over to my house to pick up a note? I'd like the lab to look it over, and I'd like a report on it as soon as possible.'

'You think we're running a private messenger service here?'

'Come on, Meyer, loosen the reins. I should be home

19

in a half-hour or so. Try to get back to me on Sokolin before noon, will you?'

'I'll try,' Meyer said. 'What else do you do for diversion on your day off? Pistol practice?'

'Good-bye, Meyer,' Carella said. 'I've got to call Bert and Cotton.'

Cotton Hawes was dead asleep when the telephone rang in his bachelor apartment. He heard it only vaguely and then as a distant tinkle. During World War II, he'd been the only man aboard his PT boat who'd earned the distinction of having slept through the bleatings of the alarm announcing General Quarters. He'd almost lost his Chief Torpedoman's rating because of the incident. But the captain of the vessel was a lieutenant, j.g., who'd been trained as a radar technician for the Navy's Communications Division and who didn't know torpedoes from toenails. He recognized, with some injury to his ego, that the man who really commanded the boat, the man who established rapport with the crew, the man who knew navigation and ballistics, was really Cotton Hawes and not himself. The j.g. (anachronistically called 'The Old Man' by the crew, even though he was only twenty-five years old) had been a disc jockey in his home town, Schenectady, New York. He wanted only to return safely to – in order of their importance – his beloved records, his beloved M.G. convertible, and his beloved Annabelle Tyler whom he'd been dating since high school. He did not appreciate Naval chains of command or Naval reprimands or Naval operations. He knew he had a job to do and he knew he could not do it without Cotton Hawes's complete cooperation. Perhaps the Admiral would have been delighted were Hawes demoted to Torpedoman First Class. The j.g. didn't much give a damn about the Admiral.

'You'll have to watch that stuff,' he said to Hawes. 'We can't have you sleeping through another kamikaze attack.'

'No, sir,' Hawes said. 'I'm sorry, sir. I'm a heavy sleeper.'

'I'm assigning a seaman to wake you whenever General Quarters is sounded. That should take care of it.'

'Yes, sir,' Hawes said. 'Thank you, sir.'

'How the hell did you manage to snore through that ungodly din, Cotton? We almost had two direct hits on our bow!'

'Mike, I can't help it,' Hawes said. 'I'm a heavy sleeper.'

'Well, somebody'll wake you from now on,' the j.g. said. 'Let's come through this damn thing alive, huh, Cotton?'

They came through the damn thing alive. Cotton Hawes never heard from the j.g. after they were separated at Lido Beach. He assumed he'd gone back to jockeying discs in Schenectady, New York. And whereas the seaman had temporarily foiled the further attempts of Japanese pilots to sink the boat, the victory over Morpheus was at best a shallow one. Cotton Hawes was still a heavy sleeper. He attributed this to the fact that he was a big man, six feet two inches tall and weighing a hundred and ninety pounds. Big men, he maintained, needed a lot of sleep.

The telephone continued to tinkle somewhere in the far distance. There was movement on the bed, the creaking of springs, the rustle of the sheet being thrown back. Hawes stirred slightly. The distant tinkle was somewhat louder now. And then, added to the tinkle, came a voice fuzzy with sleep.

'Hello?' the voice said. 'Who? I'm sorry, Mr Carella, he's asleep. Can you call back a little later? Me? I'm Christine Maxwell.' The voice paused. 'No, I don't think I ought to wake him right now. Can he call you when he . . .' Christine paused again. Cotton sat up in bed. She stood naked at the telephone, the black receiver to her ear, her blonde hair pushed back to tumble over the black plastic in a riot of contrast. Delightedly, he watched her, her slender fingers curled about the telephone, the curving sweep of her arm, the long length of her body. Her brow was knotted in a frown now. Her blue eyes were puzzled.

'Well,' she said, 'why didn't you say you were from the squad to begin with? Just a moment, I'll see if—'

'I'm up,' Hawes said from the bed.

'Just a second,' Christine said to the telephone. 'He's coming now.' She cradled the mouthpiece. 'It's a Steve Carella. He says he's from the 87th Squad.'

'He is,' Hawes said, walking to the phone.

'Does that mean you'll have to go in today?'

'I don't know.'

'You promised you'd spend the day—'

'I haven't even talked to him yet, honey.' Gently, Hawes took the phone from her hand. 'Hello, Steve,' he said. He yawned.

'Did I get you out of bed?'

'Yes.'

'You busy today?'

'Yes.'

'Feel like doing me a favour?'

22

'No.'

'Thanks a million.'

'I'm sorry, Steve, I've got a date. I'm supposed to go on a boat-ride up the Harb.'

'Can't you break it? I need help.'

'If I break the date, the lady'll break my head.' Christine, listening to the conversation, nodded emphatically.

'Come on. Big strong guy like you. You can take the girl with you.'

'Take her where?'

'To my sister's wedding.'

'I don't like weddings,' Hawes said. 'They make me nervous.'

'Somebody's threatened my future brother-in-law. Or at least it looks that way. I'd like a few people I can trust in the crowd. Just in case anything happens. What do you say?'

'Well . . .' Hawes started. Christine shook her head. 'No, Steve. I'm sorry.'

'Look, Cotton, when's the last time I asked you for a favour?'

'Well . . .' Hawes started, and again Christine shook her head. 'I can't, Steve.'

'There'll be free booze,' Carella said.

'No.'

'Take the girl with you.'

'No.'

'Cotton, I'm asking a favour.'

'Just a second,' Hawes said, and he covered the mouthpiece.

'No,' Christine said immediately.

23

'You're invited,' Hawes said. 'To a wedding. What do you say?'

'I want to go on the boat-ride. I haven't been on a boat-ride since I was eighteen.'

'We'll go next Sunday, okay?'

'You're not off next Sunday.'

'Well, the first Sunday I *am* off, okay?'

'No.'

'Christine?'

'No.'

'Honey?'

'Oh, damnit.'

'All right?'

'Damnit,' Christine said again.

'Steve,' Hawes said into the phone, 'we'll come.'

'Damnit,' Christine said.

'Where do you want us to meet you?'

'Can you come over to my place at about noon?'

'Sure. What's the address?'

'837 Dartmouth. In Riverhead.'

'We'll be there.'

'Thanks a lot, Cotton.'

'Send flowers to my funeral,' Hawes said, and he hung up.

Christine stood fuming by the telephone, her arms crossed over her breasts. Hawes reached for her and she said, 'Don't touch me, Mr Hawes.'

'Honey—'

'Don't *honey* me.'

'Christine, honey, he's in a jam.'

'You promised we would go on this boat-ride. I made the arrangements *three weeks* ago. Now—'

'This is something I couldn't avoid. Look, Carella

24

happens to be a friend of mine. And he needs help.'

'And what am I?'

'The girl I love,' Hawes said. He took her into his arms.

'Sure,' Christine answered coldly.

'You know I love you.' He kissed the tip of her nose.

'Sure. You love me, all right. I'm just the merry widow, to you. I'm just the girl you—'

'You're a very lovely widow.'

'—picked up in a bookshop.'

'It's a very lovely bookshop,' Hawes said, and he kissed the top of her head. 'You've got nice soft hair.'

'I'm not quite as alone in the world as you may think,' Christine said, her arms still folded across her breasts. 'I could have got a hundred men to take me on this boat-ride.'

'I know,' he said, and he kissed her ear-lobe.

'You louse,' she said. 'It just happens that I love you.'

'I know.' He kissed her neck.

'Stop that.'

'Why?'

'You know why.'

'Why?'

'Stop it,' she said, but her voice was gentler, and her arms were beginning to relax. 'We have to go to your friend's house, don't we?'

'Not until noon.'

Christine was silent. 'I do love you,' she said.

'And I love you.'

'I'll bet you do. I'll just bet you—'

'Shhh, shhh,' he said, and he sought her mouth, and she brought her arms up around his neck. He clung to her, his big hands twisting in the long blonde hair. He kissed her again, and she buried her face in his shoulder, and he said, 'Come. Come with me.'

'Your friend. There isn't time—'

'There's time.'

'We have to—'

'There's time.'

'But won't we—?'

'There's time,' he said gently.

Bert Kling was reading the Sunday comics when Carella's call came. He took a last wistful look at Dick Tracy's wrist radio and then went to answer the phone.

'Bert Kling,' he said.

'Hi, Bert. This is Steve.'

'Uh-oh,' Kling said immediately.

'You busy?'

'I won't answer any leading questions. What happened? What do you want?'

'Don't be so brusque. Brusqueness is not flattering to youth.'

'Do I have to go to the squad?'

'No.'

'What then?'

'My sister's getting married this afternoon. The groom received what could amount to a threatening note.'

'Yeah? Why doesn't he call the police?'

'He did. And now I'm calling you. Feel like going to a wedding?'

'When? What time?'

'Can you be here at twelve?'

'I've got to pick up Claire at nine tonight. There's a movie she wants to see.'

26

'Okay.'

'Where are you now?' Kling asked.

'Home. 837 Dartmouth. In Riverhead. Can you be here by noon?'

'Yeah. I'll see you.'

'Bert?'

'What?'

'Bring your gun.'

'Okay,' Kling said, and he hung up. He walked back to the newspaper. He was a tall blond man of twenty-five years, and he looked younger in his undershorts because his legs were covered with a light blond fuzz. He curled up in the arm-chair, studying the wrist radio design again, and then he decided to call Claire. He went to the telephone and dialled her number.

'Claire,' he said, 'this is Bert.'

'Hello, lover.'

'I'm going to a wedding this afternoon.'

'Not your own, I hope.'

'No. Steve's sister. You want to come?'

'I can't. I told you that I've got to drive my father out to the cemetery.'

'Oh yeah, that's right. Okay, I'll see you at nine then, okay?'

'Right. This movie's at a drive-in. Is that all right?'

'That's fine. We can neck if it gets dull.'

'We can neck even if it doesn't get dull.'

'What's the picture anyway?'

'It's an old one,' Claire said, 'but I think you'll enjoy it.'

'What is it?'

'*Dragnet*,' she answered.

*

The packet from the Bureau of Criminal Identification arrived at the squadroom at 10.37 A.M.

Meyer Meyer was, in truth, surprised to see it. The chances of this Marty Whatever-His-Name-Was having a record were pretty slim to begin with. Add to that the possibility of his having a record in *this* city, and the chances were beyond the realm of plausibility. But record he had, and the record was in the voluminous files of the I.B., and now a photostated copy of the file rested on Meyer's desk, and he leafed through it leisurely.

Marty Sokolin was not a big-time thief. He wasn't even, by any police standards, a small-time thief. He was a man who'd got into trouble once. His record happened to be in the I.B.'s files because he'd got into trouble in this city while on vacation from California.

It was perhaps significant that Marty Sokolin had not been discharged from the Army because of frostbite as Tommy Giordano had supposed. True enough, he had been medically discharged. But he'd been released to a mental hospital in Pasadena, California, as a neurasthenic patient.

Meyer Meyer knew nothing of Tommy's frostbite supposition. He knew, however, that neurasthenia was the modern psychiatric term for what, during the First World War, had been called plain and simple 'shell shock'. A psychiatrist probably would have defined it as nervous debility or exhaustion, as from overwork or prolonged mental strain. Meyer simply called it 'shell shock' and noted that Sokolin had been released from the hospital as fit to enter society in the summer of 1956.

He did not have his brush with the law until almost

two years later in March of 1958. He'd been working, at the time, as a salesman for a paint company in San Francisco. He'd come East for a sales convention and had begun drinking with a stranger in a midtown bar. At some point during the evening, the conversation had swung around to the Korean War. The stranger had admitted that he'd been 4-F and rather glad of it. Because of his disability, a slight heart murmur, he'd been able to make fantastic advances in his company while men of his own age were away fighting.

Sokolin had at first reacted to the man's confession with slightly drunken solemnity bordering on the maudlin. One of his best friends, he informed the stranger, had been killed in Korea because another soldier had failed to do his duty. The stranger sympathized, but his sympathy must have sounded hollow and insincere to Sokolin. Before the stranger fully realized what was happening, Sokolin was hurling curses at him for being a deserter and a shirker and another son of a bitch who didn't do his duty when he saw it. The stranger tried to get away, but Sokolin's ire mounted irrationally until finally he smashed a beer mug on the edge of the bar and came at the stranger with the broken shard clutched in his fist.

He did not kill the surprised 4-Fer, but he did manage to cut him badly. And perhaps the attack would have been considered second-degree assault had not Sokolin accompanied it with eight words spoken clearly and distinctly in the presence of the half-dozen witnesses lining the bar.

Those words were: 'I'll kill you, you son of a bitch!'

And so the assault had leaped into the rarefied atmosphere bounded by the words 'with an intent to

29

kill a human being', and the indictment read first-degree, and the maximum penalty for violation of Section 240 of the Penal Law was ten years in prison as opposed to the maximum five years for the second-degree crime.

Sokolin had come off pretty well. He was a war veteran, and this was a first offence. It was, none the less, first-degree assault and the judge could not let him off with a fine and a fatherly pat on the head. He was found guilty and sentenced to two years in Castleview Prison upstate. He'd been an ideal prisoner. He'd applied for a parole after serving a year of his term, and the parole had been granted as soon as a firm job offer was presented to the board. He had been released from Castleview two months ago – on April 3.

Meyer Meyer pulled the phone to him and dialled Carella's home number. Carella answered the phone on the third ring.

'I've got that stuff you wanted on Sokolin,' Meyer said. 'Did that patrolman show up for the note yet?'

'About a half-hour ago,' Carella said.

'Well, he's not back here yet. You're leaving about noon, huh?'

'About one o'clock, actually.'

'Where can I reach you if the lab comes up with something?'

'The wedding's at three at the Church of the Sacred Heart at the intersection of Gage and Ash in Riverhead. The reception starts at five at my mother's house. It's gonna be an outdoor thing.'

'What's the address there?'

'831 Charles Avenue.'

'Okay. You want this stuff on Sokolin?'

'Give it to me.'

Meyer gave it to him.

When he'd finished talking, Carella said, 'So he's on parole now, huh? Went back to California with a firm job offer.'

'No, Steve. I didn't say that.'

'Then where is he?'

'Right here. The job offer came from this city.'

3.

BY ONE-THIRTY THAT bright Sunday afternoon, Antonio Carella was ready to shoot his wife, strangle his son, disown his daughter, and call off the whole damn wedding.

To begin with, Tony was paying for the wedding. This was the first time – and the last time, thank God – a daughter of his was getting married. When Steve married Teddy, it was *her* parents who had paid for the festivities. Not so this time. This time, Tony was shelling out, and he was discovering that the wedding would cost, at a conservative estimate, just about half what he earned in an entire year at his bakery.

The biggest of the thieves, and he had half a mind to ask Steve to arrest the crooks, were the men who called themselves Weddings-Fêtes, Incorporated. They had arrived at the Charles Avenue address at 9.00 A.M. that morning (after Tony had stayed up all night in the bakery getting his Sunday morning breads baked) and proceeded to turn the Carella back-yard into a shambles. The Carella house in Riverhead was a small one, but the land on which it rested was possibly the largest plot on the street, stretching back from the house in a long rectangle which almost reached the next block. Tony was very proud of his land. His back-yard boasted a grape arbour which rivalled any to be found in his home town of Marsala. He had planted fig trees, too, nourished them with loving care, pruned them in the summer, wrapped them with protective tarpaulin in the winter. And now these crooks, these *brigandi*, were trampling over his lawn with their tables and their ridiculous flags and flower canopies and . . .

'Louisa!' he had screamed to his wife. 'Why inna hell we can't hire a hall? Why inna hell we have to have a *outdoor* wedding! A hall was good enough for me, an' good enough for you, an' good enough for my son, but Angela has to have a outdoor wedding! So those crooks can tear up my lawn an' ruin my grapes an' my figs! *Pazzo! E proprio pazzo!*'

'Shut up,' Louisa Carella said kindly. 'You'll wake up the whole house.'

'The whole house is wake up already!' Tony said. 'Besides, there's nobody in the whole house but me, you, an' Angela, an' she's getting married today an' she's not sleeping, anyway!'

'The caterers will hear you,' Louisa said.

'For what I'm paying them, they're entitled to hear,' Tony replied, and grumblingly he had got out of bed and gone down to the back-yard to supervise the setting of the tables and the construction of the bridal arbours and bandstand and dance-floor. The caterers, he discovered, were very fancy people. Not only were they turning his back-yard into a Hollywood set for *Father of the Bride* (starring *me*, Antonio Carella, he thought sourly) but they were also building a twelve-foot mermaid, the length of the young fish-woman's body to be sculpted from ice, a similarly sculpted ice tub to rest beneath her and contain bottles of champagne for any thirsty guests. Tony prayed to God the sun would not get too strong. He visualized the fish-woman melting into the tub, the champagne beginning to taste like lukewarm ginger ale.

At one o'clock, his son and daughter-in-law arrived. Now Steve was a boy Tony could usually count on. Before Steve had gone into the Army, he used to work nights at the bakery, even though he was going to college during the day. Steve was a boy who could be trusted. He was a boy a father could count on. So today – *San Giacinto di California!* – even Steve had turned on him. Today, of all days, with those thieving Weddings-Fêtes, Incorporateds, tearing up the lawn, with Angela running around like a chicken *senza capo*, with the world of Antonio Carella slowly collapsing around him, his own true son Steve had arrived at the house with three additional guests! Not that Tony minded the extra expense. No, that didn't matter to him at all. So he would work an additional four months in the bakery to make up the money. But it was having to explain to those Incorporateds that there would be three more people and that they would have to arrange them at different tables. Steve was insistent on that. No, he did not want to sit with his friends. He wanted one here, and one here, and himself over there! *Pazzo!* His own son, as crazy as all the others.

And the tall one, the red-headed one with the white streak in his hair – *sangue della maruzza!* He was enough to frighten all the bridesmaids in Riverhead. And Tony was sure he had seen a gun under the redhead's coat when he stooped down to tie his shoe. A big black revolver sticking out of a shoulder holster. All right, it was a good thing for his son to be a cop, but did his friends have to carry weapons to a peaceful Christian wedding?

And then Angela had started. At one-fifteen, exactly one hour and forty-five minutes before the wedding, she had begun to cry as if the world was trying to rape her. Louisa had come running out back, wringing her hands.

'Stevie,' she said, 'go up to her. Tell her it'll be all right, will you? Go. Go to your sister.'

Tony had watched his son go upstairs. The wailing from the upper-storey bedroom window had not ceased. Tony sat with his daughter-in-law Teddy – *com'é grande*, he thought, *povera Theodora!* – and the three strangers, Mr Hawes, Mr Kling, and Miss Maxwell, drinking wine and ready to shoot his wife, strangle his son, disown his daughter, and call off the whole damn wedding!

He fumed and fretted until Teddy patted his hand. And then he smiled at her, and nodded his head, and rested his hands on his paunch and hoped – please, dear God! – that everything would turn out all right and that somehow he, Antonio Carella, would survive the day.

Standing in the corridor outside Angela's bedroom, Carella could hear his sister sobbing beyond the door. He knocked gently and then waited.

'Who is it?' Angela said, her voice breaking.

'Me. Steve.'

'What do you want?'

'Come on, Slip, open up.'

'Go away, Steve.'

'You can't chase me away. I'm a police officer investigating a disturbance of the peace.' He wasn't quite sure, but he thought he heard his sister stifle a laugh on the other side of the door. 'Slip?' he said.

'What?'

'Do I have to kick it in?'

'Oh, wait a minute,' Angela said. He heard footsteps approaching the door. The bolt was slipped, but Angela did not open the door for him. He heard her footsteps retreating and then the bed-springs creaking as she hurled herself down. He eased the door open and entered the room. Angela was lying full length on the bed, her face buried in the pillow. She wore a full white slip and her brown hair tumbled to her shoulders in a riot of disarray. Her slip had pulled back to reveal a blue garter taut around her nylon.

'Pull down your dress,' Carella said. 'Your behind is showing.'

'It's not a dress,' Angela said poutingly. 'It's a slip. And who asked you to look?' but she pulled it down over her leg instantly.

Carella sat on the edge of the bed. 'What's the trouble?'

'There's no trouble.' She paused. 'There's no trouble at all.' And then she sat up suddenly, turning her brown eyes toward her brother, surprisingly Oriental eyes in a high-cheekboned face, the face a refinement of Carella's, pretty with an exotic tint that spoke of Arabian visits to the island of Sicily in the far distant past. 'I don't want to marry him,' she said. She paused. 'That's the trouble.'

'Why not?'

'I don't love him.'

'Oh, bullshit,' Carella said.

'I don't like swearing, Steve. You know that. I never could stand swearing, even when we were kids. You used to swear on purpose, just to annoy me. That, and calling me "Slip".'

'You started the "slip" business,' Carella said.

'I did not,' Angela told him. 'You did. Because you were mean and rotten.'

'I was telling you the truth,' Carella said.

'It's not nice to tell a thirteen-year-old girl that she's not really a girl because she still wears cotton slips.'

'I was helping you on the road to maturity. You asked Mama to buy you some nylon slips after that, didn't you?'

'Yes, and she refused.'

'It was in the right direction.'

'You gave me an inferiority complex.'

'I gave you an insight into the mysterious ways of womanhood.'

'Oh, bullshit,' Angela said, and Carella laughed aloud. 'It's not funny. I'm not going to marry him. I don't like anything about him. He's a worse boor than you are. And he swears more. And besides . . .' She stopped. 'Stevie, I'm afraid. Stevie, I don't know what to do. I'm terrified.'

'Come on,' he said, 'come on,' and he took his sister into his arms and stroked her hair and said, 'There's nothing to be afraid of.'

'Steve, he's *killed* people, do you know that?'

'So have I.'

'I know, but . . . we're going to be alone tonight in . . . in one of the biggest hotels in the world . . . right in this city . . . and I don't even know the man I'm about to marry. How can I allow him to . . . to . . .'

'Did you talk to Mama, Slip?'

'Yes, I talked to Mama.'

'And what did she say?'

'She said, "To love is to fear nothing." I'm translating loosely from the Italian.'

'She's right.'

'I know, but . . . I'm not sure I love him.'

'I felt the same way on my wedding day.'

'You didn't have all this church hullabaloo.'

'I know. But there was a reception. It was just as nerve-wracking.'

'Steve . . . do you remember one night . . . I was sixteen, I think. You'd only been a cop a short time. Do you remember? I'd just come home from a date, and I was sitting in this room having some milk before I went to sleep. You must have had the four-to-midnight shift because it was pretty late at night, and you were just coming in. You stopped in here and had milk with me. Do you remember?'

'Yes. I remember.'

'Old Birnbaum's light was burning across the way. We could see it through the window there.'

He looked across at the window and through it over the long expanse of his father's back-yard to the gabled house belonging to Joseph Birnbaum, his father's closest friend and neighbour for forty years. He could remember that spring night clearly, the sound of insects in the back-yard, the single light burning in Birnbaum's attic room, the thin yellow crescent of a moon hanging listlessly over the sharply slanting roof of the house.

'I told you what had happened to me that night,' Angela said. 'About . . . about the boy I'd dated and . . . what he'd tried to do.'

'Yes, I remember.'

'I never told Mama about that,' Angela said. 'You were the only one I ever told. And I asked you if this . . . happened all the time, if this was what I could expect from boys I dated. I wanted to know what to do, how I should behave. Do you remember what you told me?'

'Yes,' Carella said.

'You said I should do whatever I felt was right. You said I would know what was right.' She paused. 'Steve . . . I've never . . .'

'Honey, shall I get Mama?'

'No, I want to talk to you. Steve, I don't know what to do tonight. I know that's awfully silly, I'm twenty-three years old, I should know what to do, but I don't, and I'm terrified he won't love me any more, he'll be disappointed, he'll—'

'Shhh, shhh,' he said. 'Come on now. What do you want?'

'I want you to tell me.'

He looked into her eyes and he took her hands and said, 'I can't do that, Slip.'

'Why not?'

'Because you're not a baby in cotton slips any more, and you're not a little girl who's suddenly puzzled by her first kiss. You're a woman, Angela. And there isn't a man alive who can give a woman instructions about love. I don't think you'll need them, honey. I really don't think you'll need them.'

'You think it'll . . . be all right?'

'I think it'll be fine. But I also think you'd better start dressing. Otherwise you'll miss your own wedding.'

Angela nodded glumly.

'Come on,' he said. 'You're going to be the prettiest goddamn bride this neighbourhood ever had.' He hugged her, rose, and started for the door.

'Was . . . was Teddy frightened?' Angela asked.

'I'm going to give you one bit of brotherly advice,' Carella said. 'I won't tell you whether Teddy was frightened or puzzled or innocent or whatever. I won't tell you because marriage is a private thing, Angela, built on faith more than anything else. And whatever happens between you and Tommy – tonight or forever – you and he will be the only two people to ever know about it. And that's one of the frightening things about marriage . . . but it's also pretty damn reassuring.' He went back to the bed, and he took her hands again, and he said, 'Angela, you have nothing to worry about. He loves you so much he's trembling. He *loves* you, honey. He's a good man. You chose well.'

'I love him, too, Steve. I do. Only . . .'

'Only *nothing*. What the hell do you want? A written guarantee that life is just a bowl of cherries? Well, it isn't. But you've got a clean slate, and you can write your own ticket. And, honey, you're starting with one of the major ingredients.' He grinned. 'You can't miss.'

'Okay,' she said, and she nodded her head emphatically.

'You going to get dressed?'

'Yes.'

'Good.'

'Okay,' she said again, more emphatically. She paused. 'But I think you're a louse for not giving me at least *one* hint!'

'I'm not a louse. I'm a loving brother.'

'I feel better, Steve. Thank you.'

'For what? Get dressed. Your blue garter is very pretty.'

'Go to hell,' she said, and he closed the door behind him, chuckling.

The boy's name was Ben Darcy.

He was twenty-six years old, with bright blue eyes and an engaging grin. He wore a blue mohair suit, and he walked across the back lawn with a long-legged lope, coming to a stop before the back porch where Tony Carella sat with his guests.

'Hello, Mr Carella,' he said. 'Lots of activity going on. Are you excited?'

'The caterers,' Tony said, looking out across the lawn at what seemed to be miles of white tablecloth. 'You're early, Ben. The reception doesn't start until five.'

'But the wedding's at three. You don't think I'd miss Angela's wedding, do you?'

'I think maybe she's gonna miss it herself,' Tony said. 'You know my daughter-in-law, Teddy? This is Ben Darcy.'

'I think I've seen you before, Mrs Carella,' Ben said. Teddy nodded. Her back was killing her. She wanted to ask for a straight chair, but she knew Tony had given her the most comfortable chair on the porch, and she did not want to offend him.

'And these are some friends of my son,' Tony said. 'Miss Maxwell, Mr Hawes, and Mr Kling. Ben Darcy.'

'Just call me Ben,' Ben said, shaking hands all around. 'I've known the Carellas so long I feel like a part of the family. Is there anything I can do to help, Mr Carella?'

'Nothing. Just keep out of their way. For setting up those tables and things, they're making me a poor man.' He wagged his head forlornly.

'He's the richest man on the block,' Ben said, grinning. 'Everybody in the neighbourhood knows that.'

'Sure, sure,' Tony said.

'When we were kids, he used to give out free rolls at the back door of his bakery. But then he started pinching pennies. No more rolls.' Ben shrugged.

'It was a free Salvation Army soup kitchen there,' Tony said. 'I figured out one day I was giving away five hundred rolls a week to kids who come to the back door! I also figured out it was the parents sending the kids around to suck Tony Carella's blood. No more rolls! Absolutely not! Cash on the line! No credit in my bakery!'

'He still gives away rolls,' Ben said warmly. 'All you need is a hard-luck story, and Tony Carella begins weeping. If the story's good enough, he'll give you the whole damn bake shop.'

'Sure, sure. The Rockefeller Foundation, that's me. I'm in business for my health.'

Ben nodded, grinning. Idly, he asked, 'Are you gentlemen in the baking line, too?'

Kling, ready to answer, glanced at Hawes first. Sitting with the sunlight glowing in his red hair, the white streak starkly naked against the flaming crimson, Hawes resembled nothing less than a baker. He caught Kling's eye and said, 'No, we're not bakers.'

'That's right,' Ben said. 'You're friends of Steve, aren't you?'

'Yes.'

'Are you policemen?'

'Us?' Hawes said. He laughed convincingly. 'Hell, no.'

Teddy and Christine looked at him curiously, but they did not betray puzzlement.

'We're theatrical agents,' Hawes lied unashamedly. 'Hawes and Kling, perhaps you've heard of us.'

'No, I'm sorry.'

'Yes,' Hawes said. 'Miss Maxwell is one of our clients. She's going to be a big star one day, this girl.'

'Oh, really?' Ben said. 'What do you do, Miss Maxwell?'

'I . . .' Christine started, and then stopped.

'She's an exotic dancer,' Hawes supplied, and Christine shot him an angry glare.

'An exot—?' Ben said.

'She strips,' Hawes explained. 'We've been trying to convince Mr Carella here to let Christine pop out of the wedding cake, but he doesn't think it's such a good idea.'

Tony Carella laughed. Ben Darcy looked unconvinced.

'Hawes and Kling,' Hawes repeated. 'If you ever become interested in show business, give us a ring.'

'I will,' Ben said. 'But I don't think I'll ever become interested in show business. I'm studying to be a dentist.'

'That's a noble profession,' Hawes said. 'But it lacks the glamour of the entertainment world.'

'Oh, teeth can be pretty exciting,' Ben said.

'I'm sure,' Hawes answered, 'but what can compare to the fever pitch of opening night? Nothing! There's no business like show business.'

'I guess you're right,' Ben said, 'but I'm glad I'm studying dentistry. I imagine I'll go into periodontal work later on.' He paused. 'It was Angela who first convinced me to become a professional man, you know.'

'I didn't know,' Hawes said.

'Oh yes. I used to date her. Date her? Hell, I began taking her out when she was seventeen and I guess I camped here on the Carella doorstep for the next five years. Wouldn't you say so, Mr Carella?'

'Yes, he was a pest,' Tony agreed.

'She's a wonderful girl,' Ben said. 'Tommy's a very lucky guy. There aren't many girls like Angela Carella around.'

The screen door behind Ben clattered shut. He turned abruptly. Steve Carella came out on to the porch.

His father looked up. 'She's all right?' he asked.

'She's all right,' Carella said.

'Girls,' Tony said mysteriously, and he shook his head.

'Hello, Ben,' Carella said. 'How are you?'

'Fine, thanks. You?'

'So-so. You're a little early, aren't you?'

'I guess so. I was just out for a walk, thought I'd stop by to see if I could lend a hand. Is Angela all right?'

'She's fine.'

'Everything seems to be okay at Tommy's house. The limousine's there already.'

'Oh?'

'Yep. Sitting in Tommy's driveway when I walked by there.'

'Good. Then I better get started.' He looked at his watch. 'Honey, Bert and I will be riding with Tommy. You don't mind, do you?'

Teddy looked up at him. He could read in an instant any nuance on her mobile face. Deprived of speech since

44

birth, her face had become a tool of expression so that meaning was instantly transmitted through her eyes and her lips. He had expected displeasure at his announcement but, reading her face now, he saw only puzzlement and realized she had not 'heard' him. Standing behind her as he'd spoken, he had not shown her his lips to read. He knelt beside her chair now.

'Bert and I are going to the church in Tommy's car. Is that all right with you?'

There was still no displeasure on her face. The puzzlement remained, and with it came a suspicious narrowing of the eyes. He knew in that moment that he had not fooled his wife. He had not told her of the incident with the black widow spider, but Teddy Carella — in her silent world — had already fathomed that something was amiss. The presence of Hawes and Kling was not the fulfilment of a social amenity. They were here as policemen, not wedding guests. She nodded, and then reached up to kiss him.

'I'll see you at the church,' he said. 'Are you all right?'

She nodded again. Her back was still killing her, but she sensed her husband had more important things on his mind than the trials of pregnancy. She flashed a sudden, radiant smile. Carella squeezed her hand.

'Come on, Bert,' he said.

4.

A BLACK CADILLAC limousine was parked in the driveway on the blind side of the Giordano house when Carella and Kling arrived. The car sat far back from the street, at the end of the concrete strips, close to the garage. The driver was nowhere in sight.

As they walked up on to the front porch, Kling said, 'I make it for a gag, Steve. I think we're going to a lot of trouble for nothing.'

'Well, maybe,' Carella answered, and he rang the doorbell. 'It doesn't hurt to be careful, though, does it?'

'I guess not. I get the feeling, however, that Cotton would much rather be elsewhere with his blonde.' He paused. 'But . . . that's show biz.'

'Huh?' Carella said, and Tommy opened the door.

'Steve, hi! Come on in. I was just dressing. Do you know how to tie a bow tie? I've been trying for the past half-hour and getting nowhere. Come on in.' He looked at Kling curiously.

'Bert Kling,' Carella said, 'Tommy Giordano, my future brother-in-law. Bert's with my squad, Tommy.'

'Oh. Oh, yeah. Come on in. I feel pretty silly about all this, Steve. I think it was a gag.'

Kling caught Carella's eye. 'Well, gag or not,' Carella said, 'Bert and another friend of mine will be at the wedding and the reception.'

'I appreciate what you're doing, Steve,' Tommy said,

'but in thinking it over, I'm pretty sure it was a gag. Come on into the bedroom, will you?'

They followed him through the house. In the bedroom, Tommy took a white tie from the dresser top and handed it to Carella. 'Here,' he said. 'See what you can do with this damn thing, will you?'

He faced Carella. He lifted his chin, and Carella began working on the tie.

'I checked on Sokolin,' Carella said.

'Yeah?'

'I don't want you to start worrying . . . but he's in this city. Got out of jail in April.'

'Oh.'

'Still think it's a gag?'

'Gee, I don't know. You think a guy would carry a grudge all this time? For something that happened in Korea? Or really, for something that didn't even . . .'

'Were you in Korea?' Kling asked, interested.

'Yeah. You?'

'Yeah.'

'Army?'

'Yeah.'

'I was in the Signal Corps,' Tommy said. 'With the Tenth Army Corps at the Inchon landings.'

'I was in on the Seoul liberation,' Kling said. 'With the Ninth Corps.'

'Under General Walker?'

'Yes.'

'Hell, we linked up with the First and Ninth around Seoul!' Tommy said. 'Jesus, I'll bet we were close enough to touch.'

'You were on the drive to the Yalu?'

'Sure.'

47

'How do you like that?' Kling said. 'It's a small world, all right.'

'And you're a cop now, huh?'

'Yes. What are you doing?'

'I work in a bank,' Tommy said. 'I'm training to be an executive.' He shrugged. 'It's not really what I want to be.'

'What do you want to be?'

'I'd like to be a baseball announcer. I used to be a pretty good catcher when I was a kid. I know the game inside out and backward. Ask Jonesy when he gets back.' He turned to Carella. 'You didn't happen to see him downstairs, did you?'

'Who?' Carella said. 'There. Your tie's tied.'

'Jonesy. My best man. My best *friend*, too. He went downstairs about a half-hour ago, said he needed some air.'

'Was he in a monkey suit?'

'Yeah.'

'Didn't see anybody dressed for a wedding. Did you, Bert?'

'No.'

'Well, he'll be back,' Tommy said. 'Jesus, I hope he has the ring. What time is it, Steve?'

'Two o'clock. You've still got an hour. Relax.'

'Well, I'm supposed to get there a little earlier, you know. I've got to go back to the rectory. I'm not supposed to see the bride until she comes down the aisle. Your mother is a lulu, Steve.'

'How so?'

'I'm not complaining. She'll probably make an excellent mother-in-law. But I called a little while ago, and she wouldn't even let me *talk* to Angela. That's going a little far, don't you think?'

'She was dressing,' Carella said.

'Yeah?' Tommy's eyes glowed. 'How does she look? Beautiful, I'll bet.'

'Beautiful.'

'Yeah, I knew it. Was she nervous?'

'Very.'

'Me, too. You want some coffee?'

'No, thanks.'

'A little drink?'

'No. Do you want to hear about Sokolin?'

'Sokolin? Who's—? Oh, sure. Sure.' Tommy pulled on his jacket. 'There. I'm all set. How do I look? Did I shave close enough?'

'You shaved close enough.'

'I'll probably need another one by the time we check in tonight. I've got a heavy beard. You blond guys are lucky, Bert. Do I look all right, Steve? Is the tie straight?'

'The tie's straight.'

'Good. Then I'm ready to go. You think we ought to leave now? It's past two, isn't it?'

'I think you ought to do something before you leave,' Carella said.

'Yeah? What?'

'Put on your pants.'

Tommy looked down at his hairy legs. 'Oh, God! Oh, Jesus! Boy, am I glad you're here! How could a guy forget to do something he does every day of his life? Boy!' He shucked the jacket and took his black trousers from a hanger in the closet. 'What about Sokolin?'

'He spent a year in jail because he got into an argument about his dead Korean buddy.'

'That doesn't sound so good.'

'It sounds pretty lousy. I don't imagine he'd got much love in his heart for you.'

A knock sounded at the front door. Tommy looked up and then slipped his suspenders over his shoulders. 'Steve, would you get that, please? It's probably Jonesy.'

Carella went to the front door and opened it. The boy standing there was about Tommy's age, twenty-six or twenty-seven. He was as tall as Carella, with broad shoulders and long legs. He wore his brown hair short. His grey eyes were alight with excitement. He looked very handsome in his tuxedo and his white starched shirt-front. Seeing Carella's similar uniform, he extended his hand and said, 'Hi. Usher?'

'Nope. Relative,' Carella said. He took the hand. 'Steve Carella. Brother of the bride.'

'Sam Jones. Best man. Call me Jonesy.'

'Okay.'

'How's our groom?'

'Nervous.'

'Who isn't? I had to get out for a walk or I'd lose my mind.' They went through the house into the bedroom. 'You okay, Tommy?' Jonesy asked.

'I'm fine. I was ready to walk out of here without my pants, how do you like that?'

'Par for the course,' Jonesy said.

'You've got dirt on your knees,' Tommy said, looking down at his best man's trousers.

'What?' Jonesy followed his glance. 'Oh, hell, I knew it. I tripped on the front step going out. Damn it!' He began brushing vigorously at his trousers.

'Do you have the ring?'

'Yep.'

'Check.'

'I've got it.'

'Check anyway.'

Jonesy stopped brushing his pants and stuck his forefinger into his vest pocket. 'It's there. Ready for delivery. Jones to Giordano.'

'Jonesy used to pitch on our team,' Tommy said. 'I caught. I already told you that, didn't I?'

'Jones to Giordano,' Jonesy said again. 'He was a damn good catcher.'

'You did all the work,' Tommy said, zipping up his fly. 'There. Now for the jacket. Have I got my shoes on?' He looked down at his feet.

'He was like this before every game,' Jonesy said, grinning. 'I know this guy since he was three years old, would you believe it?'

'We used to get walked around the park together,' Tommy said. 'Jonesy missed the Korean bit because he's got a trick knee. Otherwise we'd have been in that together, too.'

'He's the meanest bastard ever walked the earth,' Jonesy said playfully. 'I don't know why I like him.'

'Yok-yok,' Tommy said. 'We've got mutual wills, Steve, did you know that?'

'What do you mean?'

'Had them drawn up when I got out of the service. Birnbaum's son made them out for us. Birnbaum and his wife witnessed them. Remember, Jonesy?'

'Sure. But you'd better have yours changed now. You're gonna be a married man in a few hours.'

'That's right,' Tommy said.

'What do you mean, mutual wills?' Carella asked.

'Our wills. They're identical. Jonesy gets everything I own if I die, and I get everything he owns if he dies.'

Jonesy shrugged. 'You'll have to change that now,' he said.

'Sure, I will. When we get back from the honeymoon. But I never regretted the wills, did you?'

'No, *sir*.'

'Birnbaum thought we were nuts, remember? Wanted to know why two such young fellows were making out wills. His wife – may she rest in peace – kept clucking her tongue all the while she signed. What ever happened to that lawyer son of his, anyway?'

'He's out West now. Denver or some place. He's got a big practice out there.'

'Poor Birnbaum. All alone here in the city.' Tommy stood at attention, ready for inspection. 'Pants on, tie tied, shoes shined. Am I okay now?'

'You're beautiful,' Jonesy said.

'Then let's go. Oooops, cigarettes.' He snatched a package from the dresser. 'Have you got the ring?'

'I've got it.'

'Check again.'

Jonesy checked again. 'It's still there.'

'Okay, let's go. What time is it?'

'Two-twenty,' Carella said.

'Good. We'll be a little early, but that's good. Let's go.'

They went out of the house. Tommy locked the door behind him, and then turned left, walking toward the driveway lined with tall poplars which shielded it from the house next door. They walked toward the car with all the solemnity of a funeral party.

'Where's the driver?' Tommy asked.

'I told him he could go get a cup of coffee,' Jonesy said. 'He should be back by now.'

'Here he comes,' Kling said.

They watched the driver as he ambled up the street. He was a short man wearing the black uniform and peaked cap of a rental service. 'Ready to go?' he asked.

'We're ready,' Tommy said. 'Where were you?'

'Up the street getting a cup of coffee.' The driver looked offended. 'Your best man said it was all right.'

'Okay, okay, let's go,' Tommy said.

They got into the limousine, and the driver began backing into the street.

'Wait a minute,' Tommy said. The driver turned. 'What's that?'

'What?'

'There. In the driveway. Where we just came from.'

'I don't see anything.'

'Have you got the ring, Jonesy?'

Jonesy felt in his pocket. 'Yes, I've got it.'

'Oh. Okay. I thought I saw something glinting on the concrete. Okay, let's go. Let's go.'

The driver backed out of the driveway and turned into the street.

'Relax,' Jonesy said.

'Boy, I wish I could.'

The limousine moved slowly up the tree-lined street. The sun was shining in an eggshell blue sky. It was a beautiful day.

'Can't you go any faster?' Tommy asked.

'We've got plenty of time,' the driver said.

He stopped at an intersection at the top of a long hill. Patiently, he waited for the light to change.

'You turn left at the bottom of the hill,' Tommy said. 'The church is on the left.'

'I know.'

'Oh, hell,' Jonesy said suddenly.

'Huh?'

'Cigarettes! I forgot cigarettes.'

'I've got some,' Tommy said.

'I'll need my own.' He opened the door on his side. 'I'll get some at the candy store. Go ahead without me before you bust a gut. I'll walk down the hill.' He slammed the door behind him and started for the sidewalk.

'Don't get lost!' Tommy yelled after him frantically.

'I won't. Don't worry.' He vanished inside the candy store on the corner.

'The light's green,' Tommy said. 'Go ahead.'

The driver put the car into gear and started down the hill. It was a long steep hill with one street bisecting it. It ran at a sharp pitch to a second street at the far end, a dead end blocked by a stone wall which shielded a steep-angled cliff of jagged rock. The stone wall was painted with alternating yellow and black lines as a warning to approaching motorists. As a further precaution, a huge blinking DEAD END sign flashed in the exact centre of the wall. Since the time that excavation for gravel had begun in the area behind the wall, leaving the rocky cliff and the steep drop, only one motorist had driven through the wall and over the cliff. He'd been killed instantly, and it was learned later that he'd been drunk, but the accident had been enough to warrant the yellow-and-black paint job and the blinking light.

The limousine gained momentum as the car hurtled toward the end of the hill and the painted stone wall.

'That's a bad turn at the corner,' Tommy said. 'Be careful.'

'Mister, I've been driving for twenty years,' the driver said. 'I never missed a wedding yet, and I never yet had an accident.'

'Yeah, well there's a steep cliff behind that wall. A guy was killed here once.'

'I know all about it. Don't worry, you ain't gonna get killed. When you been married for fifteen years, the way I have, you'll maybe wish you *did* get into an accident on your wedding day.'

The car sped for the bottom of the hill and the turn. The DEAD END sign blinked monotonously. Clutching the wheel in two massive fists, the driver swung it sharply to the left.

There was an enormous cracking sound which jolted the automobile.

The car did not turn to the left.

With something like awe in his voice, the driver said, 'Jesus, it won't steer!'

5.

FROM OUTSIDE THE car, passers-by saw only a vehicle which was wildly out of control, the front wheels pointing in opposite directions as the limousine hurtled forward toward the sidewalk, the stone wall, and the cliff beyond.

Inside the car, the passengers only knew that the driver could not, for some reason, steer the limousine. In a last desperate effort, he swung the steering-wheel to the right and then the left, his foot automatically leaping to the brake pedal. The car swung in a screeching arc toward the sidewalk, its back wheels leaping the kerb, the rear end swinging toward the wall and the cliff.

'Brace yourself!' Carella shouted, and the men in the car tensed for the shock of impact, surprised when the shock was not as great as they expected, startled with the knowledge that something had intervened to prevent the powerful smash through the stone wall, amazed when they realized the something was a lamp-post.

The car ricocheted off the unbending steel pole, swerved in another wild arc, bounced forward on to the front wheels and then lurched on to the back wheels finally, coming to a dead stop as the brakes took hold completely and irrevocably.

The men in the automobile were silent.

The driver was the first to speak.

He said only, 'Wow!'

One by one, they climbed out of the car. Kling had banged his head on the roof of the car, but otherwise no one was injured. The car itself had fared worse. The entire right side was smashed in where the limousine had collided with the lamp-post. A crowd was gathering on the sidewalk. A policeman began shoving his way through it. The driver of the Cadillac began talking to him, explaining what had happened.

Carella walked to the steel lamp-post and slapped it with an open hand. 'We can all get down on our hands and knees and kiss this baby,' he said. 'If it hadn't stopped us—' He looked over the stone wall, and then wiped his forehead.

'What the hell do you suppose happened?' Kling asked.

'I don't know,' Carella said. 'Come on.'

Together, they walked to where the driver and the patrolman were squatting on their hands and knees at the front of the car.

They waited.

'Sure,' the driver said to the cop. 'That's it.'

'Yeah,' the cop said. 'Boy, you were lucky you hit that lamp-post. A guy was killed here once, you know that?'

'What is it?' Carella asked.

'The steering linkage,' the driver said. 'There's a steering tube under there, connected to the tie rod ends. Well, the one on the right side busted. And without that tie rod end, I didn't have any control.'

'It looks like more than that,' the patrolman said.

'What does it look like?' Carella asked.

'It looks like somebody worked on that thing with a hack-saw!'

At 3.00 P.M., Tommy Giordano and his best man stepped from the rectory of the Church of the Sacred Heart and walked to the altar. In a loud stage whisper, Tommy asked, 'Have you got the ring?' and Jonesy nodded in assurance.

Angela Carella, resplendent in white, entered the back of the church on her father's arm. Her face beneath the white veil was frozen in lovely horror.

On one side of the church, sitting with the bride's family, were Steve and Teddy Carella, and Bert Kling. On the other side, sitting with the groom's relatives, were Cotton Hawes and Christine Maxwell. Organ music filled the vaulted stone vastnesses of the church. A photographer who'd snapped Angela as she'd stepped out of the Cadillac, snapped her again as she'd mounted the church steps, and again as she'd started down the aisle, now hopped with gnomelike agility to the front of the church, anxious to catch her as she approached the altar. Tommy's hands twitched at his sides.

Louisa Carella began crying. Teddy reached over to pat her mother-in-law's hand, and then reached for her own handkerchief, and blew her nose to hide her tears.

'She's beautiful,' Louisa said, and Teddy nodded, her eyes brimming.

The organ music swelled to drown out the sounds of the joyful weeping, the 'Ooooohs' and 'Ahhhhhs' which heralded the bride's steady regal progress down the aisle. The flash bulbs popped as the photographer busily kept his shutter clicking. Tony Carella, his bent arm supporting the trembling hand of his daughter, walked down the aisle with the dignity of a monarch about to be crowned, certain that the twitching of his left eye was not visible to anyone in the pews.

In the first pew on the bride's half of the church, Steve Carella sat alongside his wife and chewed his lip.

Somebody sawed through that rod end, he thought. *This was no damn black widow joke. This was serious business.*

Angela climbed the steps to the altar. Tommy smiled at her, and she returned the smile, and then lowered her eyes behind the pale white veil.

And whoever did the sawing was well aware of that steep hill and that sharp turn. Whoever did it probably sawed it through just far enough to know it would snap when the turn was attempted.

Tony Carella handed his daughter to his soon-to-be-son. Together, the couple faced the priest. The church was still with the solemnity of the occasion.

Tommy saw something glinting in the driveway as we pulled out, Carella thought. *Probably metal filings from the sawed rod. The rod is thin. Ten minutes with a hack-saw could have done a very fine job on it. And Sam Jones was gone for a half-hour walk. And Sam Jones had dirt on the knees of his trousers. And it was Sam Jones who gave the driver permission to leave the limousine in search of a cup of coffee.*

The priest said a prayer and then blessed the couple with holy water. Tommy was sweating profusely. Beneath the white veil, Angela's lips were trembling.

'Do you, Thomas Giordano,' the priest said, 'take this woman as your lawfully wedded wife to live together in the state of holy matrimony? Will you love, honour, and keep her as a faithful man is bound to do, in health, sickness, prosperity, and adversity, and forsaking all others keep you alone unto her 'til death do you part?'

Tommy swallowed hard. 'Yes,' he said. 'I do.'

'Do you, Angela Louisa Carella, take this man as your lawfully wedded husband to live together in the state of holy matrimony? Will you love, honour, and cherish him as a faithful woman is bound to do, in health, sickness . . .'

And it was Sam Jones, Carella thought, *who conveniently stepped out of the automobile to buy a package of cigarettes just before the crash.*

' . . . prosperity, and adversity, and forsaking all other keep you alone unto him 'til death do you part?'

'I do,' Angela whispered.

It is also Sam Jones, best man and best friend, who is named in Tommy's will, who gets everything Tommy owns should Tommy die. Sam Jones.

'For as you have both consented in wedlock and have acknowledged it before God and this company, I do by virtue of the authority vested in me by the Catholic Church and the laws of this state now pronounce you husband and wife.'

The priest made the sign of the cross over the young couple and, sobbing next to Teddy, Louisa Carella suddenly said, 'Now I have *another* married daughter,' and she took Teddy's hand and kissed it quickly and fervently.

Tommy lifted his bride's veil and kissed her fleetingly and with much embarrassment. The organ music started again. Smiling, the veil pulled back on to the white crown nestled in her hair, Angela clutched Tommy's arm and they started up the aisle, the photographer recording every inch of their progress.

In the rectory, the telephone began ringing.

*

The nun in the rectory held the door open for Steve Carella as he stepped into the small room. Standing by the telephone in the robes he'd worn during the ceremony, Father Paul said, 'I knew it'd take a wedding to get you into the church, Steve. But I didn't guess a phone call would bring you into the rectory.'

'Two things I never discuss are politics and religion,' Carella answered. 'Is the call from the squad, Father?'

'A man named Meyer Meyer,' Father Paul said.

'Thank you,' Carella said, and he took the receiver from the priest's hand. 'Hello, Meyer. Steve.'

'Hello, boy. How goes the wedding?'

'So far, so good. The knot's been tied.'

'I've been doing a little further checking on this Sokolin character. Are you still interested?'

'Very much so.'

'Okay. I checked with his parole officer. He's been leading an exemplary life, working as a salesman in a department store downtown. But two weeks ago, he moved from Isola to Riverhead. I've got the address, Steve. From what the map tells me, it looks as if it's eleven blocks from your father's house.'

Carella thought for a moment and then said, 'Meyer, will you do me a favour? We had an accident a little while ago that stank to high heaven. Will you put a pick-up-and-hold on this character? I'd feel a hell of a lot safer.' He suddenly remembered he was in a church rectory and glanced sheepishly at Father Paul.

'Sure thing. It's kind of slow around here, anyway. I may go out on it myself.'

'Will you let me know when you've got him? We're heading for the photographer's right now, but I'll be at my father's place in about an hour. You can reach me there.'

'Right. Kiss the bride for me, will you?'

'I will. Thanks again, Meyer.' He hung up.

Father Paul looked at him and said, 'Trouble?'

'No. Nothing serious.'

'I've been told about the automobile accident,' he said. 'Quite a freak occurrence.'

'Yes.'

'But there's no trouble?'

'No.'

'Even though the accident, to quote you, stank to high heaven?'

Carella smiled. 'Father,' he said, 'you've got me inside the church, but you're not going to get me into the confessional.' He shook hands with the priest. 'It was a beautiful ceremony. Thank you, Father.'

Outside, the limousines were waiting.

Carella walked over to where Kling was standing with Teddy.

'That was Meyer,' he said. 'I've put a pick-up-and-hold on Sokolin. I think that's wise, don't you?'

'I suppose.'

Carella looked around. 'Where's our friend Jonesy?'

'He went back to the house.'

'Oh.'

'If you're thinking what I'm thinking, don't worry about it. Cotton left right after him.'

'Good.' He took Teddy's arm. 'Honey, you look about ready to drop. Come on. Get inside that nice air-cooled Cadillac.' He held the door open for her. 'Some day,' he said, 'when I get to be commissioner, I'm going to buy you one of these all for yourself.'

*

Ben Darcy and Sam Jones were talking to the caterers when Hawes and Christine pulled up in a taxi-cab. Hawes paid the driver, and then walked around to the back of the Carella house. A huge framework was in its last stages of construction at the far end of the plot, just inside the row of hedges which divided the Carella property from Birnbaum's.

Jonesy stopped talking when he saw Christine Maxwell. Wearing an ice-blue chiffon, she rustled across the lawn clinging to Hawes's arm, and Jonesy followed her progress through the grass with unabashed and open admiration. When they were close enough, his eyes still on Christine, he said, 'I don't believe we've met. My name is Sam Jones. Call me Jonesy.'

'I'm Cotton Hawes,' Hawes said. 'This is Christine Maxwell.'

'Pleased to meet you,' he said, taking Christine's hand. Belatedly, he added, 'Both.'

'What's this monster creation?' Hawes asked, indicating the huge wooden grid.

'For the fireworks display,' one of the caterers explained.

'It looks like the launching platform for a three-stage rocket,' Hawes commented, aware of the sledge-hammer subtlety of Jonesy's ogling and slightly rankled by it. 'Are we trying for the moon?'

'We'll be shooting off a few rockets,' the caterer replied humourlessly.

'When will this be?'

'As soon as it's dark. This is going to be the goddamnedest wedding *this* neighbourhood ever saw, you can bet on that.'

'Angela deserves it,' Darcy said.

'And Tommy, too,' Jonesy added, smiling at Christine. 'Have you seen the mermaid, Miss Maxwell? Come, I'll show it to you. They've already loaded the buckets of champagne. It's fascinating.'

'Well . . .' Christine started, and she glanced hesitantly at Hawes.

'I'm sure Mr Hawes won't mind,' Jonesy said. 'Come along.' He took her arm and led her to where the ice maiden lay on her side, protected from the sun by a shielding canopy. The base upon which she lay had been scooped out to form a frigid tub into which dozens of champagne bottles had been placed. It truly looked as if this was going to be one hell of a wedding. Hawes watched Christine amble away across the lawn, aware of a growing irritation within him. It was one thing to do a cotton-picking, bodyguarding favour, but it was another to have a girl snatched from right before your eyes.

'So what is this?' a voice beside him said. 'The battleship *Missouri*?'

Hawes turned. The man standing before the fireworks scaffolding was short and slender with a balding pate fringed with white hair. His blue eyes held a merry twinkle. He studied the framework as if it were truly a wonder of the scientific age.

'I'm Birnbaum,' he said. 'The neighbour. Who are you?'

'Cotton Hawes.'

They shook hands. 'That's an unusual name,' Birnbaum said. 'Very unusual. Cotton Mather? The Puritan priest?'

'Yes.'

'I'm not a religious man, myself.'

'Neither am I.'

'Did you come from the wedding?'

'Yes,' Hawes said.

'Me, too. It was the first time in my life I've ever been inside a Catholic Church. I'll tell you something. It's a *bubemeiseh*.'

'What is?'

'That the walls will fall down if a Jew steps inside. I stepped inside and I stepped out again, and the walls – thank God – are still standing. Imagine if the walls had come down during my *tsotskuluh*'s wedding. A terrible thing to imagine! *Oi*, God, I would rather cut off my right arm. She looked lovely, didn't she?'

'Yes.'

'A beautiful girl, Angela. I never had a daughter. I got a lawyer son, he's now in Denver. My wife, poor soul, passed away three years ago. I'm alone in the world. Birnbaum. The neighbour. Well, at least I'm a neighbour, no?'

'A neighbour is a good thing to be,' Hawes said, smiling, liking the little man immensely.

'Certainly. But lest you think I'm a bum, I should tell you I am also a grocery store owner besides being a neighbour. Birnbaum's Grocery. Right up the street. And I live over there. See the house? Been here for forty years and believe me when I first moved in people thought Jews had horns and tails. Well, times change, huh? It's a good thing, thank God.' He paused. 'I know both the children since they were born. Tommy and Angela. Like my own children. Both sweet. I love that little girl, I never had a daughter of my own, you know. So Tony's having fireworks! My God, what a wedding

65

this will be! I hope I live through it. Do you like my tuxedo?'

'It's very nice,' Hawes said.

'The least I could do was rent a tuxedo when Tony's daughter got married. It fits a little snug, don't you think?'

'No, it looks fine.'

'Well, I'm not as slender as I used to be. Too much easy living. I got two clerks in my grocery store now. It's not easy to buck the supermarkets. But I get by. Get by? Look how fat I'm getting. What do you do for a living?'

'I'm a theatrical agent,' Hawes said, relying upon the earlier fabrication. If someone meant to injure Tommy Giordano, he did not think it wise to advertise his profession.

'That's a good business. Is Miss Maxwell in show business?'

'Yes,' he lied again. 'She's a dancer.'

'I thought so. A beautiful girl. But I'm partial to blondes.' He looked across the lawn. 'I guess Jonesy isn't. He's left her.'

Hawes turned. Christine was walking back toward the fireworks platform. Alone. Jonesy was nowhere in sight. It suddenly occurred to him that Ben Darcy had disappeared, too.

I'm a fine cop, Hawes thought. *I stand here talking to a grocer while the boys I'm supposed to watch vanish into the woodwork.*

'You should take a look at the mermaid,' Christine said. 'She's quite lovely.'

'Where'd your escort go?' Hawes asked.

Christine shrugged. 'Said there was something he had

66

to take care of.' She paused. 'I didn't inquire further. I didn't think it would be ladylike.' She paused again. 'He's rather cute, don't you think?'

'Adorable,' Hawes said, and he wondered where both Jonesy and Darcy had gone.

And he hoped it was not too far.

6.

THE PHOTOGRAPHER'S SHOP was not too far from the Carella house in Riverhead. In fact, a fairly slow driver could make the journey in less than five minutes if he stopped at each FULL STOP sign on the way.

The photographer was called Jody Lewis, and a sign across the front of his shop read JODY'S simply because he did not wish to name his place LEWIS'S or LEWIS', both of which he was certain would be mistakenly read as just plain LEWIS. The shop was a simple one-storey brick building with a plate-glass front window behind which were displayed the photographer's previous efforts. Across the street from the shop, sitting back some twenty-five feet from the sidewalk, was a two-storey frame house. Six windows faced the street side of that house. From a window on the second floor of the house, the photographer's shop was clearly visible.

The man stood at the window, peering across the street at the shop. The cars had not yet arrived. That was good. That gave him plenty of time to set up. He lighted a cigar and then crossed the room to where the rifle was standing against the wall.

The rifle was a Winchester Model 70 target rifle which had been developed to meet the requirements of all long-range, high-power target shooting, and long-range shooting at small game. The stock was ample in size and weight, with a large butt stock, a well-rounded comb, and a large full pistol grip curving close to the guard. The gun also featured a target butt plate and a long, wide beaver-tail forestock.

He picked up the gun and studied it, the cigar smoke trailing up past his face.

A telescopic sight was mounted to the gun.

The sight was a blued steel tube, one inch in diameter, eleven and a quarter inches in length. It weighed only nine and a half ounces and was adjustable for internal windage and elevation with either a friction lock or a quarter-inch click.

The man carried the gun to the window and rested it on the window-sill. He focused the sight on the door of Jody's shop, so that the cross-hairs were on the centre of the doorway.

Then he sat back to wait.

The two limousines pulled up before he'd been waiting five minutes.

He pulled back the bolt and slammed it home, rested the gun on the window-sill again, and took careful aim at the entrance to the shop. He looked up from the sight once to make sure he knew which of the people coming from the cars was Tommy Giordano.

Then he waited again.

Tommy stepped into the door of the shop.

The man's finger began to tighten on the trigger. And then Tommy pulled his bride to him, her back to the street, kissing her soundly. The finger hesitated. Tommy pulled her into the shop. The moment was gone.

Cursing, the sniper stubbed out his cigar and prepared to wait for their exit.

*

Jody Lewis was a dwarf of a man who looked like something which had popped out of a trick box camera when the shutter was clicked. Bouncing around his shop with undiminished energy, he said, 'These are the only posed pictures we'll take. Of the bride and groom. This is your story, the bride's and groom's. That's why I don't want any posed shots of the best man or the maid of honour. Who needs them? This is your story. That's what it'll say on the cover of the album. "Our Wedding Day". Not the best man's wedding day, but the groom's. Not the maid of honour's, but the bride's. And all I want here in the studio with the good lights is one perfect picture of the lovely bride, God bless her, and one perfect picture of the handsome groom, and one of you together. And that's all. And then we go off to the reception. But is that the end of Jody Lewis? Not by a long shot. Not by a close-up, either. I'll be with you every minute of the way, taking pictures of you when you least expect it. Click, click, click goes my shutter. A candid record of your wedding day. Right to the hotel, right to a shot of Tommy carrying you over the threshold, and you putting your shoes in the hallway. And then back to develop and print, so that when you return from your lovely honeymoon, you'll have this candid album titled "Our Wedding Day" as a keepsake forever, as a memento of events you might otherwise forget. Who can remember all the little things that have happened or are going to happen today? Nobody has a memory like that except a camera. And I am a camera! Me, Jody Lewis, from the play and movie of the same name. Now sit right here, little ones. The two of you together. That's it. Look as if you love each other, I'm joking, God only knows you're crazy in love with each other, that's it, smile a little, Tommy, my God, don't look so serious, the girl loves you. That's better. Take his hand, Angela. That's the girl, now look over there, not at the camera, over there where the picture's hanging on the wall, that's it, hold it, click! That's going to be beautiful. Now turn a little on the seat, Tommy, that's it, and put your arms around her waist, oh she's nice to hold, my friend, that's it, don't blush, you're married now, that's it, now hold it, hold it . . .'

'How do you feel, Teddy?' Carella asked.

Gently, Teddy touched the mound which began just below her breasts. Then she rolled her eyes heavenward and pulled a weary face.

'It'll be over soon,' he said. 'Is there anything you want? A glass of water or something?'

Teddy shook her head.

'Massage your back?'

She shook her head again.

'Know I love you?'

Teddy grinned and squeezed his hand.

The woman who answered the door at the private house in Riverhead was in her late fifties and didn't care. She wore a wrinkled housedress and scuffed house-slippers. Her hair hung limply on her head, as if it had followed its owner's directive and given up the struggle.

'What do you want?' she said. She pierced Meyer and O'Brien with eyes chipped from green agate.

'We're looking for a man named Marty Sokolin,' Meyer said patiently. 'Does he live here?'

'Yes, and who the hell are you?'

Patiently, Meyer took out his wallet and opened it to

where his shield was pinned to the leather. 'Police department,' he said.

The woman looked at the shield. 'All right, Mr Detective,' she said. 'What did Sokolin do?'

'Nothing. We just want to ask him a few questions.'

'What about?'

'About what he might be planning to do.'

'He ain't here,' the woman said.

'And what is your name, madam?' Meyer asked patiently. If there was one attribute Meyer possessed, it was extreme patience. An Orthodox Jew born in a predominantly Gentile neighbourhood, he'd been further handicapped by the vagaries of a whimsical father who thought it would be a good joke to give his son a double-barrelled moniker. The family surname was Meyer. And old Max Meyer decided to name his change-of-life offspring Meyer Meyer, just to get even with the powers that dictated off-season births. The joke was played. It was not a very practical one. It provided the young boy with a ready-made millstone. To say that Meyer Meyer's childhood had been only an endless round of fist fights provoked by either his name or his religion would have been a complete understatement. For coupled with the fist fights came the slow development of a diplomat. Meyer learned that only *some* battles could be won with his hands. The rest had to be won with his tongue. And so he acquired a veneer of extreme patience to cover the scars of his father's little jibe. Patiently, he even learned to forgive the old man before he died. Now, at the age of thirty-seven, the only scar he carried from an excruciatingly anxious childhood (or, to be more precise, the only scar which *showed*) was a head as bald as the famed American eagle.

Patiently, he repeated, 'And what is your name, madam?'

'Mary Murdoch. What's it to you?'

'Nothing,' Meyer said. He glanced at O'Brien. O'Brien stepped back a pace, as if anxious to sever whatever national ties bound him to the woman. 'You said Mr Sokolin was not in. When did he leave, might we ask?'

'Early this morning. He took his damn horn with him, thank the good Lord.'

'His horn?'

'His trumpet, his trombone, his saxophone, whatever you call the damn thing. He practices it morning and night. You never heard such unholy screeches. I wouldn't have rented him the apartment if I'd known he played a horn. I might kick him out, matter of fact.'

'You don't like horn players?'

'Put it this way,' Mary Murdoch said. 'They make me vomit.'

'That's a unique way of putting it,' Meyer said, and he cleared his throat. 'How do you know Sokolin left with his horn?'

'I seen him. He's got a case for the thing. A black case. That's what he carries the damn thing in. A case.'

'A trumpet case?'

'Or a trombone, or a saxophone, some damn thing. It sure makes an unholy racket, whatever it is.'

'How long has he been living here, Miss Murdoch?'

'*Mrs* Murdoch, if you please. He's been living here for two weeks. If he keeps blasting away on that damn saxophone, he won't be living here much longer, I can tell you that.'

'Oh, is it a saxophone?'

'Or a trumpet, or a trombone, or some damn thing,' she said. 'Is he in trouble with the police?'

'No, not really. Do you have any idea where he went when he left this morning?'

'No. He didn't say. I just happened to see him go, that's all. But he usually hangs out in a bar on the Avenue.'

'What avenue is that, Mrs Murdoch?'

'Dover Plains Avenue. Everybody knows the Avenue. Don't you know the Avenue?'

'No, we're not too familiar—'

'Two blocks down and under the elevated structure. Dover Plains Avenue. Everybody knows the Avenue. He hangs out in a bar there. It's called the Easy Dragon, that's some name for a bar, isn't it? It sounds more like a Chinese restaurant.' Mrs Murdoch grinned with death's head simplicity.

'You're sure he hangs out there?'

'Sure, I'm sure.'

'How can you be sure?'

'Put it this way,' Mrs Murdoch said. 'I'm not above taking a little nip every now and then myself.'

'I see.'

'Which don't make me a drunkard.'

'I know.'

'All right. You finished?'

'I guess so. We may be back.'

'What for?'

'You're so pleasant to talk to,' Meyer said, and Mrs Murdoch slammed the door.

'Well!' O'Brien said.

'Luckily, she didn't start shooting,' Meyer said. 'With you along, I always expect bullets.'

'Maybe she'll shoot when we come back. *If* we come back.'

'Maybe so. Keep your fingers crossed.'

'Where to now?'

'The Easy Dragon,' Meyer said. 'Where else?'

The Easy Dragon was named the Easy Dragon for no apparent reason. The décor was not Chinese. There was not a Chinese in sight anywhere. The Easy Dragon looked like any tavern in any suburban neighbourhood, peopled with the usual sprinkling of Sunday afternoon drinkers. Meyer and O'Brien entered the place, adjusted their vision to the dimness after the brilliant sunshine outside, and walked to the bar.

Meyer flashed the tin instantly. The bartender studied his shield with great dispassion.

'So?' he said.

'We're looking for a guy named Marty Sokolin. Know him?'

'So?'

'Yes or no?'

'Yes. So?'

'Is he here now?'

'Don't you know what he looks like?'

'No. Is he here?'

'No. What'd he do?'

'Nothing. Are you expecting him today?'

'Who knows? He's in and out. He's only been living in the neighbourhood a short time. What'd he do?'

'I told you. Nothing.'

'Is he a little crazy?'

'How do you mean?'

75

'You know. A little crazy.' The bartender circled his temple with an extended forefinger. 'Cuckoo.'

'What makes you think he's crazy?'

'He's got a fanatical gleam in his eyes. Especially when he's drinking. Also, he's a big bastard. I wouldn't want to ever tangle with him. This guy chews railroad spikes and spits out carpet tacks.' He paused. 'Pardon the cliché,' he said. He pronounced it 'cleesh'.

'You're pardoned. Do you happen to know where he might be right now?'

'You tried his house?'

'Yes.'

'He ain't there, huh?'

'No.'

'What'd he do?'

'Nothing. Would you mind, if you know, telling us where he might be?'

'Well, I'm not sure I know. You tried his girl's pad?'

'No. Who's she?'

'A dame named Oona. Oona I don't know what. How's that for a fancy name? You should see her. She's like a regular bombshell. Perfect for a nut like Sokolin.'

'Oona, huh? And you don't know her last name.'

'That's right. Just Oona. You won't miss her if you see her. She's a blonde with bazooms like pineapples.' He paused. 'Pardon the cliché,' he said.

'You're pardoned. Any idea where she lives?'

'Sure.'

'Where?'

'Up the street. There's a rooming house on the corner. She's new around here, too. The only reason I know where she lives is she mentioned she was at a place served meals. And the place on the corner is the only place serves meals. I mean, of the rooming houses.'

'I see,' Meyer said. 'Can you describe her a little more fully?'

'Well, like I said, she's got these enormous pineapples. And she's got a mouth like a trap, and a pretty nose, and eyes like blue ice and blonde hair like a field of wheat.' He paused, retracing the path of his similes to see if he'd been guilty of another 'cleesh'. Apparently satisfied of his innocence, he nodded and said, 'If you find her, you can't miss her.'

'That's reassuring,' Meyer said. 'Has she been in today?'

'No.'

'Did Sokolin ever play a horn in here?'

'A what?'

'A horn.'

'No. He plays a horn, this nut? Boy, miracles will never cease.'

'What's the name of this rooming house? Where they serve meals?'

'The Green Corner.' He shrugged. 'The house is green, and it's on the corner. Listen, who knows why people name places?'

'Is this your place?' Meyer asked.

'Yeah.'

'Why'd *you* name it the Easy Dragon?'

'Oh, that was a mistake. The sign painter misunderstood me on the telephone. So after all the signs were painted, I figured why bother changing it to what I wanted originally?'

'What had you wanted originally?'

'The place was supposed to be called the Easy Drag

Inn.' He shrugged. 'Listen, people goof all the time. That's why they've got erasers on penc—' and he stopped himself before uttering the banality.

'Well, come on, Bob,' Meyer said. 'Thanks a lot for your time, mister.'

'Not at all. Think you'll get her?'

'All we want to do is get *him*,' Meyer said.

All I want to do, the sniper thought, *is get him*.

What's taking them so long in there? How many pictures do they have to snap, anyway?

He looked at his watch.

They had been inside the shop for forty minutes already. Weren't they due back at the house? Shouldn't the reception be starting any minute? For God's sake, what was taking them so long?

The front door of the shop opened.

The sniper peered through the telescopic sight of the rifle, fixing the doorway smack on the intersection of the cross-hairs.

He waited.

One by one, the wedding party began pouring through the open door of the shop.

Where the hell was Tommy Giordano?

Was that . . . ? No. Not him.

There now, there's the bride . . . there's . . .

Tommy appeared in the doorway. The sniper held his breath.

One, two . . . now!

He squeezed the trigger, pulling off two shots in rapid succession.

From the street, the shots sounded like the backfire of an automobile. Already inside one of the limousines,

Carella didn't even hear them. Both slugs struck the brick wall to the left of the doorjamb and then ricocheted into the air, spent. Tommy, unaware, ran to the first car and climbed in with his bride.

The sniper cursed as the cars pulled away.

Then he packed his rifle.

7.

AT ONE END of Tony Carella's lot, close to the Carella-Birnbaum property line and to the left of the fireworks stage, Weddings-Fêtes, Incorporated, had constructed a bandstand. Hung with white bunting, adorned with flowers, it provided a magnificent setting for the local band Tony had hired. The band was called the Sal Martino Orchestra. The band – or the 'orchestra' as Sal preferred to call it – consisted of:

One piano player
One drummer
Four saxophonists (two tenor men and two alto men)
Two trumpeters (one lead trumpeter and one second
    trumpeter)
And a trombonist

Actually, the ensemble would have been complete – oh, sure, the rhythm section *could* have used a bass player, but why be picky – would have been complete without the trombonist. A two-man brass section in an eight-piece band (orchestra, that is) was certainly enough brass power. The lead trumpeter would carry the section, and the second trumpeter would handle all the hot solos and screech work. Since the band (orchestra, of course) had a full sax section each member of which doubled on clarinet, the two trumpets would have afforded a well-balanced complement of brass. There really was no need for the trombone.

Sal Martino played the trombone.

He also played the French horn, but never on jobs. He restricted his French horning to the privacy of his bedroom. In all fairness, he was not a bad French hornist, nor was he a bad trombonist. It was just that the band needed him the way they needed a flatted fifth. Or an augmented seventh. The band preferred their chords to be simple and major. A diminished ninth could throw their rehearsals into a tizzy for a solid week. Simplicity was the keynote of the Sal Martino Orchestra. And simplicity certainly did not call for a trombonist in the brass section. But such are the vagaries of leadership.

Besides, Sal Martino looked like a real pro when he was up there leading the band. He was a man in his late twenties, with a high crown of black hair and a small black moustache. His eyes were blue and very soulful. He had broad shoulders and a narrow waist and long legs which he wobbled with Presley-like ease while conducting. He sometimes conducted with his right hand. He sometimes conducted with the end of his trombone. He sometimes simply smiled out at the crowd and didn't conduct at all. Whichever way he did it, the band sounded the same.

Lousy.

Well, not lousy. But pretty bad.

They sounded especially bad when they were tuning up, but then all bands sound bad when they are taking their *A* from the piano player. At 4.45 that afternoon, the Martino Orchestra was warming up and tuning up and sounding very much like the Boston Pops Symphony minus the Boston and minus the Symphony. Hawes, a music lover by nature, could barely sit still as he listened to the cacophony. He was also slightly disturbed by the fact that neither Sam Jones nor Ben Darcy was yet in evidence anywhere on the grounds. In truth, it was becoming increasingly more difficult to locate *anyone* in the Carella back-yard. Immediately following the ceremony, the Carella household had been overrun by wedding guests who hugged and embraced and kissed each other as if they had not seen each other since the last wedding or funeral – which, in all probability, they hadn't. The bedroom and adjoining bathroom on the main floor of the Carella home had been set aside for the female guests, another similar set-up upstairs having been made available for the gentlemen. As soon as all the embracing and kissing was concluded, the women trotted into the downstairs bedroom to freshen up, so that there was a constant flow of traffic from back-yard to back porch to bedroom to bathroom and out again. Hawes was getting somewhat dizzy. In all that sea of strange faces, he longed only to see the vaguely familiar faces of Darcy and Jones, but for the time being he seemed to have lost them completely.

'What's the matter?' Christine asked him.

'I'm just wondering where Darcy and Jones went.'

'Oh, they're probably around somewhere.'

'Yes. But where?'

'Have you tried the men's room?'

'No.'

'Why don't you?'

'All right, I will. Don't pick up any stray men while I'm gone.'

'Now, Cotton, would *I* do a thing like that?'

'Yes.'

He went into the house. A woman coming out of the bedroom said to another woman, 'She's pregnant *again*, can you imagine it? I haven't been to a wedding in the past five years that she hasn't been pregnant.'

'She likes children,' her friend said.

'*That* isn't what she likes,' the woman said, and they both laughed hysterically, almost bumping into Hawes as he made his way to the steps.

'Oh, excuse *me*,' the first woman said. Tittering, they went out of the house. Hawes climbed upstairs. The bedroom was cluttered with near and distant relatives of the Carellas and Giordanos. A tall, blue-eyed blond man lounging against the doorjamb said, 'Full house, Mac.'

'Mmm,' Hawes said. 'I'll wait.'

'We got a choice?' the blond said.

'The Thunderbird ain't a sports car,' a man near them said to his friend. 'And neither is the Corvette. I got news for you, Charlie. There ain't no such animal as an American sports car.'

'No?' Charlie said. 'Then how come they call them sports cars?'

'What do you want they should call them: armoured tanks? You know something?'

'What?' Charlie said.

'When a *real* sports-car owner passes an American sports car on the road, he don't even wave.'

'So what?'

'So that's the sign of courtesy, like tipping your hat to a broad. And they don't do it. Because American sports cars ain't sports cars. They're considered like cockroaches on the road. That's a fact.'

'Then what's a sports car?' Charlie asked.

'An M.G., or a Jaguar, or a Talbot, or an Alfa-Romeo, or a Ferrari, or Ghia or . . .'

'All right, all right,' Charlie said.

'. . . or a Mercedes-Benz, or a . . .'

'All right,' Charlie said, 'I come up here to go to the john, not to hear a lecture about foreign cars.'

The door to the bathroom opened. A slender man wearing eye-glasses stepped out, zipping up his fly.

'Anybody else in there?' Hawes asked him.

'What?'

'In the bathroom.'

'No,' the bespectacled man said. 'Of course not. Who else would be in there with me?' He paused. Indignantly, he said, 'Who are you?'

'Water Commissioner,' Hawes said. 'Just checking.'

'Oh.' The man paused. 'Everything okay?'

'Yes, fine, thank you.' He took a last look around the bedroom. No. No Darcy or Jones. He was starting downstairs again when a cheer went up from the backyard. For a moment, Hawes thought the caterers had struck oil. And then he realized what it was.

'They're here!' someone shouted. 'They're here!'

And at that instant, Sal Martino's orchestra began playing *Here Comes the Bride*. Hawes joined the general exodus down the steps. Women were pouring out of the downstairs bedroom. Children were screaming and giggling, rushing on to the back porch, anxious for a glimpse of the newly-arrived bride and groom. Sighing, Hawes vowed never to get married.

When he got out to the porch at last, he found Christine talking to Sam Jones.

'Well, well,' he said, 'this is a surprise. Where've you been, Jonesy?'

'Why? Someone looking for me?'

'No, I was just curious.'

'Oh, I've been roaming around,' Jonesy said.

Hawes looked at him curiously and sceptically. Sal Martino's boys were pounding out their third chorus of *Here Comes the Bride*. The music trailed off lamely as the piano player attempted a modulation into another key. Failing, he blinked helplessly at Martino who gave the band a one-two-three count and, waving his trombone frantically, led them into *Let Me Call You Sweetheart*.

The master of ceremonies, supplied by the caterers, rushed on to the floor, directing Tommy to dance with Angela. He needed no prompting.

'Best man!' the caterer shouted. 'Maid of honour!'

'Excuse me,' Jonesy said, and he rushed over to the long wooden rectangle which had been put down as a dance-floor, ringed in by the long white tables. He took the maid of honour into his arms, and the M.C. beamed happily and then began pairing off ushers and bridesmaids, Tony and Louisa Carella, Steve and Teddy, and anyone else he saw in a tuxedo or a gown. The band *segued* into *Always*, and the M.C. beamed some more, and then pulled Angela from Tommy's grasp and shoved her into Jonesy's arms, filling the void with the maid of honour whom Tommy accepted with a slightly dismayed smile. Ushers and bridesmaids began changing partners. Paunch to paunch, Tony Carella and his daughter-in-law whirled about the floor. Louisa Carella found herself in her son's arms.

'So?' Carella said. 'Are you happy, Mom?'

'Yes. It was a beautiful wedding, Stevie. You should have got married in church.'

'Now, stop it.'

'All right, you big atheist.'

'I'm not.'

'You don't go to church.'

'I work on Sundays.'

'Only sometimes.'

The band had somehow successfully modulated into *The Anniversary Waltz*. The M.C. waved his arms at the people lining the dance-floor, and they began filtering on to it, two by two, joining the wedding party. Tommy politely but firmly deposited the maid of honour into Jonesy's grip and pulled his bride to him. A tall red-headed girl in a green silk dress, which had surely been applied with a spray gun, suddenly broke away from her partner and shouted, 'Steve! Steve Carella!'

Carella turned. The redhead's voice was not exactly what he'd have called dulcet. It boomed across the dance-floor with all the energy of a nuclear explosion. Teddy Carella, dancing with her father-in-law, happened to turn just as the redhead threw her arms around Carella's neck and planted a kiss on his mouth.

Carella blinked.

'Steve,' the redhead said, 'don't you remember me? Don't you remember Faye?'

Carella seemed to be having a little difficulty with the memory. He seemed also to be having a little difficulty with Faye herself whose arms were still firmly entwined about his neck. The green silk dress, in addition to having been sprayed on, was cut low in the

86

front, very low. Glancing over the girl's shoulder, Carella saw Teddy whirl by in his father's arms, and he saw a frown beginning on her face.

'I ... I ...' he stammered, 'don't seem to ...'

'New Jersey?' the girl prompted. 'Flemington? The wedding? Don't you remember? Oh, how we danced!'

Dimly, Carella remembered a wedding years and years ago. God, he must have been eighteen and yes, there was a redhead, a slender, bosomy girl of seventeen, and yes, he'd danced with her all night, and yes, her name was Faye, and oh my God!

'Hello, Faye,' he said weakly.

'Come!' Faye commanded. 'Dance with me! You don't mind, do you, Mrs Carella?'

'No,' Louisa said, 'but ...' and she shot an apprehensive glance across the floor to Teddy, who was craning her neck over her shoulder to observe any new developments.

Faye pulled Carella to her. She threw her left arm up around his neck and Carella was overpowered by the scent of a heady perfume which drifted into his nostrils. Faye put her cheek against his.

'How have you been, Steve?' she asked.

And Carella answered, 'Married.'

Across the floor, Ben Darcy cut in on Tommy Giordano. Tommy, surprised, did not relinquish his bride for a moment.

'Come on,' Ben said, smiling. 'You've got to share the wealth.'

Graciously, Tommy bowed and handed Angela to Ben. They danced in silence for several moments.

Then Ben said, 'Happy?'

'Yes.'

'Do you love him?'

'Oh, yes,' Angela said. 'Yes, yes!'

'I used to hope . . . well, you know.'

'What, Ben?'

'We saw an awful lot of each other when we were kids, Angela.'

'Yes, I know.'

'You told me you loved me.'

'I know I did. We were kids, Ben.'

'I loved you, Angela.'

'Ben—'

'I've never met another girl like you, do you know that?'

'I think they'll be serving soon. Maybe we'd better—'

'Never a girl as pretty as you, or as smart as you, or as warm and exciting as—'

'Ben, please!'

'I'm sorry, Angela. It's just . . . I used to think this would be us. It could have been us, you know.'

'Everyone grows up, Ben.'

'Angela, you once said . . . when we were younger . . . when you first met Tommy . . . I called you, I remember, and you told me it was all over between us. Do you remember that?'

'Yes, Ben. I do.'

'You shouldn't have ended it on the telephone. Not after what we'd been to each other.'

'I'm sorry. I suppose . . . I just wanted it to be clean, Ben. Over with. Done. I didn't want one of those long, drawn-out—'

'I know, I know. And okay, I don't mind. But . . . when I was talking to you on the phone, I said if . . . if anything ever went wrong between you and Tommy, I'd be waiting. Remember that?'

'Yes. I remember.'

'And you said, "All right, Ben. I'll keep that in mind." Do you remember saying that?'

'It was such a long time ago, Ben. I really don't—'

'I'm still waiting, Angela.'

'What?'

'If anything should go wrong, if anything at all should happen between you, I'll be here. You can count on me. I'll take you in a minute, Angela. I loved you once, Angela, and I still—'

'Ben, please stop it. Please.'

'Just remember. I'll be waiting for you. I'll be waiting, Angela.'

The Green Corner was a tree-shaded house with a winding walk lined with azalea bushes in full bloom. Meyer and O'Brien walked leisurely to the front door and rang the bell.

'Coming,' a voice said, and they waited as footsteps approached the door. The door opened. A wispy little woman in a dark-blue dress stood there, smiling. From somewhere in the house, a dog began barking.

'Hello,' she said.

'Hello,' Meyer answered. 'Are you the lady of the house?'

'My, do they send salesmen around on Sundays, too?' the little woman asked.

'No, we're from the police,' Meyer said. The smile dropped from the little woman's mouth. 'Now, don't be alarmed,' he added hastily. 'We only wanted to—'

'I'm only the dog-sitter,' the little woman said. 'I

don't even live here. I don't know anything about any lawbreaking that's been going on. I come to sit with the dog, that's all.'

'No one's broken any law,' O'Brien said. 'We only wanted to ask some questions, lady.'

'Well, I don't know anything about anyone who lives here. I only sit with the dog. His name is Butch, and he tears up the furniture if they leave him alone, he gets so lonely and miserable. So I sit with him. Butch is the only one I know here.'

'Do you know the owners of the house?'

'Mr and Mrs Travers, yes, but not so good as I know Butch. Butch is a Golden Retriever, but he chews up the furniture. Which is why—'

'Know any of the roomers?'

'Yes, there's old Mr Van Ness on the top floor, but he's out right now. And there's Mrs Wittley, but she's out, too. And then there's the new girl, Oona Blake, but she's out, too. And I don't know any of them real good except Butch. He's the only reason I come over here. I'm one of the best dog-sitters in the neighbourhood.'

'This Oona Blake,' O'Brien said. 'Is it Miss or Mrs?'

'Miss, of course. Why, she's just a young girl.'

'How old?'

'Not thirty yet, I would say.'

'You said she's out right now. Do you know what time she left?'

'Yes. Early this morning. I know because the Traverses are away for the week-end which is why I'm sitting with Butch. I got here yesterday. And I was here this morning when Miss Blake left.'

'What time would you say that was?'

'Right after breakfast. I also make the meals when the Traverses are gone.'

'Did anyone call for her?'

'Who? Mrs Travers?'

'No. Miss Blake.'

'Oh. Oh, yes. As a matter of fact, someone did.'

'Who?'

'Don't know him. I told you, I don't know much of the goings-on here. You ask me, the Traverses run this place too loose. Too loose.'

'Was the man carrying anything?'

'What man?'

'The one who picked up Miss Blake.'

'Oh. Him. Yes, he was. A trombone case.'

'A trombone case? Not a trumpet? Or a saxophone?'

'No, a trombone. Don't I know a trombone when I see one? A long black case. Oh, it was a trombone, all right.'

'What did he look like?'

'I didn't get a good look. He was sitting in the parlour waiting for her, and the shades were drawn. But I saw the trombone case leaning against the arm-chair.' The little woman paused. 'She won't be here long, anyway. That Oona Blake.'

'What makes you say that?'

'I was dog-sitting last week. She got three calls in the same day. All from the same place. A real-estate agent. She'll be moving soon, that one.'

'Which real-estate agent? Do you recall the name?'

'Certainly. She got three calls in the same day. Besides, it isn't far from here.'

'What's the name?' O'Brien asked.

'Pullen Real Estate. It's the next elevated stop from here. Right on the corner, under the station.'

'Can you tell us what Oona Blake looks like?' Meyer asked.

'Yes, certainly. But I don't really know very much about her. Where shall I start?'

'What was she wearing when she left here this morning?'

'A red silk dress, rather low cut. Red high-heeled pumps. No stockings. A little sort of red feather in her hair, with a rhinestone clip.'

'Was she carrying a purse?'

'One of these small things that all you can fit into are a compact and lipstick and a few odds and ends.'

'Was that red, too?'

'No. It was a dark blue. Sequins, I believe.'

'And how would you describe *her*?'

'She's a blonde. I think it's natural. She's very well developed. If you ask me, she's got a thyroid condition. Anyway, she's a very big girl. Noisy, I guess. Or perhaps she just talks loud. She's very pretty, I would say. Blue eyes. She gives an impression of . . . I don't know . . . being strong, I guess. She's got a nice smile and a pretty nose. Does that help?'

'Yes. Thank you very much.'

'You going to that real-estate office now?'

'Yes.'

'I wouldn't. He's closed on Sundays.'

The girl dancing with Bert Kling was wearing a red silk dress and red high-heeled pumps. She wore a red feather in her hair, and the feather tickled Kling's cheek as he manoeuvred her over the makeshift dance-floor. People were beginning to filter to the tables where cocktails had been placed at each setting. Kling was beginning to feel a little hungry. Perhaps it was the way the girl danced, with a sort of nervous, pushing energy that demanded all his leading skill to counter. She was a very busty girl, and she danced quite close, her long blonde hair brushing his cheek. She seemed quite feminine and lovely – even though she was a big girl – but there was none the less this pushing quality about her which gave him the feeling that *she* was leading *him* around the dance-floor. The strength seemed in direct contradiction to the blue eyes and lovely smile which had first attracted him to her. The eyes and the smile had been totally female. The dancing was the footwork of a steel magnate, a person with something to do, a person anxious to get it done.

The band, once one got used to it, wasn't really half bad. Playing a medley of fox-trots, they moved smoothly from one number to the next, keeping a steady danceable beat. Sal Martino had put his trombone on a chair which rested on the bandstand alongside him, and he led the orchestra with his right hand, smiling out at the crowd occasionally. Waiters rushed across the lawn carrying drinks. Kling's eyes moved across the dance-floor. Ben Darcy was still dancing with Angela. The pair seemed to be having an argument. Steve Carella was dancing with a redhead who'd undoubtedly leaped from the pages of *Playboy* although, Kling mused, the same observation could probably be made about the blonde who was pushing him around the floor. Teddy Carella didn't look too damn happy about the inflammable girl in the green dress. Cotton Hawes didn't look too happy, either.

Dismally, he watched Christine Maxwell dancing with Sam Jones.

This is one hell of a wedding, Kling thought. Everybody bursting with joy. Even Steve looks pretty gloomy, though I can't see why that redhead should make any man gloomy.

'I don't think I know your name,' Kling said to the blonde in the red dress.

'You don't,' she answered. Her voice was deep and husky.

'Mine's Bert.'

'Nice to know you,' the blonde said.

He waited for her to offer her name. When she didn't, he let it pass. What the hell, if a girl didn't want to give her name, there was no sense forcing her. Besides, he told himself in deference to his fiancée, he was only dancing so that he wouldn't look conspicuous standing on the side-lines.

'You a relative?' he asked.

'No.' The girl paused. 'Are you?'

'No.' Kling paused. 'Friend of the bride?'

The girl hesitated for just a fraction of a second. Then she said, 'Yes.'

'Nice wedding,' Kling said.

'Lovely,' the girl agreed, and she continued to push him around the floor as if in a hurry to get nowhere particularly fast.

On the bandstand, Sal Martino leaned over to pick up his trombone.

From the corner of his eye, Kling caught the movement. He turned to face the band-leader. Sal's coat fell open as he picked up the horn. He stood up quickly then, the horn in his hands.

Kling's arm tightened involuntarily around the blonde's waist.

'Hey,' she said. 'Easy does it, boy.'

Kling released her. 'Excuse me, miss,' he said, and he left her standing in the middle of the dance-floor.

Teddy Carella sat at the table alongside the bride's table, sipping disconsolately at a Manhattan, watching her husband cavort in the arms of a red-headed sexpot from Flemington, New Jersey.

This is not fair, she thought angrily. There is no competition here. I don't know who that damn girl is, or what she wants – although what she wants seems pretty apparent – but I do know that she is svelte and trim and wearing a dress designed for a size eight. Since she is at least a ten, and possibly a twelve, the odds are stacked against me to begin with. I am at least a size fifty-four right now. When will this baby come? Next week did the doctor say? Yes, next week. Next week and four thousand years from now. I've been big forever. I hope it's a boy. Mark, if it's a boy. Mark Carella. That's a good name.

Steve, you don't have to hold her so damn close!

I mean, *really*, goddamnit!

And April if it's a girl.

I wonder if I should faint or something. That would bring him back to the table in a hurry, all right. Although I can't really say that *he's* holding her close because *she* seems to be doing all the holding. But I guess holding works both ways, and don't think this has been easy on me, Steve, my pet, and you really needn't . . . Steve! If your hand moves another inch, I am going to crown you with a champagne bottle!

She watched as Bert Kling pushed his way through the dancers, heading for her husband.

Is he going to cut in? she wondered.

And then Kling's hand clamped down on Carella's shoulder, and he backed away from the redhead as Kling whispered something in his ear.

Carella blinked.

'What? What did you say?'

In a hurried whisper, Kling repeated, 'The band-leader! He's carrying a gun under his coat!'

8.

SAL MARTINO DIDN'T look very happy at all.

The detectives had waited until the intermission and then, as the waiters began serving the shrimp cocktail, they'd approached the bandstand, asked him to accompany them, and led him upstairs to a small bedroom in the Carella house. They stood before him in a three-man semicircle, now, Hawes, Carella, and Kling. Their faces were humourless and grim.

'Why are you carrying a gun?' Carella said.

'Who wants to know?' Sal answered.

'I do. I'm a detective. Do you want to see my badge?'

'Yes. I do. What is this, anyway?'

Carella flipped open his wallet. 'It's a few questions, Sal,' he said. 'We want to know about that gun under your jacket. Now what the hell are you doing with a gun?'

Sal studied the shield. 'That's my business,' he said. 'You got no right to ask me. What the hell is this? A police state?'

'Give me the gun,' Carella said.

'What for?'

'Give it to me!' he snapped.

Sal dug into the shoulder holster under his jacket.

'Butt first,' Carella said.

Sal handed him the gun. Carella looked at it, and then gave it to Hawes. 'An Iver Johnson .22,' he said.

'Protector Sealed Eight,' Hawes agreed, and he sniffed the barrel.

'What the hell are you smelling?' Sal wanted to know. 'That hasn't been fired in years.'

'Why are you carrying it?' Carella asked.

'That's my business.'

'It's my business, too,' Carella shouted. 'Now don't get snotty with me, Martino. Answer the questions!'

'I told you. Why I carry a gun is my business and my business alone. And you can go straight to hell!'

'Did you ever try playing the trombone with a busted arm?' Hawes asked quietly.

'What?'

'*Why are you carrying a gun?*' Hawes shouted.

'I got a permit.'

'Let's see it.'

'I don't have to show you nothing.'

'If you've got a permit, show it,' Kling said. 'Because if you don't, I'm going straight to that telephone and call the local precinct, and you can explain it all to them in the squadroom. Now how about it, Martino?'

'I told you I got a permit.'

'Then let's see it!'

'All right, all right, hold your water. I don't have to show it to you, you know. I'm doing you a favour.'

'You're doing yourself a favour, Martino. If you've got a permit and can't show it, you lose it. That's the law. Now let's see it.'

'You invent your own laws, don't you?' Martino said, digging into his wallet.

'Is it carry or premises?'

'It's carry. You think I'd be lugging a gun around with a premises permit?'

'Where is it?'

'Just a minute, just a minute,' Martino said. He pulled a document out of his wallet and then unfolded it. He handed it to Carella. 'There,' he said. 'You satisfied now?'

The document was divided into three sections separated by perforated folding edges. It was printed on a dull shade of off-pink paper. Its outer edges were serrated. Each section measured $4\frac{1}{2}$ inches by $3\frac{3}{4}$ inches. Carella took the small official-looking document from Martino and studied the first section.

Carella read each item carefully. Then he turned the permit over to read its reverse side:

The third section of the permit simply granted Martino permission to purchase a pistol and was signed by the same Riverhead magistrate, Arthur K. Weidman.

Carella knew at once that the permit was legitimate. He none the less took his sweet time examining it. He turned it over in his big hands as if it were a questionable international document prepared by Russian spies. He studied the signature, and he studied the thumb print, and he made a great show of comparing the serial number on the permit with the number stamped into the metal of Martino's .22.

Then he handed both gun and permit back to the trombonist.

'Now suppose you tell us why you carry it, Sal?'

'I don't have to. The permit is enough. I got a gun, and I got a permit for it, and that's all you have to know. If you don't mind, I'm supposed to play some dinner music.'

CITY BUREAU OF PISTOL PERMITS

23784

DATE June 9 1958   LICENSE TO __Carry__ PISTOL IS HEREBY GRANTED

TO __Salvatore Albert Martino__

STREET ADDRESS __583 Avalon Avenue__

CITY OR TOWN __Riverhead__

OCCUPATION __Musician__

EMPLOYED BY __Self-employed__

NATIONALITY __U.S.A.__

AGE __28__   HEIGHT __5'9"__   WEIGHT __157__

Arthur K. Weidman
MUNICIPAL MAGISTRATE, RIVERHEAD

This license is issued under the following conditions:
1. It is good until revoked.
2. It is revocable at any time.
3. It is VOID for any defacement or change on permit. Holder of VOID permit subject to Penal Law, Section 1897.
4. It is restricted to ~~target shooting~~, present employment, or _____
5. To add additional guns, apply for amended permit.

Salvatore A. Martino
SIGNATURE OF HOLDER

Make	Caliber	Number
Iver Johnson	.22	326912

Thumb Print

100

'The dinner music can wait. Answer the question, Sal!' Kling said.

'I don't have to.'

'We'd better pull him in,' Hawes said.

'Pull me in? What for?' Martino yelled.

'For refusing to cooperate with a duly appointed officer of the peace,' Hawes yelled right off the top of his head.

'Okay, okay, okay,' Martino said in rising crescendo. 'Okay.'

'Well?'

'I'm scared.'

'What?'

'I'm scared. I play on jobs, and sometimes I don't get home till three, four in the morning. I'm scared. I don't like to walk the streets so late at night carrying money and my horn. I'm scared, okay? So I applied for a pistol permit, and I got it. Because I'm scared, okay? Okay? Does that answer your goddamn question?'

'It answers us,' Carella said, and he looked somewhat shamefacedly at his colleagues. 'You'd better get back to the band.'

Martino folded his pistol permit in half and then shoved it back into his wallet, alongside his driver's licence.

'There's no law against being afraid,' he said.

'If there were,' Carella answered, 'we'd all be in jail.'

Pullen Alec, drug sndries, 18 N 117..TYler 8-9670
Pullen Charles, 3312 LaFontaine..ADdison 2-1074
Pullen Donald, rl est & ins
              131 Pondigo....MAynard 4-6700
      res 4251 Archer..........MAynard 4-3812

'Here it is,' Meyer Meyer called to the counter. 'Donald Pullen, 131 Pondigo Street ... no, wait, that's the office. It's 4251 Archer. That's around here, isn't it?'

'Search me,' O'Brien said. 'We'd better ask a cop. You looked up the number too fast, Meyer. I haven't finished my coffee yet.'

'Well, hurry up.'

Patiently, Meyer waited for O'Brien to gulp down his coffee.

'I've been thirsting for this cup of coffee all day,' O'Brien said. 'I've got to work out that problem with Miscolo. Do you think maybe I can subtly hint that he change brands or something?'

'I don't think that'd work, Bob.'

'No, I don't think so, either.'

'Why don't you bring your own coffee-pot to the office? And buy yourself a hot plate? One of those single-burner jobs.'

'Gee, that sounds like a good idea,' O'Brien said. 'Except for one thing.'

'What's that?'

'I don't know how to make coffee.'

'Ah right, come on, drink up.'

O'Brien finished his coffee. Together, they walked out to the unmarked police sedan parked at the kerb.

'4251 Archer,' Meyer said. 'We'll ask the first traffic cop we see.'

They did not see a cop for ten blocks. They pulled over to him and asked him where Archer Street was.

'Archer Avenue, you mean?'

'Yes, I guess so.'

'So say what the hell you mean. And pull over to the kerb. You're blocking traffic!'

'We only want to know . . .'

'I know what you want to know. You giving me an argument?'

'No, sir,' Meyer said, and he pulled to the kerb and waited while the cop directed the cars behind him. Finally, the cop walked over to the car.

'Don't you know better than to stop in the middle of the street?' he asked.

'I wasn't thinking, Officer,' Meyer said.

'Sure. Now what was it you wanted to know?'

'How to get to Archer Avenue.'

'Two blocks down and turn right. What number did you want?'

'4251,' Meyer said.

'Another three blocks after you make the turn.' He glanced at the oncoming traffic. 'Okay, go ahead.' As they pulled away, he shouted, *'And don't stop in the middle of the street no more, you hear me, mister?'*

'Nice fellow,' Meyer said.

'Gives cops a bad name,' O'Brien said glumly.

'Why? He helped us, didn't he?'

'Bad disposition,' O'Brien said, and Meyer made his right turn. 'Three blocks from here, right?'

'Right,' Meyer said. They drove up the street leisurely and stopped before 4251. 'Here it is. Let's hope he's home.'

4251 Archer, as were most of the dwellings in Riverhead, was a private house. Meyer and O'Brien went up the front walk and pulled the door knocker. A tall man in a white shirt and a red weskit answered the door.

'Yes, gentlemen,' he said, 'can I help you?'

'Mr Pullen?' Meyer said.

'Yes?' Pullen studied his visitors. 'Is it real estate, or insurance?'

'We'd like to ask you some questions, Mr Pullen. We're from the police.'

'Police?' Pullen went white in the space of two seconds. 'Wh – wh – what . . . what did—?'

'May we come in, Mr Pullen?'

'Yes. Yes, come in.' Hastily, Pullen glanced past them to make sure none of his neighbours were watching. 'Come in.'

They followed him into the house and into the living-room. The room was done in heavy furniture covered with maroon mohair. It made the small interior seem hotter than it really was.

'Sit down,' Pullen said. 'What's this all about?'

'Have you been receiving or making phone calls to a Miss Oona Blake?'

'Why, yes.' Pullen looked surprised, and then relieved. 'Oh, it's about *her*, is it? Not me? Her?'

'Yes, it's about her.'

'I knew she was a tough customer. I knew it the minute I laid eyes on her. A very flashy person. Very flashy. What is she? A prostitute?'

'No, we don't know what she is. We'd simply like to find out what the nature of her business with you was.'

'Why, real estate,' Pullen said. 'What did you think? She wanted to rent an apartment.'

'Where?'

'Well, she was very specific about it. She wanted an apartment either facing 831 Charles Avenue or else *behind* 831 Charles Avenue. That's just a little ways from here. Charles Avenue.'

'That rings a bell,' Meyer said. He thought for a

104

moment. 'Sure. That's where Steve's parents live. Did Miss Blake say why she wanted an apartment near that address?'

'Said she had friends there.'

'I see. Did you get an apartment for her?'

'Nope. Not that one. But I *was* able to fill her other request. Yep, I gave her good service on that one.'

'Which one was that?' O'Brien asked.

Pullen smiled. 'Why, the apartment she wanted near the photography studio.'

'What a dinner!' Birnbaum said. 'Tony, you outdid yourself. What a wedding, what a dinner!'

'Birnbaum, have some champagne,' Tony said. 'We got enough champagne here to start a France. Have some champagne, my friend.' He led Birnbaum to the ice mermaid and pulled a bottle from her frozen tub. Everywhere around him, champagne corks were popping, and each new pop filled Tony's heart with joy. It really was getting to be a fine wedding. Maybe all the money those lousy Incorporateds were getting would be worth it after all. He tore the gold foil from the neck of the bottle and then ripped the wire loose. Working the cork with his thumbs, he slowly edged it out of the bottle. Standing next to him, Birnbaum put his fingers in his ears. The cork moved out of the bottle neck.

'POP!' Tony shouted, and the cork exploded from the bottle at the same instant, white bubbles following it out of the green neck, spilling on to Tony's thick fingers. Birnbaum clapped Tony on the back, and they began laughing uproariously. The band was playing louder, and Jody Lewis was running all over the lawn popping his flash-bulbs, capturing the bride and groom for posterity. He followed them to the long bridal table where the ancient and time-honoured custom of collecting the connubial loot was about to take place. Angela made a beautiful hostess for the receiving line. Tommy sat beside her, grinning from ear to ear, and Jody Lewis kept the shutter clicking as the relatives filed past to kiss the bride and wish her luck, to shake hands with the groom and congratulate him. During the shaking of hands, a gratuity, a present, a ten-dollar bill or a twenty-dollar bill in an envelope was pressed into Tommy's hand.

'Congratulations,' the well-wishers said, slightly embarrassed by the handing over of money, a civilized gesture with all the inherent savagery of primitive times, the spoils offered to the newly-crowned king. And Tommy, in turn, was embarrassed as he accepted the gifts because there is nothing more difficult to do than accept a gift with style, and Tommy was too young to have acquired style. 'Thank you,' he muttered over and over again. 'Thank you, thank you.'

The champagne corks kept exploding.

'The trouble with this stuff,' Birnbaum says, 'is it makes you want to go to the bathroom.'

'So go,' Tony said.

'I will.'

'Right upstairs. The bedroom at the end of the—'

'No, no. Too crowded up there,' Birnbaum said. 'I'll run over to my own house.'

'What? And miss the wedding?'

'It'll take a minute. It'll be quick. Don't worry, Tony, I'll be back. Just try to keep me away.'

'All right, Birnbaum. Hurry! Hurry!'

Birnbaum cocked his head to one side and started off through the bushes to his house on the next lot.

At the far end of the table, unobserved by either Angela or Tommy who were busy accepting gifts and good wishes, a pair of hands deposited a pair of small bottles filled with red wine. The bottles of wine were each tied with big bows. One bow was pink, the other was blue.

The pink bow had attached to it a card which read:

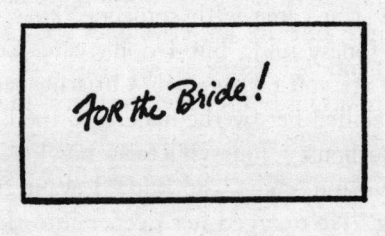

The blue bow had attached to it a similar card which, had Tommy seen it, might have struck a responsive chord. It is doubtful, however, that he would have recognized the handwriting as being identical with that on a card he'd received earlier in the day.

The card attached to the blue bow read, simply:

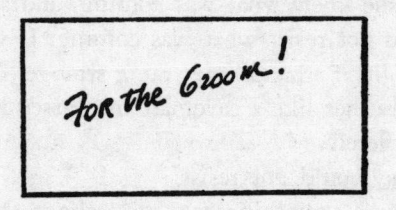

'Come with me,' Jonesy said to Christine.

'I came here with someone, you know,' Christine said

coyly. She was rather enjoying the game and, oddly because she had not wanted to come, she was enjoying the wedding, too. But particularly, she was enjoying the look of dismay which spread over Cotton's face whenever he saw her dancing with Sam Jones. The look was priceless. She enjoyed it more than the music, and more than the champagne, and more than the exploding corks, and the wonderful free feeling of gaiety which pervaded the outdoor reception.

'I know you came with someone. He's bigger than me, too,' Jonesy said, 'but I don't care. Come on.'

'Where are you taking me?' Christine said, giggling as Jonesy pulled her by the hand into the bushes at the side of the house. 'Jonesy! Really now!'

'Come, come, come,' he said. 'I want to show you something.' He dragged her deeper into the bushes on to a path which had been stamped down through constant walking through the short grass.

'What do you want to show me?'

'Let's get a little farther away from the festivities first,' he said. His hand on hers was tight. He pulled her along the path as if urgently propelled. Christine was not frightened. She was, in truth, slightly excited. She thought she knew what was coming, and she thought she would not resist what was coming. It would serve Cotton right if a handsome young stranger dragged her into the bushes like a caveman and kissed her soundly and completely.

No, she would not resist.

There was something very nice about the attention Sam Jones had showered upon her all afternoon, something reminiscent of a time when she'd been very young, when outdoor parties were standard fare every week-end during the summer. Now, running over the short grass with him, she looked forward to the kiss she knew was coming. She felt very youthful all at once, a young girl running through a tree-shaded lane, her feet dancing over the sunlight-speckled trampled path at the far end of the lot.

Jonesy stopped suddenly.

'Here,' he said. 'This should be far enough away, don't you think?'

'For what?' Christine asked. Oddly, her heart was pounding in her chest.

'Don't you know?' Jonesy said. He pulled her toward him, his back to the Carella property. Christine felt suddenly breathless. She lifted her mouth for his kiss, and someone suddenly screamed, and she felt goose pimples erupt over every inch of her body, and then she realized it was Jonesy who was screaming, screaming in a wildly masculine voice, and she pulled away from him and looked into his face and then turned to follow his glazed stare.

Not seven feet from where they were standing, a man lay face downward on the path. The man's back was covered with blood. The man was not breathing.

'Oh my God!' Jonesy said. 'It's Birnbaum!'

9.

THE TELEPHONE IN the squadroom was ringing insistently.

Hal Willis, alone, unbent from his doubled-over position alongside the water cooler and shouted, 'All right, all right, for Christ's sake! It never fails. A guy goes for a drink of water and . . . all right, I'm coming!' He threw water and paper cup into the trash basket and ran like hell for the phone, snatching it from the receiver.

'Hello!' he shouted. '87th Squad!' he shouted. 'Detective Willis speaking!' he shouted.

'I can hear you, Mac,' the voice said. 'I can almost hear you without the aid of the instrument, and I'm all the way down on High Street. Shall we try it again? *Pizzicato* this time?'

'You mean *diminuendo*, don't you?' Willis said softly.

'Whatever I mean, I think we all get the idea. This is Avery Atkins at the lab. Somebody up there sent a note down to us. We've been working on it.'

'What note?'

'It says "For the groom". Familiar with it?'

'Vaguely. What about it?'

'What did you say your name was, friend?'

'Willis. Hal Willis. Detective 3rd/Grade. Male, white, American.'

'*And* pretty snotty,' Atkins said.

'Listen, have you got information for me, or have you? I'm all alone here, and I've got a million things to do. So how about it?'

'Here it is. Catch it, wise guy. Paper used was five-and-dime stuff, trade name Skyline, sold over the counter all over the city at twenty-five cents for a package of ten cards and ten little envelopes. Go chase that one down. Ink used was Sheaffer's Skrip, number thirty-two, permanent jet black. Ditto over counters across the face of our fair city. You can chase that one down, too, wise guy. Which brings us to fingerprints. Two sets on the card, both lousy. One set belongs to a guy named Thomas Giordano. No record. Checked it through his service fingerprints, he was in the Army Signal Corps. The second set belongs to a guy named Stephen Louis Carella who, I understand, is a detective working for the magnificent 87th Squad. He ought to be careful where he lays his fat fingers. You had enough, smart guy?'

'I'm still listening,' Willis said.

'Comes to the handwriting itself, and there's a lot of crap here you don't have to know about unless you come up with a sample for comparison. There's only one thing you do have to know.'

'What's that?'

'Whoever sent this over asked us to run a handwriting comparison against the signature of one Martin Sokolin on whom we have a record at the I.B. We did that. And one thing's for sure.'

'And what's that?'

'Martin Sokolin didn't write that love note.'

The three detectives stood over the body of Joseph

Birnbaum. There was no pain, no joy, no sorrow on their faces. Impassively, they stared at death and whatever they felt was rigidly concealed behind the masks they wore for society.

Carella was the first to kneel.

'Shot him in the back,' he said. 'Bullet probably passed through to the heart. Killed him instantly.'

'That's my guess,' Hawes said, nodding.

'How come we didn't hear the shot?' Kling asked.

'All those champagne bottles going off. This is quite a distance from the house. The shot probably sounded like just another cork going off. Take a look around, will you, Bert? See if you can find the spent cartridge.'

Kling began thrashing through the bushes. Carella turned to Jonesy where he stood with Christine. His face was a pasty white. His hands, though he tried to control them, were trembling at his sides.

'Pull yourself together,' Carella said harshly. 'You can help us, but not the way you are now.'

'I . . . I . . . I can't help it,' Jonesy said. 'I . . . I feel like I'm going to collapse. That's why . . . why I sent Christine for you.'

'Is that why?' Hawes asked.

'I . . . I knew I couldn't make it myself.'

'Maybe it's a good thing,' Carella said. 'If you'd have erupted on to that lawn, you'd have busted up that wedding as sure as—'

'What were you doing back here, anyway?' Hawes said, and he looked at Christine angrily.

'We were taking a walk,' Jonesy said.

'Why here?'

'Why not?'

'Answer my question, damnit!' Hawes shouted. 'That

man there is dead, and you're the one who found the body, and I'd like to know just what the hell brought you back here? Coincidence?'

'Yes.'

'Why? What were you doing here?'

'Walking with Christine.'

'Cotton, we just—'

'I'll get to you, Christine,' Hawes said. 'Why'd you choose this path for a walk, Jones? So that you'd have a witness when you discovered the body?'

'What!'

'You heard me!'

'That's . . . that's prep — that's preposterous!'

'Is it? Then why'd you come back here?'

'So I could kiss Christine,' Jonesy blurted.

'And did you?' Hawes said venomously.

'Cotton—'

'Keep out of this, Christine. Did you kiss her?'

'What's this got to do with Birnbaum? What business is it of yours whether or not I—'

'When did you see the body?' Carella interrupted, annoyed because Hawes was dragging his interrogation down into the muck of a private and not a police matter.

'We were standing here,' Jonesy said. 'And I happened to see it.'

'You were just standing here?' Carella asked.

'I . . . I was going to kiss Christine.'

'Go on,' Carella said, and he watched Hawes's fists close into hard balls at his sides.

'I saw the body,' Jonesy said. 'And I – I screamed. And then I recognized it was Birnbaum.'

'Where does this path lead?' Hawes snapped.

'To Birnbaum's house. On the next lot.'

Kling came thrashing through the bushes. 'Here it is, Steve,' he said, and he held out the brass casing. Carella looked at it. The side of the casing was stamped '357 MAGNUM'. The back end of the casing had the lettering fixed in a circle:

In any case, there was no doubt about what kind of a gun had fired this particular cartridge. Either a Colt or a Smith & Wesson Magnum revolver.

'A Magnum,' Carella said. 'A big gun.'

'Not necessarily,' Hawes said. 'Smith & Wesson puts out a Magnum with a short three-and-half-inch barrel.'

'In any event, this casing lets out our friend Martino with his Iver Johnson .22.'

'Yeah. What do we do now, Steve?'

'Call Homicide, I guess. With three detectives on the scene, I don't think we ought to ring the local squad. Or should we?'

'I think we'd better.'

'Jesus, I'd hate like hell to break up the wedding.' He paused. 'I don't think Birnbaum would have wanted that, either.'

'Maybe we won't have to.'

'How do you figure?'

'This spot is pretty well protected from your father's lot. Maybe we can bring the photographers and the M.E. in through the next street, across Birnbaum's back-yard and through the bushes. What do you think?'

'I don't know,' Carella said.

'What precinct is this, anyway?'

'The 112th, I think.'

'Know anybody on the squad?'

'No. Do you?'

'No.'

'So what makes you think they'll do us a favour?'

'Professional courtesy. What the hell, it won't hurt asking. You only get married once.'

Carella nodded and looked down at the lifeless body of Joseph Birnbaum, the neighbour. 'You only die once, too,' he said. 'Come on, Jonesy, back to the house. You, too, Miss Maxwell. Few questions I'd like to ask both of you. Bert, you come back and call the 112th. Cotton, will you stay with the body?' He suspected that Hawes might be better equipped for the diplomacy necessary with the 112th Squad than Kling was. But at the same time, he didn't want a jealous male bellowing at an obviously frightened suspect while he questioned Jonesy and Christine further.

If Hawes appreciated Carella's tactic, he showed no sign of it. He simply nodded and went to stand alongside the prostrate Birnbaum as the rest started back for the house.

In the distance, Hawes could hear the sound of the band, the sound of voices raised in laughter, the tiny far-away pops of the champagne corks. Closer, the insects filled the woods with their myriad noises. He swatted at a fly which had settled on his nose, and then lighted a cigarette. The path, he noticed, took a sharp turn several feet beyond where Birnbaum was lying. Idly, Hawes walked to the bend in the path, surprised when the woods around him suddenly ended to become the open lawn of the Birnbaum back-yard. He glanced up at the Birnbaum house.

Something glinted in the attic window.

He looked again.

There was a sudden movement, and then the window presented nothing more than a blank open rectangle.

But Hawes was certain he'd seen a man with a rifle in that window a second ago.

A blonde in a red silk dress was sitting at the dressing table in the downstairs bedroom when Christine Maxwell entered the room. Carella had told her he wanted to question Jonesy alone and that he would get back to her shortly. She'd gone downstairs immediately in search of the ladies' room. She wasn't feeling at all well, and she wanted to wash her face and put on some fresh lipstick.

If anything, the blonde in the red silk dress made her feel worse.

As Christine put her small blue purse down on the dressing table, the blonde was adjusting her stocking, the red dress pulled back over her nylon, her magnificently turned leg rivalling that in any Hollywood boudoir scene. Standing beside the blonde in the tight, low-cut, overflowing-in-abundance red silk, standing beside the splendidly outstretched leg, Christine Maxwell felt suddenly skinny and awkward. She knew this was absurd. She'd always thought of herself as rather well-proportioned, capable of provoking a whistle or two on any street corner in the city. But the blonde who smoothed the nylon over her extended leg was so munificently endowed, so regally statuesque, that Christine suddenly imagined she'd been fooling herself all these years. The blonde tightened her garter, her shoulders and breasts bobbing with the movement. Fascinated, Christine watched the rippling flesh.

'You look kind of pale, honey,' the blonde said.

'What? Oh, yes. I guess I do.'

'Go out and have some of that whisky. Put the colour back into your cheeks.' She rose suddenly, looked at herself in the mirror, tucked a stray strand of hair back into place, and then said, 'There, it's all yours. I've got to see John.' She walked into the bathroom, closing and locking the door behind her.

Christine opened her purse, took out a comb, and began combing her hair. She did look pale. She'd better wash her face. God, that poor man lying in the path.

The bathroom door opened. 'Well, so long, dear,' the blonde said. She walked to the dressing table, snatched a purse from its top, and breezed out of the bedroom.

Apparently, she had not noticed that the purse she'd taken was Christine's.

Nor did Christine, in her agitated state, notice the error either.

Peering over the window-sill, the man in the attic room of Birnbaum's empty house saw Hawes glance up at the window and then glance up at it again. Quickly, he ducked below the sill.

He saw me, he thought.

He saw the rifle.

Now what?

Goddamnit, she knows she's supposed to keep anyone away from this house! Where the hell is she? Why isn't she doing what she's supposed to be doing?

He waited, listening.

He could hear the steady crunch of heavy feet across the lawn behind the house. Cautiously, he crawled on his hands and knees to the left of the window, and then stood up. He backed away from the window. From where he stood, he could not be seen from outside, but he had a clear view of the lawn and . . . yes, that man was heading for the house, walking across the lawn at a brisk clip.

What do I do? he wondered.

He listened.

The man was coming around the side of the house. He heard footsteps on the slate walk there, and then on the steps leading to the front porch, and then clomping across the porch to stop at the front door. There was no knock. Stealthily, the front door eased open, creaking on its hinges.

Silence.

In the attic room, the sniper waited. He could hear the footsteps again, carefully, quietly advancing through the silent house, toward the steps, hesitating on each tread, each creaking step bringing the intruder closer and closer to the attic room. Quickly, the sniper went to the door and stood just inside it. Quickly, he grasped the rifle by its barrel.

There were cautious footsteps in the corridor outside now.

He held his breath and waited.

The doorknob twisted almost imperceptibly.

The sniper swung the rifle back over his shoulder like a ball bat.

Gun in hand, Cotton Hawes kicked open the door to the attic, and the rifle moved in a sudden blurring arc, the butt catching him on the side of his face and knocking him senseless to the floor.

10.

THE STENCH OF cordite still hung in the air of the small room across the street from Jody Lewis's photography shop. Donald Pullen opened the door with his key and then said, 'Phew! What's that stink?'

'Cordite,' Meyer said immediately. The smell was as familiar to him as the scent of his wife, though not nearly so pleasant. 'Someone fired a gun in here, Bob.'

'Yeah,' O'Brien said, and immediately began looking for the spent shell casing.

Meyer went to the window. 'Nice view of the photography shop,' he said. He bent suddenly. 'Here it is, Bob.' He picked up the shell casing.

'Here's another one,' O'Brien said. He carried the casing to Meyer.

'Same gun,' Meyer said. 'A rifle.'

'Somebody fired a rifle in this room?' Pullen asked incredulously.

'It looks that way,' Meyer said.

'Why? Why would anybody fire a rifle in a small room like this?'

'A good guess might be in order to hit somebody going in or coming out of that photography shop across the street. You said Miss Blake specifically requested an apartment near the photography shop, didn't you?'

'Why, yes! That's amazing,' Pullen said. 'That certainly is amazing deduction.'

'Elementary,' Meyer said grandly, and Bob O'Brien stifled a laugh. 'Let's look around, Bob. A rifle doesn't particularly strike me as the kind of weapon a woman would choose. What do you think?'

'I never think on Sundays,' O'Brien said, but he began looking over the apartment. The place had a look of impermanence to it. There was a bed with brass bedstead against one wall, a night-table standing alongside it. A basin and a pitcher of water rested on the table. A floor lamp stood behind a worn easy chair in one corner of the room. A curtained closet was on the wall opposite the window. Beside that was the door leading to a tiny bathroom. O'Brien went into the bathroom and opened the medicine chest. It was empty. He pulled back the curtain on the closet and looked at the empty hangers.

'Whoever was here was travelling light,' he remarked.

'Any signs of a woman?' Meyer said. 'Lipstick tissues? Bobby pins? Long hairs?'

'Not even a sign of a human,' O'Brien said. 'Wait a minute, here's something.' He lifted an ash-tray from the night-table. 'A cigar butt. Know any dames who smoke cigars?'

'Anne Baxter and Hermione Gingold,' Meyer said. 'Think they also fire rifles?'

'Maybe. But most actresses don't perform on Sundays. Besides, it would never be my luck to catch a case involving celebrities.'

'I had a celebrity once,' Meyer said. 'A singer. It's a shame I was a married man at the time.'

'Why?'

'Well,' Meyer said, and he shrugged eloquently.

'It certainly is fascinating to watch you fellows at work,' Pullen said.

'It beats television six ways from the middle,' O'Brien said. 'Most people think of cops as everyday working-men who go to a musty office and type up reports in triplicate and do a lot of legwork all over the city. Just ordinary guys, you understand? Guys with wives and families. Guys like you and me, Mr Pullen.'

'Yes?' Pullen said.

'Sure. That's the influence of television. Actually, a detective is a pretty glamorous character. Ain't that right, Meyer?'

'Absolutely,' Meyer said, sniffing the cigar butt.

'He's all the time getting involved with gorgeous blondes in slinky negligees. Ain't that right, Meyer?'

'Absolutely,' Meyer said. The cigar was a White Owl. He made a mental note of it.

'He leads a life of gay adventurous excitement,' O'Brien said. 'When he ain't drinking in some very swank bar, he is out driving in a Cadillac convertible with the top down and the blonde's knees up on the seat. Boy, what a life! I'm telling you, Mr Pullen, detective work ain't all routine.'

'It sounds much more interesting than real estate,' Pullen said.

'Oh, it is, it is. And the salary is fantastic.' He winked. 'Not to mention the graft. Mr Pullen, don't believe what you see on television. Cops, Mr Pullen, are not dull boobs.'

'I never thought they were,' Pullen said. 'It certainly is fascinating the way you men work.'

'You'd imagine somebody in the building would

have heard a rifle going off twice, don't you think, Bob?' Meyer said.

'I would imagine so. Unless this is a home for the deaf.'

'Any other apartments on this floor, Mr Pullen?'

'There's one right across the hall,' Pullen said. 'I rented it myself.'

'Let's try it, Bob.'

They crossed the hall and knocked on the door. A young man in a short beard and a terry-cloth bathrobe opened it.

'Yo?' he said.

'Police,' Meyer said. He flashed the tin.

'Man, dig the badge,' the man in the bathrobe said.

'What's your name?' Meyer asked.

'Real or professional?'

'Both.'

'Sid Lefkowitz is the square handle. When I'm on the stand, I use Sid Leff. Shorter, sweeter, and with a good beat.'

'What stand?'

'The bandstand, man.'

'You're a musician?'

'I blow guitar.'

'Which name do you prefer?'

'Whichever one you like. I'm not choosy, man. Just blow your own *ad lib* chorus.'

'Mr Leff, did you hear any shots coming from the room across the hall?'

'Shots? Oh, is that what they were?'

'You heard them?'

'I heard something. But it didn't bother me. I was working on *Strings*.'

'On what?'

'*Symphony for Twelve Strings.* Don't get the wrong idea. It ain't from Bananasville. It's a jazz symphony. I'm writing it for three guitars, six violins, two bass fiddles, and a piano. The piano gets in by poetic licence. What the hell, without the strings on the sounding board, there wouldn't be no piano, right?'

'Did you investigate the shots?'

'No. I figured them for backfires. Trucks go by here all the time. They take a short cut to the parkway through this street. A very noisy pad, this one. I'm thinking of busting out. How can a man concentrate in the midst of din, man, huh?'

'Did you happen to notice who was in that apartment?'

'The guy with the slush pump, you mean?'

'What?'

'The slush pump. The trombone. A guy came out of there with a trombone case under his arm.'

'Anything else?'

'No. Just the horn.'

'You saw the horn?'

'I saw the case. A guy wouldn't be carrying an empty trombone case would he? That's like carrying a guitar without strings. That would be a little too far out, man.'

'Did you talk to him?'

'Exchanged a bit,' Lefkowitz said. 'The door was open when he passed by, and I spotted the horn case, and struck up a parley. He was going out on an afternoon wedding gig.'

'A what?'

'A gig. A job. I told you, didn't I? The guy played trombone.'

'What did he look like?'

'A big fellow with a busted nose. He had dark hair and dark eyes. He was smoking a cigar.'

'Do you make him, Meyer?' O'Brien asked.

'Judging from the description on his record, it sounds like our man.' He turned back to Lefkowitz. 'Did he have a scar near his right eye?'

'I didn't get a good glim,' Lefkowitz said. 'He could have. I don't know.'

'How do you know he was going to a wedding?'

'He said so. Said he was going on a wedding gig.'

'He said he was going to play trombone at a wedding? Did he say that exactly?'

'No. He said he was going to a wedding. But why else would a guy take a horn to a wedding, if not to blow it?'

'What time was this?'

'I don't know. Close to five, I guess.'

'All right. Thank you very much, Mr Lefkowitz.'

'Mine,' Lefkowitz said.

'Huh?'

'The pleasure.' He closed the door.

'What do you think?' O'Brien asked.

'Did you see a rifle in that first room?'

'No.'

'And Lefkowitz said our boy was carrying nothing but a trombone case. Want a guess?'

'I outguess you already,' O'Brien said. 'There ain't a trombone in that case. There's a rifle.'

'Yeah.'

'And since there ain't no trombone, it's a cinch he ain't going to *play* at a wedding.'

'Right.'

'And if he's taking a rifle to a wedding, chances are — since he's already fired it twice — he plans to shoot it again.'

'Right.'

'And the only wedding I'm sure of today is Carella's sister's.'

'Right.'

'So let's head there.'

'Does a guy walk into the middle of a reception with a rifle under his arm? A rifle isn't exactly a weapon you can conceal. Not after you take it out of that trombone case,' Meyer said.

'So?'

'So I don't think he's heading for the wedding itself. I think maybe he's heading for some place *near* the wedding. The same way he came to a place *near* the photography shop.'

'And where might that be?' O'Brien asked.

'I haven't the faintest idea,' Meyer said. 'But how many men on the street are carrying trombone cases, would you suppose?'

'It certainly is fascinating the way you fellows work,' Pullen said.

Christine Maxwell sat on the back porch of the Carella house, her hands moving nervously in her lap. Teddy Carella sat beside her, watching the dancers on the makeshift floor. The dancing was more frenetic now than it had been. Drinking had begun in earnest once the last course of the meal had been served. This was a wedding, a time for high celebration, and relatives from the far corners of the earth were out there on the floor whooping it up. The whooping up was causing consternation among many of the wives at the reception, but the consternation was tempered by the knowledge that this was a once-a-year day and that hasty kisses stolen from very distant cousins would hardly be remembered the next day. The only thing likely to be remembered the next day – when the gongs and hammers began to reverberate inside the skull – would be the fact that far too much liquor had been consumed the night before.

The children at the wedding reception had no problems at all, unless an overconsumption of soda pop could be considered a problem. This was better than an outing in the city park! This was better than a day at the circus! This was better than getting Captain Video's in-person autograph. For here was a dance-floor to run around with gay abandon, slickly waxed, perfect for sliding and spilling. Here were grown-ups' legs to dodge between, here – in the case of the more precocious eleven-year-olds – were corseted behinds to pinch, a magnificent lawn to tear up. Oh, this was surely Heaven.

Christine Maxwell had no such illusions of Paradise. Sitting beside Teddy, she dreaded the moment when Steve Carella would begin questioning her. He didn't think *she'd* had anything to do with the old man's death, did he? No, he couldn't. Then why did he want to question her? The thought frightened her.

But more than that, she was frightened by the unexpected jealousy exhibited by Cotton Hawes. She had wilfully promoted the relationship with Jonesy in an attempt to bring Hawes to an appreciation of her obvious charms. Her little game had worked only too well. Hawes was not only annoyed, he was furious. And she did love him. She would not exchange him for a hundred Jonesys. Or a thousand.

'Oh, Teddy,' she said, 'what should I do?'

Teddy's face became instantly alert. The impression she gave of devoting her complete attention to whoever was speaking may have simply been an illusion. She was, after all, *forced* to watch a person's lips if she was to 'hear' anything. But mechanical necessity did not explain the complete sympathy Teddy expressed as she listened. To the speaker, Teddy was a perfect sounding board. Her eyes, her mouth, her entire face took on a look of complete understanding. She tilted her head slightly now, and her eyebrows moved a fraction of an inch, the brown eyes focusing on Christine's mouth.

'I've made a mess of everything,' Christine said, and Teddy leaned closer, watching the lips, nodding slightly to let Christine know she was listening.

'I haven't known Cotton very long,' Christine said. 'Oh, perhaps a year – but that isn't very long as relationships go. He came into my bookshop once, tracking down some typing paper which had been used in a warning note. I have a bookshop in Isola.' She paused. 'He asked me out, and I accepted. I've been seeing him.' She paused again. 'I'm a widow, you know. Not a Professional Widow, the way some girls are Professional Virgins or Professional Mothers. My husband was a pilot during the Second World War. He crashed over Okinawa. It took me a long time to get over it, but the dead are dead, and the living must go on. So I'm not a Professional Widow, Teddy. I haven't been wearing sackcloth and rolling about in the ashes. But . . . but it was hard to fall in love again. It was hard to find any man who could live up to the memory of Greg. And then Cotton came along . . .'

Teddy nodded.

'And I fell in love again.' She paused. 'I don't think he loves me. In fact, I'm almost sure he doesn't. I really don't think Cotton is ready yet to become *really* involved with any woman. But I love him. And it's enough to be near him, and to be wanted by him. For now, that's enough.' Again she paused. 'I did a stupid thing today. I tried to make him jealous, and I think I may have lost him. Cotton isn't a man who can be pushed. Teddy, Teddy, what shall I do? What the hell shall I do?'

She fumbled for the purse in her lap as the tears sprang to her eyes. Snapping it open, she dug into it, expecting the familiar feel of her own bag, surprised when her hands struck something hard and unyielding. She stared into the purse.

A Smith & Wesson .357 Magnum stared back at her.

'They're on their way over, Steve,' Kling said as he hung up the phone. 'I explained the situation to them. They're coming in through the next street.'

'Good,' Carella said. He turned back to Sam Jones. 'Now, let's do some serious talking, shall we, Jonesy?'

Jonesy nodded. His face was still white. His hands were still trembling in his lap.

'First of all, Jonesy, would you mind telling me where you went this afternoon when you left Tommy's house for your alleged walk?'

'Alleged?'

'Yes. Alleged. Where did you go?'

'Why?'

'Because somebody sawed through a rod connected to the steering tube of the Cadillac and we had an accident which damn near killed everybody in the car. That's why, Jonesy.'

'I thought that accident—'

'*What* did you think?'

'I thought it was just an accident.'

'It wasn't. And you were conveniently out of the car at the time. Buying cigarettes, remember? Even though Tommy offered you his.'

'You don't think—'

'All I want to know is where you went on your walk, that's all.'

'I don't really remember. I was very nervous. I just walked.'

'Where?'

'I came out of the house and walked. I must have walked about half a mile. Then I turned back.'

'Meet anyone while you were walking?'

'No.'

'Stop any place?'

'No.'

'Then we have only your word for your whereabouts during the time that tie rod could have been sawed through.'

'I suppose . . . if you put it that way—'

'How would *you* put it, Jonesy?'

'Why would I want to . . . why would I want to do a crazy thing like that?'

In a deadly flat voice, Carella said, 'Tommy has a will leaving everything he owns to you.'

'That? For Pete's sake, what the hell does he own?'

'What *does* he own, Jonesy?'

'How do I know? He's not a rich man, that's for sure. If he dies, there might be some money on his G.I. insurance policy. And he's got a 1958 Buick and probably a small savings account. But that's all that I know of.'

'You seem to know an awful lot about it.'

'Well, I'm his best friend. Why shouldn't I know? Besides, this isn't something a man would keep hidden. God, you don't think I'd try to kill Tommy – *Tommy!* My best friend! – for a few thousand dollars, do you?'

'It's been done for less,' Carella said. 'With best friends. With husbands and wives. With mothers and sons. Some people like money, Jonesy.'

'Yeah, but . . . you're on the wrong track. I could never do a thing like that.'

'There's Tommy's will.'

'He's married now. He'll change that as soon as he comes back from his honeymoon.'

'Which might be a damn good reason for killing him *now*,' Kling said.

'Look, you guys are crazy,' Jonesy said. 'I wouldn't. I just *wouldn't* do a thing like that. You think I could kill Birnbaum? A nice old guy I've known since I was a kid? You think I could do a thing like that?'

'*Somebody* did a thing like that,' Carella said.

'But not me. Why would I want to?' He paused and studied the detectives. 'For Pete's sake, would I kill the only living witness to those wills? Does that make any sense to you?'

'He's got a point, Steve,' Kling said.

'Look, I'm telling you,' Jonesy said, 'I had nothing to do with either Birnbaum's—'

There was a frantic knocking at the door. Christine Maxwell did not wait for anyone to open it. She threw it open and burst into the room waving the Magnum.

'I found this in my purse,' she said. 'Not my purse. A girl took mine by accident. In the ladies' room. She left this one. I thought it was—'

'Slow down,' Carella said.

'—my bag, and I opened it to get a hanky, and this was inside.' She waved the gun again.

'Stop waving that damn thing, it may be loaded!' Carella shouted, and he took the gun from her. Then he nodded. 'This is it, Bert,' he said. He sniffed the barrel. 'We won't have to look any further for the gun that killed Birnbaum.' He turned to Christine. 'You said this was in your purse?'

'No. I only thought it was my purse. A blonde girl was in the ladies' room with me. She must have taken my bag by mistake. She left this one.'

'A blonde?' Kling said.

'Yes.'

'What did she look like?'

'A very big girl,' Christine said, 'in a red silk dress.'

'Ouch!' Kling said. 'I was *dancing* with her before dinner.'

'Let's find her,' Carella said, and he started for the door.

'She's probably a million miles—' Kling started, and at that moment Tommy Giordano came breathlessly into the bedroom.

'Steve!' he said. 'Steve, I'm . . . I'm going out of my mind with worry.'

'What is it?' Carella asked.

'It's Angela! I can't find her anywhere. She's gone!'

11.

THERE WAS THE strong smell of cigar smoke.

There was a long shaft of light far away, and a silhouette filling the piercing beam.

There was pain, excruciating pain which throbbed and vibrated and sang with a thousand shrill voices.

There was warmth, a warmth that was thick and liquidy, oozing, oozing.

Cotton Hawes fought unconsciousness.

He felt as if his body was quivering. He felt as if every part of him was swinging in a wild circle of nauseating blackness. Some inner sense told him he was lying flat on his back, and yet he had the feeling that his hands were clutching, grasping, trying to reach something in the blackness, as if his legs and feet were twitching uncontrollably. The pain at the side of his face was unbearable. It was the pain, finally, which forced away the unconsciousness, needling him with persistent fire, forcing sensibility into his mind, and then his body. He blinked.

The cigar smell was overpowering. It filled his newly alert nostrils with the stink of a thousand saloons. The shaft of light was penetrating and merciless, flowing steadily through an open window at the end of the room, impaling him with sunshine. A man stood at the window, his back to Hawes.

Hawes tried to get to his feet, and the nausea came

back with frightening suddenness, swimming into his head and then dropping like a swirling stone to the pit of his stomach. He lay still, not daring to move, aware now that the side of his face was bleeding, remembering now the sudden blinding blow that had knocked him to the floor unconscious. The nausea passed. He could feel the steady seeping of the blood as it travelled past his jawbone and on to his neck. He could almost feel each separate drop of blood rolling over his flesh to be sopped up instantly by the white collar of his shirt. He felt as if he were being born, hypersensitive to every nuance of smell, and sight, and touch. And, newborn, he was also weak. He knew he could not stand without falling flat on his face.

He turned his head slightly to the left. He could see the man at the window clearly, each part of the man combining with the next to form a sharply defined portrait of power as he crouched by the window, the late afternoon sunshine enveloping the silhouette in whitish licking flames of light.

The man's hair was black, worn close to his skull in a tight-fitting woolly cap. The man's brow was immense in profile, a hooked nose jutting out from bushy eyebrows pulled into a frown. A small scar stood out in painful relief against the tight skin of the man's face, close to the right eye. The man's mouth was a tight, almost lipless line that gashed deep into the face above a jaw cleft like a horse's buttocks. His neck was thick, and his shoulders bulged beneath the blue tee-shirt he wore, biceps rolling hugely into thick forearms covered with black hair that resembled steel wool. One huge hand was clutched around the barrel of a rifle. The rifle, Hawes noticed, was mounted with a telescopic sight.

An open box of cartridges rested near the man's right shoe.

This is no one to tangle with in my present condition, Hawes thought. This may be no one to tangle with in any condition. He looks like a man who tears telephone books in sixteenths. He looks like a man who allows automobiles to drive over his inflated chest. He looks like the meanest son of a bitch I have ever seen in my life, and I am not anxious to tangle with him. Now, or maybe never.

But that's a rifle he's holding, and it has a telescopic sight, and he sure as hell doesn't plan to pick his teeth with it.

Do I still have my gun? Or has he disarmed me?

Hawes looked down the length of his nose. He could see the white throat of his shirt stained with blood. He could see his shoulder holster strapped to his chest beneath his open coat.

The holster was empty.

There's nothing I can do but lie here, he thought, and wait for my strength to come back.

And pray, meanwhile, that he doesn't take a pot shot at anybody across the yard at the reception.

The black M.G. convertible had been a gift from Ben Darcy's parents. Unaware of his private intention to enter dental school, they had offered the sleek, low-slung car to him as a sort of bribe. Ben had accepted the bribe and then entered dental school, anyway, just as he'd planned to. Everybody was happy.

The car was capable of hitting rather high speeds on a straight run, and Ben was doing his best at the moment to prove that the manufacturer's claims were valid. The top down, his foot jammed on the accelerator, he cruised along Semplar Parkway at the low-flying speed of eighty-five miles an hour.

Beside him, her long brown hair blowing back over her shoulders, Angela Giordano, née Angela Carella, watched the road ahead with wide eyes, certain she would be killed on her wedding day.

'Ben, can't you slow down?' she pleaded.

'I like to drive fast,' he answered. 'Angela, you've got to listen to me.'

'I'm listening, Ben, but I'm scared. If another car should—'

'Don't worry about me!' he snapped. 'I'm the best damn driver in Riverhead. You couldn't be in better hands.'

'All right, Ben,' she said, and she clutched her hands in her lap and swallowed hard and continued to watch the road.

'So you married him,' Ben said.

'Yes.'

'Why?'

'Oh, Ben, really, we went through all this on the dance-floor. I wouldn't have come with you if I'd known—'

'Why *did* you come with me?' he asked quickly.

'Because you said you wanted to take me for a spin for the last time. A ride around the block, you said. All right, I believed you. But we're *not* going around the block, we're on the parkway heading toward the next state, and you're driving much too fast. *Ben, would you please slow down?*'

'No,' he said, 'Why'd you marry him?'

'Because I love him. Does that answer you?'

'I don't believe you.'

'Believe me. Please believe me.'

'I don't. How can you be in love with him? A bank clerk! For the love of God, Angela, he's a bank clerk!'

'I love him.'

'What can he offer you? What's he ever going to give you?'

'He doesn't have to give me anything,' Angela said. 'I love him.'

'I'm better-looking than he is,' Ben said.

'Maybe you are.'

'I'm going to be a dentist.'

'Yes.'

'Why'd you marry *him*?'

'Ben, please, please slow down. I'm—' Her eyes widened. 'Ben! Look out!'

The Buick came hurtling on to Ben's side of the parkway suddenly, passing a slower car ahead of it. It came like a steam locomotive, unable to cut back because of the car ahead, committed to the pass, determined to reach the safety of its own lane by a new burst of speed. Ben recognized the impossibility of the situation. He swung the wheel sharply to the right, heading for the grass at the side of the parkway. The Buick *whooshed* past with the roar of a diving jet as the small M.G. cleared the vented fender of the bigger car by no more than a foot, climbing on to the steeply sloping bank of grass, and then executing a small sharp turn to the left as Ben yanked the wheel over again. For a moment, Angela thought the car would roll over. Tyres squealed as it hit the concrete again, going into a skid, and then straightening to face the dead centre arrow of the parkway. Ben slammed his foot on to the accelerator. The speed indicator rose to ninety.

Angela could not speak. She sat beside him gasping for breath. And finally she closed her eyes. She would not watch. She *could* not watch.

'It's still not too late,' Ben said.

His voice droned in her ears over the rush of air in the open cockpit of the sports car. Her eyes were closed, and his voice sounded strange, low and meaningful, droning on monotonously.

'It's still not too late. You can still get out of it. You can have it annulled. He's wrong for you, Angela. You'd find that out, anyway. Get rid of him, Angela. Angela, I love you. You can have it annulled.'

She shook her head, her eyes closed tightly.

'Don't go on the honeymoon, Angela. Don't go with him. Tell him you've made a mistake. It's not too late. You'd be doing the right thing. Otherwise—'

She shook her head again. Weakly, she murmured, 'Ben, take me back.'

'I'll be waiting for you, Angela. Get rid of him. He's no good for you. Do it yourself, Angela. Tell him, tell him.'

'Ben, take me back,' she mumbled. 'Please take me back. Please. Please. Please please please please please—'

'Will you tell him? Will you tell him you want it annulled?'

'Ben, please please—'

'Will you?'

'Yes,' she said. 'I'll tell him.' She did not care that she was lying. She only wanted the nightmare of this ride to end, wanted to get away from the man beside her. 'Yes,' she lied again, and then she gave the lie strength and conviction. 'Yes, take me back and I'll tell him. Take me back, Ben.'

'I don't believe you. You're not really going to tell him.'

'I am!'

'Do you love me?'

She could not answer.

'Do you love me?'

'No,' she said, and she began weeping bitterly. 'I love Tommy, I love Tommy! Why are you doing this to me, Ben? Why are you torturing me like this? If you ever cared anything for me, take me back! Please take me back!'

'All right,' he snapped suddenly. He slowed the car, and then executed a screeching U-turn. His foot pressed against the accelerator once more. Angela did not look at the speedometer.

Tommy was waiting at the kerb when the M.G. pulled up before the Carella house. Angela leaped from the car and rushed into his arms, and he held her for a moment and then said, 'What's the hell's the idea, Ben?'

'It was just a wedding gag,' Ben said, grinning feebly. 'Kidnapping the bride, you know? Just a gag.'

'You've got one hell of a sense of humour. You're lucky I don't knock you flat on your ass. You had us all going nuts here until we noticed your car was gone. Goddamnit, Ben, I don't think this is the least bit funny. I don't think it's funny at all. Goddamnit, I think I *will* knock you on your ass!'

'Come on, where's your sense of humour?' Ben said, and again he grinned feebly.

'Oh, go to hell, you bastard,' Tommy answered. He

put his arm around Angela. 'Come on, honey, let's go inside.'

'You want me to go home?' Ben asked sheepishly.

'Go, stay, do what you want. Just keep away from Angela.'

'I was only kidding,' Ben said.

The men surrounding the body of Birnbaum the neighbour were not kidding at all. There was something very unfunny about murder. No matter when it happened, or where, it was still un-comical. There were some who maintained that the worst murders were those which dragged a man out in the wee hours of the morning. There were others who despised early evening murders. But each murder seemed the worst when it was happening, and each of the men who stood looking down at Birnbaum's lifeless shape agreed – though they did not voice it – that the worst time to be killed was in the late afternoon.

The 112th Squad had sent one detective over because the murder had been committed within its boundaries and because the case would officially be theirs from here on in. Homicide, informed that four bona fide detectives were at the scene, decided not to send anyone over. But a police photographer was taking pictures of the corpse fastidiously, if without the energetic grass-hopperiness of a Jody Lewis. The assistant medical examiner was officially pronouncing Birnbaum dead and instructing the stretcher bearers on how to carry him out to the meat wagon waiting next to the kerb in front of Birnbaum's house. Some boys from the lab had put in an appearance, too, and they were attempting now to find foot imprints from which they could make a cast. All in all, everyone was pretty busy compiling the statistics of sudden and violent death. Unfortunately, none of the investigators felt the need to make a telephone call. Had the need presented itself, one or another of the men might have wandered into the Birnbaum house which stood not forty feet from the shielding line of shrubbery behind which they worked.

In the attic of the Birnbaum house, Cotton Hawes felt his strength returning. For the past ten minutes, he had lain silently, his eyes flicking from one corner of the attic to another, and then back to the patiently waiting powerhouse squatting on the floor near the window. The attic was filled with the discarded paraphernalia of living: bundles of old magazines, a green trunk marked 'CAMP IDLEMERE' in white paint, a dressmaker's dummy, a lawn-mower without blades, a hammer, an Army duffel-bag, a radio with a smashed face, three albums marked 'Photographs' and numerous other items which had undoubtedly cluttered the busy life of a family.

The only item which interested Hawes was the hammer.

It rested on top of the trunk some four feet from where he lay.

If he could get the hammer without being heard or seen, he would promptly use it on the sniper's skull. Provided the sniper didn't turn first and shoot him. It would not be too pleasant to get shot at close range with a rifle.

Well, when? Hawes asked himself.

Not now. I'm not strong enough yet.

You're never going to get any stronger, Hawes thought. *Are you afraid of that big bastard crouched by the window?*

Yes.

What?

Yes, I'm afraid of him. He can break me in half even without using his rifle. And he may use it. So I'm afraid of him, and the hell with you.

Let's go, coward, Hawes thought. *Let's make our play for the hammer. There's no time like the present, the man said.*

The man didn't have to face Neanderthal.

Look, are we . . . ?

All right, all right, let's go.

Silently, he rolled over on to his side. The sniper did not turn.

He rolled again, completing a full turn this time, coming to rest a foot away from the trunk. Swallowing hard, he reached out for the hammer. Soundlessly, he slid it off the trunk and gripped it tightly in his right hand.

He swallowed again and got to his knees.

Okay, he thought, we rush him now, hammer raised. We crease his skull before he knows what hit him.

Ready?

He got to a crouching position.

Set?

He stood up and raised the hammer high.

Go!

He took a step forward.

The door behind him opened suddenly.

'Hold it, mister!' a voice said, and he whirled to face a big blonde in a red silk dress. She was reaching into her purse as he leaped at her.

12.

IT CANNOT BE said of Cotton Hawes that he did not ordinarily enjoy wrestling with blondes whose proportions matched this one's. For here was truly a blonde. Here was a handful, and an armful, and an eyeful; here was the image which automatically came to mind whenever anyone muttered the magic words 'big blonde.'

Standing on a runway in Union City, this girl would have caused heart stoppage. Third-row bald heads would have turned pale with trembling.

On the legitimate Broadway stage, this girl would have set the theatre on fire, set the customers on their ears, and set the critics rushing back to their typewriters to pound out ecstatic notices.

In a bedroom – Hawes's imagination reeled with the thought.

But unfortunately, this girl was not on a runway or a stage or a bed. This girl was standing in the doorway to a room no bigger than an upper berth in a Pullman. This girl was obviously not planning to set anyone but Hawes on his ear. She reached into her purse with all the determination of a desert rat digging for water, and then her hand stopped, and a surprised look came over her lovely features. In clear, crystal-pure, ladylike tones, she yelled, 'Where's my goddamn gun?' and Hawes leaped on her.

The sniper turned from the window at the same moment.

The girl was all flesh and a yard wide. She was also all teeth and all nails. She clamped two rows of teeth into Hawes's hand as he struggled for a grip, and then her nails flashed out wildly, raking the uninjured half of his face. The sniper circled closer, shouting, 'Get away from him, Oona! I can't do anything with you . . .'

Hawes did not want to hit the girl. He especially did not want to hit her with the hammer. But the hammer was the only weapon he possessed and he reasoned correctly that if this girl got away from him, Neander-thal would either club him into the floorboards with the stock of the rifle or, worse, plunk a few slugs into his chest. Neither prospect seemed particularly entertain-ing. The blonde herself was not entertaining in the slightest. Wiggling in his arms, she delivered a round-house punch which almost knocked out his right eye. He winced in pain and swung at her with the hammer, but she ducked inside the blow and brought her knee to his groin in an old trick she'd probably learned in grammar school, so expertly did she execute it. Hawes had been kicked before. He'd also been kicked in the groin before. His reactions, he discovered, were always the same. He always doubled over in pain. But this time, as he doubled, he clutched at the blonde because the blonde was insurance. As long as her hot little body remained close to his, the sniper was helpless. He clutched at her, and he caught the front of her dress and it gave under his hand, tearing in a long rip which exposed the blonde's white brassière and three-quarters of her left breast.

The material kept ripping, with the blonde at the

end of it like an unravelling ball of wool in the paws of a playful kitten. He swung the hammer again, catching her on the shoulder, stopping her movement, clutching again, catching flesh this time, his fingers closing tightly as he pulled her toward him. The blonde's dress was torn to the waist now, but Hawes wasn't interested in anatomy. Hawes was interested in clubbing her with the hammer. He swung her around, and her backside came up hard against him, a solid muscular backside. He swung one arm around her neck, his elbow cushioned between the fleshy mounds of the girl's breasts, and he brought back the hand with the hammer again, and the girl pulled another old grammar-school trick.

She bent suddenly from the knees, and then shot upward with the force of a piston, the top of her skull slamming into Hawes's jaw. His arm dropped. The girl swung around and leaped at him, a nearly bare-breasted fury, clawing at his eyes. He swung the hammer. It struck her right arm, and she clutched at it in pain, her face distorted. 'You son of a bitch!' she said, and she reached down, her knee coming up, her skirt pulling back over legs which would have been magnificent on the French Riviera stemming from a bikini, and then she pulled off one high-heeled pump and came at Hawes with the shoe clutched like a mace.

'Get the hell away from him!' the sniper yelled, but the girl would not give up the fight. Circling like wrestlers, the girl's chest heaving in the barely restraining brassière, Hawes panting breathlessly, one holding a hammer, the other a spiked-heel shoe, they searched for an opening. The girl's lips were skinned back over teeth which looked as if they could bite Hawes in two.

She feinted with the shoe, and he brought up his left arm to ward off the blow, and then she moved swiftly to the side, and he saw only the blur of the red shoe coming at his face, felt only the crashing pain as the stiletto-like spike hit his temple. He felt his fingers loosen from the handle of the hammer. He felt himself pitching forward. He held out his arms to stop his fall, and the girl caught him as he came toward her and his head bounced against her shoulder, slid, and he felt the warm cushion of her breast for an instant before she viciously pushed him away from her.

He struck the floor and the last shamed thought he had was *A girl. Jesus, a girl . . .*

A boy or a girl, the baby was kicking up a storm.

Sitting with her father-in-law who had surely had too much to drink, Teddy Carella could not remember the heir apparent ever having raised such a fuss.

It was difficult for her to appreciate the oncoming dusk with her son- or daughter-to-be doing his early-evening callisthenics. Every now and then the baby would kick her sharply, and she'd start from the sudden blow, certain that everyone at the reception was witnessing her wriggling fidgets. The baby seemed to have a thousand feet, God forbid! He kicked her high in the belly, close under her breasts, and then he kicked her again, lower in the pelvic region, and she was sure he'd turned a somersault, so widely diverse had the kicks been.

It'll be over next week, she thought, and she sighed. No more backaches. No more children pointing fingers at me in the street. *Hey, lady, what time does the balloon go up?* Ha-ha, very funny. She glanced across the dance-floor. The redhead from Teaneck or Gowanus or wherever had latched on to a new male, but it hadn't helped Teddy very much. Steve hadn't been anywhere near her for the past few hours, and she wondered now what it was that could possibly be keeping him so occupied. Of course, it was his sister's wedding, and she supposed he was duty bound to play the semi-host. But why had Tommy called him so early this morning? And what were Bert and Cotton doing here? With the instincts of a cop's wife, she knew that something was in the wind – but she didn't know quite what.

The baby kicked her again.

Damn, she thought, I do wish you'd stop that.

Tony Carella had drunk a lot of whisky and a lot of wine and a lot of champagne. He had not drunk so much since the time Steve got married and that was years ago.

In the glow of his stupor, he began to like the Weddings-Fêtes, Incorporateds. They were really nice fellows. It was worth all the money he was giving them. Oh, *madonna*, how much money he was giving them! But it was worth it. Every penny. They were nice boys, all of them. Look at the nice dance-floor they had made, bringing in that big flat platform and laying it right down in the centre of his lawn, *Santa Maria*, my lawn! But they were nice boys. Look at the nice thing they had built for the fireworks at the end of the property. They would be nice, the fireworks. He loved the Weddings-Fêtes, Incorporateds. He loved his wife. He loved his son and his daughter-in-law, and his daughter and his son-in-law. He loved everybody.

He loved Birnbaum.

Where was Birnbaum, anyway?

Why wasn't Birnbaum sitting next to him on this day of his joy, drinking wine and champagne? If he knew Birnbaum, the old man was probably off in a corner someplace weeping.

My old friend, Tony thought, weeping.

I will find him. I will find him and give him a cigar.

He was starting out of his chair when he heard the scream from the edge of his property.

Carella had dispatched the boys from the 112th, the photographer, the assistant medical examiner, and the laboratory assistants, wondering all the while where Cotton Hawes had gone. He'd asked Cotton to stay with the body. Well, the body was now gone – and nearly everyone concerned with the body was also gone. And so was Cotton.

But where?

He had not been working with Hawes for too long a time, but he felt certain the man would not have pulled a stunt so childish as walking out on his date. Still, he'd been pretty angry back there a little while ago. And Christine, as cute as she was, had certainly been asking for trouble. She'd wanted Cotton to do a burn, and he had, but she'd stumbled on to a corpse in the bargain, which proves you shouldn't play with fire, girls.

But would Cotton have walked out on her?

It was possible. Carella had to concede that it was definitely possible. There was no second-guessing the ways of maids and men. He'd handled many a suicide where a seemingly level-headed young man had thrown himself out the nearest hotel window because a sweet young thing in a skirt had refused a date. Why, take his own Teddy. Annoyed because he'd been dancing with that wench from Flemington. God, that had been a long time ago, he could remember every detail of that night as if it were happening now. Faye, grrrrr, she'd been a wonderful, wonderful . . .

Hey now.

Steady, lad.

He saw Teddy sitting near his father. He grinned and began walking toward her.

From the woods behind him, he heard someone scream, 'Help! Help!'

He whirled and broke into a trot, crashing into the bushes. His service revolver was in his fist before he'd covered three feet.

The boys had been standing on the corner watching all the girls go by. They had been standing there all afternoon, they said. They had been standing right under that same lamp-post near the el structure. Just standing. Just watching the girls. June was a good time for watching the girls, the boys said.

'Did you happen to notice the people who came down off the train?' Meyer asked.

'Yeah, we noticed the girls,' the boys said.

'Did you notice anybody else?'

'Yeah,' the boys said, 'but mostly we noticed the girls.'

'Did you happen to see a man carrying a trombone case?'

'What does a trombone case look like?'

'You know,' O'Brien said. 'A trombone case. Black leather. Long. With a sort of a flaring bell on one end.'

'Gee,' the boys said. 'You'd better ask Charlie.'

'Which one of you is Charlie?'

'Charlie's in the candy store. Hey, Charlie! Charlie, come on out here!'

'Is Charlie a musician?' Meyer asked.

'No, but his sister is taking piano lessons. She's eight years old.'

'How old is Charlie?' Meyer asked sceptically.

'Oh, he's a grown man,' the boys said. 'He's sixteen.'

Charlie came out of the candy store. He was a thin boy with a crew cut. He wore khaki trousers and a white tee-shirt, and he ambled over to the boys under the lamp-post with a curious expression on his face.

'Yeah!' he said.

'These guys have some questions.'

'Yeah!' He delivered the word as a cross between a question and an exclamation, as if surprised by his own query.

'Do you know what a trombone case looks like, Charlie?'

'Yeah!' he said, and again it was both a question and an exclamation.

'Did you see anyone come down those steps carrying one?'

'A *trombone* case?' This time it was purely a question.

'Yes,' Meyer said.

'Today?'

'Yes.'

'Down those steps?'

'Yes.'

'Yeah!' he said, the exclamation preceding the question.

'Which way did he go?'

'How do I know?' Charlie said.

150

'You saw him, didn't you?'

'Yeah! Why? You need a trombone player? Does it have to be a trombone player? My kid sister plays piano.'

'Think, Charlie. Which way did he go?'

'Who remembers? You think I followed him or something?'

'He came down those steps?'

'Yeah!'

'Did he turn right or left?'

Charlie thought for a moment. 'Neither,' he said at last. 'He walked straight up the avenue.'

'And then what?'

'I don't know.'

'Did he turn at the corner?'

'I don't know.'

'You lost him after he walked past that corner?'

'I don't know whether he walked past that corner or not. Who lost him? I wasn't even trying to find him. Who was interested in him?'

'Do you think he passed that corner?'

'I don't know.'

'Do you think he turned at the corner?'

'I don't know.'

'Could he have crossed the street?'

'I'm telling you, *I don't know*.' He paused. 'Listen, why don't you ask the guy in the delly on the next corner. Maybe he seen him.'

'Thanks, son,' Meyer said, 'we'll do that.'

'I'm sorry,' Charlie said. 'Does it have to be a trombone player?'

'I'm afraid so.'

''Cause my kid sister plays some gone piano, I mean

it.' Meyer looked at Charlie sadly. Charlie shrugged. 'So some guys go for horns,' he said resignedly, and he went back into the candy store.

Meyer and O'Brien started up the avenue.

'What do you think?' O'Brien said.

'Sounds as if it might be him. Who knows? Maybe we'll have some luck in the delicatessen.'

They did not have any luck in the delicatessen.

The man behind the counter wore bifocals, had been busy all day waiting on Sunday customers, and wouldn't have known a trombone case from a case of crabs, good day.

Meyer and O'Brien went out on to the sidewalk.

'Where to?' O'Brien said.

Meyer shook his head. 'Boy,' he said, 'this suddenly seems like a very big neighbourhood.'

13.

BEN DARCY LAY on his back in the bushes.

Dusk was coming on, staining the sky with purple. In the woods, the insects were beginning their night song. The city looked skyward and greeted the impending night with a sigh; this was Sunday and tomorrow was another workday. And in the city, in the imposing steel and concrete structures of Isola, in the teeming streets of Calm's Point, in the suburban outlands of Riverhead, the beginning of night seemed to bring with it a touch of peace, a restfulness which bordered on weary resignation. Another day was moving into the coolness of the past. The moon would rise, and stars would pepper the skies, and the city would suddenly be ablaze with light.

Ben Darcy seemed to be a part of the peacefulness of dusk. Lying on his back on the ground beneath the big maple which dominated the surrounding area of bushes, he looked like nothing more than a summer sleeper, a dreamer, a sky-watcher, the classic boy with the strand of straw between his teeth. His arms were outstretched. His eyes were closed. He seemed to be asleep, at peace with himself and with the world.

The top of his skull was bleeding.

Stooping down beside him quickly, Carella saw the cut at once, and his fingers moved to it rapidly, parting the hair, feeling the swelling around the gash. The cut was not a deep one or a long one, nor did it bleed profusely. It sat in the exact centre of Darcy's skull, and the area surrounding it had swelled to the size of a walnut. In the growing darkness, Steve Carella sighed audibly. He was tired, very tired. He did not enjoy chasing spectres. I should have been a prize-fighter, he thought. A good dirty sport where the combat is clearly stated from go, where the rules are set down by an impartial observer, where the arena is circumscribed from the very beginning, where the opponent is plainly visible and plainly identified as the opponent, the only man to beat, the only enemy.

Why the hell would anyone choose police work as his profession, he wondered.

We're dealing with destruction, he thought, and the destruction is always secret and our job is not so much preventing it as it is discovering it after it has happened. We seek out the destroyers, but this doesn't make us creators because we are involved in a negative task, and creation is never a negative act. Teddy, sitting out there, with a baby inside her, creating with no effort, creating by nature, is accomplishing more than I'll accomplish in fifty years of police work. Why would anyone ever want to get involved with a son of a bitch who saws through the tie rods of an automobile or kills the neighbour, Birnbaum, or takes a whack at the skull of Darcy? Why would anyone choose as his profession, as the job to which he devotes most of his waking hours, a task which must necessarily bring him into contact with the destroyers?

Why would anyone deliberately involve himself in the murky, involuted motivational processes of the criminal mind, dirty his hands with the crawling specimens of humanity who parade into that squadroom every day of the week, every week of the year?

Why would anyone want to become a street cleaner?

I will tell you some things, Steve, he thought.

I will tell you first that philosophy is unbecoming to a cop who almost flunked Philosophy 1 in school.

I will tell you secondly that free choice is something which is very rarely offered to human beings. You became a cop because you became a cop, and you couldn't tell yourself why without spending hours on a head shrinker's couch, and even then you might not know. And you remain a cop – why?

Because – discounting the obvious knowledge that a man must feed and clothe his wife and his family, discounting any insecurities about facing the world outside the police department, scrounging for a job when I'm no longer a boy, discounting any of this – I *want* to be a cop.

Not because *someone* has to clean the streets. Maybe no one has to clean the streets at all. Maybe civilization would move along just as briskly if the streets were as filthy as hell.

But the destroyers make me angry. When the destroyers take life from a man like Birnbaum, they make me mad as hell! And so long as destruction makes me angry, I'll continue to be a cop, I'll continue commuting to a scroungy squadroom in perhaps the world's worst neighbourhood, listening to bum jokes delivered by other cops, listening to corny humour, and telephones ringing, and complaints from the gentle people who – though they may not all be creators – are *not* destroyers.

In the deepening darkness, he grinned wanly.

You may not have realized it, Father Paul, he thought, but you had a very religious man in your rectory today.

He left Ben Darcy lying on his back, and he went to the house for some water and some damp rags.

The wedding jokes were beginning.

Standing before the long bridal table upon which rested the trays of *dolci* and the huge wedding cake and – at the far end – two bottles of wine marked separately and respectively for the bride and the groom, Tommy listened to the wedding jokes with mixed feelings. He was embarrassed by them, but he was also secretly pleased by them. He knew he was supposed to be embarrassed and so each new joke brought a flush to his boyish features. But at the same time, he secretly felt as if he had achieved manhood at last. Finally, he was being granted admission to a world-wide fraternity as a junior member. Years from now, perhaps he would attend someone else's wedding and tell the same ritual jokes. The knowledge pleased him, even though he'd heard most of the jokes before. The jokes had started with that hoary old standby of the man who leaves his umbrella in a hotel room which is later occupied by a honeymoon couple. About to retrieve the umbrella as they enter the room, he ducks into a closet and is forced to listen to their cooing lovemaking. Finally in desperation, after listening to the groom asking the bride questions like 'And whose eyes are these?' – '*Yours darling*' – 'And whose lovely lips are these?' – '*Yours, sweetheart*' – on and on, sparing no part of the anatomy, the joke tinged with the delicious unsavouriness of total possession and the anticipation of an outer-directed strip-tease, the man in the closet shouts, 'When you get to the umbrella, it's *mine!*'

Tommy laughed. The joke had a beard, but he laughed anyway, and he blushed slightly, and he watched his brother-in-law emerge from the bushes at the side of the property and rush toward the house, and then another joke started, the one about the midget who marries the circus fat lady, and this was followed by another, and then another, and then the jokes left the realm of scripted humour and took on an ad lib quality, each prankster, both married man and bachelor, coming up with top-of-the-head advice on the proper hotel-room behaviour. Someone threw in the hoary story about the white horse who married a zebra and spent the entire honeymoon trying to take off her striped pyjamas, and Tommy laughed, and someone advised him to bring along a lot of magazines because Angela would undoubtedly spend three hours in the bathroom preparing herself for the biggest moment of her life, and someone else said, 'He only wishes it were the *biggest* moment,' and though Tommy didn't quite get this one, he laughed anyway.

'What hotel are you going to, Tom?' one of the circle of jokesters asked.

'Uh-uh,' Tommy said, shaking his head.

'Come on!' someone shouted. 'You don't think we'd barge in on your honeymoon, do you?'

'I do,' Tommy said.

'Old pals like us? Don't you *want* us to visit you?'

'No!'

'No? Why not? Have you made other plans for this evening?'

And so it went. And all the while, Jody Lewis

scampered around the circle of jokesters, catching the expression on Tommy's face each time a new joke was told, the shutter clicking, clicking, to preserve the blush or the grin or the fleeting look of realized manhood for posterity, 'Our Wedding Day'.

'Don't forget that wine when you leave!' someone shouted.

'What wine?'

'Somebody brought you wine. At the end of the table. One for the bride and one for the groom.'

'But don't drink too much, Tommy. Too much wine, and you're going to have a very disappointed bride!'

'Just a sip, Tommy! A toast! And then to work!'

The crowd laughed. Jody Lewis kept his shutter clicking. Night was falling with a frightening rush.

Oona Blake crouched on the floor over Cotton Hawes, her skirt pulled back over powerfully beautiful legs, the top of her dress torn to the waist. Darkness had invaded the small attic room of the Birnbaum house. The vanishing light of daytime filtered feebly through the attic window, catching her blonde hair and then the white exposed flank of her thigh as she knotted the ropes securely around Hawes's body and then went through his pockets.

Marty Sokolin, chewing on his cigar, one huge hand around the rifle barrel, watched her. She scared him somewhat. She was the most beautiful girl he'd ever known in his life, but she moved with the power of a Nike rocket, and she scared him sometimes; but she excited him too. Watching her flip open the man's wallet, watching her hands as they quickly went through the contents, he was frightened and excited.

'A cop,' she said.

'How do you know?'

'A badge, and an I.D. card. Why didn't you search him before?'

'I was too busy. What's a cop doing here? How'd a cop—?'

'They're crawling all over the place,' Oona said.

'Why?' His eyes blinked. He bit down more fiercely on the cigar.

'I shot a man,' she answered, and he felt a tiny lurch of fear.

'You . . . ?'

'I shot a man, an old fart who was heading for this house. You told me to keep people away from here, didn't you?'

'Yes, but to *shoot* a man! Oona, why'd you—?'

'Aren't you *here* to shoot a man?'

'Yes, but—'

'Did you want someone coming up here?'

'No, Oona, but it's brought cops. I've got a record, for Christ's sake. I can't—'

'So have I,' she snapped, and he watched the sudden fury in her eyes, and again he was frightened. Sweat erupted on his upper lip. In the gathering gloom, he watched her, frightened, excited.

'Do you want to kill Giordano?' she said.

'Yes. I . . . I do.'

'Do you or don't you?'

'I don't know. Jesus, Oona, I don't know. I don't want cops. I don't want to go to jail again.'

'That's not what you told me.'

'I know, I know.'

'You said you wanted him dead.'

'Yes.'

'You said you'd never be able to rest until he was dead.'

'Yes.'

'You asked for my help. I gave it to you. Without me, you wouldn't know how to wipe your nose. Who got the apartment near the photography shop? Me. Who suggested this house? Me. Without me, you'd be carrying your goddamn grudge to the grave. Is that what you want? To carry the grudge to your grave?'

'No, Oona, but—'

'Are you a man . . . or what are you?'

'I'm a man.'

'You're nothing. You're afraid to shoot him, aren't you?'

'No.'

'I've already killed for you, do you know that? I've already killed a man to protect you. And now you're chickening out. What are you? A man or what?'

'I'm a man!' Sokolin said.

'You're nothing. I don't know why I took up with you. I could have had men, real men. You're not a man.'

'I'm a man!'

'Then kill him!'

'Oona! It's just . . . there are cops now. There's a cop *here*, right with us . . .'

'There'll be fireworks at eight o'clock—'

'Oona, if I kill him, what do I accomplish? I know I said I—'

'. . . a lot of noise, a lot of explosions. If you fire then, the shot won't even be heard. No one will hear it.'

'—wanted him dead, but now I don't know. Maybe

160

he wasn't responsible for Artie's getting shot. Maybe he didn't know—'

'You go to the window, Marty. You pick him up in your sights.'

'—there was a sniper in the trees. I'm clean now. I'm out of jail. Why should I fool around with something like this?'

'You wait for the fireworks to start. You squeeze the trigger. He's dead, and we take off.'

'And the cop laying there on the floor? He's seen both of us,' Sokolin protested.

'I'll take care of him,' Oona Blake said, and she grinned. 'It'll be a real pleasure to take care of him.' Her voice dropped to a whisper. 'Get to the window, Marty.'

'Oona—'

'Get to the window and get it over with. As soon as the fireworks start. Get it over and done with. And then come with me, Marty, come with me, baby, come to Oona baby, Marty, get it over with, get it over with, *get it out of your system!*'

'Yes,' he said. 'Yes, Oona.'

Antonio Carella had perhaps drunk too much wine, or danced too strenuously. In any case, he was having difficulty standing. He had carried a chair to the centre of the dance-floor, and he stood on the chair now, wobbling unsteadily, his arms flailing the air, and he tried to maintain his balance and signal for silence simultaneously. The wedding guests had also drunk too much – perhaps – or perhaps danced too strenuously. They were a long time coming to silence and perhaps they never would have were it not for the fear that Tony

Carella would fall off that chair unless someone began listening to him soon.

'I'm a very lucky man today,' Tony said to the hushed guests. 'My daughter Angela has married a wonderful boy. Tommy! Tommy? Where's Tommy?'

He climbed down off the chair and searched for Tommy in the crowd, dragging him into the light that spilled from the bandstand.

'My son-in-law!' he shouted, and the wedding guests applauded. 'A wonderful boy, and a wonderful wedding, and a wonderful night! And now, we going to explode fireworks. We going to make the whole night explode for my two children! Is everybody ready?'

And the wedding guests cheered as Marty Sokolin lowered the muzzle of the rifle to the window-sill and levelled his sights on Tommy Giordano's head.

14.

IF POLICE WORK is half doggedness and half patience, it is also half luck and half blind faith. Four halves, obviously, equal two wholes. Two holes were what Meyer Meyer and Bob O'Brien needed in their heads the way they needed the legwork they were doing in tracking down Marty Sokolin.

Meyer Meyer would have been extremely content to have lingered in the delicatessen sniffing of the savoury smells there, rather than to leave the place in search of a potential killer. The smells of a delicatessen, especially a kosher delly, had always been mysterious, intriguing scents to Meyer. When he was a boy, he had no idea that people actually went into delicatessens to make purchases. His mother would take him for a stroll away from their Gentile neighbourhood, into the nearest ghetto, and there she would seek out a delicatessen. Standing in the door to the shop, she would allow little Meyer to sniff to his heart's content. Until the time he was fifteen and bought his first *nickel a shtickel*, Meyer held the unshakeable conviction that delicatessens were for smelling only. He still felt rather uneasy when making a purchase in one, somewhat like a heathen defiling a temple.

He did not make a purchase in the delicatessen on Dover Plains Avenue. He made inquiries concerning the man with the trombone case, was promptly rebuffed, and then went into the street in further search of what was beginning to look like a rather elusive needle. The search was conducted in a very scientific manner based on established investigatory technique. The search was conducted by stopping passers-by and asking them if they had seen a man carrying a trombone case.

Now such painstaking investigatory technique is surely recommended by Scotland Yard and the Nassau County Police and the Sûreté and the Gestapo. It is calculated to separate, through a process of carefully phrased questions (such as, 'Did you see a man with a trombone case walk by here?') those citizens who had and those who had not witnessed the passage of the sought suspect. It was important, of course, to snap off the questions with the properly authoritative and universally accepted police tone. Police tone is a part of police procedure. The sentence, 'Did you see a man with a trombone case walk by here?' when delivered by a layman untrained in police tone could result in a plethora of confused answers. When delivered by a man who had attended the Police Academy, a man well versed in the ways of investigatory technique, a man skilled at the art of interrogation, the question assumed significance. Faced with its scientific inevitability, the person questioned was skilfully led to the point where only one of two answers was possible: yes or no. I did, or I did not see a man with a trombone case walk by here.

Meyer Meyer and Bob O'Brien, skilled inquisitors that they were, received a total of twelve 'no's' before they received a 'yes.'

The 'yes' led them up a street parallel to Charles Avenue. On the front stoop of a two-storey frame dwelling, they got their second 'yes' and began to feel that their luck she was running good. The second 'yes' came from an old man with an ear-trumpet.

'Did you see a man with a trombone case walk by here?' Meyer asked scientifically.

'What?' the old man yelled. 'I'm a little deaf.'

'A man with a trombone case?'

'Got one inside if you want to use it,' the old man said.

'A trombone?'

'Yep. On the hall table. Just dial any number you want. This ain't an out-of-town call, is it?'

'No, no, a trombone,' Meyer said patiently. 'A musical instrument.'

'Oh, a trombone. Yes, yes. What about it?'

'Did you see a man carrying one?'

'Fellow that walked by earlier this afternoon, you mean?'

'You saw him?'

'Yep. Walked right up the street.'

'Thanks,' Meyer said gratefully. 'That's swell. Thanks a lot.'

'You can go to hell yourself, young man,' the man with the ear trumpet said. 'I was only trying to be helpful.'

Night was falling. The sky was a multi-coloured bowl, light blue to the west where the sun had dropped below the horizon, a deeper blue above that, the blue of a sailor's eyes, and above that a blue that was almost black, drenched with stars, the velvet, diamond-sprinkled sheath of a sexy blonde in an all-night bistro.

'We're close to the Carella house, aren't we?' O'Brien asked.

'Charles Avenue is the next block,' Meyer said.

'Think we're getting close?'

'Maybe. I'm getting tired, that's for sure.'

'There's another customer,' O'Brien said. 'Shall we ask him?'

'We've asked everybody else so far. Why begin discriminating at this point?'

The new customer was an eight-year-old boy. He sat on the kerb with a penknife. He kept throwing the penknife into the air and watching it land, handle first, into the patch of earth in front of him. It did not seem to occur to him that a slight shift of the knife would have allowed it to enter the earth blade first. The boy seemed quite content to simply throw it into the air and have it land with a sickening thud. Over and over again, he repeated the impotent act. Meyer and O'Brien watched him for a while.

'Hello, little fellow,' Meyer said at last.

The boy looked up. His face was dirt-smeared in the fading light.

'Drop dead,' he said.

Meyer laughed feebly. 'Now, now, little fellow,' he said, 'we only want to ask you a question.'

'Yeah? What's that?'

Meyer phrased the question carefully. 'Did you see a man with a trombone case walk by here?'

The boy pierced him with stiletto eyes. 'Drop dead,' he said. 'Can't you see I'm busy?'

'Trying to get the knife to stick into the ground?' O'Brien asked pleasantly.

'Don't be a jerk,' the boy said. 'Anybody can do that. I got a caterpillar here in this hole.'

'A caterpillar?' O'Brien said.

'Sure. I'm trying to see how many times I can clobber

him before he dies. I clobbered him thirty-four times already, and he's still moving.'

'Have you tried stepping on him?' Meyer said.

'Where's the fun in that?' the boy asked.

'About this man with the trombone case, did you happen to see him go by?'

'Sure,' the boy said. He picked up the knife and dropped the stubby handle on to the caterpillar's back. 'Thirty-five,' he said.

'Where did he go?'

'Probably up to the wedding on the next block.'

'What makes you say that?'

'Thirty-six,' the boy said as he dropped the knife again. 'I think he's getting weak.'

'What makes you think the man went to the wedding?' Meyer said.

'Because he probably cut through the back-yard. Either that, or he went into the house.'

'What house?'

'He was heading that way, anyway. He stopped on the sidewalk and turned in right there,' the boy said. 'Thirty-seven. So he either cut across the back-yard to play at the wedding, or else he went inside. What else could he of done? Thirty-eight. I can count all the way to a hundred.'

'Which house?' Meyer said.

'Birnbaum's,' the boy answered. 'The third house on your right.' He looked down into the hole. 'I think I got the bastard,' he said. 'Wow, look at all that gook come out of him.'

Meyer and O'Brien did not pause to look at the gook. Hastily, they started up the street toward the Birnbaum house. In the distance, they could hear the beginning of a faint rumbling sound – like far-away thunder.

'Can you see him?'

Him, him, him, him, him, him . . .

'Yes. I've got him in the sights.'

Sights, sights, sights, sights, sights . . .

Don't miss this time, I won't, take careful aim, I will, they're starting the fireworks now, the little ones, I don't like the sound of fireworks, reminds me of guns going off, I hate guns going off, Marty, shut up, concentrate on what you're doing, I am, look they're setting off the pinwheels, can you still see him, yes, don't fire until the big ones go off, we need the cover of the explosions, don't fire yet, Marty, I won't, I won't.

Won't, won't, words, words, people talking, jumble of words, thunder in the distance, gunshots, fire, don't, won't . . .

Cotton Hawes climbed the echoing tunnel of unconsciousness, voices and sounds blurred meaninglessly, reverberating inside his head as blackness gave way to brightness, pinwheeling brightness outside, fireworks, yes, fireworks going off outside in the . . .

He blinked his eyes.

He tried to move.

He was trussed like Aunt Sadie's roast; his hands tied to his feet behind him, he sprawled on the floor like the base of a big rocking-horse. By turning his head, he could see the window. Beyond the window, the bright dizzy gleam of the fireworks split the night air. Silhouetted in the window was Neanderthal, squatting over the rifle, and standing above him, one hand on his shoulder, leaning over slightly, the red silk stretched taut over her magnificent buttocks, was the girl who'd clonked him with the shoe.

'Take careful aim, Marty,' she whispered.

'I am, I am, I've got him. Don't worry.'

'Wait for the big ones. The noisy ones.'

'Yes. Yes.'

'You can do it, Marty.'

'I know.'

'You're a man, Marty. You're my man.'

'I know. Shhh. Shhh. Don't make me nervous.'

'When it's over, Marty. You and me. Take careful aim.'

'Yes, yes.'

He's going to shoot Tommy, Hawes thought helplessly. *Oh my God, he's going to shoot Tommy, and I can't do a goddamn thing to stop him.*

'What . . . what happened?' Ben Darcy asked.

He pulled away from the wet cloth Carella held in his hand. He blinked and sat upright, and then suddenly clutched his head.

'Oh, my head. Oh Jesus, it's killing me. What happened?'

'Suppose you tell me,' Carella said. 'Here, keep this wet cloth on the swelling.'

'Yeah. Thanks.' He blinked again, puzzled. 'What's . . . what's all that noise?'

'They're beginning the fireworks.'

'Have . . . have Tommy and Angela left yet?'

'I don't think so.'

'Oh.'

'Tell me what happened,' Carella said.

'I'm not too sure. I was walking out back here when—'

'Why?'

'Why what?'

'What were you doing back here in the bushes?'

'I wasn't feeling so hot. All the confusion in there, and the row I had with Tommy. So I came here where it was a little more quiet.'

'Then what?'

'Somebody hit me.'

'Who?'

'I don't know.'

'You yelled first,' Carella said. 'You yelled for help. Why'd you do that?'

'Because somebody grabbed me around the neck. That was when I yelled. My God, what did he hit me with? It feels as if my head is broken.'

'It was a man, Ben?'

'Yes. Yes, it felt like a man's arm around my neck.'

'And you yelled for help?'

'Yes.'

'Did the man say anything?'

'Yes.'

'What did he say?'

'He said, "You lousy son of a bitch, I'm going to kill every one of you." '

'What kind of a voice did he have?'

'Deep. Husky. He sounded like a big man.'

'How big?'

'Very big. His arm was strong,'

'How tall are you, Ben?'

'An even six feet.'

'Would you say he was very much bigger than you? From what you could tell?'

'No, not that big. I mean, maybe six-two, six-four, something like that.'

'And he said, "You lousy son of a bitch, I'm going to kill every one of you." Is that right?'

'That's right.'

'And then he hit you?'

'Yes.'

'On the head?'

'Yes.'

'Is that the only place he hit you?'

'Yes.'

'He didn't knock you to the ground and kick you or anything?'

'No.'

'He simply put his arm around your neck, pulled you backwards, and then hit you on the top of the head, is that right?'

'Yes.'

'What was he wearing?'

'A tuxedo, I think. I only saw his arm, but I think it was the sleeve of a tuxedo.'

'You saw this?'

'Yes.'

'It wasn't too dark to see?'

'No. No.'

'What colour was the tuxedo?'

'Black.'

'Not blue?'

'No. Black.'

'You could tell that? In the darkness here? Under the shade of the tree here?'

'Yes. It was black. I think it was black.'

'And the man spoke and then hit you? Or did you yell for help first? Which?'

'First he spoke, then I . . . no, wait. I yelled for help first, and then he cursed at me, and then he hit me.'

'Only once, right?'

'Yes. He hit me on the head. That's the last thing I remember.'

'And you fell down unconscious, right?'

'Yes.'

'One last question, Ben?'

'Yes?'

'Why are you lying to me?'

The pinwheels had sputtered out, and the Roman candles had filled the night with red. And now, standing behind the platform, the caterers from Weddings-Fêtes, Incorporated, stood at the ready, anxious to light the fuses for the grand finale. Tommy Giordano stood alongside his father-in-law and his bride, bathed in the light from the bandstand, waiting for the medley of explosion and light which would come in the next few moments. He did not know that the cross-hairs of a telescopic sight were fixed at a point just above his left eye. He smiled pleasantly as the caterers rushed around behind the platform, squeezed Angela's hand when he saw the first fuse being touched.

The fuse burned shorter, shorter, and then touched the powder. The first of the rockets sailed skyward, exploding in a shower of blue and green stars, followed by the second rocket almost instantly afterward, silver fishes darting against the velvet night. Explosions rocked the peaceful suburb of Riverhead, shockingly loud explosions which threatened to rip the night to shreds.

In the attic room, Oona Blake dug her fingers into Sokolin's shoulder.

'Now,' she said. 'Now, Marty.'

15.

THE MEN WORKED together as a highly efficient team, and perhaps everything would have gone smoothly, bloodlessly, had not Bob O'Brien been a part of the team. It was certain that once the men returned to the squadroom, legend and superstition would prevail to single out O'Brien as the culprit.

They had drawn their service revolvers on the front porch of the Birnbaum house. O'Brien stood to one side of the door, and Meyer turned the knob and eased the door open. The living-room on the ground floor of the house was dark and silent. Cautiously, both men entered the room.

'If he's here and plans to use a rifle,' Meyer whispered, 'he must be upstairs.'

They waited until their eyes grew accustomed to the darkness. They found the staircase then and began climbing it, hesitating when their weight caused the treads to creak. On the second floor, they checked the two bedrooms and found them empty.

'An attic?' O'Brien whispered, and they continued climbing.

They were in the hallway outside the attic room when the fireworks started in the Carella back-yard. At first, they thought it was gunfire, and then they recognized it for what it was, and both instantly formed the conclusion that their sniper – if he were indeed in the house – had undoubtedly been waiting for the fireworks before opening up with his rifle. They did not speak to each other. There was no need to speak. The operation they were about to perform had been acted out by them hundreds of times before, either together, or as part of other teams. The fireworks in the yard across the way simply added urgency to the operation but they moved swiftly and without panic, Meyer flattening himself against the wall to the right of the door, O'Brien bracing himself against the corridor wall opposite the door. O'Brien glanced at Meyer, and Meyer nodded soundlessly.

From inside the room, they heard a woman's voice say, 'Now. Now, Marty.'

O'Brien shoved himself off the wall, his left leg coming up, the left foot colliding with the door in a powerful, flat-footed kick that splintered the lock and shot the door inward. Like a full-back following a line plunge, O'Brien followed the door into the room, Meyer crossing in behind him like a quarter-back ready to take a lateral pass.

O'Brien was not anxious to fire.

His gun was in his hand as he entered the room, following the jet-catapult of the door, his eyes sweeping first to the window where the man crouched over the rifle, then to the floor where Cotton Hawes lay tied in a neat bundle, and then back to the window again as the blonde in the red silk dress whirled to face him.

'Drop the piece!' he shouted, and the man at the window swung around with the rifle in his hands, the rockets exploding behind him in the back-yard illuminating his eyes, pinpointing his eyes with fiery light;

and O'Brien's eyes locked with his, and in that moment he weighed the necessity for firing.

'Drop it!' he shouted, his eyes locked with the other man's, and he studied those eyes for the space of three seconds which seemed like three thousand years, studied the fright in them, and then the sudden awakening to the situation, and the rapid calculation. And then the eyes began to narrow and O'Brien had seen the instantaneous narrowing of the eyes of a man with a gun before, and he knew the eyes were telegraphing the action of the trigger finger, and he knew that if he did not fire instantly, he would drop to the floor bleeding in the next split second.

Meyer Meyer had seen the eyes tightening, too, and he shouted, 'Watch it, Bob!' and O'Brien fired.

He fired only once, from the hip, fired with a calmness that gave the lie to the lurching beat of his heart and the trembling of his legs. His slug took Sokolin in the shoulder at close range, spinning him around and slamming him up against the wall, the rifle dropping from his hands. And all O'Brien could think was *Don't let him die, Dear God don't let him die!*

The blonde hesitated for a fraction of an instant. With Sokolin slowly crumpling from the wall to the floor, with Meyer rushing into the room, with the world outside disintegrating in a shower of sparks and a cacophonous welter of explosions, she made her decision and acted upon it, dropping instantly to her knees, pulling the skirt back in a completely feminine gesture as she stooped with masculine purposefulness to pick up the rifle.

Meyer kicked her twice. He kicked her once to knock the rifle upward before her finger found the trigger, and then he kicked out at her legs, knocking her backward to the floor in a jumble of white flesh and sliding red silk. She came off the floor like a banshee out of hell, lips skinned back, fingers curled to rake. She wasn't looking for conversation, and Meyer didn't give her any. He swung his .38 up so that the barrel was nested in his curled fingers, the butt protruding below. Then he brought the gun around in a side-swinging arc which clipped the girl on the side of the jaw. She threw her arms and her head back, and she let out a slight whimper, and then she came down slowly, slowly, like the *Queen Mary* sinking in the River Harb, dropping to the floor in a curious mixture of titanic collapse and fragile gracefulness.

O'Brien was already crouched over Sokolin in the corner. Meyer wiped his brow.

'How is he?'

'He's hurt,' O'Brien answered. 'But he isn't dead.'

'I knew there'd be shooting,' Meyer said simply. He turned to where Cotton Hawes lay on the floor in his rocking-horse position. 'Well, well,' he said, 'what have we here? Take a look at this, Bob.'

'Get me out of these ropes,' Hawes said.

'It talks, Bob,' Meyer said. 'Why, I do believe it's a talking dog. Now isn't that a curiosity!'

'Come on, Meyer,' Hawes pleaded, and Meyer saw his battered face for the first time, and quickly stooped to cut the binding ropes. Hawes rose. Massaging his wrists and ankles, he said, 'You got here just in the nick.'

'The Marines always arrive on time,' Meyer said.

'And the U.S. Cavalry,' O'Brien answered. He glanced at the blonde. 'She's got crazy legs,' he said.

The men studied her appreciatively for a moment.

'So,' Meyer said at last, 'I guess this is it. We'll need the meat wagon for that joker, won't we?'

'Yeah,' O'Brien said listlessly.

'You want to make the call, Bob?'

'Yeah, okay.'

He left the room. Meyer walked to the blonde and clamped his handcuffs on to her wrists. With a married man's dispassionate aloofness, he studied her exposed legs for the last time, and then pulled down her skirt. 'There,' he said. 'Decency and morality prevail once more. She had a wild look in her eye, that one. I wouldn't have wanted to mess with her.'

'I *did*,' Hawes said.

'Mmm.' Meyer looked at his face. 'I think maybe we got another passenger for the meat wagon. You don't look exactly beautiful, dear lad.'

'I don't feel exactly beautiful,' Hawes said.

Meyer holstered his revolver. 'Nothing like a little excitement on a Sunday, is there?'

'What the hell are *you* kicking about?' Hawes asked. 'This is *my* day off.'

'Lying?' Ben Darcy said. 'What do you mean? Why should I—?'

'Come on, Ben. Over to the house,' Carella said.

'What for? What did I—?' A gun magically appeared in Carella's fist. Darcy studied it for a moment and then said, 'Jesus, you're serious, aren't you?'

'Aren't *you*?' Carella asked, and together they walked out of the bushes. The fireworks were exploding behind them, the sighs of the crowd following each new display of pyrotechnic wizardry. Kling met the pair at the house.

'I've been looking for you, Steve,' he said. 'It's past eight, and I'm supposed to pick up Claire at nine. So I'd better be taking off.'

'Hang around a few more minutes, would you, Bert?'

'What for?'

'Hang around, can you?'

'Okay, but you don't know Claire when I'm late.'

'Inside,' Carella said to Darcy. They entered the house. 'Upstairs.' They went upstairs to the room that had been Carella's when he was a boy. School pennants still decorated the walls. Airplane models hung from the ceiling. A Samurai sword he'd sent home from the Pacific was hung to the right of the windows, near the desk. In the room where he'd been a boy, Carella felt no nostalgic wistfulness. He had led Darcy into the privacy of the house because he was about to conduct a police interrogation, and he wanted the psychological advantage of the cloistered silence, the four walls, all the appearance of a trap. At the 87th, he'd have used the small Interrogation Room set close to the Clerical Office, and for the same reasons. There were some cops who used the Interrogation Room as a sparring ring, but Carella had never laid a hand on a prisoner in all the years he'd been a cop, and he did not intend to start now. But he recognized his weapons, and he knew that Darcy was lying, and he wanted to know now *why* he was lying. He had drawn his gun with the same psychological warfare in mind. He knew he did not need his gun with Darcy. But the gun added official police weight. And, in following through on his line of intent, he had asked Kling to accompany him upstairs because the police weight was doubled with a second cop along; the feeling of inevitable exposure mounted,

179

the lie would root around in the suspect's mind searching for a rock beneath which to hide, relentlessly exposed to the overwhelming odds against it.

'Sit down,' he said to Darcy.

Darcy sat.

'Why do you want Tommy dead?' Carella asked bluntly.

'What?'

'You heard me.' He stood to the right of Darcy's chair. Kling, knowing what was happening, immediately assumed a position to the left of the chair.

'Tommy *dead*?' Darcy said. 'Are you kidding me? Why would I—?'

'That's what I asked you.'

'But I—'

'You said a man slightly taller than you came up behind you in the bushes and circled your neck with his arm, is that right?'

'Yes. Yes, that's the truth.'

'And then he hit you on the head, right? Once? Right?'

'Yes. That's what happened. How does that—?'

'I'm six feet tall,' Carella said, 'give or take a quarter of an inch. Bert here is about six-two. That's about the difference in height between you and your alleged attacker, isn't it? Isn't that what you said?'

'Yes, that's what I—'

'Would you mind grabbing me from behind, Bert? Put your arm far enough around me so that I can see what kind of clothes you're wearing. You *did* tell me your attacker was wearing a tuxedo, didn't you?'

'Well, I—'

'Didn't you?'

'Yes,' Darcy said.

'Okay, Bert.'

Kling wrapped his arm around Carella's neck. Carella stood facing Darcy, the gun in his right hand.

'We're pretty close, aren't we, Darcy? I'm practically smack up against him. In fact, it would be impossible for Bert to take a whack at my head unless he shoved me on the head this way. Am I right?'

'Yes, that's right,' Darcy said quickly. 'The attacker *did* shove me away from him. I remember that now. I yelled and then just before he hit me, he shoved me a few feet away from him. So that he could swing. That's right. That's just the way it happened.'

'Well, that's different,' Carella said, smiling. 'Why didn't you say so in the first place? So he shoved you away from him, right?'

'Yes.'

'Would you mind demonstrating that, Bert?'

Kling shoved out gently at Carella, and Carella stepped forward a few paces. 'About like that?' he asked Darcy.

'Well, with considerably more force. But that's about where I wound up, yes. A few feet ahead of him.'

'Well, you should have told me that to begin with,' Carella said, still smiling. 'He hit you from a few feet behind you, right?'

'Yes.'

'That makes a big difference,' Carella said, smiling pleasantly. 'And he didn't kick you or anything, am I right?'

'That's right,' Darcy said, nodding. 'He pushed me away from him and then he hit me. That was all.'

'Then suppose you tell me, Ben, why the hell that cut

is in the exact centre of your skull, on the top of your head? Suppose you tell me that, Ben?'

'What? I don't—'

'If you were hit from behind, you'd most likely have been hit either on the side or the back of your head. Unless the man who hit you was an absolute giant, the cut would not be in the *centre* of your skull. The size man you described would never have been able to get force enough into a blow that presupposes his extending the weapon above your head and then bringing it down vertically.'

'He . . . he was bigger than I thought.'

'How big?'

'Six-six, maybe. Maybe bigger.'

'That isn't big enough! The natural swing of his arm would have brought that gun down on a slant at the back of your head. Or, if he took a side swing, at either the right or the left of your head, behind the ears. How about it, Darcy? The wound was self-inflicted, wasn't it? You ducked your head and ran into that big maple, didn't you?'

'No, no, why would I want to—?'

'To throw suspicion away from yourself. Because you sawed through that tie rod end!' Kling said.

'You were out for a walk this morning, weren't you? That's what you told me when I first saw you,' Carella said.

'Yes, but—'

'Did you run yourself into that tree? Did you saw through that tie rod end on your little stroll?'

'No, no, I—'

'Did you send Tommy that black widow spider?'

'No, no, I swear I didn't do any of—'

'A note came with the spider,' Carella shouted. 'We'll compare your handwriting—'

'My handwriting? . . . But I didn't—'

'Is that blonde in this with you?' Kling shouted.

'What blonde?'

'The one whose gun killed Birnbaum!'

'Birnbaum!'

'Or did *you* kill Birnbaum?'

'I didn't kill anybody. I only—'

'Only *what*?'

'I only wanted to—'

'To *what*?'

'I . . . I . . .'

'Take him away, Bert,' Carella snapped. 'Book him for the murder of the old man. Premeditated homicide. It's an open-and-shut Murder One.'

'Murder?' Darcy shouted. 'I didn't touch the old man! I only wanted—'

'*What* did you want? Goddamnit, Darcy, spit it out!'

'I . . . I . . . I only wanted to scare Tommy at first. With . . . with the spider. I . . . I thought maybe I'd scare him enough so that he'd . . . he'd back out of the wedding. But . . . he . . . he didn't, he wouldn't . . . he wouldn't scare.'

'So you went to work on the car, right?'

'Yes, but not to *kill* him! I didn't want to *kill* him!'

'What the hell did you think would happen when that rod snapped?'

'An accident, I thought, to stop the wedding, but that . . . that didn't work, either. And then I—'

'Where does the blonde come in?'

'I don't know any blonde. I don't know what you're talking about.'

'The blonde who shot Birnbaum! Come clean, Darcy!'

'I'm telling you everything. I was only trying to scare Tommy. The wine was to make him sick, yes, but then I took Angela for a ride in my car, and I tried to talk sense to her. If she'd agreed to what I—'

'What wine? What do you mean, wine?'

'The wine. For him and her. And if Angela had told me she'd go along with me, I'd have taken the bottles back. But, anyway, it's only to make him sick, so he'll . . . he'll look like a boob on his honeymoon. So she'll be . . . disgusted with him. And then maybe she'll come to me, after all. I love her, Steve! I love Angela!'

'You gave them wine?'

'Two bottles. One for him, and one for her. To take on the honeymoon. Two small little bottles. I left them on the bridal table. With cards.'

'Where'd you get the wine?'

'My father makes it. He makes a barrel each year.'

'And bottles it?'

'Yes.'

'You put something in that wine? To make them sick?'

'Only Tommy's bottle. Only the one marked "For the Groom". I wouldn't want Angela to get sick. That's why I put two separate bottles on the table. One for the bride and one for the groom. Only *his* bottle has the stuff in it.'

'What stuff?'

'You don't have to worry. It'll only make him sick. I only used a little of it.'

'A little of *what*, goddamnit!'

'The stuff we use in the garden. To kill weeds. But I

only put it in Tommy's bottle. I wouldn't want Angela to—'

'Weed-killer? Weed-killer?' Carella shouted. 'With an arsenic base?'

'I don't know what it had in it. I only used a little. Just to make him get sick.'

'Didn't it say POISON on the can?'

'Yes, but I only used a little. Just to—'

'How much did you use?'

'It was just a small bottle of wine. I put in about half a cupful.'

'Half a – and you mix that stuff twenty to one with water to kill weeds! And you put half a cup of it into Tommy's wine! That'd kill an army!'

'Kill an – but – but I only wanted to make him sick. And only him. Not Angela. Only him.'

'They're married now, you goddamn idiot! They'll drink from *one* bottle or *both* bottles or ... you goddamn fool! What makes you think they're going to follow your instructions for a honeymoon toast! Oh, you goddamn idiot! Cuff him to the radiator, Bert! I've got to stop the kids!'

16.

DANCING HAD COMMENCED under a starlit sky.

The Sal Martino Orchestra, having imbibed of good, clean, commercially bottled wines and champagnes and whiskies all afternoon and evening, having been treated to the sweet, exhilarating taste of Antonio Carella's expensive elixir, played with a magnificently mellow lilt. Distant cousins embraced distant cousins with mounting fervour as the hours ran out. It would be a long time before the next wedding.

Steve Carella burst from the house and on to the dance-floor, his eyes skirting his wife where she sat wriggling uncomfortably in her chair, darting over the dance-floor in search of Tommy and Angela. They were nowhere in sight. He saw his mother dancing with Uncle Garibaldi from Scranton, and he rushed over to her and pulled her from the startled uncle's arms and said, 'Where are the kids?'

'What?' Louisa said.

'Tommy and Angela. Where are they?'

Louisa Carella winked.

'Mama, they didn't *leave*, did they?'

Louisa Carella, who'd had a bit of the commercially bottled elixir herself, winked again.

'Mama, did they leave?'

'Yes, yes, they left. This is their wedding. What did

you want them to do? Stand around and talk to the old folks?'

'Oh, Mama!' Carella said despairingly. 'Did you see them go?'

'Yes, of course I saw them. I kissed Angela good-bye.'

'Were they carrying anything?'

'Suitcases, naturally. They're going on a honeymoon, you know.'

'*Che cosa?*' Uncle Garibaldi from Scranton asked. *Che cosa, Louisa?*'

'*Niente. Sta zitto, Garibaldi,*' she answered him, and then turned to her son. 'What's the matter?'

'Somebody put two small bottles of home-made wine on the table this afternoon. Did you happen to see them?'

'Yes. His and Hers. Very cute.'

'Did they have that wine with them when they left?'

'Yes. Yes, I think so. Yes, I saw Tommy put the bottles in one of the suitcases.'

'Oh, Jesus!' Carella said.

'Steve! I don't like you to swear.'

'Where'd they go, Mama?'

'Go? How should I know? This is their honeymoon. Did you tell me where *you* went on your honeymoon?'

'Oh, Jesus,' Carella said again. 'What did she tell me, what did she say? She *talked* about the hotel! Damnit, what did she say? Did she mention the name?'

'What's the matter with you?' Louisa asked her son. 'You act like a crazy man!'

'Bert!' Carella shouted, and Kling ran to where he was standing. 'Bert, did you hear anybody mention the name of the hotel the kids were going to?'

'No. Why? Have they left with the wine?'

'Yes.'

'Oh, Jesus,' Kling said.

'What do we do?'

'I don't know.'

'A big hotel, she said. I'm sure she said that. Hold it, hold it. One of the biggest hotels in the world, she said. Right in this city. She said that.' He clutched Kling's shoulders desperately. '*Which* is one of the biggest hotels in the world, Bert?'

'I don't know,' Kling said helplessly.

'Do you think someone might have seen them drive away?' He turned to his mother. 'Mama, did they take a car?'

'No, a taxi, Steve. What *is* the matter? Why are you—?'

'*Che cosa?*' Uncle Garibaldi from Scranton asked again.

'*Sta zitto!*' Louisa said more firmly.

'Did you hear Tommy tell the taxi-driver where they were going?'

'No. My God, they only left a few minutes ago. If I knew it was important, I'd have asked them to—'

But Carella had left his mother and was running toward the front of the house and the sidewalk. He stopped at the gate and looked in both directions. Kling pulled up to a puffing halt beside him.

'See anything?'

'No.'

'There's somebody.'

Carella looked to where Jody Lewis, the photographer, was packing his equipment into the trunk of his car. 'Lewis,' he said. 'Maybe he saw them. Come on.'

They walked to the car. Lewis slammed the trunk

shut and then came around the side of the car quickly. 'Nice wedding,' he said, and he got into the car and started the engine.

'Just a second,' Carella said. 'Did you see my sister and her husband leave here?'

'The happy couple?' Lewis said. 'Yes, indeed. Excuse me, but I'm in a hurry.' He released the hand brake.

'Did you happen to overhear the address they gave the cab-driver?'

'No, I did not,' Lewis said. 'I am not in the habit of eavesdropping. Now, if you'll excuse me, I want to finish my work and get to bed. Good night. It was a wonderful wedding.'

'Finish your—?' Carella started, and he turned to Kling, and the same excited look crossed both their faces in the same instant. 'You going to take another picture of them?'

'Yes, I'm—'

'At the hotel? Putting their shoes out?'

'Yes,' Lewis said, 'so you can see I'm in a hurry. If you'll—'

'You've got company, mister,' Carella said, and he threw open the car door. Kling piled into the sedan. Carella was following him when he heard his mother's voice on the path behind him.

'Steve! Steve!'

He hesitated, one foot inside the car, the other on the pavement.

'What is it, Mama?'

'Teddy! It's Teddy! It's her time!'

'What?'

'Her time! The baby, Steve!'

'But the baby isn't due until next we—'

'It's her time!' Louisa Carella said firmly. 'Get her to the hospital!'

Carella slammed the car door shut. He thrust his head through the open window and shouted, 'Stop the kids, Bert! My wife's gonna have a baby!' and he ran like hell up the path to the house.

'What hotel is it?' Kling asked.

'The Neptune.'

'Can't you drive any faster?'

'I'm driving as fast as I can. I don't want to get a ticket.'

'I'm a detective,' Kling said. 'You can drive as fast as you want. Now step on it!'

'Yes, *sir*,' Lewis answered, and he rammed his foot down on the accelerator.

'Can't you drive any faster?' Carella said to the cabdriver.

'I'm driving as fast as I can,' the cabbie answered.

'Damnit! My wife's about to have a baby!'

'Well, mister, I'm—'

'I'm a cop,' Carella said. 'Get this heap moving.'

'What are you worried about?' the cabbie said, pressing his foot to the accelerator. 'Between a cop and a cabbie, we sure as hell should be able to deliver a baby.'

17.

A CONVENTION OF Elks or Moose or Mice or Masons or something was cavorting in the lobby of the Neptune Hotel when Kling arrived with Jody Lewis. One of the Elks or Moose or Mice or whatever touched Kling with an electrically charged cane, and he leaped two feet into the air, and then rushed again toward the reception desk, thinking he would arrest that man as a public menace as soon as he finished this business with Tommy and Angela. God, it was past eight-thirty, Claire would have a fit when he finally got around to picking her up. Assuming the kids hadn't tasted that wine yet – why was he calling them kids? Tommy was about his age – but assuming they hadn't tasted the wine, assuming a stomach pump and a rush to the hospital wouldn't be necessary, holy Moses what had happened to what had started out as a quiet Sunday?

'Mr and Mrs Giordano,' he said to the desk clerk.

'Yes, sir, they checked in a little while ago,' the clerk answered.

'What room are they in?'

'I'm sorry, sir, they left instructions not to be disturbed. They're honeymooners, you see, and—'

'I'm from the police department,' Kling said, snapping open his wallet to his shield. 'What room? Quick!'

'Is something—?'

'What room, damnit?'

'428. Is something—?'

Kling rushed to the elevator. Behind him, camera in hand, Jody Lewis dashed across the lobby.

'Four,' Kling said to the elevator boy. 'Hurry!'

'What's the rush?' the boy answered. Idling against the control panel, he gave Kling a bored sneer. Kling didn't feel like arguing. Nor did he feel like earning the distinction of being the first Neptune guest to be treated with rudeness in the past ten years. He simply clutched one hand in the elevator boy's tunic, yanked him away from the control panel, slammed him against the rear wall of the elevator just as Jody Lewis entered the car, and then pressed the button to close the doors and pressed another button marked with the numeral 4.

'Hey,' the elevator boy said, 'you're not allowed to—'

'Just shut the hell up,' Kling said, 'or I'll throw you down the shaft.'

The boy modulated into an injured silence. Sulking against the rear wall of the elevator, he silently cursed Kling as the car sped up the shaft. The doors slid open and Kling rushed into the hall with Lewis. Behind him, in a parting shot of defiance, the elevator boy yelled, 'You louse!' and then hastily closed the doors.

'What room?' Lewis asked.

'428.'

'This way.'

'No, this way.'

'It says 420 to 428 here.'

'The arrow's pointing this way.'

They rushed down the hall together.

'Here it is!' Lewis said.

Kling rapped on the door. 'Open up!' he shouted.

'Who's there?' Tommy's voice shouted back.

'Police! Bert Kling! Open up! Hurry!'

'What? What?' Tommy said, his voice puzzled behind the wood of the door. A lock was thrown back. A key turned. The door opened. Tommy stood there with a wine glass in one hand. He was wearing a blue silk robe, and he seemed terribly embarrassed. Behind him, sitting in a love seat, Angela Giordano tilted a wine glass to her lips as she watched the door with a perplexed frown on her forehead.

Kling's eyes opened wide. 'Stop!' he shouted.

'Wh—?'

'Don't drink that wine!'

He darted into the room past a startled Tommy Giordano, and then slapped the wine glass out of Angela's hands.

'Hey, what the hell—' Tommy started and Kling said, 'Did you drink any?'

'The wine?'

'Yes, yes, the wine!'

'No. We just opened one of the bottles. What—?'

'Which one?'

'I don't know. They're both on the table there. What is this? Did the fellows put you up to this?'

Kling ran to the table and lifted the open bottle of wine. The card still hung from its neck. *For the Bride.* Suddenly, he felt like a horse's ass. He picked up the second bottle, the one marked *For the Groom* and, greatly embarrassed, he started for the door.

'Excuse me,' he said. 'Sorry to bust in on you. Wine was no good. Sorry. Excuse me, excuse me,' he said, backing toward the door.

Behind him, Jody Lewis said, 'One last picture,

please. Just put your shoes in the hall for me, would
you? One last picture.'

'Oh, go to hell,' Tommy said, and he slammed the
door on his visitors.

'Boy,' Lewis said, 'what a temper.' He paused. 'Is that
wine you've got there?'

'Yes,' Kling said, still embarrassed.

'Why don't we open it and have a drink?' Lewis said.
'I'm exhausted.'

Steve Carella paced the floor of the hospital waiting-
room. Meyer, Hawes, and O'Brien who'd followed the
meat wagon and Sokolin to the hospital after depositing
Oona Blake with the local precinct, paced the floor
behind him.

'What's taking so long?' Carella asked. 'My God,
does it always take this long?'

'Relax,' Meyer said. 'I've been through this three
times already. It gets longer each time.'

'She's been up there for close to an hour,' Carella
moaned.

'She'll be all right, don't worry. What are you going
to name the baby?'

'Mark if it's a boy, and April if it's a girl. Meyer, it
shouldn't be taking this long, should it?'

'Relax.'

'Relax, relax.' He paused. 'I wonder if Kling got to
the kids in time.'

'Relax,' Meyer said.

'Can you imagine a nut like that? Putting arsenic –
half a cup of it – into a small bottle of wine and
thinking it would only make Tommy *sick*! A dental

student! Is that what they teach dentists about chemistry?' He shook his head. 'Attempted murder, I made it. We throw the book at the bastard.'

'Relax,' Meyer said. 'We'll throw the book at all of them.'

'How's Sokolin making out?'

'He'll live,' Meyer said. 'Did you see Cotton's face?'

'I hear a girl beat you up, Cotton,' Carella said.

'Yeah,' Hawes said shamefacedly.

'Here comes a nurse,' O'Brien said.

Carella whirled. With starched precision, the nurse marched down the corridor. He walked rapidly to greet her, his heels clicking on the marble floor.

'Is she all right?' the detectives heard him ask, and the nurse nodded and then took Carella's arm and brought him to the side of the corridor where they entered into a whispered consultation. Carella kept nodding. The detectives watched him. Then, in a louder voice, Carella asked, 'Can I go see her now?'

'Yes,' the nurse answered. 'The doctor's still with her. Everything's fine.'

Carella started down the hallway, not looking back at his colleagues.

'Hey!' Meyer shouted.

Carella turned.

'What is it?' Meyer said. 'Mark or April?'

And Carella, a somewhat mystified grin on his face, shouted, '*Both!*' and then broke into a trot for the elevators.

All Orion/Phoenix titles are available at your local bookshop or from the following address:

Mail Order Department
Littlehampton Book Services
FREEPOST BR535
Worthing, West Sussex, BN13 3BR
telephone 01903 828503, *facsimile* 01903 828802
e-mail MailOrders@lbsltd.co.uk
(Please ensure that you include full postal address details)

Payment can be made either by credit/debit card (Visa, Mastercard, Access and Switch accepted) or by sending a £ Sterling cheque or postal order made payable to *Littlehampton Book Services*.
DO NOT SEND CASH OR CURRENCY.

Please add the following to cover postage and packing

UK and BFPO:
£1.50 for the first book, and 50p for each additional book to a maximum of £3.50

Overseas and Eire:
£2.50 for the first book plus £1.00 for the second book and 50p for each additional book ordered

---

BLOCK CAPITALS PLEASE

name of cardholder ....   *delivery address*
....   *(if different from cardholder)*

address of cardholder ....

....

....

postcode ....   *postcode* ....

☐ I enclose my remittance for £..........................

☐ please debit my Mastercard/Visa/Access/Switch (delete as appropriate)

card number ☐☐☐☐☐☐☐☐☐☐☐☐☐☐☐☐☐☐

expiry date ☐☐☐☐   Switch issue no. ☐☐

signature ....

prices and availability are subject to change without notice